"*The Soul Mark* showcases Fischer's gift of creativity in taking familiar, well-worn truths and painting them in new, beautiful ways that inspire fresh wonder and appreciation. She writes worlds I want to live in, characters I can relate to, and themes I need to hear. Like her other books, *The Soul Mark* captivated me, moved me, and inspired me, and I highly recommend it as a must-read!"

~ Melissa J. Troutman, co-founder of *The Valley* and author of *Trust & Deception*

"In *The Soul Mark*, J. J. Fischer tells a fast-paced and gripping tale of restitution, redemption and love, all set in a fantastical and well-crafted world. Keep watching for more from this amazing author!"

~ Anna Zogg, author of the *Intergalaxia* novels

THE SOUL MARK

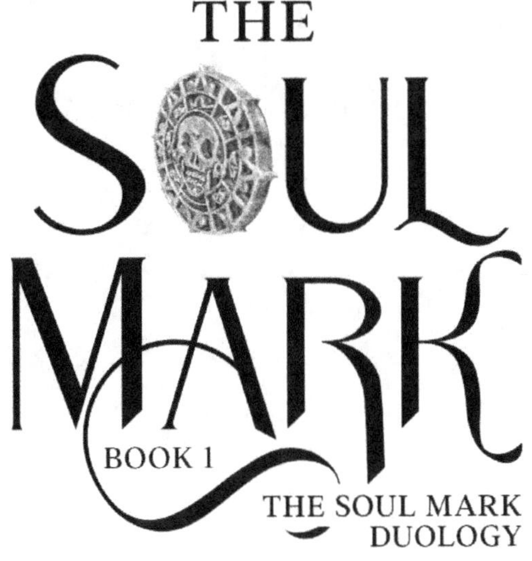

BOOK 1

THE SOUL MARK
DUOLOGY

The Soul Mark Duology

Book One: The Soul Mark

THE SOUL MARK

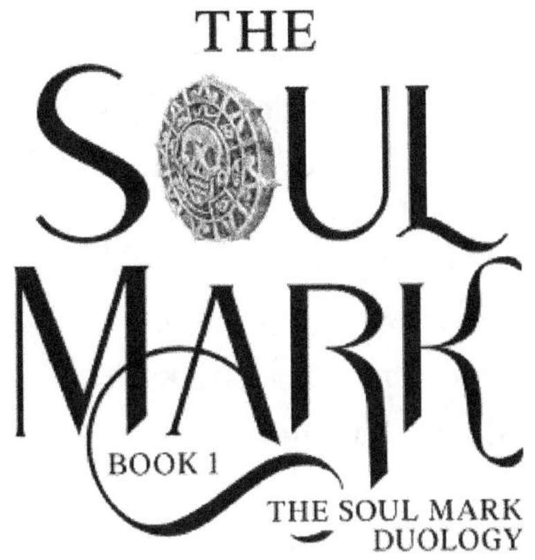

BOOK 1

THE SOUL MARK
DUOLOGY

J. J. FISCHER

For Dave, my Samwise Gamgee in the wilderness

"But the goat on which the lot fell for Azazel shall be presented alive before the LORD to make atonement over it, that it may be sent away into the wilderness to Azazel."

- Leviticus 16:10 (ESV)

THE PRISON-ISLAND OF AZAZEL
LEGEND
COASTAL PATH
FARMLAND
VOLCANIC DESERT
MILITARY OUTPOST
SETTLEMENT
W
N
S
E
WORMWOOD
LOBELIA
ANJELICA
MT. ECILA
URIAH'S HIDEOUT
PENNYROYAL
ACONITE
NERIUM
TANSY
BELLADONNA
FORT
ARNICA
HELLEBORE
THANATOS HOUSE
MAP NOT TO SCALE
COPYRIGHT J. J. FISCHER 2021

Glossary of Words

Some of the following words and their associated meanings are taken from colonial or old British English. Others are of my own invention.

Ague – Recurring malaria
Ambidexter – A double dealer
Arguefy – Argue
Cheek music – Eloquent talk, but often idle in nature
Chirk – In good spirits; cheerful
Cleverly – In good health
Cramp-words – Difficult or obscure words
Crumpsy – Short-tempered or irritable
Dauncy – Noticeably unwell
Eternity box – A coffin
Eye servant – A servant who only attends to their duties when watched
Feeze – Fretful excitement or alarm
Fishy – Drunk
Gallinipper – A large biting mosquito or other insect
Gapeseed – Any astonishing sight
Gut-foundered – Extremely hungry
Jeddarty-jiddarty – Entwined or tangled
King's picture frame – The gallows
Land pirates – Highwaymen; here used to refer to marauders
Lank-sleeve – A one-armed man
Limpsey – Limp and flaccid, usually just before fainting
Mutton-headed – Stupid
Pot valiant – Courage or valiance as a result of drunkenness
Polrumptious – Raucous, rude, or disruptive
Sevenday – A week
Slitherum – A dawdling, slow-moving person
Smug – Well-dressed
Solemncholy – Excessively solemn
Sullens – A bad mood, otherwise known as a fit of the sullens
Swill-belly – A heavy drinker
Unchancy – Potentially dangerous; not safe to meddle with

Chapter One

A large lump settled in Sela's throat, and she wondered if she and Liri would ever sing together again.

Her older sister stood sedately before the priest, her spine forced straight with the help of her overly tight stays, hands folded neatly in front of her, dressed in her sevenday best—the dark red wool gown that would likely be faded by the time Sela was old enough to claim it as a hand-me-down. Though the dress was her favorite of Liri's wardrobe, on a day like today, it looked uncomfortably like blood.

Surpassing Liri's gown in a richly tailored, ankle-length cassock was the priest, his tonsured head gleaming by the light of the paraffin wax candles scattered liberally across the room. His nasal voice droned on, dipping into the polished finery of an Old Tongue whenever his hearers showed any sign of understanding his meaning, as if the intent of his sermonizing was to remain as eloquently obscure as possible. Reaching the conclusion of some lofty vein of thought, his hoary eyebrows shot up and rheumy blue eyes lifted to survey the watching crowd.

Sela craned her neck to peer around Liron, who stood beside her holding their two-year-old sister, Cadence. She caught only a glimpse of the famed Book of Souls before the priest hefted it closed and an altar server bore the tome away. Had the priest been reading from the Book of Souls the whole time? Or were his somber-sounding reflections his own? Either way, she wished she understood more of his words. Precious few people knew the Old Tongues, and even fewer of those dared risk the censure of the Carver's servants by sharing them with an overly curious thirteen-year-old girl.

Thank the Carver for Teodoir.

The altar server returned, and the priest cleared his throat. It sounded dusty, like cobwebs had gathered there while he spoke. Liri straightened, and beside her, Tucker Alexander did the same. Sela thought she saw them clasp hands briefly. So Liron was right—they *were* sweethearts. As if he read her thoughts, she felt a nudge from her older brother, but by the time she met his eyes, a serious air had snuffed out his customary light-heartedness. He held Cadence tighter against him, as if aware that any moment, Liri could be taken away from them forever.

The Carver forbid it. Only those firstborn children divinely chosen by the lot would be stripped of their souls for the sake of their families' sins. Only those who *deserved* exile. And neither Liri nor her sweetheart, Tucker, deserved anything but a life filled with sunshine, wildflowers, and the music Liri loved almost as much as Sela.

The priests said that the lot was merciful—one child sacrificed to spare dozens more. Each year, the name of every firstborn child who had reached the age of accountability, eighteen years, went into the lot. Of hundreds of children, only a dozen would be chosen to receive the soul mark—or, more accurately, the soul *stain*. After being ritually branded on the hand by the priest, they would each recite the oath that pawned their soul for the sake of their family, and all the families whose children had escaped selection.

And then they would go to Azazel, never to be heard of again.

Since Liri was the eldest child, and Liron's older twin, they had always known she would face the lot. But Sela believed, as her parents did, that the Carver was just. The priests said that those chosen were selected by the will of the Carver. If you stood against the lot, you stood against *Him*. A fearsome accusation.

But the Carver would never choose Liri, Sela was sure of it. Beautiful, gentle Liri, who filled their house with warmth and goodness and light. Who Cadence favored in looks, with her silky blonde hair and sea-green eyes.

"We're nearly there," Liron whispered, prodding her again.

He'd seen the ceremony before, then. How? Had one of his friends undergone the sacred ritual?

The priest muttered something that sounded like an incantation, and the tension of the large, candlelit chamber drew unbearably tight, like a drawstring. Only one of the ten firstborns would be selected to make up the dozen sent to Azazel, as the Old Town—capital and largest city of Eremia—would host many such ceremonies today. Behind the firstborns, their families gathered, wringing moisture from nervous hands despite the chill wind that wove through the room.

On the other side of Liron, Sela's father curled an arm around the waist of her mother. The night before, Sela had heard Ashira weeping through the thin walls of their home, Yaron's deep voice steady and reassuring. Watching as the priest eyed the ten firstborns like a vulture assessing his prey, Sela held onto the memory and her father's conviction.

Liri was safe.

Liri had said once that she heard sounds as colors, and, sometimes, colors as sounds. Colored hearing, she called it. Tilting her head to one side, Sela tried to imagine the proceedings as Liri might experience them. Would the ring of a deep, throaty bell echoing through the chamber remind her sister of tarnished bronze, or a charcoal, ashy gray? Would the blood red of the priest's cassock remind her of a solemncholy blessing, a shouted warning, or the hacking, bloody cough of those poor souls who'd never recovered from the river fever?

Might the thud of Lord Auberon's boots across the groaning wooden dais sound like absolution, rather than finality?

Dressed in an austere black cassock and shoulder cape ensemble that seemed to promise more portentous happenings than joyful ones, Lord Auberon took the priest's place, his eyes raking the firstborn offerings and hardly straying to the families gathered behind them. Sela had never seen the esteemed elder of the Righteous before, though she knew enough about the sacred order to remember that they mostly wore white robes, unlike the common priests, who always dressed in red. But today, on the day that every person dreaded, except for those whose firstborn were grown past the age of accountability, he would wear black.

Black for death, or for justice?

As Lord Auberon took up the priest's monologue in the Old Tongue, Sela's gaze strayed to a boy standing a little behind Tucker, just as she and her family stood behind Liri. He could hardly be much younger than Tucker—seventeen, perhaps, and nearly as tall as her father, who stood to his left. More young man than boy.

Well-built, with graceful limbs designed for the flawless execution of the fighting techniques Liron had recently begun sharing with her, he stood with his arms crossed and feet nearly shoulder-width apart. Confident, then. Her eyes lifted to his face, and she understood who he was from the obvious family resemblance.

Tucker's brother, Caleb, spoken of many times, but never met. He had Tucker's striking, strong-boned features, but the hair that curled across his forehead and over his ears was chestnut rather than copper. As if sensing her attention, his eyes swiveled to her. In an odd contrast to the tension in his face, he gave a slow smile, followed by the slightest of nods.

Sela tore her gaze away, color seeping up her neck. What would he think, catching her staring at him? At seventeen, he would have finished school. As the second son, free of the ever-present threat of being sent to Azazel, he would be looking to his future. And by all reports of his keen mind and zeal for the Carver, it was a very bright future indeed.

She should be looking to hers.

Carver, please spare Liri and *Tucker. For Liri's sake. And Caleb's.*

Lord Auberon ceased speaking, and all thoughts fled. Switching to the common tongue—the *lingua franca* they shared with the mainland countries—he projected his voice so that it seemed to penetrate even the darkest corners of the room.

"Good men and women of the Old Town, and of Eremia. We are gathered here today, not for death, but to celebrate life. By the blood and sacrifice of one of these young men or women, our eternal destinies are counted as secure. 'Tis the Soul Carver's will that through the blood of the one, many will be spared…"

Lord Auberon was handsome in a classical sense, or rather, *beautiful*. His soft cheeks bore not even a hint of stubble, and Sela wondered if he ever had to shave. Somewhere in his forties, he was well past the usual age of needing to. Even Liron was shaving. Was Caleb?

Sela shunted the thoughts away. A wool-gatherer and a slitherum, her mother sometimes called her. Liron was less kind when he was trying to teach her something and he caught her daydreaming instead.

"…and now," Lord Auberon was saying, "we shall proceed with the lot."

Sela jerked upright, watching Liri do the same. The moment of truth. When this was over, they could all go home, and Liri would be free of the anxiety that had dogged her steps the last few months. She could bond with Tucker, if she wanted to. Or one of the half-dozen admirers that had darkened their doorway over the past year.

Lord Auberon snapped his fingers, and the red-garbed priest hastened forward, clutching a small chest. The lid opened with a tiny *click*, and Lord Auberon extended the same slim fingers into the velvet-lined interior, his hand devoid of the many jewels the priests usually wore. Sela knew ten gold coins lay inside, each engraved with the name of one of the firstborns. The coin of the chosen one would be delivered to the member of the Righteous who would escort them to Azazel. The other coins would be distributed to the freed firstborns, a lifelong token of their deliverance, to be borne in a spirit of gratitude. Many wore the coin sewn into their clothing or strung around their neck as a good-luck charm.

The Carver had spared them once, they reasoned. He might spare them again.

Lord Auberon selected a coin, balancing it between thumb and forefinger, then inspected it briefly. He nodded, as if unsurprised by the name scratched there. That was good. If the coin bore Liri's name, he would have looked startled. People always hated when a woman was chosen. But what about Tucker?

Sela chanced another look at Caleb. His arms were still crossed, but his hands now clutched his elbows, as if he gripped them for strength. His full mouth was pressed into a firm line.

If Tucker was chosen… *poor Caleb*. Should the bond between the brothers prove as strong as Liri had said, he would never recover.

"Liri Meriweather, daughter of Yaron and Ashira, is chosen by the Carver's lot to be exiled to Azazel. Miss Meriweather, please step forward."

Sela blinked twice, then froze. Beside her, Liron went equally rigid, and Cadence began to cry. Their mother's soft weeping quickly trumped even Cadence's tears.

Only Liri remained silent. With perfect posture, she stepped forward to stand before Lord Auberon. Looking stricken, Tucker extended a hand to touch her arm, which quickly fell to his side as if she'd burned him. Liri looked back and smiled at him, her eyes gleaming with moisture. After today, he could never touch her again.

"I offer myself as a substitution," Liron announced, handing Cadence to their weeping mother and bounding forward. He set one man-sized boot on the platform. "I am her twin, after all. I am of the age of accountability."

Lord Auberon studied Liron from above the bridge of a narrow nose. His voice was not unsympathetic. "You are the younger twin, not the elder. And you know as well as I do, Master Liron, that the Carver's lot allows no rite of substitution. Miss Liri must submit to her destiny, and you must submit to yours."

Liron's shoulders sagged in defeat. Liri turned again and sent her twin one of her most beautiful smiles. Bravery mingled equal parts with sadness. To be torn from one's family for life—horrible.

But to be torn from one's twin…the other half of one's soul, or so it was said. Was the superstition true, then, that of every pair of twins, one was cursed to live a miserable life?

The priest appeared with two altar servers, bearing an ornate black bowl that resembled a cauldron, although the outside was the color of gold and artfully wrought. Sela smelled coal smoke and felt a wave of heat even from where she was standing. Suddenly her legs worked again.

"Nay!" she screamed, bounding past Liron to where Liri had extended her palm to Lord Auberon. She jerked her sister away from him. Although five years older, Liri was small and delicate for her age, and Sela registered the heady taste of success. Now to escape with Liri somehow… Sela spun around, searching through the drifting smoke for possible exits, but a strong hand clamped onto her arm.

She looked up into Lord Auberon's pale face. If she'd been Liri, his dark gray eyes would have sounded like the hiss of water droplets landing on hot metal.

"There is no escape from the Carver's will, young Miss…" He hesitated, evidently not knowing her name.

"Sela," she shot back defiantly.

"Peace, Sela," came Liri's gentle voice. "Lord Auberon, would you allow me to speak with my sister?"

"It must be done quickly."

"Aye, it will be." Liri sank to the floor, bringing Sela with her in a puddle of mingled red and blue skirts. Sela stared into her older sister's green eyes, refusing to give in to the impulse to memorize her features, because that would mean saying goodbye forever. "Beautiful Sela, Lord Auberon is right. You cannot argue with the Carver's will. And if 'tis His will that I go to Azazel…" She briefly choked, then caught herself. "Then I must go."

"It can't be the Carver's will. Someone must have made a mistake. This is *wrong*."

Liri's slender fingers stroked her cheek, brushing away tears Sela hadn't known she'd shed. "'Tis not up to you to decide what is right and what is wrong, dear one. Before you land yourself in more than your usual share of trouble, you must go. You must…let *me* go. I will never forget you, Sela. I love you."

Over their heads, Lord Auberon's voice was indignant. "Mister Yaron, won't you restrain your daughter?"

Yaron, his arms full of Ashira and Cadence, shrugged helplessly.

It was Liron who came for her. "I'll look after her," he said to Liri, with a steadiness Sela could only marvel at, given the churning of her own insides. "You look after *you*, sis." A million things passed between them, impossible to translate into words, and, not for the first time, Sela felt like an intruder.

If twins truly shared a soul, this day theirs would be torn in two.

Liron raised Liri to her feet and then gathered Sela against his chest. When she shoved him away, he easily lifted her and dragged her from the platform, only setting her down when they were beside their parents again. Yaron sent him a grateful, albeit plaintive, look. Ashira buried her head in Cadence's soft hair and wept harder.

Liri's glance strayed from Sela to Tucker, who only bowed his head. Liri stiffened, as if registering the sudden abandonment. Would he not try to rescue her? Would he not even say goodbye?

You cannot argue with the Carver's will.

It didn't seem like Tucker was even contemplating dissent.

Fear flashed across Liri's features, but she turned away and extended her hand again. Lord Auberon took it in his, then placed his other hand over her head, near her crown.

He murmured what sounded like a prayer, too soft to hear.

"The transfer is complete," he announced, withdrawing his hands, and turned to the altar server. He withdrew a long metal rod from the hot coals which glowed orange-red. At the end of the rod was a X shape, like the cardinal points of a compass.

There were no more prayers. As Lord Auberon pressed the brand to Liri's skin, her shoulders jerked and she suppressed a gasp of pain.

Sela lunged forward, but Liron caught her around the waist and held her firmly against him. "I'm sorry, little sister. There's nothing either of us can do." She felt his tears dripping into her hair—the straight, ebony-black hair that was the same as his, and the opposite of Liri's.

It should have been *her*. Sela. Liri was light to her darkness. Liri was ordinariness to her many oddities. Sela was more twin to Liron than Liri. She even looked more like Liron than Liri did, though her brother had Liri's green eyes. Why hadn't she been born the eldest? Why hadn't the Carver chosen *her*?

"I willingly pawn my soul so that others I love may live," Liri was saying, prompted when she faltered by Lord Auberon. All of the firstborns had learned the pledge, but nine, at least, were relieved they had no need to say it.

"By this soul mark, those I love are absolved of their sins. And by this stain on my skin, all shall know that I am soulless, and unclean. After today, I swear never again to set foot on Eremian soil, or to touch or bond with"—she gave a small choke, then continued—"any unbranded person. I will never wear gloves or conceal my soul mark in any way, lest I stumble an unbranded person or jeopardize their eternal destiny. By the grace of the Carver, who gives life even to the condemned, I will live out the rest of my earthly days on Azazel. When I die, having pawned my eternal soul in exchange for the absolution of those I love, I will cease to exist. This fate is final and cannot be reversed."

Her shoulders drooped, and she clutched her burned hand. All around, the families of the firstborns and the firstborns themselves sighed, as if Liri's pawned soul had granted them eternal absolution that quickly. Only Sela's family remained as they were.

The red-garbed priest, now wearing white silk gloves, reached for Liri's arm. She followed him from the room obediently, without a single backward glance at the family she would never see again.

Sela tore herself from her brother, making for the heavy door they'd entered barely an hour ago with so much hope for Liri's deliverance. Halfway there, her foot hooked around the base of a heavy wooden pew and she lurched toward the ground.

A strong arm reached out and grabbed hers, preventing her from falling. She winced at the warmth of bare skin against hers—warmth that Liri would never experience again, at least not amongst those still in possession of their souls.

"Steady, now," said a deep voice above her. "You nearly fell."

She glanced up into the face of Tucker's brother, Caleb. He visibly started as he glimpsed her eyes. People usually did, although violet-colored eyes were generally considered lucky, along with other oddities, like a rare name or mushrooms growing close to a fence in the springtime.

Sela looked down at Caleb's tanned hand on her bare arm. "I'm steady."

He released her abruptly. "I'm sorry about your sister."

"I'm happy for your brother."

She tried not to prove herself a liar, but Caleb appeared unmistakably relieved. Although the memory now belonged to a murky haze, she recalled him embracing Tucker with an intensity she'd never before witnessed between any pair of brothers. He turned the saying "closer than a brother" into a glaring falsehood. They might as well have been twins.

She sighed and imagined her breath as pure white, vacating her lungs with the force of air escaping a pair of bellows. Did she even have a soul? Or were the priests as deceitful as she was, pretending she didn't wish Tucker had been taken instead of Liri?

"Take heart," Caleb said, still studying her from his superior height. "The Carver always makes His will known in time."

Even at thirteen, she knew Caleb Alexander was only parroting his betters. Dislike for Tucker's brother settled into the pit of her stomach. If the Carver condemned one such as Liri to a lifetime of suffering and exile, then Sela—and even Caleb—deserved no better.

You cannot argue with the Carver's will.

She imagined the wisps of her soul seeping out from her chest, as black as the locks of her hair. If she had a soul, it had vanished today, along with Liri's. Spinning around, she left Caleb standing in the middle of the room, his mouth slightly parted as he stared after her. She would leave him to his fancy future and his prim sayings.

Only outside, in the gathering dark of the streets, did Sela allow herself to cry.

Let me go, Liri had said. Liri, who sang songs to the Carver so beautiful that even the trees roused themselves to applaud her.

But Liri was gone.

And Sela would never sing again.

Chapter Two

Six years later

"Against the Corruptions of the flesh, ye must take a stand, young masters and misses. A Soul, once lost, is lost forever. A Soul mark, once given, cannot be ungiven, hence the X placed on the palm during the branding, barring the way back to the body forever. Bless the name of the Carver."

"Bless the name of the Carver," Sela repeated wearily, losing interest in Father Monroe's customary offering of bread and condemnation. Why would they thank the Carver for eternal damnation? She didn't follow the good Father's logic, though she'd long since given up trying to argue with him. She'd suffered too many days spent standing in the bitterly cold corridor without a shawl or cloak as punishment. But when she still smelled her sister's burning flesh six years after she was branded for sins not her own, she struggled against the urge to smack the man across his shiny, sweaty forehead.

He was talking about Liri.

At nineteen, Sela was nearly too old to attend the compulsory religious class. But Father Larken had insisted she take another year of instruction, desperate to beat the Defiance and Contempt out of her, as he put it. "To shape her into a good candidate for the Binding," he had said to her parents a year ago, despite—or maybe because of—her still being in earshot. She had almost laughed. If any man was drawn to her as a lifetime prospect, she would question both his judgment and his sanity.

And she didn't want to be bonded to a fool.

For Cadence's sake, she tried to pay attention, even as her eyes drifted about the room. Sixty or so children crammed the large chamber, of which she was likely the eldest. Not enough tables or chairs were available for everyone, so many sat on the stone floor, or leaned against the back wall, as she did. Cadence perched in front of her on a desk, the patched knees of her wool stockings showing beneath her plain dress.

Aye, there were better things Sela could be doing today. Like making sure her family wouldn't starve or freeze to death come winter.

This late in the afternoon, it would already be cold outside, but inside, the chamber was stuffy, making her uncomfortable in her tight stays and warmest gown. A fire to the right of Father Monroe spluttered and smoked, usually barely sufficient to warm the good Father's backside, let alone those of the sixty or so others. Watching the priest sweat profusely, Sela wondered how it was possible to be both hot and cold at the same time.

"The Book of Souls sayeth…"

Sela straightened, then slouched again as Father Monroe resurrected one of his favorite aphorisms. She hardly knew what was really in the Book of Souls and what only rolled around in the man's head like stray marbles, since they were too often conflated. The only time she'd seen the Book itself was at the ceremony that had taken Liri. Did the priests quote the Book from memory? And did the Book really say that Liri was condemned forever? Six years gone, and it felt like a lifetime.

For Liron and their parents, too.

"Bless the name of the Carver," Father Monroe finished with a solemncholy air, and Sela obediently mumbled the words, her heart lifting at the priest's dismissive tone. Like sparrows liberated from a cage, the students quickly emptied from the room. She was free for another afternoon. Perhaps Liron would spar with her again tonight, once Cadence and their parents had gone to bed.

Cadence pressed against her side, and Sela tucked her arm around the girl's shoulders. In Liri's absence, all of them had grown closer, as if fearful that, one day, another would be dragged away from them. The day after Liri was taken, Sela had moved into her older sister's bedroom, desperate to cling to any part of her. Though the room had long since given up any hint of Liri's lavender fragrance, Cadence's insistence at sleeping beside Sela went a long way to reminding her of her beloved sister. Even at eight, Cadence was a miniature Liri. For that reason, Ashira kept her closer than a favorite shawl.

"Is Liron coming to walk us home?" Cadence's sing-song tone betrayed a hint of the beautiful voice that had labelled her a musical prodigy at the tender age of four.

"He promised he would." Sela tugged her closer. "We'll meet him at the gate. Come on."

Together, they walked toward the door. Father Monroe materialized before the threshold like one of the king's guards that paced outside the palace. "You seemed distracted today, Sela."

Outside the confines of his sermons, Father Monroe usually lapsed into the common tongue, or mainland speech, as they often called it. Without his *thous* and *thees*, the man appeared oddly normal, the expression in his eyes almost kind.

"Liri was taken six years ago today." Feeling Cadence tremble, Sela wished she hadn't spoken. The girl had no memory of the ceremony, although she remembered enough to know that life before was filled with light and joy, while afterward was marked only by darkness and despair. Still, their parents tried to shield Cadence from grief and painful reminders as much as they could. Their mother would not be pleased to hear Sela bring up the subject.

"Taken?" the priest repeated. "Sela, you must know—"

"That 'twas the will of the Carver, *aye*. I know."

He looked somewhat askance at being interrupted. "Azazel is not death, Sela, nor should you think of it as such."

"Then what is it?" The only things she knew with any certainty were that Azazel was far, far away from the Old Town and Eremia, and that Liri was there…possibly suffering.

"'Tis simply…a wilderness. A place of lawlessness where the

soulless roam free. Though one might call it a final mercy to those who have no eternal destiny to look forward to." He shook his tonsured head. "I've already said too much. The only thing you need to know, Sela, is that you will not find the Carver in that forsaken place."

"Why would the Carver send Liri there, then? Surely, He would not abandon her? I thought the Carver was a God of love."

As if he hadn't heard her question, the priest patted Cadence's blonde head and stepped away. "Good evening to you both."

She could ask Teodoir. Her beloved mentor would know, having been a priest himself, although now his shoulders bowed inward with many years and their accompanying sadnesses. He'd lost his own eldest child to Azazel, before Liri was even born. Did Teodoir know what fate had befallen Liri? Six years of questioning had not softened him. But perhaps she could try again, trap him into answering, even send Cadence…

"I'm cold." Cadence shuffled her feet. "Can we go home now?"

"Of course." Sela removed her shawl and draped it around the girl's shoulders, then steered her from the room. The crisscross of dark passageways was barely lit by several candles—tallow, judging by the acrid odor—and Sela was glad she knew the way. This late in the year, the thick evening fogs descended early, and even the oil lamps did little to illuminate the dark streets.

Leaving the seminary, they crossed a courtyard dominated by starkly naked trees which had lost the last of their glorious coverings the sevenday before. At the heavy wrought iron gate, Sela paused, shifting her weight from one foot to another. Usually, their father sent Liron to escort them home, wary of the streets of the Old Town at this time of night, inhabited only by lamplighters and mischief-makers. Were they too late? Had Liron already come and gone?

"Where's Liron?" Cadence tugged on Sela's skirt. "Isn't he coming?"

"He's always here. He's probably just a little late, is all. Come here." Dropping to her knees, careful to keep the hem of her everyday gown out of the gutters, she drew Cadence close. The streets appeared deserted, the fog having descended early. Had Father Monroe waxed on for longer than usual?

They waited for half an hour, until the fog had fallen so thickly that Sela could hardly see more than a few yards beyond the perimeter of the seminary. Feeling miserable without her shawl, though glad that Cadence was warm, Sela squinted into the gloom.

Liron, where are you? Not for the first time, she wished she was allowed to bring Roux to the seminary. Roux, who was better than any guard dog. But the priests didn't permit animals to be the passive recipients of religious instruction, and so Roux stayed at home, to the disappointment of everyone who had ever met him.

"I want Mama." Cadence buried her face in Sela's gown.

Darkness had almost fully fallen. Their brother wasn't coming. Sela tried not to think of the significance of that, for she could too easily imagine Liron lying somewhere in a gutter, bleeding out from a head wound. The loss of Liri had drawn close the possibility of every kind of misery once thought only to befall others.

"Come on." She took Cadence's hand as they set off down the foggy street, unable to see even the shop windows. "We'll start without him, and maybe he'll meet us on the way." She affected a casual, unworried air. "Do you think he's been sidetracked chasing Etta?"

For once easily diverted, Cadence giggled. "She's very pretty."

"And prone to fits of the sullens."

"Don't you like her, Sela?"

"I don't like any girl who looks at Liron like he's a tasty piece of mutton she'd like to serve up for her dinner."

Though her brother was five years her elder, they'd grown close in the years since Liri was gone—so close that Sela often thought of him as *her* twin, rather than Liri's. When he'd returned from his military training a year ago, he'd been fascinated by the art of war, and after more than a little begging on her part, had agreed to teach her what he'd learned. Though firing his flintlock pistol or musket remained off-limits due to the noise it would inevitably produce, she'd practiced loading the weapons and sighting a target, in addition to self-defense, swordplay, wrestling, and even a little boxing.

"And who will you bond with?" Cadence asked with uncharacteristic slyness.

"Did Mama put you up to this?"

"Nay, Liron did."

"Why? Is he tired of fighting off suitors on my behalf?" Sela guided her sister around the shards of a broken bottle lying scattered in the street.

"I would've thought *you* would be the one doing the fighting."

Sela halted and stared at her sister. Sometimes, Cadence's perceptiveness surprised her. Was she really only eight? But then, a girl who had lived through what Cadence had—the deep grief of her parents, the void left by a beloved sister who she could not help but resemble, the ashes of a life that would never be—was no ordinary girl.

"You know about that?" Sela began cautiously.

"I know you're always sweaty when you come to bed at midnight. And there are calluses on your hands."

"Those are from the farm chores."

"Or so you say." The sly look came again. "*I* think…"

But the shadow that broke through the fog in front of them cut off whatever thought Cadence had been about to express.

Still holding Cadence's hand, Sela stepped forward. "Liron?"

"For you, pretty girl, I'll be anyone you like."

Not Liron, then. The words were faintly slurred. Was the stranger fishy? Sela stepped in front of Cadence and eyed the man as he detached himself from the surrounding gloom.

Her height or a little taller, but broad, with solid shoulders that fit snugly beneath his greatcoat. A craftsman of some kind, or even a soldier? Nay. His stained but well-tailored breeches were tucked into finely made leather boots, while an ornate flintlock pistol rested in the holster at his hip. His long hair was clubbed at the nape of his neck in the fashion of younger men who weren't old enough to wear wigs. He spoke perfect mainland speech, despite the slurring.

Well-educated and possibly wealthy, then. And not in control of his better faculties, judging by the look in his pale eyes.

Either way, he was unchancy and not to be trusted.

"Step aside, sir, and we'll be on our way."

He only came closer, and she smelled the wine on his breath. *Definitely fishy.* "What's your name, pretty girl?" His hand drifted to the black strands that had escaped her pins, and she jerked away, dragging Cadence back with her. His gaze flickered to her face and his eyes widened. "You have uncommonly lovely eyes."

"And you have uncommonly poor manners, sir." She pulled her sister in a wide berth around him, just as she had the broken glass, but his hand shot out and grabbed her wrist.

"Don't go leaving so quickly. I only want to talk to you."

"My sister and I are leaving, sir. Unhand me."

When he only smiled lazily at her, she wrenched her arm. His fingers held fast. Strong, then. No soft-pawed aristocrat, despite the stench of wealth that lifted from him. Sela thought of the knife she kept in her boot at Liron's urging. Would she be able to reach it? Not while Cadence was possibly in danger.

With her free hand, she pushed her sister away from her, in the direction of home. The house was not far, and hopefully Liron would meet her on the way. Or a kindly neighbor would see the girl and intervene, although that was less likely in the wake of the river fever whose indiscriminate kiss of death still kept many bound to their homes. Cadence stumbled and made as if to return to her side, but Sela shook her head.

"Run, Cadence! Go home!"

Curling her fingers into a fist, Sela brought her hand down on the man's wrist, delighted to hear him yowl in pain. She pulled on her arm, and it came free. But before she could scuttle to a safe distance, he reached out and jerked her back against him. His wine-soaked breath fanned her ear as his wiry arm curled around her throat, restricting her air.

"Calm down, pretty girl. We're not far from my home. Come with me, and you can cool down a little." He rubbed her chilled, bare forearm, then fingered the lacy cuff at her elbow. "Or warm up. You're half-frozen, love."

This time, her fingers curled into talons, and she raked at his arm, dragging in a full breath as her throat was freed. Pulling down hard on the limb, she twisted under his arm and out of his grasp and scampered backward, reaching for the knife in her boot and plucking it from its sheath. She held the weapon up in front of her, her chest straining against her stays, her lungs raking in air so fiercely she feared they'd burst. She glanced to her left to make sure that Cadence had gone, then sucked in another sharp breath.

Her sister had not moved.

Recognizing the frozen look on Cadence's face as blind terror, Sela tried to draw the man away, brandishing the knife. Thankfully, his attention remained on her, his mouth curved in a leer. Had he forgotten her sister was there? Sela didn't want to risk urging Cadence to run again in case he remembered her presence and tried to hold her sister hostage. What man was so brazen as to attack a woman on the street while there was a witness? Definitely part of the aristocracy. She'd wager her own soul on it.

The relaxed smile had hardened to flint. He held up his arms, showing smooth, unmarked palms. "Easy now, girl. I said I wouldn't harm you."

Unbranded or not, she didn't trust him an inch. "I don't care for your word. Or for strange, fishy men." The knife wavered in her hand. Had this man hurt Liron?

"Fishy?" He grinned. "I'm not fishy."

Without warning, he lunged at her. Despite previous assertions of his sobriety, he moved wildly off-balance, and his body collided with hers, bringing them both to the cobbles. Her hand lashed out of its own will and he yelped. The breath was smacked from her lungs—she'd broken his fall. Stunned, she lay there, momentarily breathless, as his hand shot out and grabbed the wrist that wielded the knife, trapping it against the cobbles. His weight and the heavy fog pinned her. By the light of a lone oil lamp, she saw him smirk as his hand glided over the bodice of her gown.

"Now there, my violet-eyed girl, don't you think—"

Her knee jerked upward, connecting with his groin, and his entire body crumpled. The grip on her wrist loosened and, suddenly panicked, she brought the knife up between them just as he lost his balance and fell against her. She felt him grunt, and his stale breath whooshed out. His body went limp, his head lolling against her chest with sickening familiarity.

"Get off me!" It took some effort to remove him from her person, but finally he rolled away onto his back. Or rather, she rolled *him*. She caught her breath between her teeth. The knife she still clenched was bloody. Had she injured him? Kneeling beside the man, she caught a glimpse of his staring eyes and his blood-soaked waistcoat and nearly retched. She didn't need to feel for the pulse at his neck to know that he was dead. She'd seen enough scarlet-mouthed corpses in the river fever epidemics.

Only, *she* was the one who'd killed him.

Sela dropped the knife like it was poison. She looked down at her gown. Her bodice was soaked in his blood. This time, she did retch, right there on the cobbles, until her stomach could heave no more. Finally, she looked up at Cadence, who still stood frozen, but had inched a little closer.

"Don't look, little sister," she said desperately, selecting the term of endearment Liron often used for his younger sisters. "Stay away."

"Is he…is he…dead?"

"Aye."

Oh, what had she done to the girl? How could Cadence ever be the same again? One sister was soulless, another a murderess. She couldn't escape what she'd done. Murder was punishable by death. Father Monroe had said as much that very morning.

'Twas an accident! Carver, forgive me.

"What are we going to do?"

We? Cadence still thought of them as a "we"? There was no including her sister in this. Sela scrambled to her feet and crossed the street to Cadence, careful not to touch her sister and unintentionally bloody the girl. But Cadence threw her arms around Sela's waist, burying her cheek in her stomach. The blood that stained her younger sister's face was more than Sela could bear. Nausea swelled.

"What do we do?" Cadence said again.

Sela did the only thing she could think of—the only thing she'd ever done.

She ran.

On the threshold of Mister Teodoir's house, Cadence began to sob uncontrollably. "I'm sorry, Sela, I couldn't…"

"You did nothing wrong."

"But that man came for you, and I couldn't even move to help you."

Sela dropped to her knees, at eye level with her sister. "Listen to me, Cadence. None of this is your fault. That man attacked us. And fear…" She remembered her initial reaction at Liri's ceremony. "Sometimes fear paralyses us. 'Tis not your fault."

Her lip wobbled. "Or yours, Sela."

That, at least, remained to be seen. Trying to quell the shaking in her hands, Sela stood and knocked on Teodoir's door, three smart raps that her old mentor, even with his fading hearing, would register. She hated to bring trouble to his door, but if anyone would know what to do, Teodoir would. And since he lived on the outskirts of the Old Town, on a small croft given to him by Sela's grandfather, they would be safe here.

For now.

The heavy oak door swung open, the firelit room beyond dispensing the familiar scents of tallow, pipe tobacco, cinnamon, and rosewater—the favorite fragrance of Teodoir's late bondmate, Meribah. The old man himself looked ready to bed down for the night, but when he saw Sela's bloodstained gown, his drooping eyes widened beneath snow-white eyebrows.

"Sela, my dear! Whatever happened to you? And Cadence… Quickly, girls, come into the light."

Taking both of their arms, he pulled them inside, gently steering them toward the hearth. He looked between them, evidently at a loss. "Oh, my dears…"

"'Tis not my blood," Sela said quickly. "Nor Cadence's. Neither of us are hurt."

Nodding once, he reached for a cloth, then the handle of the heavy cast iron kettle that hung above the hearth. "Tea," he muttered, as if that would fix them both.

"Mister Teodoir, we don't have—"

Catching sight of Cadence shivering, Sela bit off the reply. She pushed the girl closer to the fire, then collapsed into one of the rough chairs Teodoir had fashioned while still a young man. Even after all these years, the furniture held fast.

She watched her mentor with more than a little fascination. Although he'd unofficially tutored her for most of her life—as he had Liri and Liron, and as he would Cadence, once their mother relaxed her protective stance—she'd only once been in his house. He always came to their small farm for lessons and stayed for supper with her family afterward.

She watched his capable, callused hands as they prepared tea, one hand shaking a little as he poured hot water over the dried leaves. Because of age, or fear? She'd never known him to be fearful of anything, excepting the healthy dose of terror he nurtured for the Carver. Did he know he now sheltered a murderess? That, even now, the soldiers were probably hunting for her?

She stood abruptly. "I shouldn't have come."

"Sit, Sela." Teodoir pushed a chipped cup into her hands, then another, slightly less full one into Cadence's small fingers. Always a father. And mindful of possible spills, even when the world was imploding.

Teodoir lowered his lanky body into his favorite armchair, a faded, slouched-back relic Meribah had last re-upholstered before Sela was born. He cradled a cup of tea in his own workworn hands.

He seemed to be waiting for something.

Sela traced the smooth handle of her cup. "Aren't you going to question us, Teodoir?"

"I'm guessing you'll share when you're ready."

She understood in that moment why she had flown to Teodoir for refuge. Though he bore a great love for the Soul Carver that Sela could hardly understand—or emulate—she had always admired his wisdom, determination, and patience. He'd served as a priest in the religious orders well into his middle age, until he'd fallen in love with a woman. While some in his position had chosen to remain where they were and take the woman in question as a bondlessmate behind closed doors, Teodoir was a man of honor.

And yet, he'd had no desire to join the ranks of the Righteous, the religious order whose initiates were free, unlike the priesthood, to pursue the Binding. Sela had always wondered why he spurned them. Instead, Teodoir gave up his priesthood to bond with Meribah, and became a simple farmer, craftsman, and humble tutor.

Sela had always counted him, next to Liron and Roux, to be her greatest friend. Now, he would be her confessor.

"Teodoir, I killed a man today."

Cadence abandoned her tea on a nearby table and fled into Sela's lap, wrapping her arms so tightly around her waist that Sela sloshed her own tea, spilling several drops on the floor.

No visible reaction came from Teodoir's lined face, but he reached out and collected the hot beverage, depositing both their cups next to Cadence's. Clearly, tea was not the remedy he'd thought it was. Keeping her eyes lowered, Sela recounted the entire story, from Liron's strange absence to her decision to walk home.

"I could have asked the priests for an escort, but I didn't think…" She choked off an internal rebuke, then finished her grim tale, relating the accidental death of her attacker as emotionlessly as she could, for Cadence's sake. She'd left her bloodied knife with the dead man, having no thought to do anything but run. Would such a mistake implicate her now?

"And you came straight here," said Teodoir at last, the gravity of his baritone voice filling her with dread.

"Aye." She finally raised her eyes to his and was astounded at the compassion she glimpsed there. He felt sorry for her? "I shouldn't have involved you, Teodoir. But I didn't know what else to do. I couldn't… I couldn't come home like this." She gestured to her bloodstained gown. "Not today."

Not when today marked exactly six years since the loss of Liri.

"Oh, my dear." He scraped a hand back through thinning hair as white as the robes of the Righteous. "I am aggrieved this terrible thing has befallen you." A single tear slipped down his leathery cheek, and Sela stared at it. She'd never seen Teodoir cry, not even when he accidentally pounded his thumb with a hammer and shattered the bone. "You have borne more than any young woman your age should have had to bear."

"But I *killed* him…"

"'Twas an accident, Sela. Whatever happens from this point on, remember that truth. The Carver is merciful—"

"What do you mean, 'whatever happens from this point on'?" Sela clutched Cadence closer.

"What will you do?" he asked, simply.

"They don't know 'twas me. Assuming no one saw what happened but Cadence, I… the fog was thick, after all…"

"You intend to run?" His voice held no emotion.

"What other choice is there, Teodoir?"

"You were attacked, my dear, and bless the Carver that you and Cadence are unharmed. Bless your quick thinking and desire to protect your precious sister, as well as yourself. But a man is dead, Sela. His family will be wanting to know what happened to him."

"I can send them an anonymous letter containing the truth of it."

Teodoir frowned. "Would you spend the rest of your life running, Sela? Could you hide the truth until your dying days? More still, would you ask Cadence to lie for you?"

"You think I should turn myself in?"

Cadence raised her blonde head from Sela's middle and began to cry again. "They can't take Sela! They can't! I won't let them!"

Teodoir reached out and patted the young girl's hair. "The Carver has all of us in His hands, my dear." He met Sela's gaze meaningfully, as if there were more he could not say in front of Cadence. "We will talk later."

He stood and the chair groaned as it yielded his tall frame.

"I will escort you both home. Your parents will be frantic with worry. But first, you must both change your clothes. Meribah was about your size, Sela, although not quite so tall. And we will have something for Cadence, I am sure of it."

Though it was late to share a meal, Teodoir stayed for supper. Sela counted small mercies. Despite the sisters being nearly two hours late and dressed in different clothes than the ones they'd set out in that morning, her parents said nothing about either abnormality. Her mother gave Sela a tight hug and then swept Cadence into an even more vigorous one.

Had they expected such odd happenings on the anniversary of Liri's branding? Or did painful remembrances of such a great loss merely inspire quiet resignation to every subsequent misery?

Sela turned to her father as soon as Teodoir had followed her mother and Cadence into the living room. "Where's Liron?"

Yaron frowned. "He was summoned to the king's court this afternoon. Something about new orders. He was to come for you and Cadence on his way home."

"He didn't." Sela spun away before her father could read her expression. Thankfully, and probably due to her shivering and his weariness from laboring in the icy fields, he didn't press her. But the question in his eyes remained as she headed upstairs to the tiny room she shared with Cadence.

Even Roux was more sedate than usual. While he usually greeted her at the door, tonight she found him on her bed, curled in a tidy ball. When Sela appeared, he stood and stretched like a cat, his narrow snout split in a wide yawn as he uttered his familiar high-pitched bark of greeting.

Sinking onto the mattress, she buried her murderous hands in his soft red coat. Good thing she'd scrubbed the blood from them at Teodoir's before changing into Meribah's faded green gown. Clever as he was with that finely attuned nose, could Roux still smell the blood beneath her nails?

She'd first come across the red fox when he was little more than a cub, perhaps only six months old at most, which meant he would have entered the world around the same time Liri was taken from it. Sela had risen early in the morning to feed the chickens, her first daily chore, and found the beautiful animal writhing in the tiny space beneath the wire that fenced the coop—the very gap their father had asked Liron to fix the day before.

Easing closer, she'd realized the fox had been snagged by the wire, the sharp ends of which pierced his fine coat. Struggling as he was, blood already streaked his fur.

With Liron's help, she'd freed the fox and tended his wounds, all the while managing to steer clear of the snapping jaws with their fine black whiskers. With seemingly no trace of the vixen, dog fox, or other cubs, the animal had sought more and more contact with them, even once given his freedom, until eventually he became tame enough to eat from their hands.

She called him Roux-manteau—Roux for short—which meant Redcoat in one of the Old Tongues that had long since passed out of common use. It had been years since Roux had slept anywhere but on the end of Sela and Cadence's bed.

Teodoir would call it the grace of the Carver that Sela had such a friend to fill the void left by Liri's absence. But Sela joked with her brother that by keeping Roux—an animal which had sought to viciously end the lives of their precious chickens—she honored her father's advice to always keep her enemies close.

The vulpine version of a purr emanated from Roux's throat, and Sela moved her hand to the fox's pale belly. He sprawled across her lap, licking her hand once, as if in reassurance that no amount of blood could ever come between them. Sela stroked his ears, frowning. He seemed strangely morose. Was he sick? Or did he sense what had happened? Like a dog, he often absorbed his mistress's moods.

"I wish you had been there today, Roux." Her enemies had been rather *too* close.

"Sela! Supper is ready." Her mother's musical voice drifted up the stairwell.

Reluctantly, Sela stood and the fox scampered off her lap, eager to accompany her downstairs. He padded beside her as she descended the staircase, the sag and groan of each step mimicking the weight on her heart. How could she face her family?

Before Liri's ceremony, the lamplit, comfortable, tobacco-scented space after supper had always been filled with music. Her father's pipe, Liron's makeshift array of drums, Liri's fiddle, and all of their voices blending in perfect harmony. After Liri, there'd been no music for two years, until the discovery of Cadence's talents awoke memories of the old days like a flickering flame. Now, most nights, her father and brother played while the rest of them sang, save Sela, who refused to sing a single note until Liri's fiddle joined them once again.

Tonight, there was nothing, not even the gentle hum of her mother as she worked at her loom after the dishes had been washed and tucked away. No one questioned why Teodoir stayed, or why Ashira made no protest at Roux's noisy assault on the leftover mutton bones. The solid, earthy presence of both seemed as much a comfort to her parents as to her.

The door opened and banged closed, as if the knob had been

jerked from an unsuspecting hand by the force of the wind. Liron burst into the room, and Sela was glad that Cadence had been sent to bed an hour before. Rain beaded the shoulders of Liron's greatcoat, surely soaking into his marine's uniform beneath. The wind and rain had together turned his hair into wildly spun meringue.

Sela ran to him, and he pulled her against his chest as Roux bounded gleefully around their ankles, good humor and energy restored. "I'm so sorry," Liron whispered, though the regret in his voice was more compelling than any apology. "As you can see, I was delayed."

"What kept you?" their father demanded, his usually gentle manner absent.

Liron faced him directly, looking as if he stood down the cannons of the mainland armies with nothing more than the flintlock pistol at his hip. "They let us go as soon as we heard."

"Heard what, my son?"

"About the scuffle in the streets near the south seminary, where the girls attend the mandatory religious classes. Somebody killed a man."

"A man?" Sela's mother looked about to faint. Her father's pale face was strained. Only Teodoir appeared unrattled.

"And not just any man. The son and heir of Lord Brigham."

Chapter Three

As blood pounded in Sela's ears, Liron turned to her with obvious relief. "I was so worried about you and Cadence. Is she upstairs?"

Numbly, she nodded. At their feet, Roux yelped, and Liron bent to stroke his fine fur, oblivious to Sela's state of shock.

"Lord Brigham's son?" her father was asking. "The one the high priest was grooming to take his place?"

Sela's stomach plummeted. Not only had she correctly guessed that their attacker was wealthy, he was wealthy beyond all imagining…and powerful. She leaned against the wall, wishing she could be absorbed into its frame. Why couldn't she have been prone to fainting spells, like Liri and their mother? There was nothing she wished for more than oblivion.

"My friends," said Teodoir, before Liron could answer. "There is something Sela and I must tell you before you hear more."

All eyes swiveled to Sela, despite Teodoir's generous use of the words "and I."

She curled shaking hands into fists as she faced them. "I was the one who killed him." Seeing Liron's mouth open, she obliterated all uncertainty as to her meaning. "I killed Lord Brigham's son."

A brief, shocked silence stole over the gathering. When the room burst into questions—her father's, mother's, and Liron's—Sela's knees trembled, and she felt Teodoir's hand on her elbow, steering her to a chair.

"Easy, now," he murmured, dropping into the chair beside hers. "Tell them what happened."

But she could no longer move. Or speak. The terror that had

settled over her the day Liri was taken had returned, this time to freeze her permanently. Only when Roux jumped onto her lap and pressed his nose against her shoulder did she start to thaw.

"You killed…" Liron's face paled to such a deathly white she feared he might have caught the river fever. "I don't understand."

Teodoir squeezed her hand, and she almost jolted at the contact. "There's not much to tell. It was an accident." Slowly, haltingly, with the warmth of Teodoir's hand and Roux's fur holding the numbness at bay, she began to recount the afternoon's happenings. It seemed an eternity before she was done, every retelling of her sins carving another piece from her soul. Or was her soul already banished from her body by the Carver?

Had she already been rendered tainted?

"Cadence and I ran to Teodoir's house," she finished. "He helped us change into fresh clothes before escorting us here. And that is all of it." Tears swelled, but she angrily blinked them away. "I swear 'twas an accident. I never meant for Lord Brigham's son to fall on my knife."

"Did anyone see you?" Liron's first thoughts evidently ran along a similar vein to hers. Was he contemplating running? Hiding?

"Not that I could tell, given the near darkness and the heavy fog, but Cadence and I were both terrified. We left as quickly as we could."

"Are you all right, Sela?" Her mother's soft voice. The urgency of the question kicked up a notch. "Is Cadence…"

"Neither of us are hurt, Mama." By the stiffness of her back, she would be badly bruised by morning, but no need to share that with her mother. Ashira had not coddled her in years. Not since Liri.

Her father stood next to the hearth, and by the light of the smoldering flames she watched him age ten years. "Teodoir? What do we do?"

As with Cadence, the *we* was a small comfort.

The older man straightened. "There are heavy rumors that

Lord Brigham's son is—uh, was—an unsavory character, much too fond of drink and women. What the high priest saw in the man beyond the gold glinting from his father's purse is beyond my understanding…" He trailed off, and Sela glanced at him in surprise. He'd never spoken poorly of the order he'd left behind, not even when many of his former colleagues shunned him. Was he angry? Or only tired? Something glinted in his eyes with heat enough to stiffen his spine.

Teodoir continued, "Still, Lord Brigham has influence enough to put down any rumor. He has the ear of the king. If Sela shares what really happened, I fear they will not believe it. They may kill her for defending herself."

Ashira put her head in her hands and began to cry softly. Wordlessly, Sela's father crossed to her and enfolded her in his strong embrace. Sela felt a pang of loneliness. She didn't begrudge her parents comforting one another, but it often seemed as if they forgot her presence. Wasn't she deserving of comfort?

But nay—she was a murderer.

Liron shrugged out of his greatcoat and dropped into the chair on the other side of Sela. "Teodoir's right. They'll sentence her to death, attempted rape or not." Guilt etched every line of his face.

Sela flinched. Until now, she'd not allowed herself to contemplate the man's intentions. She'd thought only of Cadence's safety. Despite the ample heat of the room, she began to shiver.

Her father cleared his throat. "We don't know that anyone saw her."

"Would you ask Cadence to lie for you?"

Teodoir's earlier question bounced around in her mind. She paused in stroking Roux's coat. If no one had witnessed what she'd done, and no soldiers came for her, she could assume a normal life. She would finish her year with Father Monroe. After that, she could work in her father's fields or at her mother's loom. She could even shackle her broken spirit to another poor soul's, if her parents insisted on her pursuing the Binding. There were enough unsuspecting young men who would cheerfully volunteer for the lifetime work-in-progress that was Sela Meriweather.

But Cadence would know the truth. What would the forced keeping of Sela's secret do to the girl who'd already lost so much? She would never tell, Sela knew. Even at eight years old, Cadence was loyal to a fault. But to save Cadence from herself…

And if you give yourself up, Sela, what then? Cadence would lose her too. Two older sisters gone, and with Liron soon to leave with the king's ships for war. But she would be sad for the truth, and not for a lie.

Because she had a courageous sister, and not a cowardly one.

The trembling eased. She clenched her fists and spoke over the others. "As soon as 'tis first light, I'm turning myself in."

The second uproar sounded so much louder than the first that Sela feared they would wake Cadence. Roux scrambled from her lap, sending her a filthy look. But Liron grabbed her hand.

"You heard Teodoir, Sela. If you confess, they'll likely execute you."

"There'll be a trial."

"Not a fair one," he countered. "Not with half or more of the jury in Lord Brigham's pay."

"The priests and some of the Righteous will be in attendance. And 'tis often said that the Carver loves mercy…"

Though Teodoir's face betrayed the fact that he did not know how those two sentences of Sela's fit together, she saw a glimmer of pride at the last part. Did she really believe it? The Carver had also sent Liri to Azazel.

"*Nay,*" Liron said decisively, glancing to their father for support. "Listen, Sela. I received my orders today. I'm to sail two days from now." She felt her stomach fall, but his grip on her hand tightened. "I can hide you on the ship. It won't be easy—you'll have to disguise yourself as a boy, and your living quarters will be cramped—but 'tis better than what you'll face here if they come for you."

"You're headed for war." She felt the blessed numbness returning. "With the mainland."

Many years ago, before Sela was born, Eremia had broken off from the rest of the mainland countries, which had formed a central conglomerate to consolidate their power. Though the Old Town's technology was rumored to be more dated than that of their mainland counterparts, their sheer numbers, large navy, isolated position, and wealth of resources had allowed them to retain their power. But the mainland countries—at least, those which had not yet fallen to Eremia—still made for a formidable enemy.

"I'll protect you." Liron said clenched his jaw. "Once we've made berth, I'll find a place for you, and you can safely reveal yourself as a woman."

"On the mainland?" Ashira said through her tears. "We'll never see her again!"

"'Tis better than the eternity box," Liron replied, and their mother began weeping again, likely imagining Sela lying cold and lifeless in her best gown.

"I admire your ingenuity and courage, Liron," said Teodoir at last. "But 'tis Sela's decision."

Sela stared into her mentor's face. What did he believe she should do? Was it right to cast herself upon the Carver's mercy? To surrender herself, even to death? What if the Carver forsook her the way He'd forsaken Liri?

And if she left, would her family ever recover? Would Cadence?

Her father finally spoke. "'Tis late, and we have kept Mister Teodoir from his bed too long. I will accompany him home." He looked between her and Liron. "And we will decide these matters in the morning, once we have rested and broken our fast."

Always the optimist, Yaron Meriweather, believing that there would be rest this night, and clarity with the sunrise. But Sela dutifully nodded her agreement.

Teodoir folded her in an uncharacteristic hug, smelling of pipe tobacco and rosewater. Though she was taller than the average man, he stood taller still, and his stubbled chin briefly grazed the top of her head. "You are not alone, Sela," he said softly.

"Remember that. Even in the darkest places of the world where man may fear to tread, *He* is there."

She did not have to wonder which *He* Teodoir meant. The way he emphasized the word—the same way the priests and elders emphasized their words sometimes—left no room for doubt.

The Carver of Souls.

Late that night, she lay in bed listening to Cadence's light breathing and Roux's dream-induced whimpers. How was it that only that morning, she had woken in this bed with a strange squeeze of contentment, before remembering that Liri was still gone? She'd not thought she could lose more than what she already had.

How she wished she'd stayed in bed.

The rhythm of Cadence's breathing changed, and Sela felt the girl huddle closer, her small hands wrapping around Sela's stomach.

"Sela?"

"Yes?"

"Promise you won't leave me, like Liri did?"

"Dearest, Liri didn't choose to leave us. She was chosen." How Sela hated that she now echoed the priests, the same way Tucker's younger brother had. Empty platitudes had a way of propagating themselves in spaces that were otherwise impossible to fill.

"Why couldn't someone else be chosen?"

"I don't know, Cadence. But you should sleep."

"I'm not sleepy," she said, but a yawn betrayed her. "Sela?"

"Yes, dearest?"

"I love you."

"Why do you love me, little one?"

"You're always so…brave."

Her heart squeezed as tight as a fist. "I love you too, Cadence. Always remember that." She kissed the girl's forehead, and several moments later, heard her breaths lengthen and deepen.

Reassured, Cadence had fallen asleep and forgotten to obtain

Sela's sworn adherence to her request. Sela reached out to Roux, expecting him to be immersed in some vulpine dream of multitudes of chickens without wire coops to contain them, but the fox licked her hand. Wriggling over, he settled himself between her and Cadence, his luxuriant tail finer than any mane of hair.

Aye, she was thankful for small mercies—though she was on rather poor terms with the One rumored to dispense them. That Cadence would have Roux, and Liron would have his regiment, and her parents would have each other. Even Teodoir would have his memories of Meribah. Only she would be alone.

"You are not alone, Sela. Remember that."

An hour before first light, she carefully folded Meribah's gown over a chair—her mother would have to return it to Teodoir—and dressed quickly in one of her own gowns, a soft wool of darkest red like Liri had worn the day of her ceremony. Liri had Sela to help her dress, then, but Sela moved quietly, not wanting to awaken her family.

She looked in on her parents, committing their sleeping faces to memory, then at Liron, sprawled on his bed, still fully dressed except for the sodden greatcoat puddling on the floor. The straight black hair that mirrored hers slanted across his pale forehead. Tomorrow, it would likely be gathered up in a tidy queue, as Liron the brother and son became Liron the marine and soldier. What did Etta think of her brother's orders?

Last of all, she looked in on Cadence, curled around Roux. When she entered, the fox glanced up, his intelligent eyes seeming to take in everything she could not put into words, just as Liri had once looked at her twin. He gave a soft whimper, suddenly more devoted dog than indifferent cat.

"Stay, Roux. Look after Cadence."

The fox lowered his head to the mattress. Did she glimpse sadness in his eyes? Nay, it was foolishness to think so. He was only an animal.

"You're always so brave." Cadence's words, which had confirmed her decision the night before.

She tore her gaze away.

Today, for the first time in her life, she would be.

"'Tis only a year, Caleb. Why are you so anxious about it?" Pushing his empty plate away and leaning back from the table, Tucker grinned. "Is there a woman you've been pursuing whose interest might fade after a year away?"

Caleb punched his brother in the arm playfully, his frown morphing to a smile. Only his brother could get away with such an outrageous comment. "You know there isn't anyone, Tuck."

"Then why your reluctance to go?"

Dropping the silver utensils he'd used to rearrange the food on his plate for the past half hour, Caleb sighed and let his chin sink into his steepled fingers. "I don't know."

"You said it yourself when we were both home last sevenday. Last a year on Azazel, and your future is secure. The Righteous will never let you put a foot wrong."

"That's true. But I believed the position would involve…religious instruction. Matters befitting a servant of the Carver. But 'tis not that at all. The description is closer to…maintaining security. Establishing perimeters."

"As an o'er-guard, you mean." Tucker squinted at him. "So far, I don't see a problem."

"Even you've heard the rumors, Tuck. Azazel is home to the worst of men and women."

Realizing his blunder too late, Caleb watched as Tucker swallowed.

Dropping his gaze to a fascinating section of lace tablecloth, Tucker finally cleared his throat. "You can speak her name, Caleb."

Liri. Caleb didn't know the girl's last name, or anything about her beyond her pale, ethereal beauty, but he knew how much she'd meant to his brother. Sweethearts only, not potential bondmates, though given a couple of years, Tucker might've asked her. But she'd been taken in the same lot that spared Tucker. As far as Caleb knew, his brother had hardly looked at another woman since.

"Why didn't you go to Azazel?" Caleb asked carefully. "You're a year ahead of me, after all." Even as he asked, he knew why.

"The opportunity was offered," Tucker replied lightly, "and declined. I thought it best to let old wounds heal over without pawing at the scabs." He shook his head, and the clouds slowly retreated from his eyes. "But you should go, Caleb. Those who return from Azazel are highly esteemed, since they've been exposed to the worst of temptations and triumphed over them. The elders would take you under their wing. Mother and Father would be beyond proud."

Was that why Tucker remained here, a mere guard for the high priest while Caleb's future had never looked brighter? Caleb's brother had never bested him in hand-to-hand fighting—one of the first levels of training to enter the ranks of the Righteous, the elite group whose authority trumped even the priests', and was second only to the king's—but he was sharp, intelligent, fast. Had the elders viewed Tucker's decision as a snub? Did they know he hadn't yet forgotten Liri?

And likely never would?

Caleb steered the conversation to less treacherous waters. "Then you're not worried about Azazel corrupting me?"

"Corrupting you? You're the most honorable man I know, besides myself." Tucker gave his customary wink. "If anyone can resist temptation, 'tis you. And besides, Lord Auberon will be going with you. The man is as severe as they come."

"Lord Auberon?" He'd only met the man once—six years ago, to be precise—but even that brief meeting was enough to spark interest. Zealous as he was for the Carver, Lord Auberon shunned the trappings of a wealthy lifestyle and channeled a seeming contradiction of passion and restraint at every turn. Rumor had it that he'd even weeded out the thistles among the Righteous.

Beyond that, Caleb knew nothing about the man.

"Aye, I heard that he wants to see about restoring order to Azazel. Things have grown a little wild there in recent years." Tucker twisted his grimace into another strained smile. "What else is holding you back?"

Caleb considered his brother to be the closest friend he had in all the world, but even so, he couldn't tell Tucker about the sliver of unease that had begun to grow in him. Why, when everything was falling into place, did he suddenly have these doubts? His mentors among the Righteous could not be wiser. The priests had shown him and his brother kindness after kindness. His parents could not be more pleased…

He shook his head. "'Tis nothing. Probably just nerves."

"You don't have *nerves*, Caleb. I've never seen you question your judgment. Not after you've made your mind up. And you *did* agree to go."

He had, until the real purpose of his going had been revealed. Not to be an agent of mercy, seeking to reach out to the soulless— if only to offer comfort to those who had no eternal destiny—but an o'er-guard. Someone to watch the watchers, to be precise.

It had been years since he'd used his fists or fired a weapon. He hadn't enjoyed that part of his training, even though he was surprisingly good at it, and still took care to stay in shape. The elders of the Righteous said that physical training built discipline, endurance, and perseverance. All good character traits for a servant of the Carver, and of the king. But in him, the combat training had only grown unrest, a nagging disquiet that stole the comfort he'd formerly found in the Carver's words. If they were men of peace, why train him as a man of war?

Tucker was still studying him. "Lord Auberon says that the o'er-guards have very little to do with the prisoners. You're there for the other guards, mostly. Azazel presents a whole host of temptations. And not all men are as strong as you are, Caleb. Physically and otherwise."

Caleb raised his eyebrows. He'd long ago learned that the

strongest man was the one who admitted his weaknesses, not the one who boasted of being immune to them. "You won't consider coming with me?"

Tucker glanced away. "Someone has to stay with Mother and Father. As you know, Mother hasn't felt cleverly recently."

Likely a case of the recurring ague, and not enough of an excuse for Tucker to stay—or Caleb, for that matter.

He wove his fingers together, admiring the gold signet ring that Father had given him on his twenty-third birthday, a month past. Though Tucker was the eldest son and bore the real signet ring, they were so close that Tucker had insisted another ring be made for Caleb. Their parents had happily obliged, as they had most requests that maintained the harmony between the brothers.

Tucker was right. It was only a year. If it was wasted, he had the rest of his life to ascend the ranks of the Righteous and win the approval of the elders.

Nay—of the Carver. That was what mattered most.

Caleb planted his hands palms-down on the table and pushed himself away from his uneaten dinner. "Then I'll go," he said, pleased when the unspeakable heaviness of his heart minded its business and stayed out of his voice. "And I'll see you before next winter, Tuck—I promise."

The door burst open, and both men spun to face the intruder, Tucker frowning while Caleb's hand moved to his knife. It had taken a near-mugging in one of the back alleys near Tucker's house for Caleb to concede to carrying a weapon on his person, and so far, he'd had no cause to use it for any greater purpose than slitting the neck of an envelope. He dropped his hand when he glimpsed Tucker's butler, short of breath but without any murderous intentions.

"Forgive me, Mister Tucker, for not knocking, but I bring word…urgent word. Your cousin, Mister Josiah…he is…"

"Speak, man," urged Tucker, while all of Caleb's fears reared like a spooked horse.

"He is dead."

Joss Brigham, dead?

Some ten or fifteen years their elder, Caleb had only met the man twice, and disliked him as much on the second meeting as he had on the first. If not more so. But he'd never wished his cousin dead.

Tucker had visibly relaxed. "How did Joss die, Thomas?"

"He was murdered, Mister Tucker, on the streets near the south seminary. The one attended by many of the poorer folk. Stabbed in the chest with a knife—left at the scene, would you believe."

Left at the scene? What murderer would leave his weapon beside the body of his victim, potentially implicating himself?

"Have they caught the man?" Tucker continued to probe.

"The woman, you mean, sir. She turned herself in early this morning."

"The *woman*? Early this morning? Then Joss was killed…"

"Last night. A soldier found Mister Brigham and raised the alarm, but no one saw anything. They're questioning the girl now."

"The girl, you say?" Tucker pinched his jaw between thumb and forefinger. "How old is she?"

"Very young, I hear, sir. She's saying Mister Brigham attacked her—tried to force himself on her while…*ahem*, intoxicated." The butler colored, clearly embarrassed to be speaking so plainly.

From what Caleb knew of Joss Brigham, her story was not so far-fetched. But whether Joss's father, Lord Brigham, would suffer it to be widely believed…that was another matter entirely.

"Thank you, Thomas. We will attend to the matter. You may go."

"I am sorry for your loss, Mister Tucker, Mister Caleb." The butler bowed, then swiftly departed.

Tucker stroked his chin. "I can't profess to be grieving the man's passing. I ever wished his father was not so rich Joss was excused from the lot."

Caleb nodded his agreement. "Still, one of us should visit Lord Brigham. See if we can offer any assistance. His mother and sisters will be grieving."

"What do you think of the girl's claim?"

Caleb frowned, feeling the doubts of earlier descend like the fog that had last night obscured the truth of Joss's death. "I think it likely true."

"As do I. But to respond with murder…"

"In the heat of the moment, she possibly didn't have a choice. And Joss was fishy."

"She could've screamed."

"And you think someone would have come running?"

Tucker nearly grinned. "If you were nearby, *you* would have."

"But I wasn't." Nor was any other honorable man or woman, it seemed, and now Lord Brigham would pursue vengeance against the murderer of his only son…his heir. The priesthood would be furious at the scathing accusations against one of their own.

The Righteous—surely they would be more balanced in their execution of judgment.

His brother sobered. "Since I'm the eldest, I'll go. You must prepare for Azazel, given you'll leave within the sevenday. I'll make your excuses and you can apologize to Lord and Lady Brigham at the funeral."

"You'll attend the trial, then?"

"Aye, as one of us should." Tucker looked resigned.

"And should they cry out for her blood, will you plead for mercy in my stead?"

"I'll consider it, Caleb. But I think it more likely that she'll hang long before Joss settles into his earthy grave."

Chapter Four

Sela had thought the cell where the guards deposited her after being interrogated cold, but this room was colder still. She tried not to flinch beneath the icy stares of the townspeople and, more distantly, the unveiled hatred of the family of the man she now knew as Josiah—Joss—Brigham. His mother and sisters huddled on cushioned seats in the back row, but Lord Brigham assumed a soldier's posture, as if he expected that the proceedings would not be long in concluding. His eyes simmered like coals burned low.

Aye, grief made some cold, and others hot.

Heartsore, hungry, and exhausted, Sela had registered very little of the five days that had elapsed since she'd stolen through the streets to the south seminary, where she gave herself up to Father Monroe. The bewildered man was not without compassion, especially on hearing her version of events, but he was duty bound to deliver her to the king's men, as she'd expected.

"The Carver keep thee, Sela," he said as the soldiers arrived, among them the dead man's furious father. She'd had only a moment to wonder at the ease with which Father Monroe slipped in and out of the Old Tongues before Lord Brigham's heavy hand knocked her to the ground.

Surprisingly, Father Monroe seized her assailant's wrist before he could strike her a second time. "Calm thyself, Lord Brigham, lest ye circumvent the proper application of justice by taking it into thine own hands. Ye must hear her tale, then decide of what fate she is deserving."

"I've already decided," the man snarled, snatching his hand away. "Death, and death only. And I'll thank you to keep out of my business, Father. I apply my own justice."

Still on the ground, her cheek smarting, Sela stared at Father Monroe as he extended a hand to her. "Why would you help me?"

"The heart of the law is mercy," he replied, returning to the common tongue. "Though ever we mortals forget it."

Was this his answer to her question about Azazel? Or something deeper? She allowed him to help her to her feet. Were she branded, he could not have done so—perhaps he knew that. He managed a strained smile as the soldiers seized her arms.

"I will pray for you, child."

"Thank you," Sela said as she was dragged away, beholding the same gentleness she'd seen in Teodoir's face the night before, and wondering if she hadn't sorely misjudged Father Monroe.

Four full days of interrogation in a torchlit cell had followed, during which time Sela almost wished she had decided to run after all. She'd seen no one from her family. Had Liron already left on his warship? Had the soldiers harmed Teodoir for sheltering her? Or—the Carver forbid—her family?

It was only when she'd been escorted into the courtroom that she saw them, sitting as close to the front as they could get. Her mother, with eyes underscored by black half-circles like the coal-dusted miners from the outskirts of the Old Town, looking as if she'd slept as little as Sela had. Cadence sat in her lap with cheeks so pinched Sela nearly wept to see them. Her father, his arm around them both, and next to him, Teodoir, the same look on his face as when he'd sat at Meribah's funeral.

Liron sat slightly apart from them—*Liron!*—his forehead creased in a determined scowl, his arms folded in parallel iron bands across his broad chest. He wore his commoner's clothes. Had he shirked his orders? Refused to sail?

Only Roux was missing.

Sela managed a tight, reassuring smile before the soldier on her right jerked her around with a tug on her manacles. At least they'd removed the chains around her ankles. Did they consider her dangerous? Hadn't she convinced them that she'd never intended to kill Joss Brigham?

She bowed her head. It felt like a dream. A dark, terrible dream. Soon, she'd wake up in her father's chair, with Roux warming her feet and a fire crackling amiably in the hearth. Liron would beat his drums, and her father would lift his pipe, and her mother and Cadence would sing, their soprano voices so high and pure they held the power to summon any lost soul from Hel. To summon Liri and her fiddle, who would play for the Carver…

The vision melted away as seven men glided into the room. Two were soldiers—admirals, perhaps, judging by their regalia and ceremonial swords. Three wore the red garb of priests. The remaining two boasted the elegantly embroidered white robes of the Righteous. Sela saw Lord Brigham visibly relax as he scanned their faces, and her stomach cinched tighter. Whatever eased Lord Brigham's mind could only trouble hers, and if he had found himself allies, then she would be contending with enemies.

The shortest of the red-robed priests stepped forward, and Sela recognized the high priest from the few public ceremonies he'd presided over. With slow, shuffling steps, he ascended the wooden dais where Liri had been branded six years before. Today, the heavy wooden furniture had been removed, and only a single high-backed ornately carved wooden chair with a plump scarlet cushion stood on the platform.

The high priest sank onto the cushion, his red robes pooling around his feet. He braced his arms against the sides of the chair and, though she stood almost directly before him, looked past her—to Lord Brigham, she guessed. He gave a tight nod, and Sela fought the urge to glance behind her. It would only betray uncertainty and weakness. And she would not shame her family further.

"'Tis with great sadness that I preside over this matter," began the high priest in a sonorous tone that belied his small stature, "the murder of my successor, Josiah Brigham, a man of rare and noble character."

Aye, she was going to hang.

"Though the confession of Sela Meriweather has been heard

in full, it has taken some days to determine the truth of other aspects of her account. Namely, the accusation that Mister Brigham, heir to Lord Brigham, did seek to forcibly take from Sela Meriweather her virtue, after the fashion of dishonorable and debauched men."

The high priest drew in a lungful of air, then exhaled heavily, as if he savored the legacy of a fine wine upon his tongue. The rest of the courtroom collectively held their breath as he expended his.

"This court has found no evidence to support this accusation. While Miss Meriweather has maintained that she was attacked by Mister Brigham, leading to a scuffle that occasioned his unfortunate death, there are no marks on her person to support such a theory, and the murder weapon was Miss Meriweather's own knife. 'Tis determined that Mister Brigham's greeting of Miss Meriweather on the street was mistakenly interpreted as possessing foul intentions, which led to the latter drawing her weapon when none was required."

Hot anger replaced cold grief. Sela fought the urge to rush the platform and strangle the man with her bare hands. What about the bruises on her back, ribs, neck, and arms? What of Cadence's eyewitness account—had she even been questioned? Not that Sela would wish an interrogation on the girl.

"The charge of drunkenness against Mister Brigham has also proved to be false. Three of Mister Brigham's friends witnessed him leaving the establishment to walk home and have attested to his sobriety and presence of sound judgment."

A lie. An outright lie. Had Lord Brigham simply paid his son's friends to vouch for him? Or was the high priest blind to the faults of his replacement?

"Furthermore, it has become known that Miss Meriweather is in the possession of several skills consistent with the art of war, taught to her by her brother, Mister Liron Meriweather, who serves in the king's navy. 'Tis believed that Miss Meriweather's evident proficiency with a weapon, misinterpretation of Mister Brigham's intentions, and unnecessary panic are of sufficient explanation for the subsequent tragic loss of Mister Brigham's life."

The high priest's gaze eventually swiveled to her. "While Miss Meriweather is to be commended for eventually surrendering herself to the Carver's justice, it must be taken into account that she also fled the scene shortly after establishing that Mister Brigham was deceased. Thus, I find Miss Meriweather guilty of murder."

"Hang her!" yelled a man near the back, but Sela did not turn to see who had spoken. Another of Lord Brigham's minions? He seemed to be matched, decibel for decibel, by a litany of high-pitched wails near the front of the room. Her mother? Or Cadence?

"The sentence for murder is death by hanging," the high priest stated, then collapsed into an unfortunate coughing fit. By the time he finally cleared his throat, the courtroom was already in an uproar. "Quiet!" he bellowed.

After a few more cries and exclamations punctuated the chamber like stray musket fire, they obeyed.

"Several of my good colleagues—and the members of the jury themselves—have suggested the sentence of death is appropriate, given the gravity of Miss Meriweather's offense. However, I have considered that given Miss Meriweather's age, gender, and otherwise intact record, mercy may be extended in this instance.

"Therefore, I sentence Sela Meriweather, not to death, but to lifetime exile…on Azazel."

As the room exploded again, Sela bent her head. Despair yielded to a strange, piercing joy.

Not death…but Azazel.

Azazel.

Where Liri yet lived.

"I offer myself in her place," came Liron's voice, and Sela spun, catching a glimpse of Lord Brigham's mottled face before settling on her brother's, calmer than any doldrums.

"There is no rite of substitution," the high priest replied calmly, and Sela felt a crushing relief. A second time, Liron tried to save his sister from Azazel. She was glad they wouldn't let him.

"*Exile*? Your Grace, death alone can atone for the loss of my only son!"

As the high priest turned his attention to placating Lord Brigham, Liron edged near Sela, blending in with the heaving crowd. "Why didn't you run with me, Sela?"

She turned as far as her chains permitted her, keeping her voice low. "I couldn't. A life built on lies would have destroyed me. And Cadence, too."

"Better that than what awaits you on Azazel." His face was so grim, she ached to discard the manacles and throw her arms around him.

"But I'm going to see Liri."

"You don't understand, Sela." Liron's voice was pleading. "Azazel… Lord Brigham may believe otherwise, but Azazel is a fate far worse than death."

"How can seeing Liri again be a worse fate?"

"You should've run when I gave you the chance."

"And put you in danger, were I discovered by your superiors? You'd be court-martialed and imprisoned—possibly killed." Sela stared at his clothes. "But what of your orders? Why are you still here?"

"My commander granted me leave to stay until the trial ended. Listen to me, Sela. Teodoir discovered that Lord Auberon was one of the men who advocated for your death, though Father Monroe and Father Larken both pleaded for mercy. Lord Auberon is close with Lord Brigham. Watch your back, just like I taught you. They may seek your death after all…on the open sea where there is no one to look out for you."

Liron's warning fell on deaf ears. Father Monroe and Father Larken had pleaded for mercy?

One of the soldiers who flanked her had finally registered their furtive conversation, and he yanked her head around whilst simultaneously shoving Liron away. "No talking!"

Pulling against the soldier's hold, she strained her neck, trying to catch her brother's eye amidst the crowd. "Liron!"

He spun on his heel so fast the black strands of his unbound hair flicked against his cheek. "Sela?"

"Tell them I love them!" She glanced at their parents, Teodoir...Cadence. "Look after them...please. I'll find Liri, I promise. I'll make sure she's okay."

He looked like he wanted to retch, but he nodded. "I will. Stay safe, little sister." This time, he did not move, but watched her until the man to his left pushed him backward.

"Remove the prisoner," the high priest yelled over the din. The guards turned her around, and the crowd pressed so close she wondered if she would be crushed to death before they could strip her of her soul.

As they drove a path through the mass of people—some crying for death, others wailing for mercy—Sela caught sight of a familiar face, watching her from only a few paces away.

He was older now—six years older, to be exact—and a grown man rather than the boy she remembered. Hair still a striking, glossy copper, with blue eyes as cold as his brother's had been warm. The man who, as a boy of eighteen, had let Liri go without a second glance.

Tucker Alexander.

Sela saw he remembered her, although given he was present at her sentencing, he'd likely heard her name. Why had he come? He was old enough to be bonded, with one or even several children. Surely he'd forgotten Liri by now.

Suddenly, he stood before her. Her guards, preoccupied with battling the heaving mass either side of her, were momentarily distracted. Tall as she was, his eyes were at least an inch above hers. She was not used to having to look up.

His mouth was hard. He pressed something into her manacled hands, and she registered callused fingertips and the smooth caress of paper before he leaned forward to speak in her ear. "For Liri."

Someone stumbled into her, and she fell against Tucker's chest. He righted her with a hand to her waist, but she saw by the downward slant of his lips that he found touching her distasteful, even this side of the branding. Was he the last unbranded soul who would?

The Carver forbid it.

"Won't you deliver it yourself?" she said, with more than a little defiance.

"Nay, you'll do just as well."

One of her guards clamped his hand on her shoulder, breaking her focus. By the time she looked again for him, Tucker was gone.

Tucker watched Liri's sister as the guards half-led, half-dragged her through the crowd. Murderer of his cousin or not, he was glad she went to Azazel, and not to the noose—or the king's picture frame, as commoners crudely termed it. Not because he believed her innocent of the crime that condemned her, but because she would now deliver his letter to Liri.

His apology.

On the matter of her innocence, she'd managed to divide not only public opinion, but that of the jury, and of the council of priests, soldiers, and elders that met to decide her fate. It was the high priest, swayed by the testimony of Father Monroe and Father Larken—who knew the girl personally—who eventually decided for Azazel.

Not that it was the more merciful option.

Returning to his home, he found Caleb hard at work in Tucker's personal study, poring over some obscure text from the Book of Souls. His overly studious brother glanced up as Tucker entered, his unbound dark hair settling over the shoulders of his open-necked white shirt like a cloud, sleeves hastily shoved up to his elbows. Black ink flecked his fingers. Ever fastidious with his appearance, Caleb, excepting the time he spent with the Carver.

"Tuck. I haven't been outside all day. Did you come from the sentencing?"

"Aye."

"And?"

Though Tucker did not believe Caleb and Sela had ever met, he had no wish to invite an association now. Already filled with pity for Joss's victim who'd swiftly become his murderer, Caleb might be drawn to the violet-eyed girl as much as his cousin had been, and to a similar detriment. Knowing that Sela was the sister of Liri would only bind Caleb to her fate more closely. And as strong as Caleb was, Tucker had no wish to invite such a grounds for intimacy.

His brother would be gone to Azazel by the morning. Ensconced in this study, and with Joss Brigham's funeral having come and gone, he would hear nothing of the fate of Liri's sister, who would be sent to Azazel next month, according to Tucker's contacts. Thousands lived on Azazel—perhaps more. The chances of Caleb and Sela meeting were small. Better a minor lie now, and the asking of Caleb's forgiveness later, if the truth became known.

For all his pity, Caleb hadn't even asked the girl's name. Did he think so little of Joss Brigham? Or was he merely distracted?

"The sentence was death," Tucker replied, thinking of Liri. "I pleaded for mercy, as did others, but 'twas for naught. She'll hang at sunrise."

And as Tucker beheld the sorrow in his younger brother's face at a nameless girl's fate, he concluded he'd done the right thing.

"You look dauncy," said a male voice through the bars, and Sela looked up from the tightly folded and sealed missive Tucker had given her to see Liron. Her spirits rose and she clambered to her feet, tucking the letter into a pocket of her skirt.

"I'm fine," she replied hastily, not wanting him or any of the others to worry, although she could not help shivering even as she reassured him. She was ever cold in the cell where they'd stowed her after the sentencing—cold except for one moment that was filled with heat so searing, she never wished to be near fire again. "They let you visit me?"

"Teodoir pulled some strings. Only one of us was allowed to see you. The others wanted to come, especially Teodoir and Cadence, but I won the lot." His smile turned into a grimace. "The only lot in my life I was ever grateful to win."

Sela knew Liron hadn't chosen to join the king's navy. That fate, too, had been decided by lot—and deemed the will of the Carver. She quelled her rising bitterness. She would not let it poison the last few moments she would ever spend with her brother.

"How are they faring?"

He pressed his face so close to the bars that she could see every line his recent cares had worn into his skin. The bars imprinted two more, framing his earnest face in iron shadows. "In truth, Sela…shattered."

"'Twas the only way, Liron. And this way, I'll be with Liri."

"That is my only consolation," he replied. "If it means anything, Teodoir is proud of you, even through his tears. He wanted me to give you this." He reached through the bars for her hand, and she drew back with a hiss.

"*Liron*," she said, a soft apology lining her words. "You cannot touch me."

"They've branded you already?" Horror laced his tone.

She raised both palms to show the livid X burned into each one, smeared with a strange yellow-brown substance—presumably so the marks would endure to her old age. How had Liri borne such agony with grace and poise? Worse, still, was the fact that no unbranded soul could ever touch her again.

Not even Liron.

"I am soulless," she replied, with a shrug. The moment she saw Liri, she would give her the hug denied her for six long years. And she would forget that the twice-branded carried a double curse—still soulless, still without an eternal destiny, but condemned to a season of punishment following death, dependent on the magnitude of one's crimes, and eventually followed by a release to oblivion.

Or so the priests said.

Only those condemned prisoners under the age of twenty-five were offered Azazel and double-branding as an alternative to death, with the hope that they were young enough to atone for some of their sins in their lifetime. The *merciful* offer hearkened back to the days of old when the Carver had supposedly devoted entire cities to those who had unintentionally committed terrible crimes. But some of the condemned still chose death, fearful of both Azazel and the punishment awaiting them in the afterlife. Those who took their punishment via the noose were said to enjoy the blissful cessation of existence.

Another of the Carver's *mercies*.

"That explains the gloves they insisted on giving me," Liron said, with a sour glance at the white material stuffed carelessly into one of his coat pockets. He reached through the bars again. "I don't believe in that nonsense, Sela. Give me your hand."

"If you touch me, they'll brand and exile you too."

He laughed. "Let them try."

Where Liri was—or had been—soft and pliable, her male twin was defiant and unyielding, much like Sela herself. Not for the first time, Sela wondered if *she* was Liron's twin, and not Liri. Was that why, even with the consolation of gaining Liri, it hurt so much to think of being parted from him?

Liron's face softened as he saw her anguish. "Fine, then. I'll pass it through the bars. I won't touch you."

Hesitantly, she extended her burned hand, and Liron placed something on her palm. Another letter, folded and sealed like Tucker's.

"Teodoir said to read it once you arrive on Azazel. He said you'd understand it better then."

She stowed Teodoir's letter beside Tucker's. What was she,

some kind of postal service? "He's been to Azazel?"

Liron nodded. "Didn't he tell you? As a young man and acolyte of the Righteous."

"I thought he never joined their ranks."

"Aye, he did, though he later switched to the priesthood."

"Did he tell you why?"

"Is it important, Sela?" He sighed. "Nay, he didn't tell me. But listen, there's something *I* have to tell you." He glanced behind him, as if fearful of someone listening at the door, and then lowered his voice. "My ship is heading to the mainland, to the port of Consuela, where most of our fleet is stationed. There's a rumor…"

Somewhere in the guts of the prison a door clanged, and Liron flinched. When all was silent again, he pressed closer. "Have you heard the stories of Prince Magnus?"

"Prince Magnus? What has the long-absent son of the king got to do with—"

"Shh, just listen. You know that the king has not been seen in public in years."

"Aye." Her parents had told her that, prior to his long absence, the king was widely known to be just and good-hearted. But in all the years that Sela had been alive, very few professed to have actually seen him. Only his closest advisors claimed to receive his direct instructions.

"Even when I went to collect my orders, I waited half the day with the other new recruits, only for Lord Auberon to appear and tell us that the king was too ill to see us, and that we would be sailing in two days. That was why I was late to…" He swallowed. "Late to come for you and Cadence."

"All is forgiven, Liron."

"I know. But if I hadn't—"

"There's no use replaying the past. Go on."

He wet his lips. "Well, a new rumor has arisen that the king is close to death—if he isn't dead already." Liron continued as if he hadn't just spoken treason. "I'd hoped he might intervene in your trial, but he hasn't intervened in any matter in over twenty years. And Prince Magnus…"

He did not bother restating what they both knew. Prince Magnus Theodorus had gone to the mainland while still a boy, moving among their various neighbors in a bid to build goodwill between them and his father's kingdom. Even to the darkest, loneliest places of their country, reports came of his wise and honorable nature.

But since the declaration of war against the mainland countries a year past—unexpected, given the king's long-reported desire for peace—they had heard nothing more of Prince Magnus. Was he an unwitting prisoner of one of the mainland rulers? An esteemed guest? Had he gone over to their side? Ill as he was rumored to be, not even the king had made an attempt to summon his son home.

"There are reports, Sela, that Prince Magnus is alive and well on the mainland. I thought that if I could find him, I might persuade him to return to Eremia…to overrule the high priest's sentencing."

"*If* you could find him? What of your duties, Liron?"

"Once I'm on the mainland, I'll desert the king's navy."

"*Desert*?" Sela gnawed her lip. "And be shot by our own men when they catch you?"

"*If* they catch me…which they won't."

"Liron—"

"This is your only chance, Sela." His eyes seemed to plead with her. "*Liri's* only chance. I have to do this, lest our parents lose yet another daughter. If anything, I must do it for Cadence."

He was clever, her brother. He knew she cared for Cadence as much as he did. "And if you find Prince Magnus, appeal to him, and he does nothing?"

"You don't understand. I met the prince when I was still a child, though that is a story for another day. He is a good man—a very good man. I know he will pardon you. His very nature is mercy itself."

She held up her marked palms. "'Tis too late for me, Liron.

They say I'll leave for Azazel in the morning."

Seeing her tears, he reached for her, but she reared back. He sighed and snatched the gloves from his pocket, tugged them on, then extended his hands.

Gratefully, she clasped them, barely feeling the warmth of her brother's skin through the white leather. He squeezed, and the tears she'd held at bay since the branding fell with such force she did not even mind the gloved fingers that brushed them away.

"I'll come for you, Sela. To Azazel. I swear before the Carver that I'll come for you."

"Don't make promises with your lips that you can't set your mind to keeping." She sounded so much like their mother that she could see Liron almost smile.

"I *will* be keeping them." He studied her. "You did nothing wrong. You merely defended your honor. Prince Magnus will reverse the punishment."

"But a man is still dead." She smiled weakly. "Perhaps, by going willingly to Azazel, I might atone for his death. Keep myself out of Hel."

"The only Hel is the place you're going," Liron replied swiftly, and then the anger vanished, leaving him strangely stiff. "I'm sorry. Please, be careful. Don't trust anyone. Teodoir said…"

She set her mind to memorizing his face. She wished she could carve it in stone and take the rendering with her. What would her brother look like in ten years? Twenty? Fifty? Would she hear if he bonded with Etta and had children with her? She hoped they weren't prone to the sullens, like she was.

"What did Teodoir say, Liron?" she pressed, realizing he'd trailed off again.

"Time's up, Meriweather," came a voice from behind him.

She heard the jingle of iron keys as a heavy door groaned inward on tired hinges. Liron squeezed her hand as she continued to memorize the exact shade of his green eyes. At least she would have Liri to remember him by.

"Teodoir said that Azazel is a place so dark that even the robes of the Righteous do not shine their usual white. You must be on your guard. But he also said—"

Someone grabbed Liron's arm, and he was jerked away.

"—he said that even so, the Carver is there. I love you, Sela!"

"Liron!" she screamed as his voice faded and the only torch was tugged from the sconce where it had given light. She heard a low chuckle.

"Sela!"

The door clanged shut.

And she was left in darkness.

Chapter Five

Rain at the beginning of a journey was bad luck, or so those more superstitious than Caleb maintained. Or was it rain on the day of one's Binding? Sailors scurried across the deck, liberally scattering handfuls of salt over the boards which quickly melted beneath the vigorous pattering of rain. Yet another superstition, since salt was believed by many to be an antidote to poisons and repel evil.

Either way, there was nothing joyful about today, he thought, watching the sorry chain of soul-stained prisoners trudge aboard the ship from his place on the quarterdeck. At least they were alive, unlike the poor wretch who'd hung that morning for his cousin's murder. Though the more he heard of Azazel, the more he wondered if the king's noose would be a more merciful end…along with the oblivion that followed.

He forced himself not to bury his gloved hands in his coat pockets. The white leather gloves were fine and soft—the best that his father's money could buy, and warm—but they were an ever-present reminder of the coming-of-age lot he still remembered six years later. And the fact that innocents now boarded the ship that would bear them into their exile—and possibly to their deaths.

Eyes roaming the vast ship, the *Deliverance*, he surveyed the dozen or so prisoners that now shuffled their feet on the main deck—a whole year's quota. Young, as expected—eighteen years, to be precise, and slightly more boys than girls this year. Half of them looked malnourished, as if they'd been swept from the streets overnight. Which was entirely likely, given the wealthy and titled were often exempted from the lot, along with only children and the sons and daughters of the elders of the Righteous. Not Tucker, though, since their father was wealthy but untitled.

Caleb's gaze settled on one of the prisoners, a young woman in a dark red gown with raven-black hair that reached halfway down her back. Her glossy locks were as straight as a ship's mast, much like her posture, and he guessed she was tall for a woman, judging by the relative heights of the young men chained on either side of her. Though no waif, he could see she was dauncy by the paleness of her complexion, and the slight sway of her slender shoulders. How long had it been since they'd had food?

She lifted one hand to brush the loose hair back from her face and he saw the soul mark, fresh and angry red against her yellowed palm. The reason for the gloves encasing his hands. Amidst his self-enforced distance, he felt a swell of pity.

It could have so easily been Tucker standing there in her place. *But for the will of the Carver.*

"Lieutenant Alexander."

Caleb forced the grimace from his face as he turned slowly. While they were at sea, he would retain the uncomfortable naval title, though he hoped he could abandon it thereafter. He was no soldier or marine, though the sword and pistol hanging from his hip insisted otherwise.

Lord Janus Auberon stepped onto the quarterdeck with polished black boots that warred with the blinding perfection of his double-breasted cream coat, waistcoat, and crisp white gloves. As befitting his title, the cuffs and standing collar of his coat were embroidered with gold. If it were a sunny day, the two parallel columns of gold buttons would wink in the light. Today, they still emanated a faintly celestial gleam, much like the eyes of the man himself. Like the rest of the Righteous, he wore no wig. A plentiful head of wheat-colored hair was neatly restrained at the nape of his neck with a black ribbon.

An angelic face, Tucker would say. With smooth cheeks that appeared almost boyish despite his middling age and a thin build that might pass as athletic in the right company, Lord Auberon looked every inch an elder of the Righteous. He hadn't aged at all in six years. Likely, he wouldn't age much in twenty.

"Lord Auberon." Caleb bowed his head. "I am honored to meet you once again."

Iron gray eyes swept him head to booted toes. "*Again*, Lieutenant Alexander?"

"I met you six years ago at my brother's coming-of-age ceremony. I was only a boy then."

The older man gave a tight nod. "And your brother?"

"Spared, by the grace of the Carver."

Lord Auberon's smile widened. "I am glad." His gaze swept the line of prisoners and, like Caleb, honed in on the girl he'd been studying. "I have heard much about you, Lieutenant—"

"If the informality does not offend you, Lord Auberon, please call me Caleb. I am unaccustomed to military titles."

"Caleb, then. My fellow elders have told me much of your great promise." His beautiful face turned austere. "I am grateful to have such a zealous man at my side as we head into the abyss." He scowled at the girl Caleb had been pitying.

"My lord," Caleb began, raising a gloved hand to indicate his clothes. Almost rustic next to Lord Auberon's ensemble, but no less pristine—and blindingly white, with the silver trim that indicated a lieutenant's rank. "Lowly acolyte as I am, I am used to plainer dress than this. Are we to wear such garments for the entire voyage?"

"Not just for the entire voyage, but for the entirety of your time on Azazel, Caleb." Lord Auberon turned to examine him, then sighed as he glimpsed Caleb's expression. "I, too, am used to more humble dress, as you have likely heard—and witnessed, six years ago. But on Azazel, we members of the Righteous are few. Guards there are, and guards aplenty, but few men such as us. We must stand out to others. We must be light, shining in the darkness."

"Then we are to minister to the lost?" He swallowed, watching the girl sway again.

"Aye, after a fashion," Lord Auberon replied. "You must watch for our men, Caleb, lest they stray from the path. Azazel is full of dangerous temptations. Your role, amongst others, is to keep your fellow guards from turning aside to the right or to the left. Even in a place of desolation and debauchery, we must maintain a state of absolute purity."

It was as Tucker said.

The girl toppled soundlessly, collapsing into the chest of the boy behind her, who angrily shoved her aside. She sprawled onto the deck instead, causing those whose ankles were chained to hers to stumble themselves. Caleb started forward.

Lord Auberon reached out and grabbed his arm. "*Absolute* purity, Caleb. Watch thyself as much as thou watches thy peers." His sudden use of the priesthood's inflections swept aside any confusion as to his meaning.

Caleb nodded, and what Lord Auberon saw in his face must have convinced him, for the man released his arm.

He bowed, then headed for the fallen girl.

By the time Caleb arrived amidships, the white-gloved guards had already unchained the girl from the rest of the group, touching her as warily as if she were contaminated with river fever. She lay on her back, her chest rising and falling gently, her hands resting palms-down on the deck beside her. She was sweet-featured, if not conventionally lovely.

One of the guards, a ginger-haired man hardly older than Caleb, nudged her ribs with his boot. "Wake up, girlie."

"Have they had water today?" Caleb said, drawing the ginger-haired man's attention to his presence, and then to his white coat. The man's own coat was red, trimmed with silver. Another lieutenant?

"Aye, they've had both water an' food, Lieutenant Alexander."

"Including her?" He indicated the unconscious girl.

"She came from another prison early this mornin'. A last-minute addition t' this here transport. I dunno if she were fed or watered, Lieutenant."

One of the black-coated guards bent and held a cup of water

to her lips. With a soft moan, the girl came awake, lifting herself from the deck with elbows that trembled. The guard jerked away so fast the water sloshed onto his boots. She turned her gaze on Caleb and he sucked in a breath.

He'd only seen two other women with eyes the color of hers, and one of those was a distant aunt who'd passed while he was still a child. The other…

Could this girl be Liri's sister? The one he'd steadied when she fell on her hasty escape from the room? He didn't know her name, consumed as he'd been by the sweet relief of learning Tucker was saved. This woman was old enough, having been twelve or thirteen when last he'd glimpsed her. And her hair had been dark, in his remembering.

But to be Liri's sister would make her a younger child, not the elder one. And she was chained with the other prisoners of the coming-of-age lot and branded accordingly.

Besides, violet-colored eyes were lucky, or so those who speculated as to the significance of rain on the first day of a voyage or the healing touch of a royal would testify. Likely, dozens of women had her peculiar shade of purple-blue, including his aunt. And several of her own age.

Still, he'd never seen a more beautiful shade, sparking with fire as if she hadn't just pawned her own soul. Set off by her black hair, they rendered her uncommonly striking. She'd snag the attention of most men, soulless or otherwise.

The ginger-haired man was staring at her as if contemplating a similar revelation, and the understanding stirred Caleb into action. "Get her some water and food," he said to the dazed guard, without another glance at the girl. "Then send them below."

A distant jingle of chains alerted him to the several dozen other prisoners now coming on board—the doubly branded, those men and women of twenty-five or fewer years whose own sins condemned them to Azazel in lieu of the death penalty. Though he knew that from this point on no practical difference existed between the single-branded and the double-branded—not to the untainted, and certainly not to members of the Righteous, who considered both as having forfeited their souls—he could not help wincing at the thought that this innocent girl would be stowed below with those who'd needed no lot to nudge them toward a life of evil.

Carver, have mercy on her.

And he turned away.

Caleb Alexander was here.

On the ship that would bear her to Azazel.

And he was a member of the Righteous. One of Lord Auberon's favored protégés, if she'd read their distant conversation and body language correctly through the stanchions of the quarterdeck.

Though he'd been surprised by the shade of her eyes, as all who first glimpsed them were, he hadn't seemed to recognize her, nor remember her most distinctive feature. Had she been so unremarkable to him, six years ago? Or was she much altered?

That was likely. She rarely smiled or laughed, these days…and even less since she'd given herself up to Father Monroe.

Caleb remained largely unchanged, although he'd grown into a man's body in the time she'd grown into a woman's one. Handsome, after an enigmatic, scholarly fashion, with the lean muscularity of his older brother, though a little more height. Chestnut-colored, wavy hair now grown long and subdued in a queue, with dark blue eyes that would have been too serious if the lines around his mouth had not confessed his tendency to smile.

Had Tucker known that his own brother was to accompany her into exile? Why not give *him* the message for Liri? Was he ashamed to be discovered corresponding with one of the soulless?

She'd glimpsed pity in Caleb, but mingled with distaste, like one who gazes at the dying and is only the more thankful for his steady pulse. Like Tucker. And, unlike the ginger-haired guard, he did not look as if he wished to give her more than a passing glance.

It was for the better. Many times, in the years since Liri had been taken, she'd wool-gathered on the subject of Caleb Alexander, wondering where his rumored zeal for the Carver and love for his brother had taken him. Now, she knew.

Aye, it was good that he did not recognize her.

The guards ordered them below, and Sela struggled to her feet, taking care to keep her distance from the single-branded prisoners. Though she was as soulless as they, they'd seen her second brand and made it clear they wanted no part of her. She wondered, again, why she'd not been shackled to the second group. Had they come from a different area of the Old Town?

As the other prisoners crowded into the space below the main deck, Sela glanced around. The large hull of the *Deliverance* had been divided into several holds, with the present space revealing several dozen bunk beds constructed from planks of timber, extending in the forward and aft directions. Several hammocks were strung between them, wavering slightly with the swaying of the ship. A roughly hewn set of stairs in the middle of the deck— a companionway, she thought it was called—led down to another hold, presumably where the stores and ballast were stowed. The air already smelled stale.

The ginger-haired guard cleared his throat. He was better dressed than the others with him and wore a fine red coat edged with silver over breeches, a waistcoat, and tall black boots like the ones Caleb had been wearing.

"Right. I'm Lieutenant Ezekiel North. Zeke for short, though that don't affect ye none. Cap'n Foley has charged me with ensurin' yer all comfortable in yer new accommodations. Which are blessedly humble." He paused to snigger briefly. "An' simple. Gents t' the stern side, ladies t' the bow."

"But…" A young man, one of the single-branded who had pushed Sela away as she fainted, glanced at the double-branded who had come below. "We are to live…all together? Us and the…"

He trailed off, face reddening. By the cut of his clothes, he was clearly wealthier than most. Had he expected his father's money to save him from the lot?

Lieutenant North frowned. "Listen here, boy. T' us, yer one an' the same. Single-branded, double-branded, it don't matter. Yer all but soulless now." He jerked his thumb downward. "Once yer on Azazel, ye will see I'm right."

But Sela didn't need Azazel to prove the truth of the lieutenant's words. After all, it was only among the condemned that such divisions—varying increments of sin and judgment—became necessary. The unbranded had no recognition of their need.

The guards moved among them, separating the men from the women, being careful not to touch the soulless except with gloved hands. Sela eyed the double-branded prisoners. Three dozen at least, and nearly two-thirds of those were men, although she knew the oldest would only be twenty-five at most. She understood the red-faced young man's discomfort. The double-branded were a rough-looking lot—even the women. Thieves? Nightwalkers? Murderers…like herself? She gulped.

She glanced up to see Lieutenant North's eyes on her, studying her with a hint of speculation. He smiled pleasantly and strolled over to her. "What's yer name, miss?"

"Sela. Sela Meriweather."

"A pretty name." He tilted his head. "Feelin' any better, miss?"

"A little. Thank you, sir."

His smile broadened, and along with it, the extent of her unease. "I'll be sendin' food and water down shortly. Don't ye worry." He tapped her hand with his gloved one and spun away.

Despite the attentions of the ginger-haired guard, she was relieved the officers, sailors, and soldiers were forbidden to touch her. A small mercy, and one that would work to her advantage.

The other prisoners, however, were another matter. While the men were chained to their beds, the women were allowed to move freely on their side of the hold. Since all of the beds were quickly taken—mostly by the double-branded women who rushed them like a river breaking its banks—Sela sank into a hammock in the far corner of the hold, wondering if she would awaken to a knife at her throat. She didn't have anything of value, but the other women didn't know that.

A loud voice rose above the others, clamoring for attention.

"By the Carver, Molly, lay off!" The exclamation was followed by a string of words so colorful Sela's cheeks burned. She watched as two of the double-branded women faced off amidst the watching others.

The one called Molly seemed older than the rest, with bright red hair scraped into a messy chignon, square shoulders, and freckled hands drawn tight into fists at her side. Her voice, in stark contradiction to her ready posture, was calm—almost bored.

Molly's challenger was a slightly smaller woman with dark-brown hair and flashing eyes. "This bunk here is mine! I claimed it first."

"I don't care, Hester. Take your bag off my bed or I'll throw it overboard."

"You wouldn't dare."

Molly grabbed the offending bag and made to leave with it. Hester's hand shot out, but Molly's fist was waiting for her. The smaller woman crumpled to the floor, clutching her jaw. Molly dropped the bag and raised a foot to kick her in the side.

"Stop!" Sela jolted to her feet and hastened to put herself between the women. Molly's attention transferred to Sela and her foot paused mid-air. She lowered it slowly, studying Sela from head to toe.

"Stop?"

Sela scrambled for the words to end the scrap before it began. "You're fighting over nothing. Can't we settle this peacefully?"

Wrong words, Sela.

Molly's eyes darkened. Her hand tightened into a fist, and Sela had only a second to register the movement before Molly closed the space between them. She jerked her arm up in just enough time to block Molly's punch, sweeping aside the blow like Liron had taught her.

The watching women gasped.

Clearly enraged at being thwarted, Molly stepped past the fallen Hester and faced Sela directly.

"If you would defend her, girl," she snarled, exposing surprisingly perfect teeth, "then you must take her place."

Caleb was surprised to find his quarters spacious and clean. Clearly, Captain Foley ran a tight ship—or was it only because Lord Auberon was on board?

He closed the door to his cabin in time to see the ginger-haired man—whose name he'd since uncovered in a debrief with the captain—exit the adjacent cabin.

"Lieutenant Alexander."

Caleb returned the nod. "Lieutenant North."

"Seein' as we're of the same rank, why don't ye call me Ezekiel? Zeke, for short."

Caleb had no wish to invite further familiarity with anyone on board, save Lord Auberon, but as the lieutenant would be his closest neighbor for the next three months, he relented. "Call me Caleb."

"Pleased t' meet ye, Caleb." Zeke clearly hailed from the poorer districts of the Old Town—perhaps originally a dockworker's son, given his imperfect mainland speech, or the son of a tradesman. While he appeared proud of his rank, he seemed at odds with his uniform and fidgeted constantly. "Yer one of them Righteous, then?"

Caleb nodded. "Though I'm the lowest of the order."

Zeke leaned forward conspiratorially. "Is it true—"

Boots clattered toward them and a flush-faced soldier reared into view, missing Caleb standing next to Zeke. "Lieutenant North, the women…" He dragged in a breath and finally saw Caleb. "Two women be fightin'."

"Already? We've not even left port."

Caleb followed Zeke to the hold where the prisoners had disappeared, glad he'd remembered his gloves. He would have to pin a reminder to the inside of his door. Did a fight in the hold between two prisoners necessitate the presence of a member of the Righteous? Or was he only curious?

Several dozen women crowded around the fighters, though they quickly parted for the newly arrived marines, including himself. Two women stood facing each other, fists raised in front of them, the taller woman standing protectively over a third woman on the floor.

He started as he recognized the taller woman as the raven-haired girl from before. She didn't strike him as the type to start a fight—or be in one in the first place—but as he watched, her reasons for doing so quickly became apparent.

"Knock her down, Molly!" called one woman, evidently oblivious to the marines' presence.

"Get her good, Sela!" another yelled, echoed by several others.

So the raven-haired woman—*Sela*, pronounced *Say-la*—was the crowd favorite. Because she'd defended the third woman?

Molly, who was shorter than Sela but far more solidly built, threw a punch that would have floored a man. Sela reflexively blocked it, then moved out of the other woman's reach. Molly snarled and kicked out, and again Sela jerked away, every movement of her body lithe and graceful, in stark contrast to the other woman's brute strength.

Having successfully separated Sela from the girl on the floor, Molly came for the fallen woman instead, who held up her doubly branded hands in surrender. Quickly, Sela abandoned her defensive maneuvers, coming at Molly with a punch of such strength and speed it surprised Caleb. Molly failed to block the blow and grunted as Sela's fist grazed her jaw. Sela's second punch landed squarely in Molly's chest, and she skidded back, breathless.

She was exceedingly well-trained. Especially for a woman.

Beside him, Lieutenant North—Zeke—exclaimed in surprise, and Sela glanced up. Her gaze moved from Zeke to Caleb and her violet eyes widened. Her fists lowered slightly. Was she…*ashamed?*

Molly took advantage of Sela's dropped guard to rush the taller woman, and her advance brought both of them to the ground. Now at a clear disadvantage, Sela struggled beneath Molly as the other woman punched her in the stomach. She gasped and tried to dislodge the heavier woman, but Molly was enraged. Her next fist found its home in Sela's face. Caleb winced at the force of the blow. Why wouldn't his feet move?

"Cease!" Zeke broke his own enchantment and surged forward, marines to his right and left. They dragged Molly away, and Caleb found himself beside Sela, whose eye was already bruising, her lip split and bleeding as one arm cradled her stomach. He extended a gloved hand toward her. Was this the same woman who had fainted in front of him less than an hour ago?

She froze, her gaze shifting from the white leather glove to his flawless, silver-trimmed coat, then to his face, and back to the glove. Wondering if she was afraid, he turned his hand and flattened his palm so that she would not mistake his meaning. But her paralysis only intensified as her eyes flitted to his open palm. Comparing the unmarked hand beneath his glove to her soul-stained one? Caleb cursed his insensitivity.

When it became clear that she would not take his hand, he withdrew it, stuffing the apparently offensive appendage into the pocket of his coat. Slowly, like snow melting beneath the glare of the sun, she relaxed and struggled to her feet. Immediately, she turned to look for the fallen woman.

"Hester, is it?" Her gentle voice fell across his ears like silk. "Are you all right?"

Had she taken blows for a woman she did not even know? The

dark-haired woman, Hester, gave a gruff nod, and Sela extended a hand as Caleb had done—and he tried not to feel slighted at how easily she offered the help, or how quickly Hester accepted it. When both women were standing, Zeke materialized again. Beside him, a barely subdued Molly seethed.

Zeke looked between the three women. "Which one of ye started this here fight?"

Sela pressed her lips together, as did Molly, but Hester stepped forward. "There was a debate over a bunk. Molly insisted 'twas hers, though I'd clearly claimed it. Molly and I argued, and Molly knocked me to the ground. This girl—Sela—defended me."

The violet-eyed girl had gone pale, and Caleb wondered if she would pass out again. She was clearly dauncy. A touch of the ever-relapsing river fever, or mere exhaustion? The impressive bruises forming around one of her eyes only magnified the startling color contained therein.

"'Tis not true," insisted Molly, her pretty face sullen. "The bunk was mine. When I refused to give it up, Hester threw the first punch."

A quick questioning of the watching crowd of women soon proved Molly a liar, and Zeke frowned. "More fightin' like this, an' I'll see each and every one of ye chained for the entire trip, like the gents."

A ripple of unease wove through the women, and Caleb knew Zeke's threat was on-point. Deprived of their precious liberty for three full months? There was no worse punishment.

Save Azazel itself.

While Zeke's back was turned, Molly glared at Hester and then focused her full ire on Sela. She slashed her hand across her throat in a threatening gesture, and Sela swallowed.

Caleb drew Zeke aside. "May I recommend, Lieutenant North," he said softly, "that you separate Molly from the other women for a term. Allow things to calm down a little."

Zeke nodded. "Aye, Lieutenant Alexander. A good idea. T'will be done."

When Zeke repeated Molly's punishment, the stocky woman glared at the others and reached for some colorful profanity that saw her quickly dragged away by Zeke's men. Caleb watched as Hester murmured something to Sela, who merely nodded. Zeke's punishment would grant the women a reprieve, but they could not keep Molly confined forever. And what would happen when Molly returned, hankering for blood? What would she do to Sela once they were alone on the island?

You cannot protect everyone, Caleb. He reminded himself that these women were here because of the will of the Carver—or because they'd committed crimes deserving of exile. Even Sela, whose courage surprised him even more than her strange beauty, was here because of the Carver's will.

Why did the thought cause him increasing disquiet?

He turned on his heel and left the hold.

Sela heaved a sigh at Molly's going, but Caleb's sharp disappearance coaxed an even greater one. He'd seen her fight like a savage—seen her with blood trickling from her mouth and her eye probably looking like she'd tangled with an ox. And she had, she thought, remembering her surprise at Molly's extraordinary strength. Had the woman been some kind of prize fighter? Or simply labored every day of her short life?

Sela had lost the fight—but she would not have, if not for her freezing when she spied Caleb Alexander. Just like she'd frozen when Caleb reached for her…the familiar pity mingled with something foreign, like admiration. Nay, it couldn't be admiration. She was so far below his notice that she wondered at two meetings within the space of an hour.

Hester edged nearer. "Thanks," she whispered. "For before."

"Molly coming at you so suddenly was unfair. I only did what anyone would have done."

Hester stared at the other women, who had long since

dispersed to attend to various duties and activities. "But they didn't." She shook herself and eyed Sela's face. "Does it hurt?"

"Not at all. I gained far worse from sparring with my brother."

The other woman's eyes widened. "'Twas your brother who taught you to fight like that?"

"Aye. He serves in the king's navy." *For how long?* Did he truly intend to desert, and to find Prince Magnus? She hoped he'd have the sense to stay.

"Would you…would you teach me? I'm afraid…" Hester swallowed, hesitating, looking nothing like the fierce challenger of before.

"Of Molly?"

"Nay, Azazel. I've heard such things…" Hester trailed off. "Could you instruct me?"

Sela nodded. "As much as I know, aye, I will."

"Thank you." She glanced at the bunk. "'Tis the largest one in the hold, which was why I claimed it. Big enough for two. Why don't you share it with me?"

In this strange place, the comfort of an actual bed, and the presence of another person nearby, proved an oddly appealing currency. Or perhaps Hester only wanted a bodyguard. Either way, Sela relished having found a friend. Or the exiled equivalent.

She nodded.

"Aren't you going to ask my crime?" Hester raised her palms, indicating the double brands.

"Only if you ask mine." Sela indicated her own brands, and Hester's eyes widened to saucers.

"The Carver have mercy, Sela. I thought you were one of the lot."

"Nay. I just came aboard with them."

Hester stepped forward, her hand on Sela's arm. "You should be careful. You've made an enemy of Molly today. And with the way the white fists look at you…"

"The white fists?"

"The guards."

Sela thought of Caleb's extended hand. If she'd accepted his help, would he have shuddered? Grimaced, like Tucker had? She was about to reassure Hester that the guards couldn't touch her, especially the officers, but another question snagged at her.

"Why are they not called white *hands*?"

"Why do you think, Sela? There are no *hands* here. Not anymore. Hands clasp and hold and calm and reassure…hands *caress*." Hester's voice took on a gloomy tone. "Nay, from now on, there are only fists. Why else do you think I asked you to teach me how to fight?"

Chapter Six

The gentle sway of the ship in port was nothing compared to the violent lurch they were forced to endure once they reached the open sea. Sela quickly discovered that she had been blessed with a tougher stomach than most, but poor Hester was not so lucky. With five days already passed, and having run almost immediately into a storm, she'd been too sick to do anything but hurl the contents of her stomach into a chamber pot.

Sela should have been grateful for the respite from offering self-defense lessons, but she would've given almost anything to be free of the hold with the lingering stench of vomit—and worse. At least she had nothing to fear from Molly, given the other woman was still held somewhere in isolation. Or from the other women, who'd been careful to keep their distance once they'd observed what Sela could do with her fists.

On the sixth day, the storm finally calmed, and they were allowed to go up on deck after the male prisoners had taken their turn. Having changed into her spare gown—Liron had only been allowed to bring her one change of clothes—Sela followed the other women's example, cleaning her filthy gown and scrubbing her skin as best she could. Beside her, Hester worked determinedly. Her face had lost its distinctly green tinge.

After everything was done, Sela pressed the heel of her palm to her forehead, feeling oddly dizzy. A bead of sweat trickled down her neck and slipped beneath the collar of her gown. Was it getting hotter? For nearly a sevenday, they'd shivered in the hold. Sela had been glad of Hester's spare blanket more than once.

"Sela?" Hester's voice seemed to come from a long way off. "Are you dauncy again?"

Again? She was never sick, at least not at home. One of her mother's great talents was the knowledge of the medicinal herbs in her grandmother's garden, which had brought Sela through many a rogue fever. More than anything, she wished for the cool touch of her mother's capable fingers on her burning forehead.

She must've swayed, for Hester grabbed her shoulders and leaned close. The edges of her seemed fuzzy, as if the sun glared behind her back. "Sela? Stay awake. I'll call for help."

Stay awake?

Hester asked too much.

The burning was followed by the shivering. Sela grabbed the blankets she'd thrown off, wondering why the bodice of her gown was damp. The world spun, and she remembered Joss Brigham's blood soaking her…and Cadence.

She screamed. "Get it off me! Get it off!" She flung herself from the bed, but gloved hands grabbed her wrists. The surge of strength left her as quickly as it had come, and she went limpsey in the unknown person's grip. She was guided back to the bed and tucked beneath the stifling blanket again. "Father Monroe," she whimpered, spying a tonsured head gleaming by the light of a candle. "Please forgive me. Oh, Carver of Souls…"

Blackness. Was she already on Azazel? Her heart raced. Molly would find her, hold a knife to her throat as she'd threatened. But she had no strength in her limbs to stand, let alone run. The fever surged through every vein, coloring the blackness until her eyes ached and her throat felt drier than a desert. She longed for oblivion again.

Ah, water. Blessed water. Someone raised her head and relieved her thirst. The same someone then removed her gown and tugged at the laces to her stays. She should fight, but she was tired…so tired. Weaker than Roux when he'd broken his leg as a cub and succumbed to the same fever as the one that now raged through her.

Nay, not the same…

"Roux…" she said, and moaned. Why had she left him with Cadence? Cadence had access to the family Sela could never see or touch again. Sela was alone. Oh, for the feeling of his soft fur against her burning palms…

She registered the rush of cool air against her chemise, and she struggled into a sitting position, swatting away the hands that had removed her stays and gown.

"Calm yourself, Miss Meriweather," came a woman's voice. An older woman's voice, and strangely gentle. "The ship's surgeon has come and gone and left you in my care. You're safe with me."

Safe? She nearly laughed. And then, as if the Carver had finally had mercy on her, she found the blessed dark of oblivion again.

X

The woman who'd troubled his dreams for nearly a sevenday was now in the room adjacent to his.

Caleb had only discovered that the ship's healer was—next to Zeke—his closest neighbor when he heard the screams coming through the bulkheads. He'd burst from his cabin where he'd been studying a text copied from the Book of Souls and into the other in time to see the raven-haired woman lunge from the bed, only to be caught by the ship's surgeon. She fainted, and the surgeon carried her back to the bed, being careful not to touch her bare skin.

The woman—Sela—continued to writhe, a mumbled string of nonsense interspersed with ardent mentions of "Father Monroe" and the "Carver of Souls," as well as the occasional plea for forgiveness. His pulse raced at the fervency of her words.

"What's wrong with her? Is she seasoning?" Caleb questioned the balding surgeon as the man bent to examine Sela. He'd heard of the illnesses that many arrivals to Azazel contracted, unused to the tropical climate and its strange diseases. Most survived— though some died, with more casualties among the prisoners than the soldiers.

The healer, Ira, answered him. "Nay, not seasoning. Not yet, at least. But she's out of her mind with fever."

He did not need to glance at her bare hands to see the soul stains that marked the healer, a slightly plump woman of middling age. The ship's surgeon would attend to the officers, marines, and sailors—and the prisoners, at a distance—but only the branded healer was permitted to offer the prisoners direct care. Caleb had heard stories of past voyages where prisoners had died because no one would tend them.

"The river fever?"

The surgeon straightened and shook his head. "I don't believe so, Lieutenant Alexander. Likely only a fever brought on by the conditions down below."

Caleb suppressed a shudder. He'd not been to the prisoner's hold since they'd weighed anchor, although he'd heard of the terrible conditions, and he'd endured the storm the same as they, admittedly with far less discomfort than Lieutenant North, who had a weak stomach despite his many voyages. He could well imagine the horrors of down below.

As Sela twisted in the blankets, the surgeon backed away. "I'll leave her to your care, Ira."

When the surgeon had left, Caleb watched the healer raise Sela's head and press a cup to her lips. Despite her feverish state, she drank long and deeply. Her body relaxed slightly. Ira's fingers worked at Sela's gown, and then she turned to Caleb, as if realizing he was still there.

"Lieutenant Alexander? I am sorry, was there something you wanted?"

Her question chafed, for more than one reason. He shook his head. "I only came to offer my assistance."

She glanced pointedly at his fine white shirtsleeves and cream-colored waistcoat, her meaning clear. He was about as useful as the surgeon, and she knew it as well as he. "Thank you, Lieutenant. But I think we'll manage."

He nodded, and when he left the room, she closed the door firmly behind him.

Judging by the moans and occasional screams that tore across the bulkhead between them, Sela's fever continued throughout the night. Caleb discerned few of her words, but enough to glean that she pleaded for mercy from the Carver. For her deliverance from the fever, or from something else? Devoted as he considered himself to be to the Carver, he'd never offered such fervent, heart-wrenching prayers. And none so soaked with guilt and regret, as if the branding had cost her not only her eternal soul, but her earthly tranquility as well.

He prayed on his knees for her, for mercy and peace. When she continued to writhe, he sat on his bed and leaned against the bulkhead, unable to sleep.

In the early hours of the morning, she finally fell silent. Did she yet live, or had the Carver taken her?

Please. I asked for mercy and peace for her—but not the permanent kind.

He heard the healer's door open and close again, and cracked his own door open just enough to see Ira vanish down the narrow corridor. Unable to curb his curiosity, he slipped out, having not undressed the night before.

Only when he entered her cabin and saw her pale hands resting atop the covers did he realize he'd forgotten his gloves. Seeing her stillness, all thoughts of such things left his mind, and he crossed the cabin to her side. Was she dead?

But nay—she yet breathed. The fever had left her, he guessed, though he could not hold his hand to her forehead to confirm it. The covers were drawn up modestly to her chest, leaving her arms bare. Glossy locks, blacker than squid ink, fell around her head in wild abandon.

Reassured, he turned to leave, but feeling oddly thrown, he bumped into a chair.

When he glanced at her, her violet eyes were on him, one of

them ringed by the yellow-green of a fading bruise. He mentally kicked himself for his uncharacteristic clumsiness. "Are you feeling better?"

"Aye, much better…thank you."

He dropped into the offending chair, kneading the tight muscles in his neck. "I reside on the other side of your wall. I came to see if your fever had broken."

She colored. "I kept you awake?"

"I usually sleep little, so 'tis no matter, Sela."

Her eyes widened and she searched his face. "You know my name?" When he only nodded, she seemed to withdraw. Her hands curled atop the covers. Because she was upset, or because the brand still smarted? "Where am I?"

"The healer's cabin. One of the starboard cabins, if you wish to know, near the *Deliverance*'s bow." He nodded at the door. "Ira left a few minutes ago. She should be back soon, should you need anything."

"I don't need anything." She raised herself on her elbows, then tried to wrest herself into a sitting position. He darted forward to help her, then drew back as she glanced pointedly at his bare hands. "I can manage."

"You're still weak. You should rest."

"I've had enough rest, Caleb—I mean, Lieutenant Alexander. I need to return to the hold." Despite her words, she sank back against the pillow weakly.

He only stared at her.

How did she know his name?

"I'm sorry," Sela stammered, recognizing the question in his eyes as he eased back into his chair. "I heard Lieutenant North call you Caleb. I still forget…"

She could see he accepted her excuse. She still forgot that she was soulless. Were she unbranded, it might have been acceptable to use his Carver-given name, especially since they were only four years apart in age. But with the soul stain…

Did he truly not recognize her, even though he'd apparently learned her name? Or did a mark on her palm render her as unfamiliar as a stranger?

He was still staring at her. "Are you quite sure we've never met? You look…somewhat familiar." His fingers tested the slight stubble grazing his jaw.

His hands. He'd forgotten to wear gloves, or left them behind on purpose, and now she could not help doing a little staring of her own. His hands were slender but strong, the knuckles large and the elegant fingers tapering to blunt fingernails. Hands built as much for nursing a heavy tome as for wielding a knife with devastating accuracy. They were flecked with ink, and she guessed what kept him from his sleep.

Had he seen the Book of Souls with his own eyes? Did he know what lay within its sacred borders?

When her hesitation became too lengthy to respectably answer, he leaned back. "I am sorry, Sela. I don't mean to pry."

"Nay, 'tis not that." She chose her words carefully. "I would think that if you'd met me before, Lieutenant Alexander, you would have remembered me."

"Indeed." He wove his fingers together, then crossed his legs and spread his knitted hands across his thigh. "Your eyes…I admit I've rarely seen the like of them."

"Rarely?"

"My aunt boasted a similar color. And when I was still a boy, I met a girl with eyes the same shade as yours, although I met her only briefly, and I am sorry to say that I do not know her name. 'Twas she I originally mistook you for. But I know now that I'm mistaken. The girl I met was a younger sister, not an elder. And likely there are plenty of girls with the color that haven't yet crossed my path."

She understood, then, why he doubted himself. He had believed her to be Liri's sister, but then saw her arrive with those chosen by the lot, and assumed she had only one brand, not two, which would make her the eldest child—and an innocent. Then he knew nothing of Joss Brigham? A strange sense of loss turned her stomach.

Should she correct him? Reveal herself as Liri's sister? But for what purpose? He would discover the truth soon enough, especially if he had Lord Auberon's ear. He might feel sorry for her, but only for a little while. And when he found out what she had done…

Her hands curled instinctively. *Nay.* He could find out the truth on his own. And for now, she would preserve his better opinion of her, and not investigate the reason why she wanted it preserved.

"Do you have other siblings?" he asked at last.

"Three," she replied, and it wasn't a lie. "A brother and two sisters. The youngest is eight years old. The other two are twins."

"You must miss them."

"They have each other." She easily deflected his sympathy. "And you, Lieutenant Alexander?"

"One brother, barely a year older than myself."

"Are you close?"

"Closer than twins." He must have seen her wince, for he grimaced himself. "I am sorry…I should not speak of what you have lost."

For all his talk of brotherly closeness, Caleb appeared as warm as Tucker had been cold. And he'd come to her in the middle of the night, to see if she still ailed. Or did he only seek to satisfy his curiosity?

Nay. She saw the light in his dark blue eyes. For all he was a member of the Righteous, he cared for people. Even the branded.

"You go to Azazel, then?" Her voice was nearly a whisper.

He nodded. "For a year. After that, I cannot say." He ran his tongue over lips that must have been dry. "I saw what you did in the hold. For that woman, Hester…"

Then he made it his habit to learn the names spoken around

him. Why Hester, or the Sela of nineteen, but not the Sela of six years ago? Had he truly been so preoccupied by his fear for Tucker?

"I should let you rest," he said when she failed to reply again. At least he mistook her reticence for fatigue. His hand lifted, as if he would have squeezed her arm warmly, and she knew it was an instinctive gesture. Had Caleb Alexander always been so gentle? Not for the first time, she wished she'd met him before the branding. Before Joss Brigham…

Realizing his blunder, he lowered his hand and offered a grim smile instead. "Sleep well, Sela."

He'd been gone for only a few minutes when she heard footsteps in the corridor.

Ira?

"Sleep well, Caleb," she whispered to the pillow, and when the healer returned, she pretended to be asleep herself.

Caleb had difficulty concentrating on his studies with the movement of the ship—far more pronounced in the tiny cabin— but he dutifully redoubled his efforts. The passage Lord Auberon had given him to peruse was a text on the nature of the afterlife, as if the elder sought to remind Caleb that his destiny—both earthly and eternal—would forever be diverging from that of the soulless in the hold.

And from that of the ailing woman in the adjacent cabin.

Alone with the extract and his lantern in the dark of the night, his ears only just registered the shuffling of feet outside his door. When they had passed, he opened the door in time to catch a glimpse of a decidedly feminine gait and hair as black as the marks flecking his sleeves. Shrugging on his coat and tugging on his gloves, he followed Sela up the companionway and onto the deck, pausing when he saw her heading for the bulwarks.

He nodded at one of the night watchmen, recognizing the

grizzled face and knowing that the woman was in no danger from this particular sailor. Still, what made her wander? Was she out of her mind with fever again and liable to do harm to herself?

He watched her from the shadows. She leaned over the railing, angling her face to the breeze as the ship slid effortlessly through the waves. She had good sea legs, and seemed not to mind the gentle tilting of the ship from side to side, unlike the landlubber Lieutenant North. Her hair spilled over her shoulders, the exact color of the ocean depths into which she now peered. A rogue wave slapped against the belly of the ship and must have splashed her, for he heard her indrawn breath, followed by a sigh of pleasure, as if she was enlivened by the ocean as he was.

The wondering drove him forward, and though he scuffed his boots across the deck to make sure he wouldn't startle her, she barely stirred at his presence as he joined her at the railing.

She smiled at him. "Can't sleep, Lieutenant Alexander?" On any other woman's lips, the question—and the grin—would have been far too bold. But for some reason, she had no fear of him, and he in turn felt completely at ease with her. So much so that despite their short acquaintance, she was simply Sela to him, and he had not thought to ask her family name. Perhaps he could discover it from Lord Auberon.

"I could say the same for you."

She shrugged. "I've been sleeping all day."

He studied her briefly. She was no longer feverish, but still very pale. Ira had confided that Sela had thrashed so violently and burned so hot she'd feared they would lose her. The healer had insisted the woman stay a few more days in her keeping before returning to the dank hold. "A ship is no place to wander at night."

"You fear I might be swept overboard?"

"Or worse," he replied, thinking of Lieutenant North.

She frowned, then crossed her arms atop the railing and leaned her chin on the pale layers of her hands, gazing at the waves below silvered by moonlight. "Is it any different," she mused without looking at him, "if a soulless person dies at sea and not on Azazel?"

"Nay," he answered her, but without conviction. "For the soulless, nothing exists beyond death. Save the temporary punishment the doubly branded must endure for those sins which have not been atoned for in life." He glanced at the brand she concealed. "Though that will not be your portion, being a child of the lot."

Her shoulders stiffened and he regretted his candor.

"I am sorry, Sela."

"Nay," she replied softly. "Of my fate I, at least, am truly deserving."

He opened his mouth to contest her statement, but she straightened and glanced at him. "How do the sailors know the way? Azazel is so far, and yet they do not get lost."

This question he could answer with confidence—though he knew little of navigation himself. He pointed upward at a constellation almost directly above them. "Do you see that cluster of stars, shaped like a soul mark itself?"

She followed his finger to the five bright stars that formed a perfect X-shape, like the points of a compass. The star at the center burned the brightest. "Aye."

"'Twas by following those stars that our people first guided themselves to Azazel. Eventually, they became a symbol of exile for those of the lot. And later, a symbol of judgment for those who were doubly branded. Though one might say 'twas also a sign of mercy."

The moonlight full upon her profile transformed her eyes into celestial objects in their own right, and he wondered at plain features so easily rendered striking by the orbs contained therein— all the more beautiful for the way that they mirrored the loveliness of everything around her.

But it was not her beauty that moved him. He'd known many beautiful women back in the Old Town, some of them devoted acolytes of the Righteous, like himself. But he had never met a woman who beheld the Carver's world with the same sense of wonder as he did, and for that reason, he had rejected the Bindings proposed by his parents—or by the women themselves, who were not content to wait for him to present his suit.

"I never saw the stars back in the Old Town," she said. "Not like this."

"'Tis near impossible with the fog, and the pollution from coal smoke. I have only ever seen the stars away from the Old Town. Light surely appears much brighter in complete darkness." He toyed with the sleeve of his white coat, knowing the garment was but a feeble attempt to recreate the beauty of the expanse above them.

"What is it called?" Sela glanced at him, and for a brief moment, he imagined he glimpsed the glittering of celestial jewels in her eyes. "The constellation?"

"The Soul Stars. Because of the soul mark."

She sighed. "'Tis fitting."

The words of one of his favorite teachers returned to him. *"The great wonder of life is that you cannot look closely at the world and not see the Carver, Caleb, but neither can you look closely at the Carver and not see the world in a different light."*

And Caleb had spent much of his life looking closely at the Carver—the same way that Sela now gazed at the stars. How was it that after all that time, the world now looked so different to him? When Tucker had been spared, Caleb had been happy to excuse the lot, ignoring the twinge of doubt he'd felt watching Tucker's sweetheart be led away, but years in the presence of light had changed him. So much so that the presence of the soul-stained woman beside him now unsettled and alarmed rather than soothed.

Did he truly believe that the branding rendered one soulless? That nothing awaited the tainted after death, save punishment—and then oblivion?

Sela stirred and he came back to himself. He needed to keep such doubts to himself, lest he confuse her—or worse, allow her to hope.

Wishing her a brisk goodnight, he returned to his cabin.

By the time Ira had released Sela from her care—three days after first being admitted there—Molly had returned to the hold, back stiff and looking as if isolation had bred more fiery rebellion than meek compliance.

"She came yesterday," Hester whispered once they were above deck and basking in the sunshine amidships, as they were permitted to do for an hour each day. Now that Sela's fever had passed, she could tell that it was indeed getting warmer with every day they sailed southwest of Eremia. But the nights remained desperately cold, and the fever had left her weak. She wished she'd not been so hasty to leave Ira's cabin.

Beyond Molly, Sela heard a stir, and the door to the captain's cabin opened. A dark-haired man of medium height and build strode out wearing a fine scarlet coat trimmed with gold, a group of men fanning out behind him. Captain Foley, she guessed, although she'd seen the man only twice since setting sail. It was said he suffered with the ague—a recurrence of the seasoning—at times, and when he did, he kept to his cabin, relying on his officers to run the ship in his stead.

Sela spied Caleb amidst the small group, and next to him, Lieutenant North, who was directly responsible for the prisoners. And on Caleb's other side…

Lord Auberon. This, then, was the man who'd advocated for her death over exile to Azazel, wearing a splendid ensemble that had escaped the ravages of the storm several days past. What of the black cassock he'd worn at Liri's ceremony? Had he abandoned austerity in favor of extravagance?

Next to him, Caleb's dress mirrored his in almost every way, save the silver trim on his coat instead of Lord Auberon's gold. For all his gentle words some nights before, did he aspire to the heights of the Righteous?

At that moment, Lieutenant North intercepted her stare, and

he murmured something to the other two men before coming her way, one hand resting casually on the hilt of his sword.

"What does *he* want?" Hester asked, her eyebrows drawing so close together they nearly bonded across the bridge of her nose.

Sela stood as the lieutenant approached. Surprising her, he inclined his head, apparently not so restless as usual. "Miss Sela."

"Lieutenant North. Is something wrong?"

He smiled. "Just came t' see how ye were doin'. I heard about yer fever."

"I'm fully recovered, thank you."

He glanced over at Molly and frowned. "Mistress Ira were of a mind t' keep ye close at hand, miss. Thought it might be for yer benefit."

"Close at hand? But I'm better now."

"Aye, she were meaning in a more…*permanent* capacity." He scratched his clean-shaven chin as if it itched. "Just till Azazel, mind ye."

"To help Ira?"

"An' to keep ye out of Molly's way."

Sela studied the young lieutenant's face. Was there something sinister about his display of kindness? But nay, it had been Ira's idea.

"'Twould keep you from harm, Sela," said Hester, apparently still beside her. "Molly's still mad as a cut snake. And with all the sick down below, Ira likely needs the help."

Lieutenant North smiled. "Aye, but only until we reach Azazel. After that, ye must fend for yerself."

Was this the Carver's way of showing mercy? If so, she would accept it gratefully. It would be good to not have to constantly watch her back.

"Aye, until Azazel. And thank you, sir."

As if he'd abandoned the threads of their earlier conversation, Lord

Auberon watched Zeke approach Sela, who stood uneasily next to the woman she'd rescued—Hester.

"Her presence here must be difficult for you, Caleb."

Caleb frowned. Why? Because she was beautiful, or because she was an innocent? Did Lord Auberon suppose him to be tempted?

"I'm not so weak a man," he replied at last.

"Of course not," Lord Auberon murmured thoughtfully. "But I cannot say the same for our friend Ezekiel."

"He's only looking out for her, my lord. The first day she was here, she saved another woman from a beating. The wrath of that woman's attacker now falls on her."

"Did she?" Lord Auberon's eyes sparkled with interest. "Still, for all her bravery, you must know that she is here by the will of the Carver."

Unable to speak to that, he gave a tight nod.

"And while you see her as an innocent, Caleb, remember that you do not know the heart. A beautiful face can mask more evil than you can possibly imagine."

"Are you saying that she is evil?"

"Perhaps not yet. Perhaps not completely. But surely you know that, young as she is, she is already capable of great evil."

Why would he know that? Caleb frowned.

"Watch her. Not the way our friend Zeke watches her, with a spirit of unbridled lust and desire, but examine her for the defects of moral character that will inevitably show after sustained observation. Watch her long enough, and even her most admirable qualities will inevitably disappoint you."

"Is that not true of every man and woman? Do we not all have shadowed corners of our hearts that would frighten even ourselves, should they ever be viewed by the light of day?"

"Not the Righteous," replied Lord Auberon, studying *him* now. "We, by our very nature, are set apart from the rest of society, Caleb. Our souls are called to be swept clean of every cobweb, every bit of muck and grime, every blemish and every tarnish. We must be as perfectly spotless as the robes we wear. By our example, the rest of mankind is delivered from their imperfections. And through the lot, the one is sacrificed for the good of the many."

Lord Auberon watched Caleb as his attention moved to Sela. She'd relaxed, even offering Zeke a small smile. Did she know that the lieutenant was attracted to her? Did she care for him at all in return?

Did she realize yet that nothing could ever come of a spark between them?

"I recognize something in you, Caleb, a flame that I once thought burned only in myself. You are passionate, are you not? Devoted? A follower of every letter of the law?" He plucked a piece of lint from his sleeve. "Yet not a bureaucrat, not at all. With the very depths of your soul, you aspire to the heights of human experience as 'twas ordained by the Carver."

Caleb forced his gaze away from Sela. "I do. Since I was a boy, I've strived to love the Carver with every fiber of my soul, mind, and body. I was only ten years old when I realized I wanted to pledge my life to serving Him."

"I can see that." A single groove appeared in Lord Auberon's perfect forehead. "And I want to mentor you, Caleb. I rarely mentor any man of your youth, but there is something different about you. If you continue along this path, you may well rise to be an elder of the Righteous. Perhaps even the leader of the Righteous and advisor to the king himself. What do you say?"

"'Twould be a great honor, my lord," he replied. And it was, just as Tucker said. He clasped Lord Auberon's extended hand and smiled as the older man squeezed his shoulder with the affection of a father.

Across from them, Sela laughed at something Ezekiel North said. He'd never heard her laugh. It was even finer than her voice.

But nothing could ever come of a spark between a branded woman and an unbranded man.

Aye, he would do well to repeat it to himself.

The next month was filled with a series of strange kindnesses. Ira agreed for Sela to share her small cabin, and in return, Sela helped her tend the sick prisoners in the hold. While Molly remained cleverly, the other prisoners were struck down one by one by various fevers and ailments. Hester suffered worse than any of them, now so thin that Sela barely recognized her figure from a distance.

"You must eat." Sela dangled a loaded spoon in front of Hester's face, though the unappealing gruel the cook served to the prisoners twice a day would fail to tempt a cleverly person, let alone an ailing one. As Hester lay nearly motionless on the bunk she'd fought so hard to possess, Sela battled a wave of despair. Nearly two months remained on their sea journey, and every day was hotter and more stifling than the one before.

Once Hester was asleep, Sela stood and ran her hands down the front of her gown. The stench from the bilge now permeated every inch of the hold, and rats scurried freely across the deck. Not for the first time, she was thankful to be with Ira. Seeing Molly lying on her side across the hold, Sela expelled a sigh of relief and turned to go above deck.

On the main deck, in the cool night air, she spied Lieutenant North speaking with one of the night watchmen. He nodded at the man and crossed to her.

"Miss Sela. I'll escort ye to yer cabin."

"There's no need, Lieutenant."

"Aye, there is, Miss Sela. Best ye not wander alone."

She'd been surprised that Captain Foley granted her leave to roam the ship at will, for the express purpose of tending to the sick and dying alongside Ira. Was that Ezekiel North's doing, or Caleb's? She'd barely seen Caleb in several sevendays, and then only at a distance. He usually kept to his cabin, holed up with some text or another. Unlike Zeke, who braved the prisoner's hold multiple times a day and never failed to offer his protection as she moved around the ship. She hoped the guards on Azazel were as kind.

"What will you do once we reach the island?" She looked into his freckled face, liking the easy smile that quirked his lips.

"We'll stay for a sevenday or so, take on the guards that wish t' return t' the Old Town, an' fresh water an' supplies. Then we'll depart."

"You've been there before, then?"

"Aye, many times."

"What's it like?" She glanced up and realized they'd reached the narrow corridor. They stood outside the lieutenant's door.

"Azazel is…" His face darkened. "Best we not speak of it just yet, Miss Sela." Then he smiled. "I have somethin' t' give t' Mistress Ira. Some herbs she lent me for quellin' sea sickness. Hold a moment." He pushed open his door and plunged into the darkness while Sela waited on the threshold. She heard the groan of the timber deck beneath the lieutenant's boots as he moved about the cabin, lighting the lantern.

There was a soft exclamation, followed by the crash of glass shattering against the floor.

"Lieutenant?" When she heard nothing, she stepped inside.

The lieutenant was on his knees amidst the remains of a glass bottle, gingerly plucking herbs from the wreckage with his gloved hands.

"Mutton-headed, I know," he murmured, and she knelt to help him. "Mistress Ira will kill me."

"'Twas an accident." After they had swept up the glass and deposited the herbs safely into another container, Sela looked up to find the lieutenant watching her.

"Thank ye kindly, Miss Sela. Yer a gentle soul." He stood with her, seeming not to notice his mistaken reference to the state of her soul.

"You're welcome, Lieutenant North."

"Call me Zeke."

She took a step back and felt the bulkhead of the tiny cabin press against her spine. "I don't think—"

"Please. I'd like ye to."

"Lieutenant—"

With only two steps, he crossed the cabin to her, taking her face between his gloved hands. She stiffened as he trailed a gloved finger down her cheek. "Yer a lovely woman, Sela. Lovelier than the first flowers of spring."

She held up a branded hand. "And soulless."

He shuffled his feet restlessly. "I don't believe in those things. Never have. All I know is yer a flesh an' blood woman, and I'm a flesh an' blood man." His finger drifted down to her collarbone.

"Lieutenant, you don't know what you're doing. If the other officers see us—"

"No man nor woman need know."

"*I* would know. And so would the Carver."

"The Carver don't reside where we're goin', Sela." He traced the modest cut of her gown over her shoulder. "Best ye understand that right now. I'm not promisin' anythin' long-term, an' I'm certainly not plannin' t' stay on Azazel. But I would take some happiness with ye over the next little while, were ye willin'."

Then he wanted her as a bondlessmate, to pass the time on an otherwise dull journey. Hadn't Hester warned her about his attentions? But he'd charmed both of them over the past sevendays, and she'd mistaken his kindnesses for that of a friend, or an honorable man—like Caleb.

She was such a fool. A shockingly naïve fool.

Sela eyed the open door. She was his equal in height, but he was as broad as Joss Brigham had been, and he stood between her and the empty passageway. Could she scream?

The lieutenant drew back slightly, frowning. "I'm nay cad, Sela. I wouldn't force ye, I swear."

Did he speak truly? She dragged her gaze from the door. "I'm sorry, Zeke. I won't give myself to any man besides my future bondmate."

His face fell, and she thought he would step away, but then he moved closer until his body nearly pinned hers to the wall. He cradled her face once again and, before she could react, he pressed his mouth against hers. She tasted salt, and rum. Not fishy, but perhaps on the way to becoming so. The familiar paralysis stole over her limbs, as it had the day Liri was chosen, and the lieutenant must have taken it as a sign of assent, for he kissed her more forcefully, one hand encircling her waist.

A soft cry tore from her throat and she planted her hands in his chest and shoved. His arm only tightened, and she felt his warm, rum-tinted breath against her ear. "Shh, Sela, just relax. I don't believe yer soulless. Ye will see…"

"Zeke!" She shoved at him again.

This time, he skidded away, and Sela glanced up to see Caleb, looking between them with an expression like a swiftly approaching storm. He held a fistful of Zeke's coat in his gloved hand, although judging by his plain shirtsleeves and loose hair, he'd come directly from his bed.

"Lieutenant North? What is the meaning of this?"

"Caleb…Lieutenant Alexander." Zeke's freckled face was completely drained of color as he wrung his hands together. "There's nothin' wrong here, I swear it."

"And if I should send for Lord Auberon, would there still be *nothing wrong?*"

"Please, there's no need."

"I just saw you kissing this young woman, likely against her will." Sela's heart soared at his defense of her, then plummeted the next moment. "Not only do you put her in mortal danger, Zeke, but your own soul as well. Or would you try and tell me you did not know she was branded?"

Ah, but Tucker's brother was here, and gone was the gentle, warm Caleb she'd thought she glimpsed before. He might as well have called her unclean, tainted…soulless. The first stirrings of dislike swelled in her gut.

Lord Auberon's protégé, indeed.

When a sullen Zeke failed to answer, Caleb let him go with an exclamation of disgust. He shoved him toward the open door. "Wait outside. I will question the prisoner, then deal with you later. You had better do some fierce praying while you wait."

The *prisoner*? Aye, he was his brother's sibling, from head to toe.

When the door closed behind Zeke, Caleb spun to face Sela, the storm-tossed dark blue wild amidst the whites of his eyes.

"What were you thinking, Sela, putting yourself in this position?"

X

As Sela recoiled, Caleb kicked himself for his sharp words and bid his anger die.

He'd wondered briefly, when he first came across Ezekiel North drinking of Sela like a dying man slaking his thirst, if she'd come to him of her own volition. The door stood wide open— hardly the conditions for a surprise assault—and the lieutenant had grown increasingly obvious with his attentions to Sela over the past sevendays.

But then she'd visibly struggled, trying to push the lieutenant away. Caleb heard Zeke's hasty assurances and Sela's desperate cry. Nay, she was not willing. Or at least, she hadn't been by the time Caleb came along.

Still, she was a fool to place herself in such a compromising position. And with an unbranded officer, no less. Should anyone believe her a willing participant in a planned liaison, she'd be killed, even as Zeke was branded and exiled himself.

Sela had backed against the bulkhead again. "I've done nothing wrong."

"'Tis night. Most of the other officers are in their beds. And you are here, *alone*."

"'Tis not what you think, Caleb."

Softened by her use of his Carver-given name, he dragged in a deep breath before replying. "Then what is it?"

"I was returning from tending the other *prisoners* in the hold. Lieutenant North offered to escort me back to Ira's cabin. He stopped to get some herbs he'd been meaning to return to Ira, and the glass they were in shattered. You can see the remains over there." She pointed, but he kept his eyes on her face. "When I didn't hear anything from him, I feared for his safety and entered the cabin. I helped him clean up the broken glass. 'Twas then that he…" She swallowed, color surging into her cheeks. "That he proposed something most dishonorable. Even to a mere *prisoner* like myself."

He understood her emphasis. She'd been wounded by his reference to Zeke's soul, then, and her absent one. His reminder of her place.

What Zeke had proposed was not so uncommon, Caleb knew. Even on Azazel, many of the officers and guards kept bondlessmates among the branded prisoners. Few respectable women condescended to live there amongst thieves and murderers and nightwalkers. From all he'd heard of Azazel, he hardly blamed them.

Caleb studied Sela. Until now, he had believed her to be a Carver-fearing woman. But once on Azazel, might she yield to the benefits of such an arrangement? Was this what Lord Auberon had meant by the defects of moral character that would surface after long observation?

He returned to his questioning. "Did you not notice the way Lieutenant North watched you?"

"I did, but thought it innocent, given the guards are forbidden to touch the branded."

"And your friend, Hester? Did she think it strange?"

"Aye, she did."

Caleb continued doggedly. "Did the other women notice his attention?"

"Aye…and yours."

He stilled, fighting the red that was no doubt creeping up his collar. She was right, of course, though he wanted to dislike her for it. What did she make of his interest? Did she presume he had the same intentions as Zeke? He backed away. "I'm an officer, Sela. 'Tis my job to watch you. As the events of tonight have proven."

"And are you guarding me for my sake, or his?" She jerked her thumb to indicate the corridor where Zeke now skulked.

"For both your sakes," he replied honestly, with a small grimace.

She filled the space he'd vacated, her violet eyes flashing. "I don't need your help. And I certainly don't want it."

"You don't understand, Sela. If Zeke maintains you were willing to warm his bed, they'll kill you before we even reach Azazel." He saw her answering fear and reshaped his words. "'Tis a mercy I came across you both. My eyewitness testimony will prove your innocence."

"Then you're going to hand him over to Lord Auberon?"

"I haven't decided yet. If I do, Zeke will be branded and exiled to Azazel with you." *And he'd be free to pursue you without further repercussions*, he thought, fighting an unwelcome discomfort at imagining Sela as Zeke's bondmate.

Could Caleb do it? Condemn a man to a life of exile simply for touching a branded woman? The judgment was made almost every day by elders of the Righteous and the priesthood. Second only to murder or rape, to deliberately touch a branded person was to invite unspeakable condemnation down upon one's head. Those guards who reported mere accidental contact with a branded person had to spend two sevendays in isolation before undergoing the purification ceremony. But willful defiance of the law…

Queasy at the thought of the decision that now lay before him, he turned to watch Sela, only to realize she'd already slipped from the room.

"I desire mercy, not sacrifice…"

The Carver's words, which Caleb understood less with every passing year, especially since the day Tucker's sweetheart had been selected by the lot.

And the main reason why untroubled sleep would no longer deign to visit him in the dark of the night.

Chapter Seven

Fearful of both neighboring lieutenants, Sela kept to the hold or, at night, to Ira's tidy cabin, not far from the ship's galley. Zeke walked the ship like a man already condemned, and she wondered if he'd meant what he'd said—that he never would have forced her. The impulsive actions following his fervent words seemed to prove them false. Still, she had thought him kind before. Certainly not worthy of branding and exile. But Caleb would decide his fate, and, so far, he had said nothing to Lord Auberon.

The days grew hotter and the nights colder. The wide expanse of blue that had so entranced her at the beginning of their journey now seemed painfully bright and monotonous. Fresh water stores began to run low and sickness abounded, particularly among the male prisoners, who were kept chained in their section of the ship's hull. Hester remained dauncy, and despite Ira's remedies, she could keep nothing down. She had not had the energy to request self-defense lessons, let alone participate in them.

Halfway through the third month, Sela looked up from her sorry attempt at laundry to see storm clouds stewing on the horizon. Sailors scurried over the ship's main deck and up the rigging, into the crosstrees. Securing sails? Tightening ropes? She wished she'd paid more attention to Liron's stories from the naval component of his training. Another lieutenant appeared, accompanied by four marines, and ushered the women below deck. Where was Lieutenant North? Had Caleb made his decision?

In the hold, Sela hastened to Hester's bunk, since the ailing woman had stayed where she lay. The fever was gone, but her skin was pale and deathly cold. Sela stroked the woman's lank hair.

Hester cracked a single eyelid. "You're very kind to me, Sela. Whatever did you do that was worthy of a double branding?"

"I was accused of murder."

"Accused? Then you didn't kill someone?"

"I did," Sela replied, her voice wobbling only slightly. "But I didn't mean to."

"Was it a man?" Hester's own voice softened. "Were you defending yourself?"

Sela nodded to answer both questions. "His father was wealthy and powerful."

"Aye, I'm sorry to hear it, Sela. Don't you want to know my crime?"

"Only if you wish to share it."

Hester's mouth curved. "I'm a thief."

"A thief? You wouldn't steal anything."

"I would, and I did. I even picked your pockets the first day you were here, though I found naught but letters." Hester smiled as Sela feigned disapproval.

"What were you caught stealing?"

"What is anyone caught stealing these days? *Food.* A nice pie left cooling on a windowsill. If you ask me, 'twas begging to be eaten." She coughed, and winced. "That I might now die for a mere pie. It seems rather silly."

"You won't die, Hester. We're less than two sevendays from land."

"Azazel? I'm not sure I want to see it."

"I won't let you give up. You're my only friend in this forsaken place."

"Then you obviously haven't had many friends, Sela, to consider me one."

Sela laughed. "I did have a friend…back in the Old Town. A best friend, of sorts."

"What was her name?"

"'Tis amusing—her name was rather similar to yours. Esther."

A little color returned to Hester's face as she smiled again. "Esther, Hester. I like it. Was she sad to see you leave the Old Town?"

"She was taken in the lot a year ago, when we were eighteen. She was an eldest child." Another reason she desperately wanted to reach Azazel. Had Esther and Liri perhaps found each other? "You'd like her."

"Is she a thief too?"

"She never tried to rob me of my letters, if that's what you mean."

Hester laughed, then descended into a coughing fit.

Sela frowned. "I'll get Ira."

"Nay, stay with me a little while…please. 'Tis dark and lonely down here." One of Hester's eyebrows lifted. "Is the handsome lieutenant still watching you?"

"Lieutenant North?"

Hester made a face. "Lieutenant Alexander."

She decided not to share Zeke's brash proposal with Hester, or Caleb's reaction on discovering it. Better that the fate of the man rest in the hands of one, not two. "He's one of the Righteous."

"He's also a man with eyes in his head."

"Oh? And what do you suppose he sees?"

Despite her pallor, Hester's eyes twinkled. "Only something which makes him turn to watch you every time you appear on deck or cross his path."

"You're being foolish."

"Nay. The only fool is Lieutenant Alexander, for wanting what he cannot have."

When Hester had fallen asleep and a hunched shadow on Molly's bunk proved the woman was safely stowed atop it, Sela went in search of Ira, nearly stumbling on the companionway as the ship lurched drunkenly to one side. She was admitted past the cloaked guards who stood by the hatch to the prisoner's hold, though as usual, she felt their stares on her back. She shook off the weight of Hester's silly, girlish claims. If Caleb Alexander looked at her, it was only to pity her pawned soul. And if he discovered that she was not a child of the lot, but a murderer…

In the near dark, the tips of the waves already frothed and curled, the ship shuddering and groaning as it glided through a roiling, heaving mass of black. Rain spewed from a bloated sky, soaking her hair and gown, while a rogue wave smacked against the side of the ship and splattered her with icy salt spray. She gasped and stumbled to Ira's cabin.

It was empty, the lantern unlit and cold, as if Ira hadn't been there for some time. Where could she be? In the darkness, Sela tripped over a heavy chair, stubbing her toe. She whimpered as she went down.

"Oh Carver," she said to herself, rubbing her frozen arms and throbbing toe in turn. "Was Lieutenant North right? Have you truly forsaken us?"

"Hello?" A shadow filled the doorway and she recognized Caleb's voice. "Is someone here?" He peered down at her. By the dim light from the corridor lantern, she saw that he'd exchanged his usual finery for more storm-worthy clothes. The exterior of his greatcoat was soaked, and thick locks of his hair had escaped his queue to plaster themselves to his face. Had he been helping the sailors?

"'Tis me, Sela." She stood. "I was looking for Ira."

A shadow passed over his face that had nothing to do with the brief glance the swinging lantern flashed their way. "Ira's with the captain."

"With the captain? But…"

The skin around his mouth tightened. "She and the captain are…" He swallowed. "They are lovers. 'Twas Lord Auberon who discovered their relationship."

Ira and the captain were bondlessmates? It explained why the branded healer enjoyed so much freedom aboard the ship, and why Sela had seen so little of either one of them throughout the voyage. Ira had been almost pleased for Sela to assume her duties.

"What will happen to them?"

As the ship lurched to one side, Caleb reached out and braced himself against the bulkhead. "'Tis no small offense, the soul stain aside. The affair has gone on for more than a year while the *Deliverance* sailed to and from Azazel. Captain Foley is a bonded man. He has five small children to his bondmate back home."

"You haven't answered my question, Lieutenant."

"Ira will be executed once we reach Azazel," he said, with finality. "The captain will be stripped of his command, doubly branded, and left on the island while the *Deliverance* returns to the Old Town. Ira and the captain are being guarded in the captain's cabin by Lord Auberon himself."

"And do you consider this *mercy*?"

The ship shuddered and he braced himself with both gloved hands. "Ira is already doubly branded, Sela. She was shown mercy in being spared death the first time. The penalty for a second offense is death. 'Tis the law."

"Then the law is wrong." She wrapped her arms around herself, shivering as the chill of her wet clothes settled in. She could only think of the kind woman ministering to her during her fever and offering her sanctuary afterward to protect her from Molly's wrath. "And what of Lieutenant North? Have you determined his punishment?"

"I fear that…" He expelled a heavy sigh. "If I were to expose Zeke's crimes, he might try to bring you down with him. If he does, you could face death when you reach Azazel, regardless of my testimony. And I…I would not see you hang. You are innocent."

"Then you fear Lord Auberon?"

"I fear the improper application of the law," he replied carefully.

"You said you had an older brother, did you not?"

"Aye, Tucker. What of him?"

"Did he face the lot?"

"Aye, and he was spared."

"Thank the Carver. But if he hadn't been spared, sir…I wonder if you would feel so kindly toward the law now, and toward Lord Auberon. Even toward the Carver Himself."

He stared at her until the ship seemed to free-fall into the trough of a wave, and Sela lost her balance. Caleb lurched toward her and grabbed for her shoulders to steady her, but her momentum was too strong and they both went sprawling. Sela's damp skirt clung to her ankles and her legs tangled with Caleb's. He grunted as his head struck Ira's small desk on the way down. He landed on his back, while she fell against his hard chest. The lamp in the corridor was snuffed out by a gust of wind, leaving them in complete darkness.

For Caleb's sake, she was glad that her hands encountered only the cloth of his damp shirt. She struggled to disentangle herself from him, only to bump into the cursed chair again.

"Sela," he muttered, sounding distinctly annoyed. "Get off me."

The light of a lantern flooded the room. "Well, well, well. What a gapeseed this is."

Sela peered through a tangle of wet hair and saw Molly, smiling with near-vulpine charm as she held a lantern aloft. "Well, Sela, I thought you were involved with one of the white fists, but I must admit I suspected Lieutenant North. I'm surprised to find you here all jeddarty-jiddarty with Lieutenant Alexander. Enjoying a flourish while everyone else is preoccupied with the storm?"

Sela winced at the crudity of Molly's language, vulgar even despite her mainland speech, and quickly scrambled to her feet, trying not to step on Caleb. "'Tis not what it looks like. The ship hit a rogue wave…"

"So you say, Sela." She turned to leave.

Sela glanced at Caleb for help, but he looked dazed. He lifted a hand to inspect the bump at the back of his head and his fingers came away bloody. Her heart clenched, not only because he was wounded. Molly's lies could cost Sela her life, but if Lord Auberon believed the worst of Caleb…

Sela followed Molly into the narrow corridor, forgetting that she left Caleb in darkness. "Molly, wait a moment."

"Nay, Sela. I must find Lord Auberon." She deposited her lantern on a hook next to the extinguished one and hurried toward the companionway. Had it been her who blew out the light?

"Listen, *please*." Sela clambered up the companionway and through the hatch, but Molly moved fast. On deck, Sela was once more doused with rain and buffeted by winds that had only grown fiercer since she went in search of Ira. The few sailors still moving about were dressed in foul weather gear and tethered to one of the three masts. She stumbled as she ran to catch up with Molly, reaching her only a few paces from the captain's door.

"Stop!" The wind snatched up her command and swept it away, but Molly halted, a sly smile on her pale lips. Sela grabbed for her arm, only for the other woman to jerk it away. "You know what you saw, Molly."

"Aye, I do. A pair of lovers thrown together by the winds of fate."

"If you lie about me, it'll hurt Lieutenant Alexander, too."

"Aye, I'm counting on it. Two birds with one stone, and all that." Molly's grin broadened. "You know, Sela, Lord Brigham paid me good money to kill you before you reached Azazel. He'll be pleased 'twas so easily accomplished. And by your own hand, too."

Sela stared. Liron had been right to fear that Joss's father would try something on the open sea. "Lord Brigham paid you to kill me? Why?"

"You ask too many questions. Maybe that's why."

Molly turned and Sela grabbed for her arm again. At that moment, the ship nosedived into another trough, and for a second time, Sela hit the deck. This time, Molly fell on top of her, the sharp point of her elbow connecting with Sela's stomach. The ship righted itself and Molly was the first to recover her balance, planting a meaty fist in Sela's face. Her head jerked to the side and the ship followed suit, leaning hard to port. Molly rolled away across the deck and Sela staggered to her feet, grabbing for the nearest mast.

"Sela!" Her name issued from a hatch near the bow. Caleb?

She had no time to yell a response before Molly lunged at her. Sela quickly sidestepped and Molly stumbled, tumbling to the deck. Features that might have been pretty knotted with rage, and she came at Sela again. For a second time, Sela was faster, but only just. Molly was strong, having obtained the best of the food and avoiding the fever that had touched most of the prisoners. If Sela was caught, she was dead.

Thrown by the ship's momentum, and stumbling backward, Sela sagged against the ship's outer railing. The hard wood bit into her fingers. Exhaustion stole through every limb as a wave slapped against her back, soaking through her gown to her stays and chemise beneath. Molly, several paces away, narrowed her eyes. "You'll regret the day you challenged me."

A flash of distant lightning revealed the sharp point of a dagger in her outstretched hand and Molly bared her teeth savagely. A man shouted, and Sela held up a branded palm.

"Nay, Molly! Do not—"

Molly lunged, and at the last moment, Sela threw herself to the side, just as the ship tilted hard to starboard. Instead of Sela, Molly encountered only railing, which was no match for her weight, momentum, and the ship's precarious angle. Her fingernails scrabbled for a hand hold, but only one hand was free— the other clutched the dagger. Sela heard the splintering of wood and Molly's agonized scream as she plummeted over the bulwark into the writhing sea.

"Man overboard!" one of the sailors yelled.

Sela teetered on the edge herself, clutching at the remainder of the broken rail which threatened to come free. For a terrifying moment, she glimpsed the white froth of the waves below, and then a strong arm curled around her waist, dragging her backward as the ship righted itself. When she was steady, she spun and saw Caleb, his eyes so dark they appeared almost black. For a second time, he had saved her from harm.

"Molly!" she shouted, and pointed to the heaving ocean, but

Caleb was already moving toward the other sailors.

"Tie yourself to the mast, Sela!" He tossed her a length of rope, hastily tying the end of another piece around his own waist. He crossed to the broken rail and leaned over, so far that Sela feared he'd fall himself. He stayed there for several minutes, gloved hands gripping the rail, his gaze raking the depths of the sea below. Several other sailors peered over the side, but none were so bold as Caleb, who seemed to dangle over the water itself.

After what seemed like the eternity she would be denied, he returned to stand beside her. The ribbon from his queue was gone, and the wind whipped his dark hair freely around his pale face. "I can't see any sign of her. She's all but vanished."

She followed Caleb down the hatch and into the main hold, where he took her elbow and drew her aside. "Are you all right, Sela? She didn't hurt you?" His eyes roamed over her, lingering on the cheekbone Molly had sought to pound into dust.

She shook her head. "Caleb, Molly was going to Lord Auberon. She would have lied about us." Sela could not help but feel a guilty sense of relief amidst the horror of Molly's tragic end. It was a momentary reprieve. She would live…and Caleb would be safe from false accusations.

But if Lord Brigham heard that she'd survived…

Would he send other assassins to finish Molly's task? Assassins who would not be so easy to overcome? Sela was no fool. If not for the assistance of the storm—and Caleb—she would now be dead.

He studied her face, seemingly unaware that she had used his Carver-given name. "We did nothing wrong." He frowned. "I don't understand why the woman hated you so. To draw a knife—"

She could not tell him of Lord Brigham's instructions, unless she confessed all. Instead, she simply shrugged. "I'm sorry, Caleb—for before. Is your head…" She instinctively reached up to probe his wound, but he flinched and jerked away, and she remembered her place. Only the storm had caused her to forget.

Not Caleb, but Lieutenant Alexander. One of the Righteous.

"My head is fine, Sela. I'll leave you here. I must report to Lord Auberon." He nodded and exited hastily, no doubt grateful that he would not have to report himself.

Another of the Carver's *mercies*?

The rest of the women tossed and moaned on their bunks, and the hold already stank of vomit and urine. Picking her way across the filthy floor, Sela was surprised to find Hester sleeping soundly.

Nay…not sleeping.

At the sight of the woman's pale face and wide, staring eyes, Sela felt for the pulse at her neck. Had Molly killed her, simply because Sela had befriended her? Or was it the fever that had finally taken her? "Hester!" she said urgently, her heart pounding a frantic beat. "Hester, wake up. Somebody, help me!"

But she knew death when she saw it.

Where was Hester now? With the Soul Carver, awaiting an eternity of heavenly bliss, or already writhing in temporary damnation? Or had she managed to atone for her past sins and been released to mere nothingness? Sela rocked her friend's cold body, burying her face in Hester's scraggly dark hair. The woman's palms were limp at her sides, displaying the double brands that had cost Hester her life.

Carver, you are the thief, stealing away the only friend I have in this forsaken place. Not Hester. Please, don't take her too.

Only then remembering her letters, Sela stood and dug her hand into the pocket of her gown, retrieving two pieces of sodden pulp. She examined each one by the light of the sole lantern. The envelopes were ruined, and she carefully peeled them away to expose the precious missives beneath.

Both Tucker's mysterious letter and Teodoir's final instructions were a soggy mess of blurred ink. Unreadable, even in perfect light. Why hadn't she bowed to her curiosity and read both of them before? Why had she waited?

Sela lowered herself to the bunk now devoid of Hester's unconventional, lively nature. She had never cried, not since Liri had been taken, for she'd believed that no subsequent misery could approximate the loss of a beloved sister. But she'd been wrong.

For the first time since the Carver had taken what she thought was everything, Sela dropped her head into her hands and wept bitterly.

This, then, was everything.

"But if he hadn't been spared…I wonder if you would feel so kindly toward the law now, and toward Lord Auberon. Even toward the Carver Himself."

Caleb shrugged aside Sela's words and tried to focus on the page blurring in front of him. He'd seen her up close yesterday, for the first time since the storm, and had been shocked by the deep circles beneath her eyes. But then, Molly had been lost overboard and Hester pronounced dead in the space of an hour.

And now Sela was friendless, alone, confined to the hold like all the female prisoners in the wake of Lord Auberon's fury over Captain Foley's and Ira's betrayal. In the days following the storm, and with Ira's absence, more prisoners had succumbed to sickness as unsanitary conditions and low rations made living corpses of many. And genuine corpses, ten of which had been carried onto the main deck from down below, sewn into sails, weighted, and tossed into the sea.

Until yesterday, he'd feared every morning that Sela would be one of them.

Caleb's pen paused above the parchment. The relief in Zeke's eyes on hearing his reprieve had been palpable. Lord Auberon would not hear of the lieutenant's misdeeds, providing that Zeke never made an advance on Sela or any other branded woman. Zeke had nodded soberly at the conditions of his freedom, and his eyes had not once rested on Sela since the judgment. He would return to the Old Town as soon as the ship had restocked and minor repairs were made.

Captain Foley had pleaded with Lord Auberon to pardon Ira and himself, and Caleb had added to his calls for mercy, but the elder had not relented. Ira would hang their first morning on Azazel, just like the poor soul who'd had the misfortune of murdering Joss Brigham.

"Land! Land, ho!"

Caleb dropped his pen and moved to the porthole. Aye, land, and land so vast it momentarily surprised him. Despite having known Azazel to be an island home to thousands, he'd still imagined it as small and cramped. Otherwise, how could the guards account for every one of the prisoners?

As he made his way to the quarterdeck, he beheld a strip of earthy golden-brown hovering above the shimmering turquoise blue, and beyond the tawny beach, a mass of emerald green crowned in cloud. They drew closer, and Caleb discerned the lush green arms of an enormous bay, the stony fingertips of which were so close together that the entrance to the bay could hardly be more than a half-mile apart, though that might well be an illusion. The opposing headlands both ended abruptly in sheer, rocky drops, the sea cliffs plunging down into water so deep that it appeared nearly black.

Tugging at his collar in an attempt to resist the humidity, Caleb looked past the headlands to the cove where civilization stretched from ear to ear along the flatter, more hospitable parts of the bay. He knew without asking that the settlement was Belladonna, the largest on Azazel.

"Beautiful lady," Zeke translated beside him, as if quoting a poet, and Caleb raised an eyebrow in query.

"From one of the Old Tongues?"

"Aye," replied the other man. "Though 'twas meant ironically. All the settlements are named for plants with poisonous qualities. Belladonna be the most deadly of 'em all."

Caleb understood, though he could appreciate the wild, unruly beauty of the island, especially after three months at sea. Behind the settlement, mountains rose sharply—volcanic, judging by the shape of them. They hunched shoulder to shoulder like stoic sentries, though the tallest were bent at seemingly impossible angles and wreathed with cloud. Waterfalls descended from some of the rocky heights, disappearing from sight into narrow folds of earth below. Though everywhere he looked was thickly forested, patches of lighter green swarmed the base of most of the mountains. Sugarcane? Or some other crop? He had not expected so many farms, and certainly not on an island-prison.

He squinted, trying to see beyond the mountains to the wilderness rumored to lie beyond—the wilderness of which he'd heard stories since he was a child, supposedly filled with deadly adders and animals that could tear a man apart with one swipe of their claws. Some said it was a jungle so dense and impenetrable that none could find their way through it, while others claimed it was more desert than jungle.

Certainly, the inhabitants of Azazel made little attempt to disprove any of the rumors, since Lord Auberon had explained that most traversed the longer coastal routes to access the other settlements. The ships of Eremia could sail around the island, but preferred to anchor a little way off Azazel while smaller boats navigated the sharp reefs and treacherous coves. Only Belladonna's bay was deep enough to enter directly.

"How do the guards keep track of all the prisoners?" he asked Zeke, who stood silently beside him.

Zeke shrugged. "Aye, 'tis difficult. But there be no way off the island, Caleb, not with any cap'n who values his head. Few smugglers would dare take a man off the island, for fear they be condemned t' his fate. 'Sides, the soul stain be hard t' mask."

The hatch to the prisoners' hold opened, and the female prisoners climbed out one by one. Caleb recognized Sela, looking like a shadow of the woman he'd glimpsed the first day of their voyage. Her black hair was bound in a loose plait that hung lifelessly over her shoulder, and her collarbones seemed more prominent above the neckline of her faded gown. After making a valiant attempt to corral his gaze, Zeke murmured something and moved away. Caleb stared at her openly, but she never once looked his way. Instead, she surveyed the approaching land, her shoulders drooping as she likely imagined what lay in store for them.

For her.

"Good evening, Caleb."

Caleb briefly turned to acknowledge the man who'd appeared so suddenly beside him. "Good evening, Lord Auberon."

The older man tracked his gaze to Sela before Caleb followed Zeke's example and shifted his eyes away. "What are the results of your observation, my son?"

The results of his observation? He remembered the warmth of her hands through his damp shirt when she fell against him in Ira's cabin. Her eyes, the exact hue of which was somewhere between bellflowers and irises. The slenderness of her waist when he'd saved her from falling overboard. The tangible relief in her face at realizing she was saved—and that he was her savior.

The fire in her as she effortlessly challenged the teachings of the very Righteous itself.

She was not so far from his own age. An appealing mix of sharp intelligence and easy kindness, like no woman he'd ever met. Despite her comparatively lower status, she'd evidently been well-schooled. Were she unbranded, he would have pursued her for the Binding.

"Our friend Ezekiel has reconsidered his interest," Caleb said at last. "He sees that his pursuit of a branded woman is impossible...nay, immoral."

Lord Auberon studied him, as if fully aware that Caleb spoke of more than Zeke. "That is wise. And the inevitable evils of which I spoke?"

"No doubt we will witness more of them once we reach land." Despite the calm seas, and the fact that he had never suffered from sea sickness, he felt oddly nauseous.

The older man's lip curled, and he turned to study Belladonna with the air of a man surveying a meal that he'd already sampled once before and found wanting. "I agree, Caleb. Now, let us look to brighter things. Once we arrive..."

Mindful of the vow he'd forced Zeke to swear, Caleb tried not to watch Sela as the *Deliverance* neared the settlement and dropped anchor. Before darkness fell, the prisoners would be rowed ashore and set free to roam Azazel at will. There were too many, Lord Auberon told him, for the guards to keep them permanently bound or manacled. And there were no slave owners to keep watch over the prisoners, since all the exiles were slaves for life, excepting the guards, the officers, and the families some dared to bring to this forsaken place.

Was the threat of Eremia's punishments enough to keep the prisoners from attempting to escape the island? He posed the question to Lord Auberon and the elder simply pointed at a long line of stakes on the shore that Caleb had assumed was part of a fence, guarding the ramshackle sheds and tottering warehouses that crouched beside the water's edge to the north of the docks. He shivered as the grim reality of the vision asserted itself in the fading light.

Impaled on the stakes were human skulls—dozens of them, perhaps hundreds. It seemed that, though vastly outnumbered by the soulless, the guards were zealous in tracking down escaped prisoners. No doubt they would search every ship for those who carried the soul mark but had no papers authorizing their travel.

"...the soul stain be hard t' mask..."

As Lord Auberon expounded on the evils of Azazel's various settlements, Caleb hoped that Sela would find a place of safety, possibly with one of the farmers who resided far from the debauchery and maintained honorable trading with Eremia.

His mind reached for the past, six years now gone. Was Liri— likely the reason why Tucker shunned Azazel—out there even now? Surely, she was not corrupted like the rest of the populace. Perhaps she'd found a good man in place of his brother, if any such men existed in such a desolate place.

Would Sela bond with another branded soul? A farmer, perhaps? His heart squeezed painfully at the thought. But Caleb had always prided himself on facing bitter realities with courage.

And if he couldn't have Sela, he hoped that an uncorrupted man would take her in his place.

Chapter Eight

The first thing Sela glimpsed as she set foot on Azazel was an enormous tree, its limbs pale and ghostly by the light of the full moon. It seemed dead, or nearly so, although she thought it might have been beautiful at one time, like the trees in the south seminary in the fall. A far more noble sight than the line of human skulls that had greeted them as they rowed ashore, some still covered with skin and hair and crawling with crows and maggots.

One of the marines chuckled behind her, just as he had when he saw the human carrion. "Rottin' from the inside, like the soul of Azazel itself. An' like t' topple at any time, crushin' some poor soul on its way down."

"Why has no one felled it?" she asked as the marine removed her manacles.

"Because 'tis a hangin' tree, that's why."

"A *hanging* tree?"

"Used when the gallows be full up," he said, with a sly grin. "Or when there's…less official business t' be done."

Where would they hang Ira, come the morning? Seeing ragged shadows drifting in the stale breeze in the branches above, and understanding what they were, Sela shuddered and rubbed the raw skin on her wrists.

The marine waved a hand in the direction of the settlement. "Be off with ye, then."

"What, you're…letting me go?"

The man glanced at his friend and laughed heartily, exposing an array of teeth more silver than white. "There's no 'lettin' ye go' on Azazel, girlie." He nodded at her branded palms. "Seein' as ye can't go anywhere else."

She understood. The docks were crawling with soldiers and marines who stood guard to every ship, boat, and seaworthy vessel that anchored in the bay. It was probably impossible to gain passage off the island while bearing the soul stain.

The marine lifted a gloved hand and pushed at her shoulder. "Get goin'."

"How do I go about seeking employment? Or a place for the night?"

"Ye can start by walkin' thattaway." He jabbed his index finger in the direction of raucous music and the occasional gunshot, rolled his eyes, and spun away.

She reluctantly turned in the direction of Belladonna. Fittingly, the narrow strip of land between the docks and the settlement was occupied by a large cemetery, the graves marked not with the ornate, lovingly tended gravestones she'd seen in the Old Town, but heavy rocks painted white. Eight graves were packed with fresh earth, as if their inhabitants had just been laid to rest that morning. She turned back to look at the hanging tree. From its branches, a victim fighting for air and life would only see the hundreds of graves—a final, cruel reminder of their inevitable fate.

Did nothing flourish on Azazel but death?

Aware that the half-dozen female prisoners who had come ashore with her had all but dispersed, Sela gripped her small bag and started toward the music. After Molly had fallen overboard, the other women had kept away from her, even the doubly branded ones. Did they think she had pushed Molly to her death?

For the remaining two sevendays aboard the ship, she'd kept to herself, missing Hester's teasing, wicked smile. At last, she'd gone through Hester's bag, but she found only a spare change of clothes and undergarments and an assortment of odd objects—a bronze coin dating back to the Old Times, a pressed flower, and a glass marble shot through with streaks of vivid color.

Though Sela could not bring herself to wear Hester's clothes, she stuffed the remaining treasures into her bag, along with

Hester's two blankets, which were likely crawling with disease and vermin. When she could, she'd scrub them with the most potent soap she could find. Along with her own hair and body, she thought, feeling an itch on her scalp and hoping it wasn't lice.

Praying that she would be lucky enough to sight Liri and find a place with her, Sela headed directly for the busiest establishment. The settlement of Belladonna, the largest on Azazel—or so the soldiers said—sprawled across the flattened lip of the bay on either side of a vast, muddy street. Looking like a grim, upturned mouth, it was lined on the waterside with thickly tangled underbrush and the occasional palm tree, and sheltered on the other by the wrinkled folds of the vast mountains she'd seen from the ship, which seemed to simultaneously overlook and frown at the exuberance below.

The heart of Belladonna itself was a long string of multi-storied buildings, built nearly on top of each other—like a black-gummed mouth of crowded, disorderly teeth—as if the earliest inhabitants had been ignorant of the vast sections of fertile land available beyond Belladonna. Then again, just as misery preferred company, debauchery was no different, and festered all the better for its close confinement.

Dodging two men shouldering barrels and weaving around an open-topped carriage bearing two finely dressed women and an elegantly tailored man through the chaos, Sela picked her way across the street with shoes that clung to the mud like a newborn calf to his mother's teat. Her hem was already filthy from the long sea voyage, but she raised it past her ankles anyway, being careful to avoid the droppings from various animals. Would Liri recognize her, six years past?

Certainly, Esther would.

The establishment she'd selected, an enormous three-storied building with a wraparound porch and dozens of gleaming windows, seemed to have almost as many patrons gathered outside as within, and Sela clutched her bag closer as she registered more than one leer, even from the men with women already draped over them. As she gained the stairs, she felt a bare hand on her arm.

"Fresh off the ship, are we, miss? Can I help ye?"

Sela looked up into the red face of a man with hair so greasy he seemed more sea monster than human. "I'm fine, thank you."

"Ye must be gut-foundered after spendin' three months a' sea." He squeezed her arm, as if to prove his point. "Aye, but Murphy'll put some meat on yer bones." He leaned closer and Sela blanched at his stale, rum-soaked breath. "The girls upstairs are always looked after, ye know."

With what she hoped was a pleasant expression, she pulled her arm away and stepped back. "I'm not looking for work upstairs. Is Murphy the owner of this establishment?"

He sniggered. "Aye, Murphy be the owner of this here *establishment*, miss. Shall I take ye t' him?"

"If you please."

He pushed open the tavern doors and Sela was immediately assailed by the mingled stenches of whisky, rum, tallow, sweat, and tobacco. Not the pleasant kind that Teodoir smoked, but something acrid that burned the back of her throat. Dozens of tables were arrayed in a semi-circle around a stage where women danced in gowns that plunged so low and ended so abruptly that Sela blushed and turned away.

Several fiddles and even a few pipes accompanied a piano in the corner, but the lively, bawdy melody was so unlike anything she'd enjoyed with her family back home that she wished she could stuff candle wax in her ears.

The greasy-haired man led the way through the throng of people, several men turning from the display on the stage to stare at her. Powdered, garishly painted nightwalkers wove their way among them, occasionally casting Sela the odd, curious glance. Did they think she'd come to join them?

Never. Gut-foundered or not, she'd die before she sold herself.

The man waved his hand at a broad-shouldered gentleman— if she could think of him as such—behind the bar and gave a slight bow. "The great Murphy himself, miss. He'll answer yer questions. If ye shud need anythin' else…"

Sela shuddered as his gaze drifted down her. Not for the first time, she wished she still had her knife, even if the blade was now stained with Joss Brigham's blood. "Nay, thank you."

As the man departed, Murphy turned from polishing a glass to study her. "Miss—" His voice turned inquiring.

"Meriweather."

"Miss Meriweather, how may I help you?" Surprisingly, he spoke near-perfect mainland speech, and his thick hands betrayed only a single brand. One of the lot, then. His smile was worldly, but not lascivious.

"I'm new to the island."

"Aye, I can see that." He seemed to take her measure in one sweep. "Watch your step, Miss Meriweather, with those pretty eyes of yours."

A friendly warning, not a threat. "I will, thank you. I'm looking for my older sister."

His eyes clouded with sympathy. "One of the lot?"

Sela nodded. "She's young, only twenty-four years old. Blonde hair, green eyes. Shorter than I am, and slim. Very beautiful."

"Name?"

"Liri Meriweather."

"I know most of the soulless in Belladonna," he said at last, "but I don't remember your sister. And by your description, it sounds like I'd remember her."

Sela's stomach twisted. "Are there other settlements?"

"Half a dozen or so, littered around the island. Some you can walk to in a few hours. Others take more than a day to reach by horseback. Using the coastal routes, of course."

More than a day? How large was Azazel? And why did Murphy imply that no one would want to brave the heart of the island itself? Surely the coastal routes were longer and more treacherous.

Murphy's expression had grown grim. "If your sister is as pretty as you, Miss Meriweather, she may not have had much choice as to her future here."

"Liri would never sell herself."

"I wasn't talking about the nightwalkers." Murphy's gaze flitted to the stage. "Have you heard of Uriah Smith, Miss Meriweather?"

Several men within earshot stopped mid-conversation to stare at Murphy, and Sela was surprised by the fear on their grizzled faces. "Nay, I haven't."

"Then consider this a warning to stay away from him."

"I don't understand."

Murphy leaned close, propping meaty elbows across the bar as his voice dropped several notches. "Mister Smith has an eye for a pretty face. And an aim so good that any man who dares to challenge him finds himself suspended from that hanging tree you likely snared a glimpse of when you came ashore."

"I'm not afraid of any man."

"Nay? You should be." Murphy glanced at the dancing girls again. "Azazel is a dangerous place for a woman, Miss Meriweather. Should you need a roof over your head, good food, and safe employment…"

"Thank you for your help," Sela said, not so naïve she failed to understand his meaning. Leaving the bar behind, she marched to the door, determined to question as many tavern owners as were willing to answer her. She'd been so distracted with thoughts of Liri, she'd forgotten to ask about Esther. Should she return to question Murphy? Nay. He would only think she'd decided to accept his offer.

The greasy-haired man sidled up beside her again. "Did ye find what ye were lookin' for, miss?

"Aye, thank you." She darted around him, only to come face to face with an enormous man, taller than her by at least a head. Seeing that both his arms ended at the wrists in reddened stubs, Sela jerked her attention to the man's face. Both of his cheeks were branded, though the scars had faded with age.

"Don't mind ol' Reed," said her unwanted guide in her ear.

"Seein' as he has no hands, they branded his face just to be sure he wouldn't try an' bluff his way off the island."

"I'm sorry to hear it," she muttered, and pushed between both men, bursting into the fresh air with a momentum that almost made her tumble down the stairs.

Ignoring the glances of the men, and the squeals and bursts of rum-drenched laughter, she stumbled onto the muddy street, already despising the slow squeeze of humidity that dampened the chemise beneath her stays and petticoats. Had Caleb come ashore yet, or would he first witness this place by the sober light of day? She wondered where he would live. Were there decent parts of Azazel where men and women could live honestly…honorably? She wished she'd asked him.

"*Sela?*"

She turned to see a nightwalker approaching, her steps slow and hesitant, as if she yearned to run in the other direction. With uncharacteristic modesty, she crossed her arms over the bodice of her low-cut gown.

Sela stared at the young woman without recognition, trying to see beneath the elaborately curled hair, powdered face, and painted lips. "I'm sorry…do I know you?"

"'Tis Esther." The young woman fought back a sob. "Esther Gray. We were friends back in the Old Town."

"Esther?" Sela's eyes widened as she recognized the tentative smile and honey-colored curls. "Esther!" She threw her arms wide to embrace her friend, but the other woman stiffened and jerked away before Sela could touch her.

"Are you…are you an officer's bondmate?"

Did Esther think she was still unbranded? "Nay." She held up both palms. "Soulless, same as you." It was the first time she had been happy to admit as such.

"Oh, Sela." Esther's eyes swelled with tears, borne more of despair than of joy. "I imagined you safe in the Old Town, snuggled up with Roux and Cadence in your bed."

"A lot has happened since then." She embraced her friend

again, and while Esther did not pull away, she remained stiff and unsure.

"I didn't want you…to see me like this."

Sela drew back. "I've already witnessed enough of Azazel to know that you likely weren't given much of a choice."

Esther bowed her head, clearly ashamed. "If my mama were here…"

"She'd be as happy to see you as I am."

"Murphy looks after us, you know. Some of the other establishments…they beat the women. Or allow the customers to beat them. Murphy is kind, in his own way."

"While you're bringing in gold coins to line his pockets, aye. But what of afterward?"

Esther's lip trembled.

Sela cursed her outspokenness. "I'm sorry. I know nothing of what you've been through."

"I wouldn't wish you to."

A man behind Esther called her name with a suggestive smile. When Sela glared at him, he winked at her instead. She fought the urge to retch.

"I have to go, Sela—"

"Wait." Sela grabbed her friend's arm. "When you first came here, Esther…did you see Liri?"

Esther glanced away. "I *must* go."

"Please. If something's happened to her, I want to know."

"Liri…" Esther heaved an enormous sigh and turned to Sela, resignation in the powdered arch of her mouth and the graceful curve of her slim shoulders. "I saw Liri the first month I was on Azazel, when she came to Belladonna."

"She came here? Then she lives in one of the other settlements?"

"Nay, Sela. Your sister…she lives on the edge of the wilderness—beyond the mountains, but on the other side of the island."

"But you saw her—"

"Only for a minute, Sela, and you must promise me that you will not seek her out." Esther's voice turned pleading. "*Promise me.*"

"On the contrary. I'm setting out at first light tomorrow to find her." Sela lifted her chin.

"Nay. Where she has gone, you cannot follow her."

"She's not dead, is she?" Despite her efforts to appear brave, Sela's stomach fluttered.

"Of course not. Liri lives, but...have you heard of Uriah Smith, Sela?"

"Less than ten minutes ago, from Murphy himself."

Esther nodded. "Uriah Smith and his men make their permanent camp on the edge of the wilderness—on the richest, lushest part of the island. They're land pirates and smugglers, thieves and murderers and kidnappers. 'Tis said they live like kings, in defiance of Eremia, and that they have a vast cave beneath a mighty waterfall, full of all their treasures. They frequently raid the settlements for slaves to serve their every whim."

Sela remembered Murphy's admonition and felt a rising dread. "Then Liri is there? She was taken as one of Uriah Smith's slaves?"

"Nay, not his slave, Sela. She is his bondmate."

Sela's knees wobbled as her stomach went into free fall. Liri, her beautiful, fragile sister, bonded to a murderer? A kidnapper of women?

"When was she taken?" Sela finally asked, weakly.

"She wasn't taken," Esther replied. "Liri bonded with Uriah willingly. A love match, 'twas said, though I can't speak to her feelings thereafter."

"A love match?"

"They have several children together. Three, I think."

Children? It was more than she could possibly take in. At least Tucker would never know Liri's fate.

"I have to find her."

"Nay, Sela. Bonded or not, Uriah is always on the lookout for new, pretty captives to serve him and his men. If you go in search of Liri, I do not doubt that you will not return."

For the first time, Sela understood the true motivations behind Esther's decision. Better to be a willing slave than an unwilling one. "I won't abandon my sister."

Esther's powdered face softened in sympathy and she eyed Sela's filthy gown. "Have you eaten at all today?"

"Not anything that could be said to resemble real food."

The young woman's arm looped through hers. "Come with me. I'll find you supper and a place to sleep. Murphy won't mind the expense, since we're not full up tonight. And he can take the cost out of my wages."

This time, Sela pulled back. "I can't stay in a place like this."

Fine lines pulled at Esther's lovely mouth, as if an invisible puppeteer worked at her strings. "There's a lock on every door, Sela. And there's an empty room next to mine. While I'm not at liberty to join you this evening…" She glanced at the man who'd beckoned her, now preoccupied with another woman, and her heated cheeks showed even beneath her powder. "…you'll be quite safe." She looked pointedly down the muddy street. "Unless you have other options."

Esther was right. She had no place to go. If she stayed on the streets, she'd be subject to far worse conditions. And Esther had said that this was the least vile of the establishments. "You're right." She lifted her bag. "Thank you."

She only hoped the locked door would keep the greasy-haired man and his friends at arms' length.

Caleb pulled at his collar, already resenting the stifling humidity. Even by the frank light of morning, Azazel was everything he'd imagined—and worse. The night before, the bawdy music and gunshots issuing from several taverns had travelled across the water to the ship, confirming every story he'd been told about this place of depravity. Now, by the light of dawn, the main street was almost deserted, with the nighttime revelers having finally returned to their beds.

Had Sela found a safe place to sleep the night before? He wished he'd come ashore with her, and personally ensured her safety, but Lord Auberon had insisted he stay another night on the *Deliverance*. Not wanting his mentor to question his honor—or Sela's—he'd reluctantly agreed.

As Ira had been dragged to the fort where she would meet her end at the gallows that very morning, Caleb had walked the other way, trying to forget the broken expression in her eyes. The captain had been sent ashore and branded the night before. Might Foley foolishly attempt a rescue?

A lone chicken squawked across his path and Caleb dodged a muddy puddle, nudging aside the splintered remains of a glass bottle with his booted toe. It was well known that one of the chief exports of Azazel was whisky and its cheaper, equally unsavory cousins, offered to the Old Town at a far lower price than it would eventually be sold. The Righteous had tried their best to abolish the roaring trade, but any attempts to ban it only sent the merchandise underground. And the guards could not patrol every treacherous bay or hidden cove on the island, not when many of them were apparently in cahoots with the smugglers. One of Caleb's tasks, Lord Auberon had said, was to weed out the traitors.

What good would that do, though, when they would only be branded and returned to Azazel to continue their trade?

Caleb paused as he saw the door to one of the taverns open. Activity, at this hour? Two women emerged, the one with her back to Caleb carrying a small bag. The other was clearly a nightwalker, with a low-cut gown that was more showy satin than sensible wool or cotton.

The two women embraced, the nightwalker brushing tears from cheeks that were powdered white and spotted with rouge. She pressed something into the hand of the taller woman, who shook her head. The nightwalker insisted, and finally the other woman tucked it into the pocket of her gown. The nightwalker abruptly returned inside, and the tall woman turned to descend the stairs.

Caleb sucked in a breath. It was Sela, her raven-black hair loose around her shoulders, wearing a dark-blue gown he did not recognize. The dress was far more modestly cut than the nightwalker's, but why was she in the company of such a woman? And, more importantly, why was she leaving the unsavory establishment as if she'd stayed the night?

She finally intercepted his stare and started, the same expression in her eyes as when she'd noticed him watching her fight. Because she was ashamed?

She headed directly for him.

"Lieutenant Alexander."

"Sela." He could not help noticing that her hair looked clean and satiny, as if she'd bathed the night before. She smelled uncomfortably like roses. Like a woman seeking to attract a man, though her pretty face was devoid of makeup. "What were you doing talking to that woman?"

"She…" Sela hesitated, her gaze as deeply mired in the mud as her low-heeled boots. "Esther is a friend of mine."

"Esther?" Did she think him a fool, inventing an alias that was obviously false? "Like *Hester*?"

Her eyes swept up to his and he was struck anew by their startling color. "Of what are you accusing me, Caleb?"

"What were you doing in…in that place?" He waved a hand to indicate the vile establishment. Not even her use of his Carver-given name could soften him this time.

"Esther procured me a room. And she lent me one of her gowns." She indicated the dark blue dress.

"You stayed overnight in a brothel? In the company of *nightwalkers*?" Lord Auberon's predictions returned to haunt him.

"Look around you, Caleb," she snapped. "Do you see any *decent* establishments willing to welcome a woman with no money? Were you here last night to witness any of the dangers awaiting a woman alone? Esther was my closest friend back in the

Old Town, though she was taken in the lot a year ago. Nightwalker or nay, she is the only one on Azazel to show me any kindness thus far. Out of her own wages, she paid for a room with a locked door, a bath, and food. Even branded, she is a finer woman than any I have ever met."

Still entranced by her violet eyes and rosewater scent, he struggled to hold on to his anger. "Keep such company, Sela, and you'll taint your reputation."

"More than I already have, Caleb?" She raised her palm and he winced at the soul stain there.

Sometimes, he nearly forgot it existed. He forced himself to stare at it, permanently affixing it in his memory.

He dug in his pocket, extracted a handful of gold coins, and reached out for her palm. "Then here is some honest money to keep you from the tainted sort."

She pulled her hand from his gloved grip and backed away. Looking into her eyes, he realized he could not have hurt her more deeply. Pride and pain mingled equal parts in the depths of her soul. "I don't want your money, sir. Or your pity."

"Sela—"

Turning, she ran from him. He pocketed the money, retrieved the two coins that had fallen into the mud and firmly lodged themselves there, and moved to follow her, but a firm hand gripped his shoulder.

Caleb turned to see Lord Auberon, his white coat looking starkly out of place amidst the filthy, muddy street. "My lord." He dipped his head.

"Did you believe her story, my son?"

"Story?"

"Her explanation for where she spent the night."

"She said the nightwalker was a former friend. Esther." Was he a fool to be swayed by the apparent sincerity in her eyes? Or was he too taken in by beauty?

"Esther, hmm? Though I cannot imagine you are surprised, Caleb. Many a woman turns to prostitution for the ease and comfortable living it provides. Lovely as she is, she was bound to be tempted." He clicked his tongue. "Though I am taken aback that she took to it so quickly."

"I don't know that she did anything wrong. Certainly nothing like *that*."

"The appearance of doing wrong is as grievous as the doing of wrong itself, Caleb. That is why you must always watch your feet, lest they stumble and falter."

"I wanted to help her. Keep her from…from that kind of life." Caleb's voice sounded as desolate as he felt.

"I know, my son, and your compassion does you credit. The first time I visited Azazel, I was the same. I emptied half of my father's coffers to assist every person I met. But every time I did so, even with my coins in their pockets, the men and women returned to the lives I'd tried to rescue them from. You must leave the woman to her fate."

"But she is innocent." She'd slowed to a walk, but she still moved as if the devil snapped at her heels.

And maybe he did.

"She may have been once." Lord Auberon laid his arm across Caleb's shoulders with fatherly familiarity. "But she is innocent no longer."

Chest heaving, Liron ducked into a narrow alley and leaned against a stone wall, trying to catch his breath.

That was much too close.

Though he wore a heavy hood and had abandoned his marine's uniform, he was sure that one of the officers marching past had recognized him. Features like his were hard to disguise, and the king's navy kept a vigilant lookout for deserters. He'd run fast through the streets of Consuela and not stopped until he nearly reached the docks.

Liron tossed back his hood and scraped his fingers through his roughly chopped hair. He'd cut it to appear less like a soldier and more like a street urchin, though he doubted he would fool anyone up close. Nonetheless, the partial disguise, a rough beard, and the commoner's clothes he wore allowed him to move freely in the port of Consuela, searching for the one face he remembered almost better than his own.

The one man who could save them from despair.

Instead, he saw his sisters in every face he passed. Liri, with her pale, ethereal beauty and her heartfelt smile, and Sela, with her darker-complexioned looks so like his own. He had meant every word of his promise to his younger sister.

He would save them both from Azazel if it was the last thing he did.

Sela had doubted his plan, but then, she had never met Prince Magnus. Liron had been six years old when he met the king's only son, who had been leaving Eremia for the mainland in an elaborate procession. He was already a young man, and though not physically impressive—tall, but not broad, slim, but not muscular, richly tanned, but not handsome—the respect with which his soldiers and servants regarded him was clearly evident.

And then the accident…

Something or someone had spooked the horses of one of the supply wagons, and they had raced off, plunging into the watching crowd. Screams and agonized yells ensued, and as the wagon hurtled toward the place where he stood, Liron had frozen, realizing he'd wandered too far from his parents. He remembered staring into the crazed eyes of the approaching horses, the whites flashing dangerously, their mouths foaming at their bits. What would it feel like to be trampled by iron hooves?

But then a shadow blocked the sight, and he felt himself caught up in a man's arms. Something bumped the man's shoulder, and he gasped in pain and stumbled, but managed to keep his balance and get them both out of the way. As the horses finally slowed and were caught by a handful of servants, he carefully lowered Liron to the cobbles.

"There, now," came a voice, gentler than any he'd ever heard—even his father's. "Are you all right?"

Six-year-old Liron gazed up into a set of noble but undeniably plain features. The kind face of Prince Magnus—his savior—was crinkled with pain, and he held his shoulder awkwardly, as if the bone was out of place. Had he been jolted by one of the horses?

"My lord, your arm! Let me see to it at once." A manservant bustled into view, looking with horror at the prince's shoulder.

Prince Magnus gave a slight but firm shake of his head and looked back to Liron. "Have you parents nearby, young man?"

It was exceedingly generous to call a boy of his age such, but six-year-old Liron had swelled with pride. "Aye, my lord. Yaron and Ashira Meriweather. My name is Liron."

As if on cue, his parents had arrived, bowing and thanking the prince profusely. If Prince Magnus hadn't intervened, his father said, Liron would have been trampled. His mother, who held a one-year-old Sela, variously sniffed and blew into a handkerchief and wondered aloud how he had strayed so far from them.

The prince only smiled, once again looking at Liron. Despite his injury, no rebuke hovered on his lips. He glanced briefly at the infant Sela. "Are you a big brother, then, Master Liron?"

Another question to inflate his boyish pride, and at that, Liri had emerged from behind their father, standing shoulder to shoulder with Liron, as if anxious to put the story straight. She looked shyly up at the prince, who knelt and glanced between them. "Ah, you're twins?"

"How did you know?" Liron asked. "We don't look at all alike."

"Your eyes," said Magnus. "They tell me everything I need to know."

Even then, Liron had known he spoke of more than color.

"I'm the oldest," said Liri self-importantly, at that time too young to understand that her firstborn status was neither boast nor privilege. "By three whole minutes!"

The prince smiled. "Three whole minutes? You know, I

thought you seemed a little taller than your brother."

Liron had been indignant until he saw Prince Magnus's eyes sparkling with mirth. Settling for a shrug, he allowed his twin sister to usurp the prince's attention.

"My lord," said the servant at Prince Magnus's elbow, "we must tend to your injury."

Liron's parents, caught up in their fears for the prince's welfare, offered another round of apologies and thanksgiving, which Prince Magnus received with as much sincerity as if they were of the nobility. Preoccupied with little Sela, they missed the prince's next words as he tousled first Liri's hair, then Liron's.

"One day soon," he had said softly, so only Liron might hear, "you and your sisters will be free. I give you my word."

Then the prince had straightened, nodded at Liron's parents, and consented to be led away.

Six-year-old Liron had not understood the words—at first, he believed he'd dreamed the exchange—but an eighteen-year-old Liron had begun to comprehend them. On the day he'd lost his twin sister to the lot, he'd wondered if somehow the prince had foreseen Liri's fate. In addition to the healing touch, the royal family was rumored to possess gifts of prophecy, and Prince Magnus had not seemed like an ordinary man, despite his humble appearance. And so Liron waited, accepting his sister's fate—and his own—and hoping that the prince would make good on his promise.

Until the day Sela had been condemned to Azazel.

Twenty-four-year-old Liron had grown tired of waiting and taken matters into his own hands. How could he sit by and watch as his family was hacked apart, piece by piece? It was *his* fault, after all, that Sela had been attacked by Josiah Brigham. He knew the prince would help his sisters—if only he could find him.

Liron dragged his hood over his hair again as a light rain began to fall. Determination swept through his taut body, firming his jaw.

Aye. Prince Magnus would help.

Chapter Nine

By the time the sun sagged low in the sky again, Sela had despaired of ever finding honest work on Azazel. She'd knocked on nearly every door in the settlement, excepting the taverns, asking for any vacancies. She had helped her father in the fields and her mother within their home, and could cook, weave, and sew. Thanks to Teodoir, she could read and write and do sums. Inwardly, she'd hoped for a tutoring position.

Of the doors that didn't immediately close in her face, all offers were unsuitable, and she was not too proud to shun menial labor. Twice, the male proprietor had looked her up and down and hinted that another kind of work might suit her better. One even offered to be her first customer.

Sinking against the wall of a building, Sela fought the urge to weep. If she hadn't stormed away from Caleb that morning, she might have asked after work at the fort—not so far from the settlement. Did they allow branded souls to toil for them? And what of the farms she'd seen from the ship? Many were more than an hour's walk from Belladonna, and she was already weary and footsore. What if the farmers reacted the same way as the other settlement men? Out there, alone, no one could help her.

"Sela?" She glanced up to see Esther, concern creasing her forehead. "It will be dark soon. Why don't you come back with me? You look like you could use another meal."

"I can't rely on your generosity forever, Esther."

Her friend looked thoughtful. "You know, there's work in the taverns, besides the obvious. Cooking, serving, and waiting on tables. Can you still sing as beautifully as you once did?"

"Aye, but I won't."

"Because of Liri?"

Sela gave a tight nod. She would not think of music in this place. Music belonged to decency and civilization, and she was far from such things.

"Did you have any luck in the settlement?"

"Nay. The women looked at me like I might ensnare their bondmates, and the men looked at me like they wanted to be ensnared."

Esther's mouth softened. "There's one other option you might consider."

"I won't—"

"Nay, Sela, not that." She bit her lip. "There's a house not far from here, owned by a man called Thaddeus. You might call him a settlement leader of sorts, though he'd probably resent the title. He has a fearsome reputation and a colorful history, but 'tis said he's a changed man these days. Good, honorable, Carver-fearing. He lives with his sister and several others, and they're known for their kindnesses. The sister, Miss Briella, often comes to visit the nightwalkers. Stitching wounds and birthing babies and such."

"And you think they'd offer me work?"

"Miss Briella has a little girl…Temperance, I think her name is. Perhaps she has need of a nursemaid or a tutor. Miss Briella is often dauncy, you see."

"Which house is it?" Perhaps she'd knocked on the door already. And was it not *Mistress* Briella? What of the woman's bondmate?

"You likely missed it." She pointed past the settlement to the northern arm of the bay. "'Tis up on that hill, at least twenty minutes' walk past the fort, but before you reach the end of the northern headland. It looks over Belladonna and the bay, though it doesn't have nearly as impressive a view as the outpost. A big two-story place with a wide veranda. Painted completely white. Folks jest that Thaddeus got confused and built himself a lighthouse instead of a house. But I think the only paint that ever gets shipped to Azazel is white paint." She grimaced.

"Thank you, Esther." She squeezed the woman's hands. "You've been so kind to me."

Tears pearled beneath Esther's eyelids. "You were my closest friend, Sela."

"*Are,*" Sela corrected, and hugged her. "Carver willing, I'll see you tomorrow. And if Mister Thaddeus and his sister are as kind as you say they are, I promise to come back for you."

She left Esther standing in the street, clutching her arms as if she feared she would fall apart if she let go. Sela trudged down the main thoroughfare for the hundredth time that day, dodging animal dung, horses, and those who looked too long. A soldier slowed to her right, his smile appreciative, and she briefly wondered if it was Caleb. *Nay.* Even if it were, she wouldn't look at him.

Or speak to him, ever again.

After ten minutes of following a rutted road, she left Belladonna behind, and soon after that, she passed the fort, an orderly but ominous wooden structure crouching almost on the shore, just like the cemetery. A reminder that the soulless could only leave Azazel manacled or escorted by Death. She clutched her bag closer, her weary fingers aching to release the handle. The hill Esther had indicated loomed large in front of her, a worn path winding upward to the large, somewhat run-down house that crested it, the paint peeling in places, like flakes of dead skin.

Did she have the strength to climb it?

The recollection of Caleb's face as he'd spied her leaving the tavern spurred her onward. He'd believed she'd sold herself, at least at first, though the doubt in his eyes remained even after she'd explained her actions. Did he truly think her so wretched? And what of the kind, considerate Esther? Would a man of Caleb's pedigree even speak to her?

Aye, he was Tucker's brother. Though Tucker wouldn't have pretended he didn't despise her. He would have let it show in his face.

Halfway up the hill, she sank against the trunk of a tree she did not recognize—exploding in glorious purple color—to catch her breath. How was she so tired? She had not eaten since the small breakfast Esther had smuggled her, but she had gone without meals before. The lingering fever? Or the dreaded seasoning? Though her friend had always been slighter than Sela, even Esther's gown hung loosely on her.

She glanced to her right, noticing what had before been concealed by a fold of jade green. This curve of the bay hugged a tiny beach, now below her, but not so far that she could not see the small breakers and golden sand. A well-worn path snaked down from the white house to the beach, as if the occupants of the house frequently descended to partake of the warm ocean waters.

Looking up, she saw that past the white house, the grassy elbow of the bay continued to drive steeply upward until it reached the northern headland, the whole effect giving the appearance of a raised arm with a voluminous dark green sleeve, the wrinkled folds of which trailed in the turquoise waters below. The setting sun glanced off a building poised on the edge of the cliff—no more than a half-mile away. The outpost Esther had briefly mentioned? She shut her eyes for a moment.

She jerked awake, not aware that she'd been dozing, and found she'd slumped to the base of the tree. It was fully dark, save for a sliver of moonlight, and Sela glanced around, drawing her knees up against her chest despite the thick humidity. Was it too late to ascend the hill and ask for work? They might think she sought the dishonorable kind.

She looked down the hill and easily glimpsed the long stretch of taverns, badly tuned fiddles grating against squeals and rum-edged laughter. Nay, she could not go back—only if Mister Thaddeus and his sister turned her away.

Registering footsteps behind her, she spun to discern three shadows stalking her from below. A scrawny fist shot out and caught her off guard. The world lurched dizzily, as if she were still on the ship.

"Grab her bag," said a voice, too high to belong to a man but too low to be paired with a woman. By the moon's glow, she glimpsed a thin, hungry face, flanked by two more. Boys, then, not more than thirteen or fourteen years old.

Though she knew the pointlessness of it, she scrambled to her feet and clutched her bag tighter. She had very little, but Esther had given her some money that morning, even after she tried to refuse. She would not part with it now, not when Liron had taught her to stand up to bullies. "Get away from me. I don't want to hurt you."

A knife flashed silver in the moonlight. "Hurt us? Miss, I doubt ye'll be the one doin' the hurtin'."

She stilled. What could she do against a knife? Turning, she moved to escape down the hill, but her foot snagged one of the tree's raised roots and she went sprawling, her bag flying from her grasp. Her ankle wrenched and she gasped in pain before her head struck the ground. Her vision blurred, and she was dimly aware that one of the boys had pounced on her bag. The first boy advanced on her, still holding the knife.

"Hi, you! Get away from her!" Another voice splintered the night, coming from farther up the hill, and the boys abruptly scattered. Her bag went with them and she groaned, rolling onto her side.

A face came into view, and she blinked twice. Another boy, not above fifteen, but his face seemed to be…peeling? She struggled to focus, certain she'd hit her head harder than she'd first thought. Though the boy was dark-skinned, large sections of his face, neck, and arms were nearly white, giving him a mottled look. His hands were almost completely pale, as if he'd dipped them in the white paint that so distinguished the house above him.

He crouched beside her. "Miss, are you all right?"

Footsteps pounded behind him and a large, dark-haired man came into view. Sela scrambled back a little. As tall as old Reed, but solidly built, he would tower over any other man, even Teodoir. His left arm was bound to his chest in some kind of sling and, even restrained, it seemed smaller than the other, which dangled at his side.

He knelt beside the boy. "Easy, miss. You're safe with us."

He seemed to be somewhere in his forties, and though his features might have been called hard by some, his deep voice was soothing. He turned to the boy. "Did you see who attacked her, Jax?"

Jax shook his head. "One of the settlement gangs, I'd say."

One of?

"What's your name, miss?" asked the man, kindly.

"Sela Meriweather."

"Can you stand, Miss Meriweather?"

She curled her legs beneath her and tried to rise, only to crumple. The man's right arm shot out and prevented her from falling. "Jax, why don't you get on her other side, and we'll help her to the house."

But the moment she touched her ankle to the ground, she moaned. The man frowned. "I can carry you up the hill, Miss Meriweather, but as you can see, I have the use of only one arm. If you don't mind, I'll have to carry you over my shoulder."

She nodded, and the man stepped close, grabbed her around the legs, and lifted her easily, though she knew she was no sapling girl. He began climbing the hill, the strange boy trotting beside him. Sela forced herself not to stare. What had happened to his skin?

The man carried her up a flight of five steps, and his boots crossed a veranda that shone white even in the cloud-veiled moonlight. "Noemia!" he called as soon as he passed the threshold of the house.

They moved into a lamplit room, stuffed with well-worn, brightly upholstered chairs arranged around a large hearth. The man carefully lowered her into one of the chairs, and she registered the pleasant scent of pipe tobacco before he straightened. His gaze moved to her face, but he seemed not to be surprised by her eyes. The boy with the odd skin had disappeared.

A woman bustled into the room wearing a gown of canary yellow, so bright it briefly resurrected Sela's headache. White streaked her dark hair, but her eyes were as alert as any bird of prey. She smiled, and Sela felt an instant, inexplicable liking for the woman.

"Noemia." The man turned to her with a smile of his own. "Jax and I thought we heard a commotion down near the old jacaranda tree. It turned out to be Miss Meriweather in need of rescuing."

Normally, Sela would have answered such a statement with a glare and an assertion that she didn't need *rescuing*, but her ankle was throbbing and her head ached. Never mind that her first day on Azazel had already proved such a declaration moot.

The older woman's smile dissolved into a frown. "What were you doing up here in the middle of the night, Miss Meriweather?"

"I arrived on Azazel yesterday evening, on the *Deliverance*. I came to see if..." She refused to glance at the man, lest he misinterpret her meaning. "To see if you were in need of workers."

Noemia exchanged a look with the man. "You arrived only last night?"

"Aye." She extended her palms to reveal the twin brands. Guessing they were former children of the lot, she expected the pair's compassion to evaporate, but Noemia only clucked her tongue sympathetically.

"You came to the right place, my dear."

"But you...you saw my brands."

In answer, the man raised his own palms, and Sela was surprised to see a second brand marring his tanned, callused skin. "You weren't chosen by the lot, then?"

"I was," he replied, his manner solemncholy. "I received my second brand *after* I arrived on Azazel."

She studied his face. He didn't seem to be the kind of man to commit a crime worthy of double branding, although she hardly fit her own criteria, either. "I didn't catch your name," she said at last.

"Thaddeus."

"Mister Thaddeus—"

He smiled again. "Just Thaddeus."

"*Thaddeus,* then..." She dragged in a breath. "My friend, Esther, told me about you and your sister. I spent the day looking for work, but there's nothing in Belladonna, certainly nothing of the honorable kind."

A muscle in his jaw twitched.

She continued, "Esther said that your sister had a small child, and I wondered if I could be of help to her. I can cook and clean and tutor, and I would even work in the fields if there was nothing for me to do in the house. If not, I wondered if you knew of any Carver-fearing men or women that might offer me employment. I'm sorry to arrive on your doorstep so late." She indicated her ankle. "I certainly never intended to impose on you like this."

Thaddeus nodded, but instead of answering, he turned to Noemia. "Briella is feeling poorly again?"

Noemia bobbed her head. "She's resting upstairs. Tempe is finally asleep, bless her little soul."

Bless her little *soul*?

The man scratched his day-old stubble, then glanced at Sela. "You may be the answer to our prayers, Miss Meriweather. But before you agree to stay, you should know a few things about us."

A shiver of unease wormed its way into her gut. "You don't have to tell me—"

"Nay, but you should know, Miss Meriweather. It might influence your resolve to stay here. Besides, you will learn the truth soon enough. I would prefer it came from us directly."

"Esther already said that you were good people."

"No one is good, Miss Meriweather, not even the men and women of the Old Town." Thaddeus kept speaking, not even stumbling over his heresy. His gaze narrowed and turned sorrowful at the same time. "I came here as a boy of eighteen, many years ago now. Shortly after, I turned my hand to a life of crime. By the age of twenty-five, I was second-in-command of a gang far more wicked than the one that just attacked you."

He met her gaze directly and she instinctively knew he spoke the truth. "I was—am—a murderer. That is why I received my second brand, though I should have received death. I won't sanitize my past, and no one else you meet in the settlements will either. I was the worst of men." He spoke the confession like he'd done it many times before—without hesitation or heaviness, although she saw the regret in his eyes. "Have you heard of Uriah Smith yet, Miss Meriweather?"

She nodded, though she was helpless to think of anything but Liri.

"I was second-in-command to his father, a brutal, depraved man. I am ashamed to admit that I was not only privy to his atrocities, but also a participant in many of them. I used people for my own selfish ends. I used women. Like I said, I was the worst of men, and I wasn't exhibiting false humility when I said it. Are you running yet, Miss Meriweather?"

"Nay." She offered them both a hesitant smile and pointed to her ankle. "Although I couldn't run, even if I wanted to."

Another grin escaped Noemia. "Tell her the end of the story, Thaddeus. The good part."

A light lit in Thaddeus's eyes. "At the bottom of the pit I found myself in, I discovered the Carver. His grace…His mercy. Or rather, *He* found *me*. You see, I was injured in the same confrontation that killed Uriah's father, many years ago now. Noemia took me in, and 'twas she who first told me of the Carver's love. Some years later, once I'd healed—in more ways than one— I built this house, and soon after that, Jax arrived on Azazel. I eventually brought my sister and her daughter to live here with us. Noemia is a good mother to us all."

Then Thaddeus wasn't Jax's father? The boy was surely too young to be branded. But he also hadn't been born on the island. And Thaddeus's crippled arm…was that the injury he'd spoken of?

But the man had not finished his confession. "This house is full of the worst kinds of people, Miss Meriweather. Misfits, exiles, sinners. Not only ourselves, but also those we shelter and try to rescue from the pit, as I myself was rescued."

"Speak for yourself, Thaddeus," the older woman said haughtily, and the man chuckled.

"Noemia jests, but 'tis true. Nightwalkers, thieves, murderers like myself…we help all we can, in any way we can. The only criterion for permanent residency here is a heart willing to discover a different way—to live as soul-bearing rather than soulless—though many seek temporary aid and leave here to return to the lives they have known."

Should she confess her own crime? They'd already seen her second brand. And she was no danger to them… But what of Liri? What if Thaddeus learned that she was sister to the bondmate of Uriah Smith?

"I don't mind," she said at last. "And I'm grateful for any shelter and work you can give me."

He nodded. "My sister, Briella, is feeling more dauncy of late. Since Noemia has more than enough work with the household chores, she will appreciate your help with Tempe. But even if Briella doesn't need your assistance, you are still welcome here, Miss Meriweather. We have beds aplenty."

She fought tears. "Thank you, Mist…Thaddeus."

"What's your Carver-given name, my dear?" Noemia leaned close, brushing the hair from Sela's eyes with such obvious affection that tears threatened to overwhelm her normally staunch control. After the day she'd had—after Caleb—she was at a loss how to deal with such warmth. Even her own mother had never been so openly caring, at least not with her.

"'Tis Sela."

"Well then, Sela, let's get that ankle tended." She crouched in front of Sela and, undoing the laces, eased off her boot. The ankle had already swollen and bruised beyond recognition. As Noemia's cool fingers probed her foot, Sela glimpsed a single brand on her right palm. A child of the lot, then. What would Noemia think of her, double-branded as she was?

"I didn't expect to find such kindness outside the Old Town." She hastily amended her words. "Not that I found much kindness within it."

"The Carver is everywhere, Sela," Noemia replied with Teodoir's conviction and none of Father Monroe's fear. "And no matter how dark the world grows, He always leaves a remnant."

After surveying much of his home for the next year, Caleb was footsore and heartsore—though his stay would be far less than a year if he counted the voyage to and from the Old Town, and returned to Tucker before winter's end, as he'd said. Nevertheless, he was glad that Lord Auberon ordered an open-topped carriage to take them to his lodgings. He would not reside at the fort, as his mentor would, but at one of the many outposts that ringed the island. It was good for a member of the Righteous to keep watch over the other officers, Lord Auberon said, which necessitated him to stay in their living quarters as he attended to his other duties.

The driver, a singly branded man with thin shoulders who wore a low-brimmed hat even as darkness swept over the bay, guided the horses with very little effort. Passing the fort, Caleb glanced over his shoulder at the shimmering turquoise water, spying the impressive silhouette of the *Deliverance* as it rested at anchor. They climbed steadily upward, already high above the fort that shackled itself to the main settlement like a ball and chain. To the right of the rutted road, a single white house atop a small but steep hill reflected the splintered spectrum of dying light.

The horses strained against their harnesses as they ascended another incline that rose sharply behind the white house. This one, he knew, led to the northern head and the outpost that crested the clifftop—his new home. The humidity had eased somewhat, and he relished the cool breeze against his heated face.

"You are very quiet, Caleb." Lord Auberon turned in his seat to study him, a somewhat precarious endeavor given the steepness of the incline. He seemed not to sweat in his closely fitting coat and pristine clothes, and his queue looked as neat as it had that morning when he escorted Ira to the fort.

"I am grieved at the healer's passing," he replied honestly. He'd barely known the woman, but he could not help but view her execution as a tragic waste of life. Aye, he was sorrowful.

Regardless of whether or not Ira had still possessed her soul when she died.

"As am I," Lord Auberon said at last. "The executor of judgment sometimes pays as high a price as the recipient of justice himself."

Hardly true, when Lord Auberon yet lived, but Caleb nodded anyway. "Notwithstanding the wrongness of their choices, Ira and the captain were sweethearts as children, before Ira was chosen in the lot. I would have hoped the Carver would show her mercy."

"Mercy and justice are strange bondmates, my son. Only the Carver understands the intricacies of their Binding." He glanced at Caleb. "Do you know why we call the Carver such?"

Caleb shook his head.

"When men and women first walked the earth, many thousands of years ago, the Carver fashioned them like different varieties of wood. Oak, cedar, yew, cherry, hemlock. Some hardy and some delicate. Some for ornamentation, and other types for building and industry. Some to provide the materials for the throne of a king, and others to fashion a coffin for the poorest of men."

Lord Auberon seemed not to notice their driver, who likely heard every word.

"Like wood, not all souls are equal, Caleb. Some are weak and some are strong. Some are pure, destined for greatness…set aside for noble purposes. And others, like the hanging tree in Belladonna below us, are tainted…rotting from within. And one day, they will fall."

Where was it said thus? He'd read much of the Book of Souls and nothing therein even echoed Lord Auberon's assertions.

"I don't understand, my lord. Why would the Carver fashion men from rotting wood?"

"Not all wood is rotten at first, Caleb, and likewise, not all souls. But when a weak soul yields itself to the whims and desires of the world, it quickly becomes tainted from the inside. The soul stain is a physical sign of the irreversible changes that have taken place within the heart. For some, those changes are only made visible after the lot has taken place. For surely, the Carver knows those souls which are prone to weakness and destined for corruption."

Caleb tried to recall what he'd learned about lumber from a classmate whose father had worked in the industry. "But every tree is vulnerable to the demise of its heartwood. Every soul is prone to corruption."

"Nay, Caleb, not every soul. Did you not hear me say that some men are oak, and others are hemlock? Those who are strong will resist human weakness. Men like you and me. And in the places where you are still weak, my son, I will teach you to be strong."

The carriage pulled around the curve of a particularly steep incline, and by the last dregs of sunlight glancing against the clifftop, Caleb saw the outpost. It was large and spacious, more cabin than house, but with a wide porch that ran the length of the structure. Leaning against the cabin was a sturdy building that looked like a stable, with room for perhaps four or five horses. Overlooking Belladonna, the fort, and the bay, the view from the wind-ravaged cliffs would be beautiful come morning. Behind and below him, he could still see a flicker of white—the house they'd glimpsed before.

Jumping down, the branded man dragged Caleb's heavy trunk from the carriage, knifing a glance at Lord Auberon's back that would have earned him a place at the gallows if the elder were facing the other way. Caleb ignored it, remembering the harshness of Lord Auberon's words and unable to blame the man for his ire. Disembarking from the carriage, he hefted the trunk and carried it to the porch himself.

Lord Auberon inclined his head. "I will see you tomorrow, Caleb. I will expect your first report by the end of a sevenday."

"Aye, my lord. T'will be done." Caleb watched as the driver returned to his place and slapped the reins against the horses' backs. And hoped that he would not kill Lord Auberon on his way back down the hill.

After shucking his heavy coat with audible relief, Caleb entered the cabin and found a large, spacious sitting room with an empty hearth, solid wooden table and chairs, and several comfortable armchairs. Though he could not imagine lighting a fire in the sticky heat, he guessed it would be cold up here come winter. In Eremia, they'd neared the end of fall, but here on Azazel, it was the height of summer. The island was prone to 'sooners, or so Lord Auberon had warned him. He hoped there were no gallinippers.

Four bedrooms bookended the open-plan sitting room, two at each end, and Caleb stuck his head inside the only one with an open door. Finding it empty, he retrieved his trunk from outside and deposited it in one corner. The room was far larger than his cabin aboard the *Deliverance*, boasting a double bed, washstand and basin, a large hearth flanked by two comfortable-looking chairs, and two armoires. The bed was draped with a sheer, transparent netting.

"No such luck about the gallinippers, then," he muttered to himself.

"You must be Lieutenant Alexander," said a voice from behind him, and Caleb turned to see a young man leaning against the doorframe, perhaps in his late twenties, with sandy-brown hair, laughing eyes, and Tucker's grin. He was shorter than Tucker, with a palm-sized, wine-red birthmark that splashed against the side of his neck.

"Caleb," he replied out of long habit before he wondered if his status as a member of the Righteous warranted more formality with the other guards.

"Lieutenant Beckett Arkwright. Call me Beck." He studied the white coat draped over Caleb's trunk with a sly smile. "You must be one of those Righteous, sent to keep us all in line."

Aye, this man was a lot like Tucker Alexander. "I am. Are there other officers staying here?"

"Lieutenant Killian is down with the ague at the fort. He's not likely to make it this time." Beck's grin didn't dim.

"You don't like him?"

"I don't *know* him. He spends most of his time down at the settlement. If you ask me, 'tis not the ague that ails him."

Uncomfortable with the topic, Caleb surveyed the room. "I hope I didn't offend anyone or presume anything by putting my trunk in here."

"No offense or presumption taken, Caleb. It has been empty since the last representative of the Righteous left to return to Eremia."

He eyed the large bed and twin armoires. "It seems designed for two."

Beck's mouth curved mischievously. "Aye, 'tis, and I'll not report you if you use it for its intended purpose, just as I didn't report the last representative of your order, nor even Lieutenant Killian."

Caleb's stomach twisted and all merriment fell away. "I'm not that kind of man, Beck."

"Nay." Beck surveyed him as he had done the room. "Nay, I can see that you're not. You're as stiff-collared and Carver-fearing as they come."

He stared at the other man, trying to see if he was jesting, but Beck appeared serious. "What do you do up here?"

Beck shrugged. "This is only one of many outposts all over the island. From here, we can oversee many of the happenings in Belladonna below, and can easily discern any new arrivals entering the bay. We patrol the farms, watch the mountain passes for land pirates…generally maintain order and discipline. No wonder Killian was bored out of his brains."

"This Uriah Smith…" He'd heard the name many times since arriving on Azazel, though Lord Auberon had not mentioned him on the voyage. "Is he truly a threat to Belladonna?"

"Aye, Uriah is as bad as they come. Worse, if that's possible. Murders, rapes, pillages. He moves around the island, but no one has ever been able to find his permanent hideout. He frequently raids the settlements for slaves, right under the noses of our soldiers."

"Slaves?"

"Beautiful young women, mostly. One time, he even kidnapped one of the officers' bondmates, purely to spite the man. She was returned after a sevenday, but given she was tainted, her bondmate had to put her aside. She took her own life a few months back."

The gut that had barely untwisted itself coiled again, like a snake about to strike. He had to warn Sela. But how could he protect her up here on the headland?

"You look worried, Caleb. Don't you Righteous have a thing about trusting the will of the Carver?"

Aye, they did. And even though the timely reminder issued from Beckett Arkwright's mouth, he'd do well to heed the words as if they came from the Soul Carver Himself.

After two sevendays of uneasy sleep, Caleb left the cabin before first light, hearing heavy snores from behind Beck's door and knowing the man would not rise for hours yet. Finding the cliffside path he'd seen on previous rides to and from Belladonna, he headed down to the secluded beach he'd spied his second full day on Azazel, a steep descent, but barely a half-mile from the outpost as the crow flew. Through the screen of low-lying shrubbery, he could see the strange white house, gleaming in the first of the dawn light.

Lord Auberon had kept him busy, meeting the officers and soldiers and various dignitaries who mostly holed themselves up in the fort, barring the occasional carriage ride through Belladonna with their bondmates. Caleb quickly learned that he and his mentor were the only resident members of the Righteous, Lord Auberon's and Caleb's predecessor having been sent back to Eremia in disgrace a few months prior. The man had kept a young woman from the settlement in Caleb's very quarters.

Though Lord Auberon took to his role with gusto, much of Caleb's earlier enthusiasm for his work on Azazel had waned. Why had his predecessor not been branded, as Captain Foley had been, or executed, as Ira had been…like the young woman herself? When he asked Lord Auberon, his mentor appeared not to hear his question.

Caleb suppressed a gnawing dissatisfaction. No priests served on Azazel, nor were regular services held beyond his sevenday meetings with Lord Auberon. It almost seemed as if the Carver truly did not reside on the island. And despite the occasional sermon from Lord Auberon about some aspect of the law, his mentor seemed more concerned about government and soldiering than matters of faith.

Two reports had been composed and delivered, with little information to impart except what Lord Auberon likely already knew. Even without Caleb's espionage, five soldiers and two officers had received reprimands for fraternizing with the soulless. Caleb hated to imagine what punishments they had endured…or worse, the punishments of the women who'd been caught associating with them.

Caleb sighed as he reached the empty beach, letting his cares slip away. Though he missed his family and friends—particularly his brother—there was one great advantage of living on the island. His memories of the Old Town felt gray and lifeless in the face of Azazel's color and wild beauty.

He recalled his brief tour of Belladonna. Azazel was an island of surprising variety. Some of the beaches, his guide had told him, even had black sand instead of white, probably because of the volcanic minerals and rocks. The beach he headed to now was small, but the sand was smooth and fine, already warm to the touch despite the early hour. How many millions of shells had been ground nearly to dust to make that tiny strip of perfection?

No one was about, and likely wouldn't be for an hour yet.

Only the white house above would have a view of the beach—as would the outpost, though Beck would sleep till at least midday. Caleb tugged off his boots and stockings, then his coat, waistcoat, and gloves. Finally, he peeled off his shirt and loosed his hair, leaving only his breeches. With a freedom he'd hardly known, even back home, he sank his bare feet into the wet sand, feeling it squelch and fan between his toes. He sprinted forward and waded into the sea, surprised at the warmth even after two sevendays of living in the tropics. Wave after wave splashed against his bare chest. When he was up to his waist, he dove beneath a wave and came up feeling as alive as when he spoke with the Carver.

He plunged back into the surf. After only a few minutes of swimming, he felt the pull of a current beneath his feet, tugging him from the shoreline. He fought it, but it was strong—far stronger than him, or indeed any man.

A rip.

Captain Foley had warned him about ocean currents, but he'd not expected to find one this close to the beach. What had he said? *"Go with the current, then as soon as you can, swim out the side of it, parallel to the beach."*

Though it went against every instinct in his body, Caleb let the powerful river of water carry him out to sea. Eventually, when the beach seemed so far he could scarcely see the place where he'd left his clothes, the current weakened, and he swam to the side of the rip, toward the breaking waves. He breathed a sigh of relief as the ocean pounded his back once more, driving him toward the shore.

Thankfully, he was a strong swimmer, and he swam until his muscles ached with fatigue and his throat burned with salty thirst. As the first glimpse of the sun turned the peel-oranges, salmon-pinks, and lavender-purples of the horizon to gold, his feet found the sand again.

"Thank you, Carver," he murmured, turning to look at the current that had so easily ensnared him. All he could discern was the deceptively calmer surf he'd eagerly headed for, flanked by larger waves.

He made for his clothes, conscious that he'd been out for longer than he'd originally intended. As he reached them, he looked up and spied someone standing on the hill, below the white house but far above him, dressed in a plain white gown that fluttered in the wind.

A woman, watching him as much as he now watched her. The ends of her black hair snapped around her pale face, her stiff posture betraying her fear at being discovered. Though she stood nearly too far away to tell, he guessed it was Sela.

He'd thought of her often in the two sevendays since he'd seen her last, though he tried to drown his wool-gathering in zeal for his duties. She pressed against his mind like a burr on yarn, his every glance toward the settlement hopeful—nay, hungry—for the sight of her. Was she still staying at the tavern with her friend? Had she found work at one of the farms beyond Belladonna? Or had she pursued a loveless Binding with another man?

He snatched up his clothes and boots and started after her, and in that moment, the spell was broken. She turned and ran, so swiftly he knew he'd never be able to catch her, not with her head start and his lack of shoes.

He slowed to a walk, the sand that had felt so smooth and welcoming before now searching out every nook and crevice of his body. He had no doubt that it would find the insides of his boots— if it hadn't already—making for a pair of gritty, uncomfortable soles as he went about Lord Auberon's work that day.

Aye, Azazel was beautiful. But it was also dangerous.

Chapter Ten

Sela let herself back into the house, winded from her long run up the hill. Her ankle throbbed, reminding her that it had yet to fully heal. She jumped as she saw Noemia, dressed in another cheerfully blinding gown, this one a pale green. The older woman had six or seven different gowns, all of them dyed pleasantly obnoxious colors.

"Are you all right, my dear?" Noemia's knowing eyes roamed Sela's wind-reddened cheeks. "You look like you've been startled."

Aye, she had been, by the sight of Caleb swimming at the beach below the house, shirtless with hair unbound. The shadow-smudged dawn and distance between them had failed to mask the fact that Caleb's zeal for physical discipline evidently matched—or even surpassed—the passion he afforded his scholarly pursuits. She'd gone down to bathe herself and seen him returning to the shore, dripping wet. He'd moved to come after her, but she'd known she could not stay.

His company was forbidden, more than any man on the island save Lord Auberon. And besides, she hated him.

"I'm fine," she said hurriedly, not wanting Noemia to think poorly of her. "I thought to bathe, but the water is cold today."

Noemia said nothing, but only nodded sagely. "Breakfast awaits."

As she devoured a generous portion of bread and fried eggs in the kitchen, Sela watched the older woman go about her duties. Though she tended to everything capably, Sela had begun to notice some clumsiness in her movements. A dropped egg, a bag of flour knocked over, a spilled glass. Was Noemia ailing? Did Thaddeus know?

The morning after she'd woken in a strange room and a strange bed—her ankle bound and pleasantly free of pain—she had thought Thaddeus would put her to work straightaway. Instead, the man had insisted she rest from the sea voyage and her recently sprained ankle.

"You have the look of one who's barely recovered from fever," he'd said after she'd dressed in a gown Noemia had left for her and hobbled downstairs. "Pale and a little too thin, though I mean no offense in pointing it out. Nay, Sela. There'll be no working for at least two sevendays."

"But your sister and her daughter—"

"Are both ailing now, sadly. There'll be no teaching Tempe until she's better. In the meantime, recover your strength. We'll need you soon enough."

Most days, Thaddeus traveled via horseback to the nearest farm, where he and the boy with the mottled skin labored in the humidity on the lower slopes of the mountains. They evidently worked hard, for both frequently returned too weary to engage in conversation. On her second day, Sela had plucked up the courage to ask Noemia what was wrong with the boy.

"He's not dauncy, if that's what you mean." Noemia had glanced at the door, as if to confirm Jax was absent. "From the time of his boyhood, Jax has lost his coloring like some lose skin after a bad sunburn. We don't know why it happens, and it has no effect on him beyond the physical. Though back in the Old Town, it was enough to cost him his soul."

Some days passed before Sela heard the full story. Once his condition was discovered, he'd seen the priests, who had told Jax's parents that the boy was cursed. Despite the protestations of his parents, Jax was sent to Azazel, where Noemia had witnessed him being pelted with stones by the other homeless boys. She'd rescued him and claimed him as her son.

He'd been only five years old.

After ten years of being shunned—even by those on Azazel— the boy was shy and wary of people. He never went down to

Belladonna if he could help it, though Thaddeus proclaimed him a good worker in the fields. The first morning in the house, Sela had called good morning to him and the boy had skittered away like a frightened colt. He avoided her most mornings, although twice she'd caught him staring at her, and she could not forget his bravery in facing the boys who had attacked her. It was a pity that most never risked a glance beneath the skin, for she'd already witnessed his kind, gentle nature.

She'd not glimpsed Briella or her daughter, as both were still dauncy. She did what she could to help Noemia as her ankle healed—chopping vegetables, kneading bread dough, and doing the household laundry, though Noemia was still run off her own feet with the sickness upstairs. Sela wished that the older woman allowed her to visit Briella and Temperance. Perhaps she could read to the little girl, if Thaddeus had any books. But mother and daughter were still contagious, and Noemia proclaimed that Sela was too weak herself to risk exposure.

Sela looked up from her wool-gathering to find Noemia's eyes on her. "You're looking better, my dear. 'Tis good to see a little more flesh on those bones."

Aye, soon she would be healed enough to leave the house to inquire after Liri's whereabouts. She could not ask Thaddeus, with his past links to Uriah Smith's father, or any other member of the household. Not if she did not want to risk their ire, and they might well forbid her to go in search of Liri. She sighed inwardly.

Liri had waited six years. She would have to wait a little longer.

Noemia reached for a bowl but misjudged the distance, and her hand encountered empty space. She bit her lip and stepped closer. This time, she was successful, and she carried the bowl to the opposite bench.

"Noemia?" Sela hoped her voice reflected her concern. "Are *you* dauncy?"

The older woman sighed, swept floury hands down her apron, and turned around. Weariness and resignation etched her sweet face. "Nay, I'm not dauncy, Sela. Not in the way of the poor souls upstairs."

There it was again—the poor *souls*. Sela brushed the curious statement aside and continued. "But you are ailing?"

Noemia glanced at her, and her gray eyes seemed oddly unfocused. "'Tis happening little by little. So slowly, I didn't notice it at first. But soon, it will all be gone, just like my great-grandmother and grandmother at my age…and likely my mother, though I wasn't there to see it happen. Soon, I'll be completely blind."

Compassion stirred in Sela's gut.

"That is why you are an answer to our prayers, my dear. I've known 'twould happen for a year or more now. I've made preparations—changed the layout of the kitchen and the ordering of the cupboards, and memorized the steps from here to there and back again. Don't fear, Sela. Very little will be different, though I'll need you to be my eyes at times, and to visit Belladonna in my place. Besides that, there's the teaching of little Tempe to consider. I can't do that blind."

"Does Thaddeus know?"

"Aye, he realized even before I did."

"Then your gowns…"

Noemia grinned. "I want to remember colors long after I've ceased to see them. Aye, the ones I choose are mostly ghastly— cast-offs from the fashionable ladies at the fort. But they're all I can see some days, and I figure a garish yellow is better remembered than a delicate shade of lavender."

Sela smiled. "I like your gowns."

"Aye, you would, wouldn't you? I'm not so blind I can't discern the fine color of your eyes, or the way the settlement men stop to admire you in the streets." She chuckled. "Or the pink on your cheeks right now."

Sela reached out and took Noemia's flour-smudged hands. "I want to help with everything. Whatever you need."

"I don't tell you this so you can coddle me." But she smiled and squeezed Sela's fingers. "Not to worry, my dear. I'll certainly make use of you. Now, my guess is your ankle will be hurting from that flat-out run up the hill from the beach. Why don't you go upstairs and rest for a little? Then I'll need your help with churning the butter."

Sela slipped off the stool gratefully and hobbled to the door. She snatched a final glance at Noemia, blushing as she realized that if Noemia had seen her run, she had probably witnessed her gawking at Caleb.

Going blind as she was, the woman still saw better than most.

Sela paused on the threshold of her room, surprised when the door opposite hers opened. As she watched, a small girl of about five years came into view, wearing a nightgown and raised on her tiptoes. With blonde hair and striking blue eyes, the girl reminded Sela of Cadence, and she smiled.

The girl looked up and quickly held a finger to her lips. "Shh! Mama's resting."

Sela drew closer and knelt, noting the girl's bare feet. They, along with her face, arms and legs, were covered with tiny red spots. "I'll be quiet, I promise," she whispered back. "Are you Temperance?"

"Tempe," the girl corrected, drawing herself up and propping her palms against her hips as if she were fifteen and not five.

"Are you feeling better, Tempe?"

"Oh, yes. I'm ready to play now."

"Did your Mama say you could?"

"Mama's asleep, but Noemie says I'm not con-tage-jus anymore." Impressed by her own successful use of such a large word, Tempe studied Sela, evidently as fascinated by her eyes as most. "Who are you?"

"I'm Sela."

"Your eyes are like the flowers in Noemie's…" Having

forgotten to whisper, Tempe turned as the bed from within the room groaned. Or was that its occupant?

"Tempe?"

"Here, Mama!" Tempe bounded into the room and Sela followed her to the threshold.

"I'm sorry we woke you," she apologized into the sun-streaked room.

"Come in, please," a woman called, and Sela reluctantly obeyed.

Tempe bounced on a bed opposite a woman who reclined against the pillows, her face free of spots but still pale. Pretty in a weary kind of way, she had the same hair as the girl, though hers appeared lifeless against the white of the pillow. She was younger than Thaddeus, perhaps by ten or even fifteen years, and smelled distinctly of rosewater.

"I'm Sela. Thaddeus and Noemia took me in, not two sevendays ago now. I'm sorry to disturb you."

"I'm glad for the company, though I'll warn you not to come closer, Sela. I'm still dauncy and possibly contagious, whatever Noemia says." The young woman smiled, and her eyes sparkled a little. "Noemia told me about you. As you've likely already guessed, I'm Briella." Her hands reached for her daughter, and Sela caught a flash of twin brands before Tempe crossed to the other bed and wriggled close to her mother. She was so like Cadence in personality that Sela was momentarily lost in recollections of her younger sister.

"When did you arrive on Azazel?"

Sela dropped the bittersweet memories like a hot stone and dragged her attention to Briella's sympathetic face. "A little over two sevendays ago. Thaddeus and Jax rescued me from a street gang and your brother carried me here, since I'd turned my ankle."

"You came here looking for work?"

She nodded. "My friend, Esther, mentioned your kindnesses helping her and the other nightwalkers. She told me to seek you out."

"I remember Esther. A gentle and lovely girl. I wish I'd met her when she first arrived here a year ago." Her expression turned rueful.

Did Briella regret that Esther had been forced to sell herself? Or did she believe that Sela had done the same? What would a Carver-fearing woman think of a rumored nightwalker wanting to tutor her daughter?

Briella glanced up. "I can tell you are also gentle and lovely, Sela. Noemia speaks highly of you."

The woman had misunderstood. "I'm not like Esther," she blurted. "I'm not a—" She suddenly remembered Tempe's presence. "I'm not of Esther's profession."

A cloud came over the other woman's face, like the thick fogs that Sela had seen descend over the waters of Belladonna's bay. "Nay, Sela. I never thought you were. But perhaps you should know that I once was."

Briella had been a nightwalker? Was that why she was *Miss* Briella and not *Mistress*? And the reason why Tempe had no father?

As Sela's heart squeezed, Briella motioned to Tempe. "You can go downstairs now, sweetheart, although make sure you take the stairs slowly. I can hear Noemia in the kitchen. She might have a treat for you if you use your manners and ask nicely."

"Yes, Mama."

As the girl happily bounded away, Sela met Tempe's mother's gaze. "Briella, I am sorry, I did not mean—"

But Briella's face bore no resentment. "All is forgiven, Sela, and I take no offense." She sighed and shifted against the pillows, her beautifully embroidered chemise failing to disguise her thin frame. "'Tis good that you know why I was branded. Thaddeus rescued me from that fate nearly five years ago. Any shame that still lingers is mine and mine alone."

"He mentioned that you and Tempe came to live with him."

"Aye, from one of the other settlements. Noemia was glad to have more children in the house, especially after her own were—"

Briella bit her lip. "She's likely not shared that yet."

"Noemia had children of her own?"

"Aye, but…" She gazed toward the door where Tempe had departed. "'Tis not good to borrow misery by speaking of it too often." But then she sighed and seemed to change her mind. "Do you know of the lot?"

"The coming-of-age lot, aye—"

"Nay, Sela. Not that. I can see in your eyes you don't know of what I speak. On Azazel, all are considered soulless, save the unbranded. But our children, when they are born, are not branded, and are still believed to be in possession of their souls."

Briella appeared haunted as she raised her palm and examined the brand there, faded but still clearly visible.

"After they pass their first birthdays, all children born to the branded on Azazel enter another lot. A reverse lot, if you will. The Righteous consider it a bounty—a blessing of the Carver to the forsaken, a second chance at redemption. But to every branded woman, 'tis a curse, a final punishment that burns more deeply than any soul mark. Fear drives many to hide their children from the soldiers."

"Hide their children?"

"Aye. Those children selected by the lot—one from every dozen—are called the Restored. Allowed to keep their souls, they are taken from their parents, forcibly if necessary, and returned to Eremia to be fostered with strangers. 'Tis said that even there, they are seen as lesser, having lived their first year on Azazel. I have heard that many eventually join the religious orders, where they work as lowly servants and laborers. Those children who escape the lot—like my sweet Tempe—are branded once on the hand and allowed to remain on the island." Her fingers curled, as if she wished Tempe in her arms again. How many times had Briella drawn her daughter close in the dark of the night, thankful for the Carver's mercy?

"But Noemia—"

Briella's face was stony amidst her grief. "Noemia birthed

three children to her bondmate, who has since passed on. Two sons and a daughter. Whether by the Carver's will or as a result of the worst of luck…all three little ones were taken by the lot."

All three little ones.

Unable to comprehend the enormity of what Noemia had lost, Sela abandoned all thoughts of rest and threw herself into the household chores. Ignoring the woman's protests, she helped Briella downstairs for supper and listened to Tempe's animated chatter. The girl seemed content for Sela to do the listening while she did the talking, which suited Sela, utterly lost in her own thoughts. She was dimly aware of saying goodnight to the others—excepting Thaddeus, who was away on some errand—and returning to her room.

The Old Town's sentence of banishment carried a double curse—a second cruelty, as if the first were not enough. Sela might have entertained thoughts of the Binding, should she find a good man to love, or one she might grow to care for. But to birth a child, only to lose him or her to the Old Town, as Noemia had lost her little ones…

How could she ever endure such agony?

Her anger swiftly sought other prey. Was Caleb aware of the second lot? How could he follow a man like Lord Auberon, who certainly knew of the law? She had thought him a different man. A *gentle* man. Even Tucker would find the idea of tearing a woman's child from her breast abhorrent.

Esther had said that Liri had had three children with her bondmate. Had she lost any of them to the Old Town? Surely, Sela's family would have been told of a child who was of their own blood. They would have fostered *any* outcast from Azazel, even if they weren't Liri's offspring.

But Uriah Smith, from all she'd heard of the man, would have prevented the Old Town from taking what he considered to be his.

For once, the man's ruthlessness was a comfort.

Hearing a knock on her door, Sela wrapped one of Noemia's shawls around her chemise and opened it.

Seeing a man's shadowy form, she started, then recognized Thaddeus. He held a large box awkwardly between his good arm and the crooked elbow of his bad one. "May I come in?"

Understanding the box was for her, she stepped aside for him to enter. He lowered it to the floor and gave her a satisfied smile.

"Did you find my bag?" She barely suppressed her pleasure. Though the money would no doubt be long gone, it showed great kindness on Thaddeus's part. And she might have Hester's possessions and her own clothes returned. No doubt Briella tired of lending Sela her gowns.

"Nay, though something else long lost."

He opened the box to a swathe of red fur. Sela stared, not understanding, until the fur began to wriggle and a pair of snapping jaws emerged, white teeth flashing by the light of her candle. Thaddeus quickly pulled his hand to safety.

"Roux!"

The fox heard her voice and barked, the high-pitched noise becoming a squeal. He leaped into her arms, his tongue covering every part of her face that he could reach. His whiskers were unbearably ticklish, but in that moment, she hardly cared.

Roux was here.

Sela sank to the floor, clutching the fox in her lap. With tears streaming down her face, she looked up at a grinning Thaddeus. "I don't understand. Where did he come from?"

"A friend was riding though Belladonna when he heard a man calling your name, holding this box. He said he was come from the Old Town, with a package for Sela Meriweather from her brother, Liron. My friend knew that you lived here and passed the message to me. I eventually found the man, who gave the package into my keeping." Roux pressed against his leg, and he cautiously reached down and patted the fox. More ardent dog than sly cat—at least for the moment—Roux licked his hand.

"A most unusual pet. Your brother evidently loves you very much, Sela, or else he feared for your safety. It seems he paid a man to personally deliver your fox via the next ship to Azazel. It must have cost a hefty sum to do so—almost an entire year's wage of a common laborer, I would think."

All of Liron's savings. And possibly some of her parents'. An unfathomable, precious gift, though she regretted that Cadence would now be alone.

"I don't know how your brother's man fed this fine fellow without drawing the attention of the marines and soldiers on board. If one of them had seen or heard him, they would have confiscated him."

She hugged the fox closer and Roux's tail twitched, the white tip making her think of Jax and white paint. "I don't know how to thank you, Thaddeus."

Thaddeus's eyes twinkled, much like Briella's. "There's no need to thank me, Sela. Thank your brother. And thank the Carver, from whom comes every good gift."

"Smith's *here*."

Even from her place by the potatoes, Sela heard the uneasy whispers that followed the announcement. Shouldering her mostly empty basket, she strode through the musty store in the direction of the first voice. Her shopping for Noemia would have to wait. If Uriah Smith was here, in Belladonna, she might find Liri.

The man who'd spoken crushed his hat between meaty fingers, sweat beading down his neck. Sela stashed her basket on the counter and stopped in front of him. "Where is he?"

Hardly seeing her, the man jabbed a thumb over his shoulder. "Over by the hangin' tree. Doin' some hangin'."

She nodded her thanks and turned to go, but his hand grabbed her arm. At her side, Roux offered the vulpine approximation of a growl and he quickly let go. "I wouldn't leave here yet, miss." He glanced to the other men and women who now huddled near the back of the store. "Wait until he's gone."

"Thank you, but I have to go now. I must speak with Mister Smith personally."

At his disbelieving look, she nodded and moved past him.

The street was quiet, some of the shops having locked their doors, despite it being only early afternoon. Though her knees trembled a little, Sela forced herself to cross the street in the direction of the dying tree, the first thing she'd seen on Azazel.

She had to go. Because of Liri.

Roux trotted alongside her, his lithe body tense and alert, as if he realized they were no longer running errands, but stalking prey. Not for the first time, she was glad for his diminutive but intimidating presence. In the sevenday he'd been by her side, he'd stayed the unwelcome attentions of many a settlement man, so much so that Noemia allowed her to go down to Belladonna alone. Tempe was delighted with him and begged her mother to let him sleep on her bed. Briella had eventually relented, but Roux had returned in the night to Sela, unwilling to leave her side for long.

A dozen men and their horses were arrayed around the hanging tree, looking as if they'd spent several nights bearing the brunt of a 'sooner. Despite their rugged appearance, nearly all were well-dressed, with coats and waistcoats made of broadcloth or even silk brocade, embroidered with gold, silver, blue, or red thread, and breeches held up by ornately wrought buckles, some of them gilded and jeweled. Every man carried a holstered flintlock pistol and a sword, most in double baldric holsters crisscrossing their chests.

In the middle of the crowd stood a woman and two men, one of the men on horseback. The woman was young, barely older than Sela, but already held a tiny babe. Terror filled her beautiful face, and her eyes were pleading.

The man on horseback was also young, not above thirty, with a noose around his neck attached to a branch far above him. His hands were tied behind his back, but despite his precarious position, he only had eyes for the young woman and the baby she carried.

Sela pushed closer, and the watching men turned to survey her. She ignored their leers, weaving through the crowd until she was only several paces away.

"Please, Mister Smith," the young woman was saying. "Please, let Ross go. He hasn't done anythin' wrong."

Uriah Smith was as tall as Caleb, but thick brawn to the other man's natural athleticism. Ten or so years Caleb's senior, Uriah was almost as impeccably dressed as Lord Auberon himself, though his fine attire bore several layers of dirt, making a mockery of the garments that had likely once been creamy white.

He smiled. A slow, steady smile, like a cat stalking his prey who had no pressing need to pounce. "My dear Bess," he said in a honeyed voice, "your bondmate, Mister Bryant, is anything but innocent. With mine own eyes, I saw him betray us to the white fists. He's an ambidexter, a double crosser."

"Ross wouldn't do such a thing," she insisted, tears tracking down her dirty cheeks as she held the baby tightly against her stained bodice. The child began to wail.

The man on the horse glared at him. "You'll pay for this, Uriah."

The watchers chuckled softly. "Methinks ye will pay first, Bryant," called the man beside Sela, and they laughed louder. She was dimly aware that he had primed and loaded his pistol. Several of the others were spitting on their hands, as per the old superstition that such a routine would bring them good fortune in a fight.

"Don't think I don't know what this is," Ross Bryant said with more defiance, his eyes roving the crowd as if he knew them all personally. "Uriah wants Bess for himself. Always has, always will. You're fools to follow him."

"Enough cheek music, Bryant." Uriah raised his hand to slap the horse's rump.

"*Nay!*"

As the others were distracted by Bess Bryant's scream, Sela

darted to the side and wrestled the pistol from the hand of the distracted man next to her. Striding forward, she fully cocked the hammer and pointed it at Uriah's head.

Behind her, the men went quiet. Bess shushed her crying baby, looking between Uriah and Ross, who had both gone still. The horse nickered to Roux, who pranced around Sela's heels as if he believed the whole thing a game.

Uriah looked Sela up and down—an unhurried, languid glance that paused several times in its assessment before he finally met her eyes. When he did, he smiled, two dimples appearing. Uriah Smith had a face that would have been devastatingly attractive on any other man, excepting the cruel slant of his lips and the brand on his cheek. He held out his hands in a gesture of surrender, exposing brands that mirrored hers.

Three brands?

"What's your name, miss?"

"Sela Meriweather."

"*Meriweather*?" Uriah's grin revealed twin rows of perfect teeth. "Beauty runs in the family, I see." He stepped closer and whistled. "But not those eyes. Those, my girl, are uniquely yours."

"I'm not your girl." She cradled the gun in both hands. He obviously recognized her name, but she would not think of Liri—not yet. "Come any closer and I'll shoot you."

"You, a murderer?" He laughed, seeming to look through her, as if the soul she'd thought she'd possessed was glaringly absent, and the truth of it was evident only to him.

"I am doubly branded, like you, Mister Smith. My brother taught me how to shoot. Like I said, don't come any closer."

"I like a little fire and steel in a woman." Uriah's reply gained the ribald laughter of his men over her head, several of whom called out increasingly vulgar descriptions of her. She remembered Joss Brigham and Ezekiel North and refused to blush.

"Let the Bryants and their babe go free. Do it now, or I'll shoot."

Roux added his growl to hers, and Uriah looked down. "An intriguing animal, Sela. Is he yours?"

"He'll be at your throat if you don't do what I say." She waved the muzzle of the gun at him. "Whatever the sins of this man, you cannot think to leave this child fatherless."

He shrugged. "Ah, Sela, but there you are mistaken. *I* am fatherless, and I have survived all these years."

"Survived? And what of your soul?"

He laughed, his men with him. "Do not worry on that account, pretty Sela. I grew up on Azazel—the one place where even the Carver will not tread. I have no eternal destiny. So you see, nothing I do on this forsaken island can condemn me. I might as well please myself." His gaze drifted down her again, making her feel even more unclean than when she'd first received the soul mark.

"Then please, Mister Smith—let this man go. For the child's sake, if naught else."

"Let Ross Bryant go?" Uriah's eyes narrowed dangerously and he stepped back. "Aye, Miss Sela, I'll do as you say."

Before she could react, he'd slapped the rump of the horse. Ross Bryant was jerked from the saddle as the beast leaped forward. Someone shouted her name just as her finger started to squeeze the trigger. Before she could, she saw a flash of silver and Uriah's flintlock was in his hands. A multiple-barreled firearm, if she wasn't mistaken.

He leveled the pistol at Bess and her babe, cocked the hammer, and fired.

X

Having heard that Uriah Smith was terrorizing the settlement, the last thing Caleb had expected as he rode in with Lieutenant Arkwright and the other soldiers was Sela, holding Smith at gunpoint.

Slender as she was, she stood with her feet a shoulder-width apart, holding the pistol level with Smith's head, unwavering, though Caleb heard the slight tremble in her voice as she answered Smith's taunts.

Did she know the man Smith had condemned to hang, or his bondmate and child? Or had she simply stepped in again to defend an innocent? If so, she had more courage than any woman—and possibly any man—he had ever met.

Still, she was a fool. As the men laughed behind her, a red fox bared its teeth at her heels—a *fox*? Caleb blinked twice and forced his attention to Smith. The man was far more dangerous than Sela realized.

"Aye, Miss Sela, I'll do as you say," he heard Smith quip, and then all chaos broke loose. The horse surged forward and the man dangled in the noose, writhing like a hooked eel. Out of instinct, Caleb reached for his knife and threw it. The rope snapped neatly, and the man slumped to the ground. Probably a lucky throw, but at least his aim was as good as it used to be, even with his gloves.

Smith drew his pistol.

"Sela!" Caleb yelled, and her finger moved on the trigger.

But instead of firing at Sela, Smith aimed at the woman holding the child. A shot rang out, and the woman crumpled.

"Nay!" Sela screamed. She fired, and Smith stumbled and staggered back, clutching his bloodied shoulder.

One of Smith's men lunged for Sela, and Caleb spurred his horse forward, drawing his sword. With frightening ease, his long-dormant training returned to him, and he cut down the man with the first sweep of his blade. Sela spied him and froze, the pistol falling from her hand.

As Lieutenant Arkwright and his men engaged the land pirates, Caleb dismounted. Seeing that Smith's prisoner was alive, he turned to the woman, who was drenched in blood. Even at that distance, he knew she was dead.

Sela pushed past him and sank to her knees beside the woman. "Bess," she called as the baby in her arms wailed louder, another kind of deafening amidst the gunfire and clash of steel. The woman's bondmate, having freed his hands and tugged the noose from his neck, knelt beside Sela, rocking the woman and sobbing her name.

Remembering Smith, Caleb turned as the injured pirate climbed atop the horse that had borne the condemned man, grabbed its reins, and whirled it around. The men who had been fighting the soldiers mounted and followed him. Leaving it to the soldiers to catch the pirates, Caleb focused his attention—and his wrath—on Sela.

Sela was now rocking the dead woman's baby son, whose father seemed to at last remember that the boy was still among the living. She carefully handed the child to him—mercifully unharmed—and squeezed his shoulder comfortingly. "Mister Bryant? I am so sorry about Bess. I wish I could have saved her."

She either knew the family or was an exceptionally fast study of names.

"You did your best, Miss Meriweather." Bryant lifted his eyes to hers, and though he knelt beside his bondmate whose corpse was not yet cold, Caleb detected a trace of admiration in the man's visage. "'Tis a better fate than what would have awaited her had I died and Uriah taken her for his own."

Caleb hadn't known Sela's last name, though it seemed familiar. Certainly, it was spoken with familiarity by the man Sela had saved. Was Bryant already seeking a replacement bondmate? As if she suspected the same, Sela took her hand from the man's shoulder and stood.

"Come with me, Miss *Meriweather*." Leaving the man to grieve his bondmate, Caleb planted his gloved hand on the small of her back and propelled her away from the grisly scene. Beck passed them and glanced inquiringly at Sela, then raised an eyebrow at Caleb. "I'll see you back at the outpost, Lieutenant," Caleb called over his shoulder, grabbing for his horse's reins with one hand and tugging Sela along with the other.

Ezekiel North was gone, returned to the Old Town two sevendays past. But here Sela had gone and acquired another enemy, far more dangerous to her than Zeke had ever been—and madder than a taunted bull, now that she'd wounded him.

And—the Carver forbid—he wanted her too.

Caleb had called her by her last name. Did he know who she was? Sela dragged her feet as he pulled her into the first narrow alley they came across. Uriah and his men had frightened every living soul from daylight, like cockroaches scattering from under a lifted stone, and they were alone.

"Sela." He grabbed her wrist and she jerked backward, but succeeded only in hurting herself. How did a mere scholar have a grip like a vise? Or the skill to sever a taut rope with a hurled knife from yards away, as he'd so effortlessly done?

She forced herself to remember Liron's lessons. Maneuvering her hand in a circle, she seized his forearm and tried to twist his arm behind his back, but he anticipated her, grabbing her bodily and pulling her back against his chest. His gloved hand came around her waist, as it had the day he'd stopped her from falling overboard. Though she'd seen him shirtless, she was still astonished at his strength.

She felt his warm breath against her ear, closer than he'd ever been to her. The exertion of restraining her would be nothing for him, so why was he breathing so fast? "Don't try that again. I'm not going to hurt you."

"You *can* fight."

"Aye."

"You just don't like to."

He didn't answer.

She glanced at his sable mare, standing placidly by, and wondered where Roux had gotten to. The last time she'd seen him, he'd been biting the ankle of the man who'd lunged for her. "You know, I half-expected your horse to be white."

Ignoring the comment, he let her go and stepped back. "What were you thinking, Sela?"

"I wasn't thinking. I simply tried to stop a ruthless man from committing murder."

"And nearly got yourself murdered in the process."

Her voice quivered. "I didn't think he would shoot her. I thought he'd shoot *me*."

He stepped closer. "Do you care so little for your own life?"

She turned away and spied Roux trotting down the narrow alley. But instead of baring his teeth at Caleb, as he usually did to strange men who stood too close and looked too long, he simply crossed to her side and leaned against her.

"The fox is *yours*?"

Sela studied his incredulous expression, wondering if he would confiscate Roux as Thaddeus had suggested the white fists might. "Aye. My brother smuggled him here from the Old Town."

Incredulity morphed into bemusement. "Foxes aren't tame animals."

"Nay, not usually, but Roux is. I've cared for him since he was a cub."

"Roux?" His anger seemed to have died as abruptly as it had arisen.

"*Roux-manteau*."

"Redcoat."

"You know the Old Tongues."

"Aye, some of them." Roux purred and brushed against Sela's leg, heedless of the blood on them both. Finally, Caleb shrugged. "I'll escort you back to the tavern."

The tavern? Seeing that he'd again judged her too hastily, Sela once more resolved to hate him. Exceptional aim with a knife or not.

After all, foxes, while clever friends with numerous remarkable qualities, were hardly reliable judges of good character.

Caleb watched as the warmth in Sela's eyes hardened into defiance. "I'm not living at the tavern."

"Then where are you living?"

"With Thaddeus and his sister, Briella. Since my second night here."

Thaddeus Gaskell? The woman went from one bad situation to worse. "You don't know what that man's done, Sela. Thaddeus—"

"—told me everything himself. The very first night, after he and Jax rescued me."

Jax? "Rescued you?"

"Some street boys attacked me. I twisted my ankle trying to get away. I'm fine."

Forcing down more questions and a flicker of worry, he returned to his original point. "Thaddeus's sister is a nightwalker."

"A *former* nightwalker."

"They are one and the same."

"Perhaps to the Righteous." She eyed his cream-colored sleeves and pure white gloves. "What business is it of yours?"

"I am…concerned for you."

"I'm not your concern, Lieutenant Alexander. And I never have been."

Aye, she spoke reason, like Tucker would, if he were here. "Your impulsive actions today drew the attention of the most dangerous man on the island."

"I injured him badly. Perhaps he'll learn to stay away from Belladonna from now on. Besides, I don't fear death."

Then she was oblivious to Uriah Smith's interest in her, more as a woman than a corpse.

She narrowed her eyes at him. "And I can defend myself."

"Like you defended yourself against me?"

He saw that his words pierced her naiveté, and her fists tightened defensively. "I knew you wouldn't hurt me. Besides, you're clearly well-trained."

"As is Uriah Smith. And dozens of other men on this island." He sighed. "You're a good fighter, Sela, and your skills would keep most at bay. But Smith has a small army of followers. And you are no match for brute strength." Seeing the hint of vulnerability in her expression, he fell on his sword for her. "Even at the height of my skills, I doubt I could have prevailed against Uriah Smith. His aim with a pistol is reputed to be the best of any man or woman on Azazel, if not elsewhere."

She seemed to choose her words carefully. "I must speak with him again. That's why I came here today."

"You need to *speak* to him? Whyever would you want to speak to him?"

"It concerns a friend," she replied stiffly.

"Esther?"

"Nay. Another woman I knew in the Old Town. Uriah Smith is holding her captive."

"Smith seeks more than your death, Sela. Promise me—" He sighed, knowing better than she did that he had no claim on her. "Promise me you'll stay away from him."

Instead of answering, she spun on her heel and left him standing there, the strange animal ambling after her as if the fox supervised heated conversations with armed men in alleyways every day.

Knowing Sela…perhaps he did.

Chapter Eleven

"How are you settling into life on Azazel?"

At the sound of Lord Auberon's voice, Caleb looked up from his reading on the cabin porch steps, surprised that the elder would venture so far from the fort in the stifling heat. "Well, my lord. There is much to occupy me."

It was only half a lie, and therefore partly truth. The last sevenday had thankfully passed without further trouble from Uriah Smith, though they also had a passing 'sooner to thank for the respite. The dead woman, Bess Bryant, had been buried, and Caleb had secretly arranged for food and a young goat to be delivered to her grieving bondmate. Lord Auberon would not approve of the gesture, but the babe was small. He only hoped Ross Bryant had found a wet nurse to care for the boy, since he had not looked old enough to be weaned.

"And the other officers?" Lord Auberon lowered himself to the step beside Caleb. "Have you a good rapport with them?"

Thankfully, Beck was out on a patrol, though Caleb had never once hidden the reason for his presence on Azazel. "There is only one other man here at the outpost. Lieutenant Arkwright. His activities are unremarkable."

An educated guess, since Caleb saw very little of the man. He was thankful for it—and that Lord Auberon did not press him further on the subject. He disliked spying on his fellow men when his own thoughts were so often in disarray.

Lord Auberon eyed the parchment in his hands. "What are you studying?"

Caleb handed it over. "The creation account."

"Ah." His mentor fingered the extract—mere copy as it was—

with reverence, and some of the tension slipped from Caleb's body. Surely, he could speak freely with Lord Auberon, of all people.

"After our conversation the other day, my lord, I thought to read it again for myself."

"A wise thought, Caleb." Lord Auberon returned the parchment and leaned back. "But the account which I gave you does not appear in these passages." He stroked his clean-shaven chin, as if he'd had a beard once and had not yet grown used to the absence of it. "That story belongs to a supplementary text."

"But surely the account from the Book of Souls takes precedence compared to—"

The elder turned his head in a slow circle. "Do you doubt the authenticity of my explanation, Caleb?"

"Nay, but—" He prayed his courage would not desert him. "The creation account in the Book of Souls makes no mention of the things we spoke about, my lord. From my reading of the Book in its entirety, 'twould seem that in the eyes of the Carver, all men stand equal. In nature, sinfulness, and the state of their souls. And that, by the grace of the Carver alone, they are able to be redeemed." He swallowed. "*All* of them."

Lord Auberon's face blanched. "Careful, my son, lest you mistakenly utter heresy. Since you are young and yet untrained, I will excuse what I have heard here today as the conclusions of a student who sees the part but not the whole." His voice softened from steel to honey. "The words of the Carver must be interpreted alongside other sources of evidence, my son. The lot has existed for thousands of years—even before the time when the Old Tongues were spoken by all. The current system of atonement has long been decreed as the Carver's will. Or would you seek to challenge that as well?"

Caleb shook his head, feeling a bead of sweat glide between his shoulder blades, despite his coat and waistcoat lying abandoned beside him. He found himself already longing for the cooler months. "Nay, my lord. I seek only to discern the Carver's will. And to honor it."

"'Tis already discerned, my son. For that, we can thank our forebears." Lord Auberon stood in a fluid movement that belied his age, brushing imaginary dirt from his spotless coat and breeches. When he looked at Caleb, something new gleamed in his eyes. "Come to the fort tomorrow, Caleb, and we will pore over the extracts together. What do you say?"

Perhaps Lord Auberon's offer was a genuine invitation for collaboration and scholarship. Might Caleb, young as he was, be at liberty to explain his discoveries of the last few sevendays of near sleepless nights?

"You have a fine mind," his teachers had always told him.

He would put it to use in service of the Carver. Shrugging aside a niggling uneasiness, he shook the hand his mentor extended to him. "'Twould be an honor, my lord."

Later that day, Caleb was heading down the hill from the outpost for an evening swim when he glimpsed Sela sitting on the sand, her fox capering beside her. She laughed as the animal's antics flung a wall of sand into a sudden breeze, then blinked, trying to rub it from her eyes. The fox's timing worked to Caleb's advantage. By the time she could see again, he was almost upon her.

She scrambled to her feet and the fox danced around her, kicking up more sand as he simultaneously dragged and chewed a stick like a dog. It was such a strange sight—a fox wanting to play fetch—that a chuckle escaped him.

"Caleb!" Sela brushed the sand from her gown, a dark green—his favorite color—that muted the vivid hue of her eyes. Though the evening was cool, she wore no shawl and her feet were bare. Seeing his glance, she blushed and arranged her gown to cover them.

Leaving his boots on, Caleb dropped to the sand near her, removing the hated gloves and tossing them beside him next to his heavy coat. Immediately, the fox pounced, thrusting front legs downward like a cat. Catching one soft leather glove in his teeth, he tore off across the tiny beach, faster than the wind.

Sela moved to go after him. "Roux! Come back!" The fox ran wide circles around her, the glove dangling like a limp rabbit from his jaws.

Caleb waved his hand. "He can have it."

"He loves a game of chase." She glanced after her pet despairingly. When she tried to approach him, he leaped out of her reach, only to sneak close again, taunting her. She lunged, and the fox jerked away at the last second.

Caleb eyed Sela. A little like the woman herself.

As Sela tired of the game, Roux entered the surf and dumped the glove in the frothy waves, looking back at him as if to gauge his reaction. Caleb suppressed a grin. Even an animal knew where such petty divisions belonged.

Sela sat beside him, digging her bare feet into the sand, and shot him a quick glance. "He'll chew it to pieces. I'm sorry."

"'Tis no matter. I have another pair."

When he looked at her next, she was staring at his hands. Because they were unbranded, a reminder of everything she'd lost? Or because she was as drawn to him as he was to her?

He flattened his palms against his thighs. "Your brother must care for you greatly to risk smuggling Roux to Azazel. If he'd been caught, there would have been serious consequences for you both."

"So said Thaddeus."

"Is your brother as stubborn as you are?"

"Even more so."

He smiled. "Then you're close?"

"Not in years, but otherwise, aye. He is now in the king's navy, heading for the mainland. 'Twas he who taught me to fight."

Caleb frowned. If Sela was the oldest sibling, her brother could not be more than seventeen. How could he have entered the navy? And who would have taught a mere boy to fight? Only those of eighteen or older were usually trained, though those entering the religious orders were often younger. And she'd also said she and her brother were not close in years.

She chewed her lip with more zeal than her fox had shown toward his glove, and he wondered if she'd noticed her slip. "Do you like living at the fort?"

"I don't live at the fort." He pointed up the incline to the clifftop. "I live at the outpost with Lieutenant Arkwright."

She didn't reply.

"Listen, Sela. You can't stay with this Thaddeus. I don't know what he's told you, but certainly not the full truth—"

"That he was a thief, murderer, and user of women."

He quelled his surprise at the man's surprising transparency and continued doggedly. "You can't stay in the house of such a man. Not a murderer with a horrific past—not when you are a young, beautiful woman. Look, I've made inquiries. There are positions open at the fort, some of them to branded women. If you applied, they would give you accommodation as well as honest toil—"

Her cheeks were red. Because he'd called her beautiful? "You warned me about the tavern, Caleb, but you'd recommend the fort? Do you have no sense of the men beneath your command?"

"They're not *my* men. But at the fort—near Lord Auberon— you would be safe."

"Lord Auberon? Who had Ira executed for what is as much a man's crime as a woman's one?"

He turned to her, dimly aware that Roux had returned to snuggle against her, his bushy tail swishing against her thigh. The mangled, thoroughly drowned glove lay several yards away. She was right, of course, but he could not speak against his mentor…or the law.

"The nature of man is the same," she said when he didn't reply, "whether he is branded or not."

Lord Auberon would have her flogged for the heresy, though Caleb increasingly agreed with her. Certainly, the Book of Souls did. "Careful, Sela, lest someone hear you."

"Why should I be careful? I was just as guilty before my branding as after it."

"Guilty?" He stared at her, unable to help his softening. "Nay. You were innocent."

She turned away, looking heartsick, and his gaze strayed to her hands as she stroked Roux. Her fingers were long, slim, the epitome of feminine loveliness. A flash of her left palm as she rubbed the fox's belly revealed her fresh brand, and he frowned. Hadn't she been branded on the right?

"Sela?" Snatching up his remaining glove, he tugged it on and reached for her right hand. She offered it to him freely, her expression sorrowful, as if she already knew what he would find.

Seeing her right palm, he nearly jerked away as Roux had done. Instead, he forced himself to examine the weal.

She was branded on both hands.

Sela knew the moment Caleb guessed her secret. She'd grown more complacent of late, almost as if she no longer cared what he thought of her…or she wanted him to know the truth. The reasons behind the second sentiment were far more frightening to comprehend than the cold logic of the first.

Still, it was done. And now, he would seek her out no longer. What had surely been attraction in his eyes as he looked at her a moment before—proclaiming her innocent—would be replaced by disgust or even hatred.

As she'd seen in his brother.

Caleb still clutched her palm in his gloved hand. "I don't understand. You arrived with the first group of prisoners. I believed you to be one of the coming-of-age lot. You don't look above eighteen."

"I'm nineteen," she replied coolly. "And I was brought to the ship from another prison. We met the prisoners of the lot along the way."

His eyes ran over her face, hardening as he realized she'd known of his misunderstanding and chosen to keep the truth from him.

"Aren't you going to ask me my crime, sir?" Hester's challenge, and now her own. Best that she shattered any illusions he had about her before she could spend any more time contemplating the untainted, almost childlike beauty of his laughter as he'd watched Roux annihilate his glove.

"Would you answer such a question honestly?"

"More importantly, Lieutenant, would you believe that my answer was honest?"

His dark blue eyes narrowed. "Don't play games with me, Sela."

"Very well. I killed a man." She pulled her hand from his.

His face showed his shock, and she knew he believed her. "For what reason?"

She stood, but her cursed fox only yawned and stretched before sidling up to Caleb, sniffing his abandoned coat as if lieutenants carried around strips of dried meat in their pockets.

"Come, Roux."

At the sound of his name, the fox raised his head, but didn't budge.

"*Roux*. Now."

She left without him, but she'd only gone a few yards before Caleb caught up with her. He grabbed her wrist with his gloved hand and turned her to face him. He studied every inch of her face until she squirmed. "Sela Meriweather. *Liri's* younger sister?"

Surprised, she could not mask her reaction to the name, and he nodded.

"I thought so, though you concealed that from me as well, even when I guessed the truth." He stared at her. "You knew who I was, didn't you? You recognized me the first day we met. That's how you knew my Carver-given name. And why you had no fear of me, even though you knew I was one of the Righteous."

"Aye, Caleb. I knew you as Tucker's brother."

His shoulders relaxed, but only by a degree. "The young girl I met the day of Tucker's ceremony would not have become a murderer lightly."

"Believe what you want to. I don't care." She tried to pull away, but he held her fast.

"Liri's here on the island, isn't she?" When she nodded, he frowned. "How does she know Uriah Smith?"

"According to Esther, she's his bondmate."

Caleb sucked in a sharp breath, like wind sheeting beneath a door. "His *bondmate*?"

"Aye, they have several children together."

"Tucker will be sorry to hear it." He seemed to have forgotten she was even there.

"I don't care about your brother." Since she'd lost the letter, she had no wish to reveal that Tucker knew she was headed to Azazel and had spoken with her directly. Best that Caleb not know the intricacies of Joss Brigham. He likely didn't even know the man.

His gaze sharpened. "You dislike Tucker?"

"I despise him. He didn't even try to save Liri when she was chosen."

"There was nothing he could have done, Sela. 'Twas the will of—"

"—the Carver. I know."

His gloved hand moved from her wrist to her chin, and he tilted her face up, as if he had no interest in the loveliness of the sunset behind him. Not so long ago, he'd called her beautiful, and it had been no slip of the tongue. He'd said it matter-of-factly, and it had sent a thrill through her chest down to her toes.

Then. Before she'd shattered his impossible regard for her.

"The man you killed. Did he try to assault you?"

The truth he sought in her face, she tried to deny him, but he was older than she and better trained at discerning emotions in others…and guarding his own. Finally, to save herself from his scrutiny, she nodded.

"And you defended yourself? His death was an accident?"

Though she said nothing, he seemed to determine the truth of the matter.

After a long moment, she shrugged. "'Tis already a long time ago, Caleb. And I did not let him hurt me."

He thought for a long moment, and finally, a heavy weight seemed to lift from him. "I am sorry for Liri. But if she is Smith's bondmate, there is naught you can do to rescue her. Only the Carver can save her now."

She could not resist a final jab. "So Tucker concluded, six years ago."

X

The second brand on Sela's palm explained so many oddities. Her ease in saying his Carver-given name, as if she'd met him before. Her estrangement from the single-branded prisoners, who had formed tight alliances while Sela had only the doubly branded woman, Hester, as a friend. Her reference to a brother who was clearly older—Liron, he thought, now that he strained his mind to think of the man's name. Liri's younger twin, who would be a year older than Caleb.

Had Lieutenant North and Lord Auberon clearly glimpsed what he had failed to see—that Sela was a woman doubly condemned?

Remembering Joss Brigham, and the nature of his cousin's crime, he'd wondered for several long, dreadful moments if Sela might be Joss's killer. Tucker had said that she was a young woman, after all, who had accused Joss of assaulting her while fishy.

But nay—that woman was dead. Hung the very morning Caleb had departed for Azazel. Tucker had said as much. And Tucker would never lie to him, not about something so important. Likely, there were hundreds of such incidents each year in the Old Town. Sela's only misfortune was to have fought back against her attacker—and won.

Why had the arbitrators of her case not shown mercy? She was only nineteen years old, and a woman at that. Tall, but not robust. If she was Liri's sister, her family was well below Caleb and Tucker's in status. Like many families, they likely lived from winter to winter, the threat of starvation always a distant possibility.

But they had not shown Ira mercy. Sela was no different.

Was it any wonder that Sela hated Tucker...and possibly Caleb, too? But for the terrible consequences of a man's lust, she'd be safely back in the Old Town with the family she clearly adored. Nowhere near Uriah Smith and the dangers of Azazel.

After delivering her biting retort, she had stilled. His hand was still at her chin, and he stroked the skin beneath her bottom lip with his gloved thumb. She was tall enough that if she tilted her face, she would reach his lips. The perfect height for him.

She didn't move. "Caleb," she said, gripping his bicep. Without his coat, he could feel the heat of her skin through his shirtsleeves. It had the opposite result to the one she intended.

But for one man's selfishness, she might have been his.

"Caleb," she said again, more softly. "If someone sees us, we'll both suffer for it."

He stepped back abruptly. Aye, she was right, and though he might weather any accusations, *she* would not. Having already been twice branded, any further offenses could cost her her life.

His every glance, his every attention put her in danger. Was he truly so thoughtless?

Like Tucker had been, letting himself care for Liri when their fates were not yet known?

She slipped away into the growing darkness, calling for Roux to follow. This time, the fox obeyed, trotting past Caleb with what would have been a sanctimonious smile had it appeared on a man.

Sela reached down and patted the fox. She was still limping a little, proof that her twisted ankle was not nearly so healed as she insisted. She paused, turned, and offered him a slight smile. The opposite of Roux's, and devoid of female charm or promise. He recognized it for what it was as he dragged his gaze away, searching the beach for his mangled glove.

She was saying goodbye.

"My lord Auberon." Caleb bowed his head and strove for a respectful tone. "I have news from Belladonna."

His mentor turned from the large chest he was counting coins into, his eyes glittering with interest. Had Lord Auberon truly been called away on urgent business the day that Caleb came to discuss his study of the Book of Souls? Surely the elder would not have lied to him. And yet, he'd said nothing since of his offer.

"Uriah Smith?"

"Nay, my lord. Smith's not been seen since the attack that killed the young woman, Elisabeth Bryant." He'd managed to persuade Beck to keep the truth of Sela's involvement from his report to Lord Auberon, though the lieutenant had smiled knowingly as he agreed to do so. "'Tis Captain Foley."

"*Mister* Foley now, I would think."

"Aye, Mister Foley."

"What of him, Caleb?"

"He has been…mistreated by the settlement men, sir. Shunned."

Lord Auberon turned and elevated a single eyebrow. "Shunned?"

"They won't speak to him or associate with him because of his formerly privileged position. He has no work, no way of feeding or sheltering himself. I wondered…the positions open to branded prisoners at the fort…Cap—*Mister* Foley is intelligent and well-educated. Might he apply for one of them?"

"And how did you come by this information, my son?"

"I saw Foley in the street." And he'd given him money for food, though it wouldn't do to share that with Lord Auberon. Caleb had been unable to turn his back on such obvious desperation. The man had been distraught, not only because of Ira's death but because of the bondmate and five children he'd left in the Old Town. Children who would never see their father again, and who would face disgrace and poverty every day of their lives due to his thoughtless actions.

Lord Auberon plucked a small coin from the chest he'd been crouching over and handed it to Caleb. The name scratched there was unfamiliar, but he knew what he held.

The coin of one condemned by the lot.

He stared at the chest. It was filled with hundreds, possibly even thousands of the engraved coins, identical save for the names etched upon each one. Liri Meriweather's coin would be in there, and the coin of Sela's friend, Esther. He recalled the coin that Tucker had carried every day of his adult life, pierced with a small hole, lashed to a chain, and worn as a necklace. A joyous reminder of his freedom? Or a crushing weight around his neck, given his deliverance had coincided with the loss of his sweetheart?

"I don't understand, my lord." He handed the coin back to Lord Auberon, who returned it to the chest and ran pale, ringless fingers through the gleaming mass. It was the only extravagance in Lord Auberon's otherwise spartan chamber.

"The man you and I knew as Captain Foley was spared of this terrible fate, Caleb. He was given a privileged position and blessed with a loving bondmate and five devoted children. Should a man who has known such bounty choose to turn from the right path, there is no mercy left available to him."

"Surely we should leave matters of repentance and the heart to the Carver, sir."

"We are the Carver's representatives, my son. Pure and unsullied by the evils of this world. 'Tis up to us to judge the men and women who stand before us, their souls rotting from within."

"But the Book of Souls—"

"This matter does not concern the Book, Caleb. As for Foley, you are to offer him no further assistance."

Then Lord Auberon knew what he'd done. Did his men watch

Caleb as he watched the other officers and guards? But a greater heaviness weighed on his heart. Lord Auberon dismissed the Book of Souls as if it were the mere ramblings of an excommunicated priest.

Fighting a gnawing disappointment, he returned his thoughts to Foley. "And if he starves to death, my lord?"

"Then you must leave him to his fate."

Caleb rode back to the outpost in the dark, mulling over his mentor's words. What Lord Auberon believed went against every fiber of Caleb's soul—and everything he'd read in the Book of Souls. Was not the Carver a God of mercy *and* justice? Did He not see Foley's misery and repentant heart? Was He not aware of Sela's grief?

And Caleb's?

Beck was still awake when he entered the cabin, reading a book beside the hearth with his feet crossed at the ankles. He snapped it shut as the door closed. "Ah, Caleb. You've eaten?"

"Nay, but I'm not hungry."

"Preparing yourself for another night on your knees? Or heading down to the beach for one of your long swims?"

He had not realized Beck was so aware of his nocturnal activities. "I haven't been to that beach in a sevenday."

He hadn't—not since he'd discovered the truth about Sela. Instead, he'd forced himself on long runs along the coast of the island, across vast stretches of sand well beyond Belladonna, until the throbbing in every limb overtook the ache from his heart. His body had never been in better shape—his soul and heart, significantly less so.

"Have you been spending time with the Accuser?"

"The Accuser?"

"The men's nickname for Lord Auberon. Not mine." Beck grinned. "You look as if you've been stripped of your soul."

Had he? He'd entertained many thoughts about Sela that were unworthy of an initiate of the Righteous, though he strove to banish each and every one of them. Certainly, he was no better than Ezekiel North.

Caleb sighed. "Perhaps I have."

"You seem different than when you first arrived on Azazel."

"How so?"

"Less sure of yourself. Certainly, more serious. You never smile, except when you're thinking about *her*."

Caleb turned on him. "Her?" he growled.

"The woman you're pining for. Miss Meriweather, isn't it? I saw you two down at the beach a sevenday ago."

He stared, having briefly forgotten that from the outpost, a man could see the settlement, the bay…his private beach. "You've been watching me?"

"As you've been watching *me*, Caleb. I won't pretend to be ignorant of what's in those sealed missives you give to Lord Auberon." Beck shrugged. "Your problem has an obvious solution."

Caleb folded his arms. "I'm not my predecessor."

"I wouldn't accuse you of hypocrisy if you entertained such an arrangement."

"But I would be guilty of it, nonetheless."

"You want her, don't you?"

"Not for one night, Beck. For life."

"Then keep her for life." Beck's smile turned sly. "Like I said, I wouldn't say anything."

"I'll not dishonor her, or myself." He rubbed his aching forehead, feeling the long nights of studying the extracts of the Book of Souls he'd brought with him…and the early starts that began with him on his knees. "There must be a way to redeem her."

And myself, he added silently, thinking of the state of his own soul before the Carver.

"There isn't." Beck's voice held a note of sympathy as his normally chirk manner yielded to a gravity Caleb had never before glimpsed in the lieutenant. "But it speaks to the man you are that you would think to look for it."

Chapter Twelve

By the time Sela had lived three months on the island, Noemia had lost most of her sight. Between helping the older woman to adapt to her blindness, befriending the skittish Jax, and teaching Tempe her letters, Sela had had very little daylight left to mull over her losses.

The night time was a different story.

Roux was a comfort, but his presence seemed to usher close memories of her family, even on the nights when she might have pushed them away. Was Azazel truly for life? How the vibrant chatterbox that was Tempe would have got on with Cadence, and how Ashira would have loved working alongside Noemia. Yaron and Thaddeus might have been friends, and Teodoir could have mentored Jax, with his patchwork skin and fractured self-confidence.

And Liron…

This was the worst of the banishment, that she was cursed to forever remember her family as they had been, while they moved on to ages and forms she might not even recognize were she to see them face to face. Cadence would grow into a lovely young woman and pursue the Binding with some unworthy soul, and Liron would become a hardened, embittered soldier like those she'd frequently glimpsed outside the taverns in the Old Town. If he died in battle with the mainland armies, would she even know?

In an attempt to draw Noemia out of the house, Sela summoned Jax and asked him to escort them down to Belladonna. Though he hated to be seen by the settlement children, the boy quickly agreed to his protector role, standing a little taller than he had before. Since it was cooler now, Sela placed Noemia's shawl atop the shoulders of her favorite gown, the canary-yellow, and took her arm to guide her down the stairs.

"You needn't worry," Noemia insisted, looking at Sela through eyes that were nearly sightless, but still managed to know exactly where she was. "I know this hill like the mark on my palm."

"I know you do, Noemia."

Jax flanked the older woman on her other side, sneaking the occasional glance at Sela. The first month she was on Azazel, Thaddeus had taken Sela aside and quietly informed her that the boy was infatuated with her, and talked incessantly about her while they worked. She had tried not to smile at the knowledge. When Jax was old enough, she hoped that he would find a girl of his own age who could look past his visually puzzling exterior to the gold that glimmered within.

They walked quickly at Noemia's insistence and found the market busy, crowded with farmers selling their produce and others hawking their various trades and crafts.

Arriving on Azazel, she'd found it difficult to adjust to the strange fare that accompanied the familiar staples from Eremia. Her favorite was a spiky-topped fruit whose flesh was stringy and sweet despite its prickly exterior, followed by the brown, hairy spheres that harbored both milk and bone-white flesh. She wished Cadence and Liron could have sampled both. How Liri would have loved—

The marketplace blurred before her, as if she and Noemia had momentarily exchanged places. In three months, she'd heard nothing of Liri, or even Uriah Smith, though she'd asked after their whereabouts whenever she could. Every settlement man or woman she questioned advised that she not seek them out, just as Caleb had insisted. Only one man had offered to take her to them, and she hadn't liked the look in his eyes.

She could go herself, but for Thaddeus, who locked the doors tightly at night and slept downstairs in the room next to Jax's, guarding the women and child upstairs. He was a light sleeper, and though she guessed he had a weapon, she did not know where he kept it. Probably on his person.

And then there was Esther, who still refused to leave the tavern for the safety of Thaddeus's household. What would become of her friend if Sela did not return?

Ironshod hooves pounded their way and her vision returned sharply. She pulled Noemia aside as several men on horseback rode into the marketplace, Lord Auberon in front on a dappled gray mare, presumably the closest he could find to white in the wild of Azazel. To his right rode Caleb on his sable mount, his coat as spotlessly white as his mentor's, his chestnut hair scraped into a sedate queue as he sat straight-backed in the saddle. Behind the two men, another lieutenant with a red birthmark on his neck and several soldiers made up the somber procession.

Caleb glanced at Sela once, his gaze encompassing Noemia and Jax, then abruptly looked away. The other lieutenant, who had come alongside him, spoke several inaudible words, but Caleb's attention remained on the crowd, his horse's reins gathered in one gloved hand as the other rested near the ornate hilt of his sword.

Sela understood.

Lord Auberon stopped near them, his sharp gray eyes raking the crowd. Were they here on some matter or simply displaying the power and presence of Eremia?

"Who is it?" Noemia whispered.

"Lord Janus Auberon and his retinue of hired thugs." The memory of Caleb's compassion pricked Sela, but she shoved it away. He'd made it clear he wanted nothing more to do with her, at least not in proper company. Though she knew that, honorable and Carver-fearing as he was, he would never ask her to be his bondlessmate.

"Janus Auberon?" Noemia chewed her lip. "I have…never seen the man. Might you describe him to me?"

She did, noting that Caleb's gaze never once strayed her way. He was as sober-faced as a pallbearer at a funeral. How the expression changed every Carver-rendered line and angle of his handsome face.

As if Lord Auberon had found what he sought, he whirled his horse around and headed back in the direction of the fort. Caleb and most of the other soldiers followed, although two detached themselves from the main group. The lieutenant and one of his men.

Dismounting, the officer headed directly for her.

"Miss Meriweather," he said, with a nod. The chirk smile he offered her brought Ezekiel North to mind, and she stepped back.

"Lieutenant."

"Beckett Arkwright. I live with Lieutenant Alexander—Caleb—at the outpost."

"How may I help you, Lieutenant Arkwright?" She kept her tone deliberately cool.

"I would speak with you privately, miss." He glanced at Noemia and Jax. "Alone, if possible."

Jax squared his thin shoulders, though the top of his head barely reached the base of the lieutenant's throat. "We don't want any trouble."

"I'm not liable to cause any." Beckett flashed Noemia a grin, lost on the blind woman. "Not today, anyway."

Noemia squeezed Sela's arm and reached for Jax instead. "We'll watch for you at a distance, my dear," she murmured. "Or rather, Jax will watch, and I will counsel him to keep his head."

Sela nodded at Lieutenant Arkwright. He bowed, handed his reins to the soldier who had accompanied him, and led the way through the crowd to a patch of empty space near the alley where Caleb had taken her, sevendays ago now. Jax's eyes followed their every movement.

As soon as they were out of earshot of the others, Sela turned on him. "Did Caleb—Lieutenant Alexander—send you?"

"Nay."

"But you come on his behalf?"

He grinned. "You're a sharp-witted girl. No wonder he likes you."

She turned to leave and he reached out and grasped her arm,

though not tightly. "Don't get yourself in a feeze, Miss Meriweather." He let her go. "I know who you are. Or rather, I know what you are to him."

She straightened. "'Tis not what you think."

"Aye, I know." His mouth turned rueful. "Caleb is too good for his own good."

"Then why have you detained me, sir?"

"Caleb is the closest thing I've had to a friend since I arrived on Azazel five years ago, Miss Meriweather. A genuinely good man, though inwardly tortured by principles for which, I freely admit, I care little. But he's been solemncholy of late."

"Solemncholy?"

Beckett Arkwright's eyes narrowed. "I think you know what I mean, Miss Meriweather, being a native speaker of our language and a woman with sense enough not to deny what is obvious to us both. I want to help him. I want to help you both."

"I don't understand your meaning, sir."

"The outpost where we reside is isolated. Under the cover of darkness, you could arrive there unnoticed and slip away before the first light of dawn."

She backed away and he caught her arm again. She shook off his gloved hand. "Is Caleb aware of what you're proposing?"

"Nay, but he will welcome my intervention once he realizes that the Carver vacated Azazel a long time ago and cares little for what we do. If He exists at all."

It was the same logic Uriah used to justify his evil. This time she staggered back, and he did not stop her. "Regardless of the dishonorable thing you ask of me, you would seek to destroy the very good you see in Caleb—the good that makes him a better man than any on Azazel."

Was she now defending him? The lieutenant shook his head. "I only want to relieve his suffering."

"His *suffering*?"

"Aye." He eyed her. "He suffers."

"Did you hear nothing of the fates of Captain Foley and Ira?"

"You'd be careful. And I would not betray you, Miss Meriweather. Either of you. I've kept darker secrets than yours over the years I've been on Azazel."

"You're assuming I care for Caleb."

"I saw the hurt in your eyes when he ignored you just now. Save yourself the deliberation, Miss Sela. Admit what I knew after only a single glance."

"I don't have to admit anything."

Turning, she strode away from him, forgetting her friends waiting with the lieutenant's man. Halfway back to the hill, Noemia and Jax caught up with her. The older woman was nearly breathless, and Sela quickly slowed.

"I'm sorry," she said, and Jax's eyes swept her face in obvious concern.

"Did the lieutenant harm you, Sela?"

"Nay, Jax. He only proposed something dishonorable."

Jax curled his fists. "I'll bruise his smug face."

"And you'll spend a sevenday locked up in the fort in isolation for your trouble." She reached around Noemia and squeezed his shoulder. "You're already a better man than Lieutenant Arkwright, Jax. You'll make some young woman very happy one day."

The boy blushed and was silent the rest of the way to the house. On the porch, once he'd disappeared inside, Noemia turned to Sela, her soft gray eyes probing.

"What did the lieutenant propose, Sela?"

She shrugged, then realized that Noemia could not see the gesture. "Nothing of concern."

"But I *am* concerned, my dear."

She sighed. "On the ship, there was a young man—Caleb Alexander, a member of the Righteous—who looked out for my safety. That lieutenant we just met resides with Caleb and he believes...he believes that Caleb cares for me."

"*Caleb*? You know this young man well?"

"I first met him while we were still children. My sister and his brother were childhood sweethearts."

"And is he a man of honor, this Caleb?"

"Aye. For certain, he would never entertain the kind of arrangement that Lieutenant Arkwright proposed."

"But you are more than childhood friends."

"Nay. But even if I did care for him, there is no future in any such feelings. Not unless I am redeemed."

Noemia bowed her head. "Or Caleb Alexander condemned."

"You're doing exceedingly well for one so young, Caleb. Go on."

At Lord Auberon's urging, Caleb continued his reading of the extract, all the more difficult for being penned in several near-unintelligible Old Tongues. As the room grew stifling, he plucked at his collar and would have shirked his coat if not for the stern look from his mentor when he reached for the first button.

He tried not to squirm like a child. The ancient text Lord Auberon had asked him to read spoke of the first lot, when twelve of the youngest citizens of Eremia had volunteered to go into exile in exchange for the forgiveness of their families' sins. It was only much later that, faced with prisons full to bursting, the king of Eremia had offered the same fate to those young people accused of crimes punishable by death.

Like Sela.

Many hundreds of years had passed since the writing of the document, but to Caleb, the lot seemed as senseless now as it had been then. What of the Carver's provision of animals for the purposes of sacrifice? And what of the Carver's proclamation that the essence of the law was mercy? Caleb's thoughts returned to Sela.

Mercy indeed.

Caleb felt a hand glide across the edge of the volume and realized he had trailed off in the middle of a sentence.

"Are you well, my son?" Lord Auberon's voice bore a hint of concern, his forehead faintly lined.

With an apologetic look, Caleb found his place. "I am sorry, my lord. I am only tired."

"Yet I see that 'tis not only fatigue that weighs heavily on your mind of late."

"Aye, you are right, my lord. Azazel is…" Caleb thought of all he'd seen as he'd ridden around the island with Lord Auberon, visiting the various settlements as his mentor's second. So much poverty, and such pain he hardly wondered why the inhabitants of the island-prison were so deep in their cups. Aye, there was depravity. But suffering also abounded in equal measure.

Caleb finally settled on, "Azazel is not what I expected, my lord."

"Ah, I thought you were troubled after we visited Hellebore." Lord Auberon sank into the chair beside him and rested his chin on webbed fingers. "Perhaps I have done you a disservice, Caleb. I took you to Hellebore by day, but I should have taken you to see it by night. At night, one witnesses the raging fire of debauchery that is but reduced to piteous, contemptible ashes by daybreak. Had you glimpsed Azazel in the darkness, you might not be so discomfited by how sorry it appears in the light."

"But my lord—is compassion so incompatible with disgust? Can we not despise wicked deeds while pitying the one who performs them? Are they not just as lost as we might have been, had we not been exposed to the light?" After his brief but impassioned speech, Caleb fell silent, conscious that his mentor's eyes had hardened to flint.

He and Lord Auberon skirted around the edges of Azazel, but no one—not even his mentor—went near the heart, where Uriah Smith was rumored to make his permanent camp. There, dozens of slaves labored and suffered in untold misery. Women were used and discarded, their children born of violation and heartbreak. For all his promises of taming the wild of Azazel, Lord Auberon had all but ignored the lawlessness and decadence at its center. It was even rumored that his predecessors had made various bargains and compromises with Smith's men to keep the peace.

Caleb's thoughts returned to Sela. If he was honest, Beck's proposition taunted him, not the least because the barrier between him and her was of human origin, not divine. But he had resolved that, wrong as the lot was, a second wrong would not right it. The Carver taught that women were to be cherished, not used.

"My lord?" Caleb prompted, realizing his mentor had failed to answer his questions.

"Careful, my son," Lord Auberon replied at last, with an iron grip on the sides of his carved chair. "You include yourself too readily in the ranks of the soulless. Remember that you are set apart for the Carver's purpose. You have a soul. You are Pure." His tone brooked no argument, and his spine was rigidly straight.

Aye, it could have been true—except that Caleb knew his own heart. Lord Auberon might consider himself a saint, but Caleb was most assuredly not. And while Caleb lived in fear of the state of his soul, the rest of Azazel lived in defiance of the existence of theirs. What could be done?

"My lord," Caleb repeated, inclined his head, and returned to the text he had been reading. Only by the end of the second page did Lord Auberon finally relax.

Aye, from now on, Caleb would do well to keep his doubts to himself.

Sela trudged down the main street of Belladonna, hardly noticing the skies gathering overhead while Roux strutted along beside her. Catching herself drifting aimlessly in memories of her lost family, she looked down and tried to smile at her companion.

"You know Noemia won't give you the mutton bones like Mama used to," she chided.

The fox gave a throaty whine, then parted his black-lipped maw in a sly grin.

"Your charm won't work on her. She's blind, Roux."

In response, the fox leaned meaningfully against her calf, emitting a soft purr like the growl of her stomach as he stared up at her through his eyelashes.

Sela laughed lightly. "Oh, you're incorrigible."

A flash of white caught her eye, and she looked up and squinted. They had nearly reached the edge of the settlement. Beyond lay the fort, overlooking a beach similar to the one not far from the white house. She gripped her basket and started after the figure that had disappeared behind the corner of an outbuilding. Was it Caleb?

Rounding the corner, she caught a brief glimpse of blonde hair before the figure startled. "Wait!" she exclaimed, seeing it was a woman. "I won't harm you."

But the woman ran, and Sela was forced to gather her skirts in order to follow. Roux bounded along beside her, his loping strides quickly outpacing hers.

The woman reached the beach and spun around, her posture alert and defensive. Roux bolted forward, but instead of growling, he only ran around the woman in circles, barking. The woman shrank back, retreating until she was nearly standing in the surf, the hem of her dress trailing in the foam. The wind whipped strands of pale blonde hair from her loose braid.

Hair like Cadence's.

At Sela's approach, the woman glanced up from Roux, and she bunched her hands into fists, though she looked as if she would rather flee than fight. She was small and slight, with narrow shoulders tapering to a slim waist and a face that would have been angelic if not for the cares that years had carved into her forehead.

As if a 'sooner descended even now, it began to rain, soaking them both as they stared at each other. The woman's blonde hair quickly became limp around her sagging shoulders, and the tension drained from her fists as she seemed to realize she was in no danger. She was a haunted shadow of a woman.

But Sela would have known that slight frame and those green eyes anywhere.

"Liri?"

Her sister's eyes were unfocussed like Noemia's. Slowly, Liri's gaze ran over Sela, moving from her face to Briella's dark blue gown, then back to her eyes.

"*Sela?*"

She held her hands up, exposing the brands, so Liri would not make the same assumption as Esther. "Aye, 'tis me."

When Liri didn't move, Sela stumbled forward and embraced her. Only then did Liri seem to react, her body dissolving right there on the sand.

"Sela?" she choked out.

They collapsed together, Liri's arms going around Sela's ribs, holding her so tightly she gasped. Tears ran down both their faces, impossible to separate from the monsoonal rain that drenched them. A rogue wave glided across the sand and curled around the pooled hems of their gowns, but neither woman reacted. Roux assumed a defensive position beside Sela's abandoned basket.

Grasping Sela's shoulders, Liri pressed her face into her younger sister's hair. "*Sela.* I thought I'd never see you again. Why are you here?"

"There's hardly time for the tale."

"The abridged version, then." Liri's slender fingers traced her face. "You look different—not a little girl anymore—but your eyes are the same. As vivid as lobelias."

"Your eyes are the same, too." Sela pulled back and studied her sister. She was more than six years the senior of the girl who had been exiled from Eremia, though she still possessed much of the rare beauty of her youth, if not in its fullest measure. There were grooves around her eyes and mouth, curved in such a way that Sela knew she rarely smiled. She was the same height, but thinner. And she no longer smelled like lavender, her signature scent. "Did you manage to get away from Uriah?"

Liri paled and dropped her hands. "You know about Uriah?"

"Aye. I met him some sevendays ago."

"You *met* him? Sela—"

"I was the one who shot him."

Liri only stared.

"Is he dead?" *One can only hope…*

"Nay, Sela. He isn't dead. He's fully recovered from the wound. How did you come to shoot him? Did he…" She blanched. "…did he hurt you?"

Sela shook her head. "I tried to stop him from hanging Ross Bryant. I succeeded—with a little help—but he shot and killed Bess instead."

Her sister frowned, as if struggling to comprehend Sela's tale. Taking her sister's cold hands in hers, Sela gave Liri a shortened version of everything that had happened since the day of Joss Brigham's attack, including Roux's unexpected arrival on Azazel.

Liri briefly eyed the fox, who was watching a blue-footed crab dance sideways across the sand. "Mama and Papa are well? Liron and Cadence? Teodoir?"

"Aye, they're all cleverly." She squeezed Liri's fingers, trying to stir her sister back to life. "But they never recovered after you were taken."

Liri's voice was very soft. "Nor I."

"You never said how you came to be here. I've searched for you ever since I arrived on Azazel, but heard naught. Did you escape Uriah?"

"Nay. Some of the women came to town to buy supplies. Uriah allowed me to go with them, providing some of his men came too. One of them was kind and looked the other way while I came here to bathe my tired feet."

"Uriah *allowed* you to go? Liri, he doesn't own you."

Her sister's silence was her answer.

"Stay here with me. Better still, let's run away together."

"This is an island, Sela, albeit a large one. Uriah knows every cave and hollow of it. There's nowhere to run. Believe me. Whatever you can think of, I've already tried."

"Then stay here with me. I'll protect you."

Liri dipped her blonde head. "Even if all the settlement men rallied behind you, there's no protection you can offer that will keep him at bay." She looked thoughtful. "But you haven't asked me why I bonded with him."

"I admit, I was surprised when I learned of it. Esther said you weren't captured."

"Not in that way." Her sister seemed to shrink even further. "I met him almost the first sevenday I was on Azazel. He seemed different, then—brave, charming, kind, clever. I fell in love with him, and he offered me his name and his protection. You see, Sela…Uriah is not the only one who is too easily captivated by a beautiful face. 'Twas only after I bonded with him that he became a different man. Sharp-tongued, brutal…cruel. He only worsened after he became leader of his band of marauders."

"Esther said you have little ones."

"Aye." Liri's shoulders curved inward. "Three. A boy and two girls. Uriah let me name my son for Liron. He looked so much like our brother."

"Looked?"

"My son was taken in the lot more than four years ago and returned to Eremia. Had Uriah been there when he was stolen by the guards, he would have torn them all to pieces. As 'twas, he was elsewhere, with another woman." Her next words were dull and lifeless, and even her remarkable eyes appeared to lack luster. "Little Liron would be five years old now." Liri raised her head hopefully. "Did you ever hear of him?"

"Nay. I'm sorry." Sela gripped Liri's forearms. "You have two daughters?"

"Aye. Anwen Rose, who is younger twin to Liron. Anwen was Uriah's grandmother whom he wished to honor." Liri reached out and touched Sela's cheek. "And little Sela Ashira, who is only three years old."

"You named your daughter after me?"

"She is a miniature you. She even has your eyes." Liri's own eyes filled with tears, more evident now that the rain had eased.

"Where are they now?"

"With the other women. I must return to them." Her hand curled over her flat stomach. "There will be another to join Anwen and Sela, soon. Though every time, I fear to face the lot."

Sela understood, but could hardly comprehend the depths of her sister's despair.

"Does Uriah know who you are?" Liri's face had gone bone white. "Does he know we are sisters?"

Wishing she could lie, Sela nodded. "I'm not afraid of him, Liri."

"You should be." Her lip trembled. "Don't leave Belladonna. With the fort here, 'tis the only place you might be safe from him. I'll try and see you whenever I can get away. But please, swear to me you won't try anything foolish. Swear you won't come after us."

"Your bondmate is a monster. How can I leave you with him?"

"Because you can do nothing, Sela."

"Caleb is here, too." When her sister's eyes showed no recognition, Sela gripped her hand. "Caleb Alexander. Tucker's brother."

A wave of pain stole any remaining light from Liri's expression, and Sela regretted mentioning the name. Perhaps it was best not to mention the letter from Tucker that she had lost.

"Tucker's brother is soulless?"

"Nay. He's one of the Righteous. He might be able to help you."

"Short of killing Uriah, he is powerless, Sela. 'Tis…" She trailed off. "The Carver's will."

"How do you know what the Carver wills, and what is merely your bondmate's wickedness?"

Liri stood abruptly. "I've stayed out too long. The others will be searching for me."

Sela hugged her, but her sister was as limpsey as she'd been at the beginning. "I love you, Liri."

"I love you too."

As Liri turned to go, Sela thought of one final question.

"Liri?"

She spun around.

"Do you still see the world in colors?"

"Aye."

"And what do you make of Uriah?"

Liri shuddered. "Black, Sela. Complete, utter, soulless black."

Chapter Thirteen

As the door of Ross Bryant's small hut swung open to admit him, Caleb was surprised to see another merciful soul already there in his place, rocking a tiny boy in Bryant's faded armchair.

"Lieutenant Alexander," said Bryant with surprise, waving his hand for Caleb to enter. "I didn't think you could come again."

At the sound of his name, Sela's face lifted and she met his gaze squarely, a questioning look in her eyes, likely at Bryant's unwise mention of "again." Did she think him heartless?

Forcing down the alarm he felt at the sight of her in Bryant's home and Bryant's chair—located as he was on the outskirts of Belladonna, on the opposite side from the fort—he nodded at her and then returned his attention to the man.

"I'd appreciate if you wouldn't mention my presence here," Caleb said in a low voice, and Bryant bobbed his head. He extended the basket he'd been carrying and the man took it with a grateful smile and murmured thanks, the brands on both palms flashing briefly.

Though Bryant was proud, he knew how to accept help. Perhaps fear of the Carver had led the man to abandon Uriah Smith's camp and protection and try to carve out a new life of his own…a decision that had cost him his bondmate and nearly his own life, if not for Sela's intervention.

"Do you know Miss Sela, sir?" The sharp-eyed Bryant seemed to have noticed the connection between them.

"Aye, I do." Though Sela, her head bent over the child as she gently cooed to him, gave no indication of knowing him in return.

"How so, sir?"

"We knew each other as children."

At that, Sela's eyes came up, flickering with lambent fire. "That is a generous way of putting it, Lieutenant."

Caleb looked to Ross Bryant, whose warm regard for the young woman holding his child was obvious. A hand squeezed the heart that beat rapidly in his chest. Had he run too far that morning?

Bryant stared back at Caleb, a hint of challenge in his brown eyes. "Miss Sela is good with young Thomas. She gets him to sleep when everyone else despairs of the enterprise, including myself."

"You come often?" Caleb directed the question at Sela.

"When I can."

No doubt she had her hands full at Thaddeus's house, with the blind woman and the boy with the strange skin condition. And Thaddeus's sister, the nightwalker—*former* nightwalker, as Sela insisted. Did she long for her own home?

Did she long for a man like Ross Bryant?

Sela stood, crossed the small room to a cradle that sat alongside the double bed, and gently placed the child therein. Though Caleb was aware that Bryant watched her just as he did, the other man was the first to break the silence.

"Won't you sing to him, Miss Sela? Thomas loves the sound of a woman's voice."

Caleb was pleased to see Sela's frown now directing itself at Bryant.

"I don't sing, Mister Bryant." She turned her back on them both.

Not "I can't," but "I don't." Whyever not?

"Lieutenant Alexander," continued Bryant, "I spoke to Foley, just as you asked me to. He'll come by here in the future. We'll see about some work for him."

By the stiffness of Sela's spine, she was obviously listening. "Thank you, Bryant. We'll speak of it more later, perhaps."

Leaving the babe sleeping, Sela retrieved a cloak from a peg near the door and wrapped it around her shoulders. "I must be getting back. I'll see you tomorrow, Mister Bryant."

Tomorrow?

"Thank you, Miss Sela. You're very kind to us."

Caleb nodded at Bryant, then turned to Sela. "'Tis near dark. I'll escort you home."

"I don't need an escort," she huffed and pushed past him.

Leaving Bryant still staring after her, Caleb followed her into the cooling night air, untied his horse from the sapling he'd fastened her to, and, against his better judgment, hastened after Sela, leading his horse behind him. Despite her long legs, he caught up with her easily. Her strange pet was nowhere to be seen.

"Slow, Sela. Belladonna is a dangerous place at night."

She skidded to a halt. "More dangerous than being seen with you, Caleb?"

At least she was calling him Caleb again, not the hated address of *Lieutenant Alexander*. "Says the woman visiting a man on her own, far away from the rest of civilization." Though he was still not sure Azazel qualified as such. "You shouldn't be alone with him."

"As I was—*am*—alone with you?"

She was impossible to reason with. "Do you intend to bond with Bryant?"

"Bond with Bryant?" She stepped a little closer, and by the last light of the day, he saw the dark, puffy circles beneath her eyes. Had she been crying? "Why would I bond with Ross Bryant?"

"Because he clearly wishes it."

She stared at him a long moment. "You have a nerve, Caleb." She spun on her heel and started back toward Belladonna, but at a slower pace this time. After ten yards, she turned and faced him again. "Ross Bryant's son will face the lot in several months. Do you know of what I speak?"

He nodded, feeling as sickened as he had the first time he'd heard about the reverse lot. Lord Auberon had described it as the settlement children's sole chance for redemption—a better life— though Caleb could not reconcile it with what he knew of motherhood and children, little as that was. He'd never met a child of the reverse lot back in the Old Town, but he guessed that the children taken experienced as much misery as those youths torn from their families to endure lifetime exile on Azazel…if not more so, being unable to remember the faces they'd left behind.

"Bess weaned her child early in the knowledge that her son might be taken from her. Her foresight turned out to be a blessing after she was murdered by Uriah Smith. But I fear for little Thomas, as does Ross."

He noted her use of the man's Carver-given name. "Is it Bryant's son you've been weeping for, then? Or Bryant himself?"

"Neither, but you're being unfair. Ross is a good man."

"Aye, he is." Never had more reluctant words been wrested from him.

"And he's still mourning Bess."

"For a few months longer, Sela, then he must look to his future." He rubbed the nape of his neck, wishing he could abandon the hated gloves that made him feel a stranger, even to his own skin. "'Twould seem he wishes it to be spent with you."

"Spoken out of concern, Caleb, or jealousy?"

He scowled.

She propped her hands on her hips. "Lieutenant Arkwright seemed to think the latter."

His mouth nearly fell open. "Beck spoke to you?"

"Aye."

"Of what?" But he was afraid he already knew.

"Why don't you ask him yourself?" At that moment, she seemed to glimpse something behind him, and he turned, expecting to see Bryant hurtling after them with either a wailing child or a proposal. But instead, a young woman stood there, gazing at Sela as if transfixed by the sight.

"*Liri!*"

Sela had found her sister? The young woman turned and ran, and Sela darted after her.

"Sela!" Caleb called, tugging on the mare's reins. Sela reached the other woman and spun her around. Tears slipped down the older woman's face, and Liri shook her head decisively.

Gripping her hand with the urgency of a hapless rider clutching the saddle of a bucking horse, Sela spoke rapidly. As Caleb neared, he heard the end of their exchange.

"…you must come back with me, please. Liri, if you return to him, he'll hurt you more."

"*Nay*, Sela. He'll only search us out and kill us both. Let me go." She tugged her hand from Sela's grip and nervously glanced up at Caleb as he approached.

Never had two sisters been less alike in face, form, or, he guessed, personality. Liri was pretty like Sela—he imagined that at one time, she had been even more so—but possessed none of her sister's fire or temerity. Though her posture was dignified, her manner and voice were hesitant, and she appeared almost timid. Had Azazel—and Smith—done that to her, or had she always been so flighty?

"Caleb," Liri said, then noticed the silver trim of his coat that signified his rank. She bowed her head deferentially. "I'm sorry…Lieutenant Alexander."

"Caleb," he corrected gently.

Her eyes still on his face, Liri blanked, as if she'd gone somewhere else in her mind. Did she see Tucker in him? Or worse, Smith?

Sela turned to him, sounding oddly desperate for all that she had no need of his company. "Uriah Smith is terrorizing the island, Caleb. Hurting Liri and, at times, their two daughters. You must urge Lord Auberon to do something about it."

Smith was vicious enough to harm his own bondmate and children? Yet it matched what Caleb knew of the man's savagery.

"I will try, Sela."

Though Lord Auberon would be unlikely to spend their limited resources on capturing a man who had evaded the soldiers for more than a decade. He'd summoned reinforcements from Eremia, but it would be months before any appeared.

He glanced at Liri. "Should you require it, there would be refuge in the fort for you and your children."

"There is no place Uriah cannot control. He has friends everywhere." She shrugged. "Even at the fort."

"Smith will meet his match in Lord Auberon."

"His match? Or another ally?"

He frowned. Of what was Liri accusing his mentor? Misguided as he was, Lord Auberon was far from corrupt.

Sela reached for her sister's hand. Liri quickly sidestepped, evading her touch. This time, the older sister appealed to him. "Would you please take Sela home, Caleb?"

"I don't need anyone to take me home." Sela abruptly tore away from them both, heading toward Belladonna again. He watched her for a long moment, then looked back to Liri to find her eyes on him. She wore a slight frown.

"I'll go after her before she gets too far." He indicated his horse.

"I know you will, Caleb."

Her gentle yet multi-layered words indicated that Liri had seen in a glance what her younger sister still failed to discern, for all Sela's brash accusations of jealousy.

"You should know, Liri, that Smith noticed your sister when she intervened to save Ross Bryant's life. I fear he won't forget her."

"Every moment I am near her, I put her life in more danger." Liri's voice softened, not without genuine sympathy. "As do you."

She sighed, absently rubbing a fading bruise on her collarbone. More of Smith's handiwork?

"From all I know of you, Caleb, you'd never do anything to hurt her."

He shook his head. He would swear it on his own life.

"Right now, Uriah and his band are camping outside the settlement of Hellebore, at least until winter comes. After that, I'll try to turn his attention to one of the other settlements. Arnica, perhaps, or maybe Wormwood. In time, the Carver willing, Uriah won't remember her. And Sela—"

Tight bands encircled his chest as he realized what Liri was going to say.

"Whatever Uriah says about him being an ambidexter, Ross is honorable. Even Carver-fearing, though like many men on Azazel, he has a rough past. Sela would do well to bond with him…though she might need to be persuaded." Her suddenly steely gaze held no uncertainty as to who she expected would be doing the persuading.

"Ross couldn't save Bess from Smith. If your bondmate comes for Sela, Ross won't be able to protect her."

"Perhaps. But she could still use a protector. And she deserves a little happiness."

The weight on his chest became unbearable. The thought of Sela with Bryant, tending his child, giving birth to their own… "You think Ross will make her happy?"

Her stare pierced him. "The only other alternatives would make her miserable." Her narrow shoulders drooped as the fight went out of her. "Though she masks the change with defiance, Sela is different than the girl I left behind six years ago. She used to have so much spirit, so much…joy. We used to sing together, you know… Our whole family was full of music."

"She doesn't sing anymore." He remembered her blunt statement to Bryant and the way she'd clammed up before swiftly departing the hut. He'd never even heard her humming.

Would the love and security of a man who clearly admired her—as well as the inevitable blessings of her own children, even if the lot cast a shadow over that particular joy—restore the things she'd lost? He could not deny her the chance to secure lifelong contentment.

Even if it came at the cost of his own.

After a long moment, he nodded, agreeing to Liri's request. "I will persuade her to bond with Ross, if I can. And I'll try to protect her…though from a distance, so I might keep her safe from speculation."

Liri offered him a grateful smile. "And I will do my best to make Uriah forget her. Though he may seek to use Sela against me."

"You know, Liri…Tucker's never forgotten you." He

wondered if Liri harbored the same hatred for his brother that Sela did.

Liri's trembling lip eradicated such a suspicion. "Nor I him."

Caleb thought of Uriah. "You deserve a chance at happiness, too. There are some who might stand up to your bondmate."

Like Lord Auberon—or so he hoped.

She said nothing in reply, but placed her unbranded hand on his clothed arm, her touch featherlight. "Goodbye, Caleb. Please look after my little sister."

Aye, he always would. "One day you might hear Sela sing again."

"I ever dream of it." Her expression turned wistful and she gazed toward Belladonna, where Sela had all but vanished. He'd be hard-pressed to overtake her. Still, a small part of his curiosity remained unsatisfied.

"She had a lovely voice, then?"

"Aye, Caleb. The most beautiful voice I've ever heard."

When Caleb returned to the outpost after escorting an obstinate Sela home, Beck was not around to be chastened for his interference, so Caleb changed his clothes and headed outside again, hoping for the evening run his body had begun to crave like some men craved whisky or rum. Instead, he found Lord Auberon standing next to his horse, holding a letter.

"Good evening, my son," Lord Auberon said, and Caleb reached for the missive the older man handed him. "This was to be delivered urgently. Not knowing the contents, I thought to bring it myself."

Caleb broke the seal and read quickly, feeling the blood drain from his face.

"Is it bad news, my son?" Lord Auberon studied him with what looked like genuine concern.

Six months ago, he might not have found it bad news. But now…

"'Tis from my father. He has arranged my…" He swallowed. "…my bonding with a young woman from the Old Town."

Sorrow mingled with anger. Few Bindings among those of his class or higher were not arranged, though Caleb had hoped to bond for love like the lower classes. Certainly, his parents had always said he would be given the choice, as would Tucker, though he doubted his parents would have permitted his brother to pursue Liri.

Why had they now changed their minds?

"When will the Binding take place, Caleb?"

"As soon as I return from Azazel."

"And do you know the young woman?"

"Nay." He barely recognized her name. He waved the letter at his mentor. "Did you support this, my lord?"

The elder looked askance. "Of course not, Caleb. And I am sorry the news does not please you."

And yet, the timing of the letter suited Lord Auberon's purposes. No doubt the man knew of his friendship with Sela and sought to prevent it from becoming more. Though he frequently questioned the rightness of the branding, Caleb would honor a pledge to bond with his intended, something his mentor surely knew.

Lord Auberon had somehow guessed the importance of the letter's contents, enough to deliver it himself when any messenger might have done. Had he corresponded with Caleb's father? Recommended the hasty union? But how, when any letter sent from Azazel would not arrive for three months, and any reply from the Old Town would take another three to reach them?

Was it the will of the Carver that he and Sela remain apart for life? If it was—and Liri's words seemed to echo the voice of reason in his own head—then he would surrender to the calling. Before next summer, he would depart Azazel forever. By that time, Sela would be bonded, and possibly expecting a child. Before he left, he would do his best to fulfill his promise to Liri and rid the island of Uriah Smith permanently.

"Caleb, my son? Are you feeling well?" Lord Auberon's youthful face creased in concern.

Caleb. His parents had chosen the name for its ancient meaning—faithful and whole-hearted. The selection had gone into a lot with other names, but it was the name Caleb which had been bestowed by the Carver. His entire life, it had suited him well, for he threw himself into everything he did with steadfast devotion. When other children were skipping in the street, playing tag, and shooting marbles, he was on his knees beside his bed, pleading with the Carver for a life set apart. The elders and priests taught that the sun rose and set by the Carver's hand. The intricate details and workings of Caleb's life were no different.

Could it be that he was meant to become the leader of the Righteous one day? If so, perhaps Sela Meriweather was a fleeting distraction, a momentary temptation. Perhaps the love he'd thought he'd felt for her was only the lust that glimmered in the eyes of men like Ezekiel North and Uriah Smith. If it was such a weakness, he could conquer it, as he'd conquered every other shadow that lingered over his soul.

If it wasn't lust but love, he would pray that the Carver would take it away. If He didn't, Caleb would love his future bondmate with as much of his heart as still remained free. He would return to the Old Town and never see Sela Meriweather again.

In exchange, he would gain all he'd ever wanted.

Straightening his spine, he faced Lord Auberon.

"Nay, I'm well, my lord. I will do as my father asks. I believe…" Aye, he *would* believe, given time. "I believe 'tis what's best for me."

In response, his mentor gave a slow, soft smile.

Chapter Fourteen

As Noemia washed the supper dishes, Sela stared at the tattooed band on the fourth finger of her right hand, her friend's blindness making it safe to do so. Noemia never spoke about her deceased bondmate, but Sela had caught her caressing the tattoo, as if remembering the intricacies of the twisted rope pattern and double knot.

Would Sela ever love a man the way Noemia had loved her bondmate?

The couple of times she'd seen Caleb, he had been distant— almost cold. Even as Roux frolicked around their ankles, he stood still, his thoughts heavily veiled, whereas before his mind had seemed open to her. He'd hinted at the benefits of pursuing the Binding with Ross Bryant, though he seemed as unenthusiastic about the prospect as she.

Did he know what Beck had attempted to arrange on his behalf? Was that why he now held her at arm's length?

Ross had done more than hint. The day before, he'd asked her to bond with him, saying that Thomas needed a mother, and she a protector. She'd told him that he was still in mourning for Bess, at least for the customary three months.

After that, she'd give him an answer.

Briella entered the kitchen and Sela turned, glad that the woman seemed to be recovering from whatever illness ailed her.

Briella sank onto a stool. "Tempe's finally asleep."

Noemia chuckled. "Praise the Carver for that."

The little girl's energy nearly rivaled that of Jax, who threw himself into the daily chores and farm work like he'd been laid up with a broken leg for several sevendays. Tempe loved to learn, and she was progressing well under Sela's tutelage. Eventually, Sela hoped to teach the other children who ran wild through the streets of Belladonna, dirty and half-naked. Years ago, Noemia had taught Jax, whose skills were now invaluable to Thaddeus. If she had her way, in time there would be dozens of Jaxes.

Coming back to herself, Sela intercepted Briella's close study. "Tempe adores her lessons, Sela. She spent most of the evening telling me about your horticulture excursion."

They had spent a morning identifying different plants and herbs, with Jax along as guard. Tempe had seemed shy and reticent, and Sela guessed she was a little sweet on Jax, despite the ten years between them. "I'm glad she enjoyed it."

Something seemed to weigh on Briella's mind. "You know, Sela, you'll have a place in our household wherever you are."

If she bonded with Ross Bryant, she meant. But Briella's interference—unlike Caleb's and even Liri's—was kindly meant. "Thank you, Briella."

"Tempe swears she'll never let anyone else teach her."

Noemia winked in her direction—an odd gesture with sightless eyes, as was Sela's returning smile.

"She's one of the brightest children I've met," Sela admitted.

Teodoir would have known how best to extend her, but Thaddeus had several precious books, and Briella was always on the lookout for writing supplies from the Old Town, however infrequently they were delivered, and no matter the inflated price that usually accompanied them.

"Aye, she gets that from her uncle," Briella said. "And her father." But then her lips firmed, the smile in her blue eyes disappeared, and she said no more.

In all the months Sela had lived under their roof, Briella had never mentioned Tempe's father, or the circumstances surrounding her birth. All Sela knew was the sharp reality of the tiny X mark on Tempe's left palm, given to her when she was only one year old. Most mothers back in Eremia would have mourned the branding of their children, but for the settlement women, such a mark was considered a symbol of deliverance.

They finished the dishes, and Noemia and Briella retreated to their rooms. Sela watched Jax slide the bolts across the front door.

"Where's Thaddeus?" He hadn't been at supper or participated in their usual companionable conversations in the sitting room afterward.

"He's gone to the settlement of Hellebore," replied Jax. "To help with the harvest over there. He'll return tomorrow evening."

Hellebore was less than an hour away on horseback, outside of which Uriah's men were rumored to be camping until the winter. Sela had not seen her sister since Liri had refused to return with her, though recent inquiries suggested that the women and children were at the camp with the men.

Until tonight, there'd been no way of going after her sister. But Caleb had promised Liri refuge at the fort, if Sela could only persuade her to leave Uriah.

Was this her chance?

As Jax entered his room and shut the door, Sela leaped into action, snagging some of Jax's freshly laundered clothes from the clothesline—she'd return them before morning came—and stealing upstairs to her bedroom. She removed her gown and petticoats, donning the wool stockings and breeches, into the waistband of which she stuffed her chemise. The breeches were a little large for her, but they would do for a short journey. She left her stays on but laced them as tightly as possible, dragging Jax's shirt on over the top. The material was voluminous, but thankfully gathered at the wrists, and amenable to stuffing into the breeches, which made them fit better, too.

After shrugging into the waistcoat and coat and stuffing her braid beneath the collar—Jax's hat was unfortunately in his room, and Thaddeus never wore a wig—Sela looked around for Roux. He was curled on the edge of the bed, and she thought to leave him there, but the fox raised his head and gave a tiny squeal as he surveyed her masculine clothing.

"Fine, you can come," she said, and he bounded off the bed.

Foxes could easily keep up with a horse, and Roux was swifter than most. Besides, it would be good to have his protection from those her disguise didn't fool.

A half hour later, she was crouching low on Jax's horse as she rode away from Belladonna, grateful that Jax was a deep sleeper who had not noticed the unlatching and unbolting of the main door, and that Thaddeus had recently taught her how to saddle a horse. Roux trotted beside them. In the event that she didn't return, she had left a note on her small writing desk explaining where she'd gone and thanking her friends for everything they'd done for her.

The Remenant, as she'd started to think of them—after a word from one of the Old Tongues—had saved her from the life she might have been forced into, like many women who arrived on Azazel. Like Esther, who still resisted Sela's attempts to rescue her from under Murphy's thumb. And like Briella, though Sela didn't know her story.

For all his compassion to young Thomas Bryant, not even Caleb could have saved Sela from Esther's and Briella's fate. He was pure, unsullied, instructed to keep away from the tainted lest they injure his soul. And so it was Thaddeus and Briella, with their gentle manners and terrible pasts, who demonstrated the mercy that the Righteous only philosophized about. And Noemia and Jax—who had every reason to turn away from the Carver after everything they'd lost—who spoke of little else but His kindness.

Thankful for the warmth of Jax's coat which held the night time chill at bay, Sela swung her thoughts to Liri.

"Some animals have to be driven, not led," her father had told her once. Aye, Liri was stubborn and fearful. She'd spent six years being terrorized by Uriah and had no comprehension of the freedom beyond his reach. Sela needed to show Liri what kind of life she could have for her daughters, if only she would leave him.

If only she would trust Sela.

Conscious that the full moon was nearing its zenith, she spurred the horse faster, Roux easily matching their pace as he darted through the undergrowth. Sweat slicked down her back.

She'd long since passed the outpost and now hugged the meandering coastline closely. The path would take her to Hellebore, which backed onto sea.

"I'm coming for you, Liri," she said under her breath, and though she had barely spoken to the Carver since arriving on Azazel, she bit her tongue and sent up a single, heartfelt plea for Liri's deliverance.

Draped across the porch steps in his shirtsleeves, Caleb relished the cool night breeze fanning his face after so many months of stifling humidity and sticky heat. It brought his body, if not his mind, welcome relief. Perhaps now he could pursue the peaceful slumber that his impending Binding—and Sela's—had stolen from him.

He stood, brushing dirt from his breeches, and abruptly straightened. Down below, a lone horse and rider picked their way through the underbrush, a small dog ambling along beside them.

The moon slipped from behind a cloud and fell upon a glossy, dark head. But the glint of reddish fur betrayed the identity of the rider, and most men might have puzzled over it, but for Caleb's prior experience with the firebrand.

Sela.

What was she doing, riding alone in the middle of the night? And in men's clothes, no less? The curve of the coastal road had forced her close to the outpost, allowing him a glimpse of her, but she would be visible to many on a night as clear as this one.

Remembering his promise to Liri to keep Sela safe—albeit, at a distance—Caleb quickly crossed to the lean-to stable and the horse he'd groomed and stabled only an hour before after his own nighttime ride. Seeing the sable-colored mare was exhausted, he decided to take Beck's mount, a spirited bay gelding which would easily catch up to Sela. He would explain in the morning.

Or the theft would be penance for Beck's dishonorable proposal to Sela.

After a moment's thought, he fetched his coat, gloves, sword, and flintlock pistol. It would not do to be caught unawares, especially if Sela was headed where he thought she was.

Sela and the fox moved fast toward Hellebore, and it took him some time to catch up to her, skirting the steep cliffs to his right that would prove fatal if his gelding lost its footing. She was a competent horsewoman, though he guessed she had rarely ridden astride. Once he'd spotted her again, he drew back, knowing that the moonlight would reveal him as easily as it had revealed her, especially if she glanced behind her. But she never did.

Foolish woman.

Sela slowed her horse as they reached the outskirts of the settlement. Hellebore was smaller than Belladonna, but far more colorful—nay, depraved—at night. Out from under the watchful eye of the fort, nightwalkers stalked the streets with uncharacteristic boldness. Twice, he'd been here on Lord Auberon's business in broad daylight, and both times a woman had approached him on his horse, one even going so far as to lay a powdered hand on his thigh. He'd quickly pulled away, thankful that Sela had not followed in the footsteps of her friend, Esther.

He suspected that Beck—who was soft-hearted but weak in the ways of men—often spent the night in one of the settlements like Hellebore, especially since Belladonna was more sober-minded and straitlaced of late. At times, the man seemed like a shadow, slinking in just before dawn and sleeping until it was time for his next night watch. Knowing that a word from Caleb to his mentor could mean Beck's branding or even death, and that Beck had remained silent about Caleb's regard for Sela, he had said nothing.

And the doubt that had first sprouted in Caleb back in the Old Town only grew with each moment he spent with Lord Auberon.

Sela dismounted and Caleb followed suit, grateful for a cluster of trees that concealed him from her view. At last, she looked around, and he stilled, hoping Beck's gelding would not nicker to the horse she had tethered to a tree.

All remained silent, and he rubbed the horse's velvety nose. "Good boy," he whispered, and the fox went still, his nose pointed into the breeze.

"Come on, Roux," he heard Sela say, and the fox followed her reluctantly. Even in men's clothes, and with that determined, feigned swagger, Caleb would have known she was a woman—and the woman who would not keep out of his thoughts, no less.

Tethering his own horse, he forced himself to crouch in the shadows. On such a night, and with very little undergrowth to conceal him, she'd easily see him following her. She might even scream and alert potential enemies to their presence. He would wait a few minutes and then continue.

Aye, and then he'd stop her from pursuing whatever reckless mission she planned for herself.

A long, lush valley dipped before Sela, the only thing lying between her and the settlement beyond, whose exuberant nocturnal festivities lit up the shore like fireworks. With the terrain more thickly forested than the coastal scrub she'd been traversing for the past hour on horseback, she summoned Roux closer and felt for the handle of the kitchen blade she'd taken with her. She mentally knifed every shadow and imaginary attacker as she descended the steep incline to the valley floor, then crouched next to a thick-waisted tree draped in a shawl of gray-green moss. Did snakes come out at night? She had heard rumors of various wild beasts prowling the Azazelian jungle, seeking human warmth and human flesh.

An owl hooted nearby, and she was pleased she didn't jump. If she was to rescue Liri, one of them needed to be brave. While Sela's horse would quickly tire carrying two women and two small children, the moon shone brightly enough for her to walk alongside them.

Her heart pounded faster. She was anxious to meet her namesake. And for Liri to be free at last.

Having seen a cluster of tents circling a large fire on the far side of the valley while she was still atop the ridge, she moved in that direction, but the sound of men's voices stopped her in her tracks.

"Aye, Turner, Smith's confirmed it. That fancy-dressed, polrumptious white fist has controlled the settlement long enough. Before spring comes, we'll take it for ourselves."

Holding her breath, she peered around the wide trunk of the tree, discerning four men standing beside a shallow stream, two of them leaning against saplings, and the others shifting their weight from foot to foot. Had she stumbled upon a plan to attack Belladonna?

The shortest of the four—Turner, perhaps?—scowled at the broad-shouldered man who'd spoken. "Smith's getting too ambitious. We'd need at least a hundred men to take the white fists at the fort alone."

"Smith has 'em," a wiry, silver-haired man put in. "An' since we've been pilferin' firearms for years now, we likely have more guns than the white fists."

The men laughed.

Turner crossed his arms, a mutinous look carved into his stony features, unsoftened by moonlight. "We'd do better to wait until we're stronger. Then we can take the *whole* island, not just Belladonna."

The broad-shouldered man glared at him. "Auberon has sent for reinforcements, or so says Smith's man in the fort. If we don't strike now, we'll never overcome them."

The fourth man, who had so far remained silent, offered a sly grin. "Are you sure Belladonna's not just about the woman?"

Sela stiffened, thinking of Liri. As if he sensed her distress, Roux flattened his body against her calf, his teeth bared in a silent snarl.

"The violet-eyed one who shot him? Smith'd sooner kill her than take her for his own, Flores."

The palm holding the knife grew sweaty. They were talking

about *her*. She moved closer to the tree, feeling the bark dig into her shoulder.

"You're crumpsy tonight, Turner. Maybe *you* should have the woman."

As the men bickered in reply, the silver-haired man interjected again. "It does no good t' arguefy, lads. Smith is raging hotter than a brand, aye. But the girl what shot him is sister t' his bondmate. He'll take the girl, all right—if only t' spite the blonde-haired witch—an' make sure she rues the day she pulled that trigger."

Sela pressed against the tree, her chest heaving beneath her overly tight stays. Perhaps they would leave. But for certain, she couldn't continue until they did. They were close enough to hear a cough or the snap of a stick beneath her booted foot. And if they found her...

She caught a flash of silver, and the older man who'd proclaimed her fate with such confidence moved past her hiding place, fumbling at his breeches. Understanding his intention, she shrank back into the shadows, but the owl hooted in the branch above her head and he startled, glancing her way.

His eyes widened and then narrowed, and he drew his curved sword. "Lads! There's someone here that's been eavesdroppin' on us."

Roux bounded forward, teeth bared and claws outstretched, and the man encountered his second fright of the night, dropping his sword as if it had tried to brand him. As he turned to fend off his attacker, Sela saw the other three men coming toward her.

She scrambled away, holding the knife out in front of her. Turner approached her first, his gaze roving over her hair and face. His beady eyes flared with recognition and he gave a mercurial smile.

"'Twould seem Uriah's woman has come to give herself up."

Had he seen through her disguise so easily? But she couldn't disguise her eyes, or her hair. As Uriah's men snickered, she brandished the knife again. "I've come for my sister. You will not touch either of us."

"Aye, she has more spirit than the blonde witch," said the broad-shouldered man.

He lunged for her, and her knife moved almost of its own accord, tracing an arc of moonlit silver more vibrant than the old man's hair. The man yelped as blood sprouted along his arm.

Sela grinned defiantly. "Touch me again, and you'll be wounded more sorely than that."

Turner and the man called Flores now advanced on her, swords drawn. Seeing the silver-haired man's weapon lying on the ground, Sela grabbed for it, bringing it up just in time to cross blades with Flores. In the process, she dropped the kitchen knife, and Flores glanced at it briefly.

"You should stick with your knife, girl. A sword is another weapon entirely."

She offered him what she hoped was a fearless grin. "So said my brother when he trained me in the use of it."

The surprise on his face melted to anger as she slashed at him. He met her blow with a force that rattled every bone in her arm, but she held the saber steady. This time, he stepped to the side in an elegant grapevine, raining blows on her with the fury of a 'sooner.

Despite his superior strength, she managed to nick his upper arm and then his thigh before the sharp point of his blade slipped past the basket guard and caught her left wrist. She gasped and kept hold of the weapon, but blood slicked down to her palms, and her heart quailed a little at the sight of so much red. With effort, she gripped the hilt with both hands.

Flores watched her with a small smile. "You've fought well, woman, but now 'tis time to surrender."

Roux yelped and skidded into her vision, the blood matting his fur a far worse sight than her own. The silver-haired man was now clutching a knife, and he scowled at the fox as he reached for his flintlock. He leveled it at Roux.

"Nay!" she screamed, and pulled away from Flores to

intercept the gun. But someone else was quicker, and another shot split the night.

The silver-haired man fell backward into the undergrowth, and another man ran into the clearing, a smoking flintlock in his left hand and a drawn sword in his right. Gunpowder stung her nose as she peered through the haze.

"Sorry," Caleb said with a quick grin at her, "I got a little lost."

All three assailants came at him, and he shoved the flintlock into its holster and darted forward, Roux now at his heels as both man and fox dove into the fray. With more power and agility than Sela would have thought to ascribe to a man who spent most of his boyhood with his nose in a book, Caleb clashed swords with Turner and whirled to fend off the broad-shouldered man, whose sleeve was bright with blood. She marveled at the beauty of his movements for a long moment, realizing that he was left-handed, same as she.

Spying Flores creeping up to strike Caleb from behind, Sela yelled her fiercest war cry and attacked. This time, Flores was ready for her, and the strength of his blows drove her backward. Parrying more strikes than she initiated, she found herself nearly at the stream the men had been clustered around. Oddly dizzy, she blinked sweat from her eyes and concentrated on gripping the sword hilt. Had she lost so much blood already?

"Give up." Flores's lips curled in a snarl. "Uriah will want you alive."

"I'd rather die," she shot back.

"Very well." Flores reached inside his coat and drew out a flintlock. Before she could react, he cocked the hammer and fired.

Sela glimpsed a blur of red fur and heard Flores scream before her own voice joined him in a kaleidoscope of anguished, fractured sound. Pain exploded across her right shoulder, and she dropped the sword and stumbled back, water filling her boots and then drenching her stockings. She dropped to her knees and threw out her hands to stabilize herself, her injured wrist turning the stream to scarlet. Her vision swam nauseatingly.

I must stay awake.

The last thing she saw was Flores on the ground, Roux at his throat.

And then black overran the red, and she slumped forward.

Just as the stocky man was nearly overcome—the short man already lay unconscious on the ground, clearly better at wordplay than swordplay—Caleb heard Sela's scream and an accompanying gunshot. Though his breathing turned ragged, he was mindful not to let down his guard by turning. He swung his sword at the stocky man, whose earlier injury made him slow to react. Sweeping aside the man's blade, Caleb pierced him in the abdomen, and the man howled and lunged at him. He was still strong, but several weakening blows later, he fell to the ground beside the short man.

Caleb spun on his heel and looked for Sela and the opponent she'd so bravely lured away from him. His heart lurched. She was face down in the stream, her shoulder bloodied and her body limp, while the man she'd been fighting lay face-up a few yards away, the red on the fox's jaws and his victim's throat ample explanation for the vacancy of the man's staring eyes.

He threw down his sword and ran to Sela, easing her onto her back as the stream doggedly persisted past them both. Long months of training solidified into instinct rendered him cautious to touch her, and he was briefly thankful he'd remembered to put on his gloves. Lifting her sodden form, he carried her the short distance to the bank before he realized the reason for her utter stillness.

She wasn't breathing.

"Sela!" he called urgently as the fox crossed to his side and emitted a high-pitched whimper, gently nuzzling his mistress. "Wake up!" Caleb shook her twice, then pressed his ear against her chest. Her heart still beat, but it was faint and slow. "Sela!"

She didn't respond. Her skin was deathly pale, the coat she wore drenched with her blood.

He hesitated. To touch a tainted soul was to almost guarantee the forfeiture of one's own. And while the accidental touch of skin might be forgivable for the Righteous or even the guards, for one of the Pure to willingly come into contact with blood… In that instant, he saw in his mind's eye everything he would be giving up to save her—brother, family, friends, career. A future among the Pure, mentored by one of the most powerful men in Eremia.

His chosen bondmate.

But in return for such a sacrifice, Sela Meriweather might live.

The pause lasted only a moment before he parted her lips and lowered his mouth to hers.

After several breaths, Caleb tugged off his gloves and felt for the pulse at her neck. It was stronger, but she still wasn't breathing. Her lips were icy cold from the stream and she was losing blood. Realizing that she had likely swallowed a lot of water, he pumped her chest.

He parted her lips again, tilted her head back, and blew air into her mouth, hardly comprehending the taste and feel of her amidst his fear that she would soon be a corpse beneath him. She looked already lifeless, her hands splayed against the moss, revealing the twin brands that had violated her skin and her innocence, her damp hair escaping her braid in lank strands around her porcelain face.

He stroked her cheek, leaving slashes of blood against her jaw. For what felt like the twentieth time, he bent and gave her his air, willing the dark-lashed eyelids to open. But she remained limp. He pulled her against his chest, pressing his face against hers in an attempt to keep her warm.

"Carver of Souls, have mercy!" he mumbled against her lips, fighting a rising desperation. "Please…save her."

For a long moment, he thought the Carver hadn't heard him.

But then Sela's body convulsed, and he jerked back as she dragged in a ragged, spluttering breath. He helped her turn onto her side, and she vomited a lungful of water. As his bare fingers threaded through hers, she sank onto her back, her violet eyes caressing his face.

"I hoped 'twas you," she said softly, and then went limp again.

He exclaimed and bent over her, but she still breathed, and her heartbeat was steady. "Thank you, Carver," he murmured, halting his rebellious thoughts before they attempted to further unravel the meaning of Sela's heartfelt admission.

The fox nudged her injured wrist with his black snout, licking her hand.

Caleb's gaze ran over her. She was injured in at least two places, though she would likely be cut and bruised in many more. They were far from the camp he'd spied at the ridge of the valley, but the others would have heard the gunshots. He had to hurry.

With his clean handkerchief, he bound the slash at her wrist, which still bled profusely. He retrieved his sword, ignoring the four bodies variously lying prone and supine on the ground. At least three were dead—one Roux's grisly victim, another Caleb's flintlock's, and a third his sword's, but he could not stop to see if the broad-shouldered man yet lived to tell of his assailants.

He lifted Sela and looked for Roux, but the fox came without being called, following him a little forlornly as Caleb carried his mistress through the trees. As he'd told Sela, he had indeed gotten a little lost, but only because her movements were difficult to track through the thick undergrowth, and he'd given her too much of a head start. Only when he heard the clash of swords had he discerned her whereabouts, and he quickly drew his already primed and loaded pistol.

He remembered the startling sight of her skillfully wielding a man's sword, whirling impossibly fast, with the feminine grace common to all her movements. How had she ever thought she could disguise herself as a man? Her war cry had stirred something in his blood, as had her scream when Roux was threatened. She showed the same compassion toward a fox that she did toward Hester and the Bryants.

By the time he reached the lip of the steep incline, Sela's slight weight had become distinctly heavier, and he paused to catch his breath before hurrying onward. Reaching the place where she had unknowingly tethered her horse not far from his, he lay her on the ground, pleased that his handkerchief seemed to have stemmed the bleeding from her wrist.

He turned his attention to her shoulder wound, thankful for the moonlight. Unsheathing his knife, he removed her coat and cut away the waistcoat beneath, exposing the bloodied, roughly spun shirt. From whom had she taken the clothes? Careful not to cut her, he sliced through the remains of the shirt, leaving her clad only in stays, chemise, and breeches. Besides the nightwalkers who brazenly roamed the settlements, on whom he forced his eyes never to linger, he'd not glimpsed a woman in a state of undress, and he was glad that she was unconscious, or at least unaware enough not to see the red that would surely be gathering at the tips of his ears.

The sight of her wound stole all such embarrassment away. She'd been shot in the shoulder, almost the same place as she'd injured Uriah Smith, the lead ball entering just above the prominent edge of her collarbone. Peeling back the blood-stained material of her chemise, he turned her and immediately saw the matching wound on her back. He heaved a sigh of relief. The ball had passed straight through her.

Using what remained of the shirt, he bandaged both wounds, then retrieved his coat and draped it over her. Quickly, he stuffed the bloodied clothes into his saddlebags.

Lashing Sela's mount to the gelding's saddle with a length of rope, he lifted her atop his horse and mounted behind her. Urging the animal forward—the fox once again trotting beside them—he rearranged her so that her head fell against his shoulder, her braid flicking against his back. Her warm cheek grazed his stubbled one, and he hauled in a long breath before expelling it slowly. He'd never held any woman so intimately, and this one was branded…soulless.

Sela had wished him to be her rescuer, though he was quite sure that blood loss and pain had caused her to voice the sentiment. It had been relief that he saw in her eyes when he came to her aid, along with a warmth that he'd never seen her direct at any man…not even Ross Bryant.

Caleb hoped it would be enough—for both of them—when she woke.

Chapter Fifteen

Sela opened her eyes to a room more richly appointed than any she'd ever seen, including back in the Old Town. She lay in the center of an enormous bed, the ethereal netting that surrounded it drawn back to reveal several pieces of ornately carved furniture, including a large, dark-wooded armoire. Light seeped through a white-trimmed pair of multi-paned windows that framed the view of the ocean beyond. She counted twelve panels before her attention was seized by the pain in her shoulder.

Her moan roused the man slumped in the chair beside her bed, and she caught a glimpse of rumpled chestnut hair, followed by a tentative smile.

The Caleb before her would not even be a cousin to the man she'd glimpsed only a sevenday ago in all his tidy perfection. Unshaven, clothes wrinkled and unkempt, and looking oddly rattled, she caught her breath at the intensity of his dark blue eyes.

He reached for her hand and she almost let him, before realizing that he wore no gloves. She snatched her fingers away.

"Caleb!"

Reluctantly, he retrieved his hand, a weight in his eyes that matched the one that bowed his shoulders.

"How long have I been unconscious?"

"Less than a day. I brought you here early this morning. 'Tis now nearly evening—sunset—though the days are a little shorter now we are headed for winter."

"You brought me here?" Before he could answer, she registered her bare legs beneath the covers and the softness of the chemise that covered the rest of her. Her front-lacing stays were gone. "Did you…"

Caleb looked anywhere but at her, but at least he didn't evade her question. "Aye, I undressed you. Beck, who has more experience with women than I do, helpfully advised on the proper removal of your…" He cleared his throat. "…uh, stays."

"More experience than you do?" she replied, trying to conceal her rising embarrassment.

"Experience," he amended after a moment's thought.

Her mortification seemed to match, then quickly exceeded his, as she realized that she wore not a woman's chemise, but a man's shirt. Caleb's?

He tried for a grin. "If 'tis any consolation, Sela, it looks far better on you than it ever did on me."

Her mind moved to other, less tender matters. Jax would bemoan the loss of his clothes—some of his best. But Sela would repay him.

Jax…

It all came back to her in a rush. Her hasty plan to rescue Liri…overhearing Uriah's men's plans…their discovery of her…

And Caleb's unexpected arrival. What had happened after she lost consciousness and fell into the stream?

Her shoulder seized her attention again and she winced. With her left hand, she probed the thick white bandages beneath the shirt, then noticed the other bandage encircling her left wrist. "Where are we, Caleb?"

"The outpost." He sank back in his chair. "The bedroom next to mine."

"The outpost?" she echoed, faintly. "Where is Roux?"

"He slept on the end of your bed until Beck lured him away half an hour ago with the promise of food. He's fine, Sela. The blood covering him wasn't his."

She sighed her relief. "Nearly a day, did you say? The others will be worried about me."

"I've sent word to Thaddeus and his sister. They don't know where you are, of course, but they know you're safe."

"And Uriah's men? Did they pursue us?"

Caleb shook his head. "Three of the four men were certainly dead. The other may not live to tell the tale."

Because of her foolish venture, at least three men were dead, possibly four. Caleb could have been killed. "Were you injured?" she asked, her eyes stealing over him from his loose hair to his casual shirtsleeves, the cuffs of which were flecked with ink.

"Nay."

"I am glad of it. But Caleb, if Lord Auberon finds out that you brought me here…tended my wounds…" She searched his face, wondering if that was why he seemed so ill at ease. "Why did you not summon a branded healer?"

"There was no time. And…afterward…I did not know if they would be trustworthy."

"Afterward?" She struggled to sit up. "Caleb? What are you not telling me?"

"Of course, you wouldn't remember," he murmured. He cleared his throat again. "When I got to you, Sela, you were lying face down in the stream. You weren't breathing."

"Not breathing?"

"Aye. Your heart was still beating, but your lungs were full of water. You'd been drowning in only a few inches of river."

"What did you do?"

"The only thing I *could* do." He took her hand, and when she tried to wrench it away, he only gripped it harder. He met her eyes directly and she watched him soften. "I gave you the breath from my own lungs, but nothing happened, Sela. You were still dying. Then I pleaded with the Carver to save you…and He gave you back your life."

Sela stared at him, as shocked by his revelation as Beck had been when Caleb had arrived at the outpost at four in the morning with two horses, a red fox, an injured woman covered in blood…and no gloves.

"Oh, Caleb." Tears slipped down her ashen cheeks. "What have I done to you?"

Any anger he'd still held on to at her foolish behavior evaporated. At the pain on her face, he nearly offered her more of the laudanum from the outpost's private supply, but he realized that nothing could take away her agony at understanding what her choice to pursue Liri had cost him.

Aye, the Carver had given her back her life…by taking Caleb's.

"'Twas my choice to follow you," he said at last, discomfited by her weeping. Shame cobwebbed her pale features, so thickly he doubted any man would ever be able to brush it away—including himself. "And 'twas my choice to save your life."

"You followed me?"

"I saw you from the outpost. I knew you were going after your sister." Why hadn't he stopped her once he'd overtaken her? But he'd known how fiercely she would react to his presence—even if he'd returned her home, she likely would have slipped away again—and he hadn't trusted himself to be alone with her. And perhaps a small part of him had wanted to help her save Liri.

To make up for Tucker's indifference…and his own.

Not for the first time, he was glad he lived so far from the settlement. No one had intercepted him on the coastal path from Hellebore to Belladonna, and Beck had promised his silence, though Caleb would never have demanded it. Taking Sela from her place on his saddlebow, Beck had first carried her to Caleb's bedroom, until Caleb insisted she be moved to the spare room.

"'Tis not what you think," he'd protested as Beck smirked, though Sela's disheveled appearance and bloodied stays attested otherwise.

"There's no shame in it, Caleb," Beck had replied with amusement.

But there was. Aye, there was shame aplenty.

"What will they do to you?" Sela asked, tugging on her hand.

He finally let her go. Her skin was as soft as he'd imagined it would be, and the observation haunted him. "I'm more concerned about what they'll do to you." He stood abruptly. "Rest, Sela. You lost a lot of blood. I'll bring you some food when you wake."

He was almost to the door when she spoke. "Why did you save me, Caleb?"

Why indeed? He resolved to be honest, though it cost him more than a little of his pride. She deserved to know the truth. Perhaps it would help with her guilt.

"Because I could not bear the thought of a future in which you were not living."

He left the room without waiting for her reaction.

When he checked on Sela again, she was sitting up, gazing out the window, even though it was well past sunset. A lone candle flickered beside her bed where he'd left it, as troubled and uncertain a spirit as the one that occupied the bed.

At the creak of the floorboards beneath his boots, her gaze moved to him, and he could tell that she was glad to see him, though sorrow lined her every illuminated feature. Her dark hair, which he'd released from the braid while she was still unconscious, tumbled over her good shoulder.

"I have to tell you something, Caleb."

He set down the tray he was carrying next to the restless candle and sat on the side of the bed. "Eat first."

"I'm not really hungry." She shrugged, then grimaced.

Leaning closer, he studied the bandage poking out from under her—his—shirt. "Would you like some laudanum?"

"Will it put me to sleep?"

He nodded.

"Then nay." After a moment's thought, she reached out and grabbed an apple from the tray. She bit into it, but without hunger.

He frowned. Was she ailing already? Without thinking, he reached out and felt her forehead, finding it pleasantly cool.

His gaze slid down to Sela, who had frozen mid-bite and was watching him. She swallowed, and he withdrew his hand.

"I'm sorry." She lowered the apple to her lap. "'Tis hard to get used to, is all."

"For me, too." He handed her the cup of water and then retreated to the chair. "What did you want to tell me?"

"Before Uriah's men discovered me, I overheard what they've been planning." She set down the empty cup. "Uriah plans to attack the fort and Belladonna. To kill all the white fists—I mean, guards—and unseat Lord Auberon."

Caleb's head came up sharply. "Attack the fort? But there are hundreds of soldiers stationed there alone, not to mention those in all the other settlements. The branded would never have a chance."

"Uriah's men believed they were numerous enough to present a challenge. And they have a plentiful supply of weapons from years of trading and thieving."

He rubbed the stubble on his jaw. This development was disturbing, and made the possibility of invasion more plausible. Lord Auberon had suspected that his predecessors had allowed the land pirates to buy weapons in exchange for food and resources, particularly when the shipments from Eremia became scarce, waylaid by storms or sea pirates. The smugglers that landed in secret coves around the island brought cargo that eventually found its way to the fort and its officers, many of whom remained silent in exchange for certain luxuries.

Further still, Smith's reign of terror—and his father's rule before him—had kept many of Azazel's inhabitants confined within the bounds of Belladonna and the other settlements for protection, which obviously benefitted the soldiers. Scattered sheep were harder to monitor, corral, and plunder—for the soldiers and pirates both. But if the pirates were stockpiling weapons…

"Tell me everything you overheard," he prompted, and she did, recounting how Smith's men had disagreed with each other on the extent and timing of the attack and questioned their own readiness. When Sela confessed that they'd mentioned her particularly—though he suspected she left a few details out—his fists clenched instinctively. "Smith will be coming for you."

"Nay, 'twas only speculation."

She met his stare, and only when Caleb heard the scuffle of footsteps behind him did he turn to survey the open door.

Beck grinned at them both. "I'm heading to bed, Caleb. Goodnight, Miss Sela. 'Tis good to see you looking so cleverly. You were as limpsey as a cotton fish when Caleb brought you here this morning."

Sela blushed, but recovered enough to manage a small smile. "Thank you for your…uh, assistance, Lieutenant Arkwright."

"Beck," he corrected her. "And I was glad to render it." With a flirtatious wink, he closed the door that Caleb had left open.

Caleb sighed. "There's no need to fear him. Beck is no Ezekiel North…or Uriah Smith. Even so, I will try not to leave you alone with him."

"Won't you be missed at the fort?"

"Lord Auberon is gone to the settlement at Wormwood for a few days. I'm to observe my usual duties while he's away."

"And when he returns?"

"He'll need to be warned of the possible attack. As for the rest—"

"The rest?"

He avoided her gaze. She didn't know of his impending Binding, and he loathed to tell her, especially since he doubted it would now proceed. Beck had suggested that he remain silent about his rescue of Sela, thus allowing him to retain his position as Lord Auberon's second-in-command and protégé. But the other half of that suggestion…

"I haven't decided yet," he admitted.

"Did your friend Beck have anything to say on the matter?"

"Aye, though he already believes you're my…" He glanced at her, surprised to see she wasn't embarrassed. "I told him he was mistaken."

"I didn't believe you were aware of the arrangement he

proposed to me, some sevendays ago now."

He met her eyes directly. "Nay, Sela. I wasn't. And I wouldn't agree to any such plan." He held her gaze, hoping she understood that he would never dishonor her, nor any other woman.

"You tried to persuade me to bond with Ross Bryant for the protection he offered, though you know as well as I do that 'twas because of Ross that Bess was murdered. If Uriah Smith believed I belonged to you, would he leave me—us—alone?" She flushed as he blanched. "For pretend, Caleb, not for real."

"I'm not that kind of man. For real, or for pretend."

"You care, then, what the others think about you? About us?"

"I'm an overseer. I must set an example."

"And what if while doing the honorable thing, you appear to be doing the dishonorable one? What then? Do you still consider yourself to have sinned?"

The muscles in his face tightened, and he turned away.

"Doesn't the Carver see the heart, Caleb?"

"Aye. But everyone else sees only the man."

He had always been conscious of what others thought of him, and even more so as he entered the ranks of the Righteous, whose activities were always under scrutiny. In the Old Town, his reputation was spotlessly white—pristine. His name had never been linked with corruption or debauchery. He'd never broken a law, Carver-given or those forged by man—until Sela. First, he had been forced to spare Ezekiel North for her sake. And now…

Did I do wrong, Carver, in trying to save her life? Surely You would not have let her die…

Though he already knew Lord Auberon would have done so without compunction.

"I'm sorry, Caleb." Her soft voice broke into his tortured thoughts, and the regret on her face stole away his anger. He had never seen her so humble…so broken. "For your sake, I wish you would have let me die."

"Nay, Sela. You're right—the Carver does see the heart. I only pray that all men may see as the Carver does." He saw her wince of pain as she shifted, and he leaned forward. "I should change your bandage."

Reluctantly, she offered him her wrist, and he slowly unwound the bandage. Seeing that the deep cut had stopped bleeding, he re-wrapped it.

"Who stitched my wound?"

"I did." He was glad she'd been unconscious.

"You know how to stitch wounds?"

"The art of healing is one of the first tiers of training to become a full member of the Righteous. After the physical arts, which includes bodily discipline and weapons drills." He sat beside her. "Now, if you wouldn't mind…" He indicated her shoulder.

"A branded healer—"

"—is an unnecessary risk, Sela. If he or she were to talk of what they believed to be true about us, it might cost you your life."

Her shoulders drooped and she reluctantly turned her back to him. Sweeping her hair onto her left shoulder, she gingerly slipped her right arm from the sleeve of his shirt so that the top of her shoulder was bared. After stitching both holes closed, he'd wound the bandage beneath her arm. He had dutifully corralled his gaze, and preserved her modesty where he could, but had still seen more of her than he'd planned to see of any woman, save his future bondmate.

At the first brush of his fingers against her bare shoulder, she shivered, and he understood her reaction, feeling a strange sensation like a breeze weaving beneath his own skin. He unwound the blood-soaked bandage as quickly and gently as those two qualities might be achieved in tandem and was pleased to find that his handiwork had prevented both wounds from bleeding further.

"I don't think the ball harmed the collarbone in any way," he said to the back of her head, "though you'll be sore for a long while, and you may find that the muscles in your arm are somewhat affected. I will pray that they are not."

He re-bandaged the wound, this time with fresh lengths of cloth. When he was done, he moved her hair to cascade down her back again, and the silkiness of the tresses momentarily undid him. One hand resting on her shoulder, he trailed the other through the obsidian strands.

"Caleb," she said softly, and he pulled his hands away, but she reached her good hand back and caught his fingers over the bandage. "Thank you for saving my life. Back outside Hellebore, and then again here."

She didn't know of his intended bondmate. If she did, would she be happy for him or devastated? And what would happen to her if he shifted the guilt from his soul and confessed everything to Lord Auberon?

Without replying, he disentangled his fingers from hers, stood, and left the room.

Aye, the Carver saw the heart, just as she said. And Caleb's was slowly being rent in two.

✕

The next morning, Sela would have returned to Thaddeus and Briella, but Caleb insisted she stay another two days to recover. Why, when he was so obviously fearful of her presence at the outpost—and her discovery?

He'd knocked on her door shortly after she awoke, carrying a bundle of clothes. From Briella and Noemia, he said, and she wondered that he had gone down to the white house in broad daylight for her. Inside the bundle, she found a fresh chemise, stays, petticoats, gown, stockings, and even shoes. Inside one of the shoes was a note from them all in Thaddeus's handwriting, communicating their concern for her injuries and hope that she would return soon. It was too risky for any of them to be seen coming to the outpost—or so Caleb asserted. *The Carver keep you*, Thaddeus had finished, and she cooled a sudden wave of anger.

As the Carver had *kept* Liri? And now Caleb?

Though Caleb had offered to help her dress—as had Beck, with another flirtatious smile—she refused his help and resolved to accomplish it herself. Gritting her teeth against the pain as she tightened the laces on her stays, she remembered the way that Caleb had so obviously spurned her thanks—and her display of warmth—the evening before. Perhaps he did regret saving her life.

Why did she care? He didn't love or esteem her, at least not as highly as he esteemed the opinions of others. Namely, Lord Auberon. And desire was vastly different than regard. She had learned that lesson from Joss Brigham and Ezekiel North.

Unable to lift her arm high enough to braid her hair, she left it hanging down and joined the two men at their breakfast, pleased to see Roux curled up on one of the armchairs. Caleb glanced at her once and then returned to studying the fragment of paper he had been surveying with scholarly intensity. She noticed that he sipped tea instead of the beer or cider that many men—including Beckett Arkwright—traditionally drank with the morning meal. She took a piece of buttered bread from the plate that Beck offered her and murmured her thanks as Caleb handed her a cup of tea. She tried not to stare at his gloves.

"Well, Miss Sela, you're looking even better this morning."

"Thank you, Lieutenant Arkwright."

He leaned forward, and she caught a glimpse of his birthmark, more obvious than any brand. "*Beck*."

"'Tis not proper."

"Since when do any of us care about *proper*?" Beck's cheerful gaze bounced between them, but Caleb ignored him, tapping a section of the extract with his gloved finger, his forehead scrunched as if contemplating a revelation.

"I thought to go home this morning."

At least that brought Caleb's head up. "Nay, Sela. You're not fit to move so far."

"Every moment I'm here, I'm a danger to you." She glanced pointedly at Beck. "*Both* of you."

"I don't know about Caleb, but I for one quite enjoy a brush with danger. Especially if 'tis wearing a pretty dress."

"Rest here one more day," Caleb said at last. "And I'll take you back tonight, as soon as 'tis dark."

At the fervency in his expression, she relented. One more day would matter little, especially if she remained hidden.

Once Beck had left the cabin, she squinted at the tract Caleb was studying, his breakfast only half-eaten and his tea likely gone cold. "What are you reading?"

He startled, as if he'd forgotten she was there. "A copied extract from the Book of Souls."

"The Book of Souls?" She could not disguise her surprise. "You're allowed to read it? Copy it?"

"You weren't?" he returned instead of answering, his eyebrows raised.

"The priests quote it, aye, but usually in the Old Tongues. My tutor, Teodoir, taught me many of the words of those ancient languages, but when the priests speak, I am never sure what is from the Book of Souls and what simply arises from their own thoughts."

"Then you've never read it for yourself?"

"Nay. I've only seen the Book once. The day of Liri's coming-of-age ceremony."

Frowning, he pushed the extract toward her. "You are welcome to it, and the others in my collection, too. But I will admit, I wasn't sure you believed in the Carver."

She thought of her plea to the Carver to save Liri. "Aye, some days I wonder how He can claim to be good and yet preside over so much evil and suffering."

"Like Azazel."

"Aye, like Azazel." She studied his face. "When I first met you, six years ago, you told me that Liri's fate was the Carver's will. Do you still believe it?"

He hesitated, sipped his tea, then wrinkled his nose. Cold, or perhaps bitter. But he downed the cup anyway. "The Book says that the Carver delights in mercy. That He richly demonstrates it to thousands through the depths of His forgiveness."

"The thousands safe from the lot?"

"Nay," he said, after a moment's thought. "*Every* man, woman, and child."

"Since I am a murderer, I understand my fate," she replied, surveying her branded palms. "And I understand yours, Caleb." She looked at his gloves. "You are kind and good and…Pure. From everything I have heard, you have always been so. But Liri—"

He looked pained. "I don't claim to understand the Carver's will, Sela."

"If you don't understand it, then how can you truly walk in it?"

Caleb's body jerked as if she'd struck him, and he sealed his lips together.

Undaunted, she pressed him harder. "Are the priests and the Righteous afraid to let the people read the Book for themselves because it might condemn them?"

"Nay, Sela," he replied quickly. "Because it might redeem them."

At her frown, he sighed.

"Over the past five years of my training, I've read most of the Book of Souls. In the past few months—between the extracts I brought with me, and those in Lord Auberon's possession—I've read all of it. I've not found anything in the Book to support the lot. Not in its present form, anyway. Nor the division between pure and tainted—between soul-bearing and soulless. In the eyes of the Carver, 'twould seem that we are all corrupted in our heartwood. That we all stand equally condemned, soul mark or nay." His eyes flicked to her brands, and she glimpsed his despair. "But Lord Auberon and the other Righteous—"

"They maintain they are Pure." She stared at him. "Then the lot is the Righteous' invention, not the Carver's decree?"

"I cannot believe that the Righteous would do such a thing. I must conclude that they've only been mistaken in their interpretation of the Book." He reached out and gripped her hand, his dark blue eyes sparking. "You must understand, Sela. If I keep my place in the ranks of the Righteous, then when I return to the Old Town, I can go to the elders and share what I have discovered with them. I am sure that they will realize their mistake. The lot will be abolished. You and Liri will be set free."

"Have you discussed your findings with Lord Auberon?"

"Aye, a little, but he believes…he believes that the sacrifices of those like Liri are the means by which our people are restored…redeemed. He refuses to listen further."

"Then what makes you think others like him will listen to you?"

Hopelessness once again crowded his fervor, and he withdrew his hand. "'Tis your only chance, Sela. And without the elders' approval, we cannot…" He abruptly choked off the sentence.

They could not *what*? What did Caleb want from her?

Regardless, Sela understood. She gained her feet. "I may not know the Carver as well as you do, but this conflict in you, at least, I understand. Who are you afraid of more, Caleb? The Carver, or those who claim to be His servants?"

When he didn't answer, she left him to his cowardice.

Though Roux wanted to be outside, Sela kept indoors for Caleb's sake, even staying away from the windows. By the time night had fallen again, she was exhausted, and almost asked for a dose of laudanum to ease the pain. But it wouldn't do for Caleb to have to carry her down the hill to the white house, not when he once again shunned touching her.

Bundling the remnants of Jax's ruined clothes into a small sack, Sela stepped out of the cabin. Seeing Caleb's tall silhouette poised on the edge of the cliff, she dropped the sack at the base of the stairs.

"Stay," she said to Roux, and the fox whimpered but remained where he was.

She approached the cliff, surprised at the winds that swelled as she neared the edge, buffeting her injured shoulder. Caleb perched only a yard from the precipice, his white coat whipping about his body, thick strands of his hair escaping the rest clubbed at his neck as he gazed out toward Eremia—thousands of miles away. How long had he been standing there?

"Are you missing your brother?"

He turned slowly, as if his gaze was connected by invisible strings to the horizon and he was reluctant to sever them. "Aye, Sela, and everything else."

"Are the rumors true, then? That you and Tucker are twins?"

"Twins?" He chuckled. "True, but for my mother's sworn testimony that we arrived a year apart."

She shuffled her feet, disliking the cool after months of hardly needing a shawl. "I'm ready to return home."

"Home?" His eyes traced her face wonderingly. "You said that before, though I didn't realize it at the time. Is Thaddeus's house truly home?"

"Nowhere is home—not truly."

"Perhaps one day you will make a new home for yourself, and fill it with your voice."

"My voice?"

"Liri told me you sing beautifully."

She turned away. "Those days are well past."

"I am praying that they will come again."

At the hope in his voice, she met his gaze. Invisible threads tethered her to him, too. "I have a far less optimistic opinion of our fellow man than you do, Caleb."

He took her uninjured wrist and drew her away from the edge. "The Righteous will listen to me. I am sure of it. Soon, you will be as free as the Carver intended."

"I still don't understand, Caleb. Why didn't you let me die?"

He stepped closer, his eyes so dark she could scarcely discern their color. "Because of this," he said huskily, and then he cradled her face between his hands, his long fingers sliding into her hair, liberating black tendrils from her braid. Tilting her head and inclining his own, he fitted his mouth to hers. His lips were as warm, strong, and smooth as his bare hands had been the night before.

She would have never guessed that a man who professed so

little experience with women could be so boldly passionate, but from what she knew of the scholar in him, he had planned this kiss for some time. As she leaned against him and slid her arms around his waist, he murmured her name and deepened the kiss. Though before, when she'd been unconscious, he'd bestowed his breaths on her, now he seemed to relish snatching hers away.

His fingers brushed against her cheek, and she startled as she finally registered the sensation of his gloves, so foreign compared to the warm, heartfelt caress of his mouth.

Abruptly, she drew back, and he frowned. "Sela?"

She backed away from the clifftop. "You must decide what you want, Caleb. The Carver's truth, or the life that Lord Auberon has promised you."

"Sela…" She could see his anguish, but she steeled herself against it.

"The white house is not far. I'll see myself home."

Chapter Sixteen

It was all he could do not to slam the cabin door. Caleb had seen Sela safely home, but at a distance, so she wouldn't object to his presence. Then he'd all but sprinted up the hill, earning a stitch in his side for the trouble.

She was right, of course. Not only because he'd yet to put aside his intended bondmate, but because in concealing his love for Sela and returning to Eremia, he would be living a double life. After enduring yet another sleepless night poring over the Carver's words, he'd thought she would see his determination to free her and the other prisoners as admirable. Instead, she believed he was running.

And perhaps he was.

Sprawled in an armchair nearest the fire, Beck tilted his head and studied him. "Meeting with the Accuser again?"

"Nay, I took Sela home."

"Ah. A heart to heart with your conscience, then." He grinned. "Miss Sela is a lovely girl. One with integrity, too. If you reject her, I can't imagine she'll be lonely for long."

Caleb didn't reply.

"You know what your problem is, Caleb?" Beck wasted no time in leaving him hanging. "You're too honorable."

"An honorable man would stay and fight for her here, Beck."

"*Here*?" Beck frowned. "You don't mean to confess all to Auberon?"

"Sela's right. If I return to Eremia, there's a good chance they won't listen to what I have to say. Or even let me return to Azazel."

"'They'?"

"The elders." Caleb hauled in a breath. "She might not say it, but she believes I'm a coward for not remaining to fight my battles here."

"It doesn't matter what the girl thinks"—Beck stretched lazily—"or even what Auberon thinks. You're your own man, Caleb, capable of deciding your own destiny. Your mind is a prison that keeps you bound more tightly than a brand and a lifetime sentence to Azazel."

Was that what he feared the most? Not the loss of his soul—from everything he'd read, the Carver would never forsake him—but everything that accompanied the branding—poverty, isolation, exile. If he surrendered himself to Lord Auberon's judgment, he would likely lose his place as a member of the Righteous. He would never be able to spar with his brother, debate with his father, or hug his mother. He would never again spend hours with his friends and colleagues, wise and learned men and women who understood the depths of the Carver like no one else.

He would lose everything he thought he was.

But to remain silent—to abandon Sela to Uriah Smith, and to leave Janus Auberon and the lot unchallenged—would betray the principles of the man the Carver had shaped him to be.

"You're too honorable," Beck had said.

Nay, the truth was that he was not honorable enough.

After a round of scolding followed by a second round of tearful hugging, Noemia and Briella sent Sela to bed to rest while Thaddeus and Jax stabled the horse she'd returned. Tempe chattered on the end of Sela's bed and played with Roux until Briella summoned her to bed.

Thaddeus knocked on the open door. "May I come in, Sela?"

"Of course."

He took the armchair Briella had placed beside her bed. "'Tis good to have you back. When Lieutenant Alexander knocked on our door early this morning, we feared the worst, even with the anonymous letter sent the day before." He nervously ran his branded palms up and down his thighs. "I'm guessing there is more to the tale than you shared with the others."

Caleb, she'd quickly realized, had simply told them that she'd gone to look for her sister and had been injured along the way. He'd said nothing of Uriah Smith or being shot.

She nodded. "There is." She told him everything, then—that she was sister to Liri, Uriah's bondmate, that she'd longed to save her from his clutches, and that she'd been shot pursuing her sister, before being saved by Caleb, an acquaintance from her childhood.

"I'm sorry, Thaddeus. I shouldn't have concealed the truth, especially after you told me that you were second-in-command to Uriah's father. Have I put you or the others in danger?"

He sighed. "Nay, though I wish you'd trusted me with this earlier. Smith has been inquiring about you in the settlement. He knows you're here."

"He's been inquiring about me?"

"Aye. Though I heard that you shot him in defense of a family, his particular attention makes sense to me now." He leaned forward. "You have to understand, Sela. Smith is no ordinary man. His mind is—"

"Twisted?"

"Aye. He thinks of naught but possession—more money, guns, food…women. If he could boast of having both you and your sister…"

"Caleb—Lieutenant Alexander—believed I should bond with Ross Bryant." She said it in past tense, because she didn't know what he believed anymore. How could he kiss her as he did and still insist on returning to Eremia?

"Ross Bryant? He cannot protect you."

"As I said to Caleb." She repeated everything she'd overheard from Uriah's men, and Thaddeus's expression only grew more troubled.

"'Tis true. Smith's men have many guns and supplies aplenty to encircle the settlement. Not to mention that Auberon's numbers are fewer after his latest crusade of purity. No doubt many of the soldiers he branded will have gone over to Smith's side out of pure spite."

"Pure"? Had he chosen his words deliberately? He stood, and she wondered that he was so gentle for such a large man. She could hardly imagine him as a member of a violent gang.

"You were treated well by Lieutenant Alexander?"

"Of course," she replied, hoping her tone was cool and unaffected. "Caleb would never dishonor me."

"I thought so, especially given his impending Binding, but I wanted to hear it from you."

She felt a wave of heat rise to her face and her heartbeat stuttered. "What do you mean, his impending Binding?"

"I heard an officer tell that 'twas arranged not long ago, by his parents. According to that man and his rumor mill, it came as quite a surprise to Lieutenant Alexander. He will bond with the woman once he returns from Azazel." Thaddeus studied her carefully. "He didn't tell you?"

"Nay." And it seemed that she was last to know. "I'm sure he would have told me, in time." But she was anything but sure.

And now she knew why Caleb wanted to return to Eremia.

Sinking onto the flea-infested mattress, Liron fought the inevitable despair of a fruitless mission.

Months of searching among the mainland countries—and watching his finances and supplies dwindle—had led to naught. The prince of Eremia had not been seen in years, and Magnus was a common enough name among the mainlanders. Several times, Liron had had to run for his life when he was sighted by Eremian soldiers. Once, he had barely escaped capture by the unified mainland armies.

Still, he held to his last remaining hope.

In this tiny inn where he counted his dwindling coins and

thought longingly of his bed in the Old Town, Liron had heard stories of a man named Magnus—not Magnus Theodorus—who travelled and worked as a simple craftsman, but seemed more than he appeared. He was headed to the port of Consuela, where the navy of Eremia consolidated their strength for another assault against their mainland enemies.

Liron had been to Consuela—months ago, now. It had been the very start of his journey. Was it possible that the Magnus of the stories was the prince who had saved his life when he was a child? Or would it be yet another dead end?

That Prince Magnus would head for Consuela was not so surprising. Perhaps the prince would finally reveal himself to his own forces and assume command of his army. Perhaps he only disguised himself as a craftsman because he feared for his life. Had he been forced into exile himself? The mainlanders had been welcoming of him, all those years ago, but now they were at war with Eremia…

Liron heaved a sigh and rolled off the filthy mattress. He headed to the window of the room, looking out at another nondescript outlook in another ordinary village. Farmers and laborers toiled beneath a hot sun that blistered and blinded, carving out a living from soil that was rock-strewn and troublesome. Yet this village had yielded something at last.

He would return to Consuela—to the very mouth of the lion. And he would pray for deliverance, and not just for his sisters.

This time, he would pray for himself.

After an uneventful sevenday had passed, Sela resolved to go about her duties as if nothing had happened, though she kept an ear out for news of Liri. As if they'd heard of Uriah's intentions, the settlement inhabitants had grown restless, and there was less than the usual amount of nighttime revelry. Sela was glad of it, for Esther's sake.

Thaddeus had insisted that she not go anywhere in Belladonna without him or Jax, and Sela had seen him teaching the boy how to fire a flintlock, which he now carried everywhere on his person. Jax had rather easily forgiven the theft of his clothes and his horse and now made it his personal mission to follow Sela everywhere, even when she was inside the house. Stifled by his zeal, she tried to remind herself that he was only concerned for her.

And that the threat to her safety was real.

She visited Esther every chance she could, and Ross Bryant and his son, though she knew that the man's period of mourning neared its end. Someone had continued to send him supplies, and Sela guessed Caleb was the culprit. She wondered what Ross would do when Caleb returned to Eremia.

His immediate needs met, Ross had turned his attention to rallying the settlement men, and his house was frequently filled with one or more of them. Only on her third visit did she realize he spoke not of rallying against Uriah, but joining with the pirate's men to overthrow the soldiers.

"How can you think of allying with him?" she asked him when the men were gone and Thomas put to bed. "Don't you remember how Uriah murdered Bess and nearly sent you to join her?" She almost told him that Uriah's men had shot her, too, though the wound was well hidden beneath her gown and shawl. Only her bandaged wrist was visible, and she'd told him she'd accidentally cut herself with a kitchen knife.

He shrugged uneasily. "The soldiers are the worse tyrants, Sela. You haven't been here long enough to know what they're like. They murder our men and use our women and steal our children. Young Thomas…" His gaze trailed to the cot where Sela had placed his son. "They may yet steal him too if we do not act."

"And you think Uriah will be a more benevolent leader?"

"We only need to ally with him to overcome the soldiers. After that, we will be our own men. And we'll protect our own." His steely-eyed stare left her in no doubt as to his meaning.

"What of Lieutenant Alexander and his kindnesses?"

"The good lieutenant will be spared, as will any who surrender to us."

"You think Uriah will be so merciful?"

"I'll make sure of it, Sela." He placed his hand over hers and she pulled away.

"Join with Uriah, and I swear to you I'll come here no more." She found Jax waiting outside with Roux, and ignoring Ross's beseeching look as he stood outside his house, she headed back to Belladonna.

"There's talk of a battle coming," ventured Jax as they approached the main street. "Thaddeus speaks of sending you, Noemia, Briella, and Tempe to another settlement."

"He does?" Thaddeus hadn't said anything to her.

"Aye," he replied, his eyes scanning the street. "'Tis not safe in Belladonna anymore. Not for women and children."

She opened her mouth to object to his statement, since he was still a child himself, but then closed it. Jax was no boy anymore. Azazel had shortened his childhood, if he'd ever had one in the first place.

Some of her anger toward Caleb died. How could she ask him to choose a path that might cost him everything he loved? Even if he stayed on Azazel—was branded—she couldn't pursue the Binding with him. Not when another lot could so easily tear a piece of them away.

Aye, she should be merciful to Ross as well. But to choose the brutality of Uriah over the tyranny of the soldiers…

When she returned to the house, Jax went to feed the horses, and she took advantage of his absence to slip down to the beach. As Roux scampered up and down the tiny stretch of sand, Sela turned her face to the wind and briefly remembered Caleb's hands caressing her skin before she shoved the memory away.

"'Tis good to finally find you alone," said a rich, baritone voice behind her, and she turned, expecting Caleb, but the man standing there made her draw her knife and Roux bare his teeth.

Uriah laughed and held up his branded palms in a gesture of surrender. "Easy, Sela. I don't want to hurt you."

"You may not want to, but you will."

He smiled, exposing dimpled cheeks—one of them branded. "Nay. I only come to talk. Your sister sent me."

"Liri?" Sela narrowed her eyes and gripped the knife tighter. "She'd never send you."

"She has only your wellbeing in mind, Sela."

He paused well out of range of her knife and Roux's teeth, arms folded across an expansive chest. Aye, she could see how Liri might have found him handsome, even charming. But he would never be able to mask the coldness of his slate gray eyes.

"You may have heard, my dear sister-in-law, that war is coming to our island."

"War brought by you and your men."

His gaze flicked to her bandaged wrist and shoulder, and she knew he was aware of her injuries—and possibly the identity of her savior, too. "You know, Sela, I am willing to forgive the fact that three of my men lie in their earthy graves because of you…not to mention the sevendays of practice it took to recover my aim with my injured shoulder." He kept on smiling.

"I only shot you because you shot Bess." She fought the lump in her throat. "You *killed* Bess."

"From what my men tell me of your frequent visits to her widower and child, 'twould seem I did Ross Bryant a favor."

"What do you want, Uriah?" she asked, sickened by his implication.

"Your sister is concerned for you. You are very nearly alone in that big old house, with only a one-armed man and a boy for protection. A ragtag band of misfits. Should anyone come knocking with sinister intent, they'd be hard pressed to defend you." His gaze moved to her shoulder again. "And you so recently injured yourself."

"Is that a threat?"

"An offer of protection. Come with me, and I'll take you to Liri right now. She and the girls long for you, Sela. Your little namesake speaks of naught else but meeting you. And Anwen, a miniature of your sister, is also anxious to make your acquaintance."

Despite the man's cruelty, he seemed a proud father. Would such a quality extend to the protection of his sister-in-law?

Nay—he couldn't be trusted.

"Thank you, but I think I'll stay with my band of misfits."

Something flickered in his eyes, like a forge stirring to life. "Did you know, Sela, that violet eyes are considered good luck?"

"I'm not superstitious."

He fingered something at his throat—a coin, like the ones given to those survivors of the lot in the Old Town. Hadn't he said he had been born on Azazel? Whose coin did he then hold? He smiled at her, as if she were a good luck charm he'd dearly like to possess.

He drew his flintlock, and Roux growled.

"Stay, Roux," she said urgently, not wanting Uriah to shoot the fox.

"Aye, *stay*, Roux," he mocked.

Keeping the gun leveled at Roux, Uriah approached her. She stood still, urging her pet to remain where he was.

He pried the knife from her fingers, reached for her braid, and in one smooth movement, he hacked off the last three inches of her hair. Liberated thus, the rest of her tresses spilled around her shoulders. Smiling, he dropped the knife at her feet and tucked the braid into the pocket of his coat. No doubt he would use it to taunt Liri.

Uriah stroked her cheek with the back of his fingers, and she stiffened. "You should know that I rarely exhibit such patience— such restraint—with any woman."

"Perhaps you only need someone to stand up to you. To show you right from wrong."

"You think me a candidate for redemption?" When she said nothing, he grinned. "Why should either of us care for our eternal destinies? We are already soulless, are we not?"

"So believes most of Belladonna. But not all."

He laughed. "Old Thaddeus is a fool."

Mindful that his flintlock was once again trained on her fox, she raised her chin defiantly. "I'll die before I let Liri spend another year under your thumb. And if you hurt anyone I love, I'll shoot you again…and this time I'll be aiming for your heart."

Her fiery words only seemed to amuse him. "So much for redemption. But let me offer a warning of my own. The next time I see you, Sela, I won't be coming for those you love. Before Belladonna falls, I'll be coming for you."

He shot at the sand beside them, causing an explosion of grit, and she flinched as Roux snarled.

By the time the sand settled, he was gone, somehow vanishing in broad daylight.

When she'd finally calmed herself, she returned to the house via the back door, hoping Noemia would be pounding bread dough, so she could join her. She needed to thump something. Instead, she found the house in uproar.

Thaddeus's large form filled the front doorway, but beyond him, Sela clearly glimpsed two soldiers. Noemia and Jax stood behind him, tears on the older woman's face. What had happened? Was it Thomas Bryant?

"Move aside. We've come for Miss Meriweather."

"On what charges?" Thaddeus demanded.

"They will be read when she presents herself at the fort before Lord Auberon."

Sela spied Briella perched on one of the armchairs, Tempe on her lap. When she saw Sela, she bit her lip and waved her away, toward the kitchen. "Shh, they don't know you're here."

But Jax turned around, his worried face contorting at the sight of her. Seeing his reaction, the soldiers pushed past Thaddeus and forced their way into the sitting room. One of them seized her arm while the other blocked Thaddeus bodily. Roux and Jax growled together, but at a word from Sela, they stayed back.

"You are to come with us, Miss Meriweather," said the guard holding her arm. "If you struggle, the blood of your friends will be on your head."

Aye, it ever was.

With a final pleading glance at Thaddeus and Jax to stand down, she let them lead her away.

When Sela was dragged through the fort gates between two guards, Caleb glared at Lord Auberon. "What is *she* doing here? She has nothing to do with this."

Lord Auberon leaned close. "Are you quite sure, Caleb? You've confessed to contact with a branded prisoner. The other men have witnessed you speaking with Miss Meriweather on a number of occasions."

When he had confessed to having saved a branded prisoner from death to his mentor, Caleb had hoped Lord Auberon would be merciful. Even so, he wisely did not name Sela, fearing that his confession would jeopardize her safety—if not his own. Without his intervention, Caleb had insisted, the prisoner would have died. But instead of understanding, his mentor had called for his guards and had Caleb arrested. Now, it appeared that he had called for Sela to be seized as well.

Had Beck betrayed them?

Sela eyed him fearfully as she approached. Her hair had been hacked off past her shoulders and hung in disarray around her pale face. Though he could not see her bandaged shoulder, one wince of pain from her and Lord Auberon would know whom Caleb had saved.

Meeting her gaze, he looked pointedly at her shoulder, then gave a tiny shake of his head, hoping she would understand.

Lord Auberon nodded at the guards, and Caleb and Sela were dragged from the parade ground and past the soldiers' barracks to the commanding officer's house, whose quarters his mentor had originally shunned in favor of even plainer accommodation.

"Bind their hands and leave us," Lord Auberon said once they had entered the gloomy hut. A soldier Caleb didn't recognize pulled his arms behind his back and bound his wrists with manacles. A second man did the same to Sela, whose face showed no pain despite the roughness of her captors.

She was a brave woman.

His mentor had lit several lanterns by the time the soldiers departed. Pursing his mouth, he studied them both from behind the dusty, cluttered desk of his predecessor.

"My lord Auberon," Caleb said quickly, hoping to alert Sela to the situation, "Miss Meriweather is an innocent in this situation. I told you that I saved a branded prisoner from death, but 'twas not her…"

Carver, forgive me the lie—

"Miss Meriweather." Lord Auberon rounded the desk and stopped in front of Sela. "That wound on your wrist. How did you get it?"

She drew herself up to her full height. "I cut myself with a kitchen knife, my lord." Despite her rigid posture, her tone was almost demure. Caleb inwardly praised her composure.

"A kitchen knife, you say?"

"I am sometimes clumsy, my lord."

"Yet your hands were steady enough to shoot a man in the shoulder from several yards away."

The fort seemed to be full of Lord Auberon's spies. "Aye, I shot Uriah Smith to save Ross and Bess Bryant."

"But Mistress Bryant died."

She nodded.

"And are you on friendly terms with Lieutenant Alexander, Miss Meriweather?"

Sela refused to look at Caleb. "Aye, the lieutenant has prevented harm from coming to me on several occasions."

"An uncommon kindness from one of the Pure. And what of saving you from certain death?"

Lifting her chin, she eyed Lord Auberon directly. He was almost exactly her height. "I recall no such event."

"You would have been unconscious at the time," Lord Auberon replied dryly.

"Nay, my lord. Lieutenant Alexander has never touched me."

She lied for him—and easily. Did she know that if she faltered even a little, Lord Auberon would hang her as he had Ira?

"Have you ever thought he held affection for you?"

"Affection?" She laughed—heartily, as if Lord Auberon had proposed an afternoon expedition to the moon. "Nay, my lord. Besides, I hear Lieutenant Alexander is soon to bond with another."

As Lord Auberon turned his back on them both, Caleb met her gaze and found it accusing. Then she knew of his impending Binding and condemned him for the liberty he'd taken with her.

She had every right to do so.

But she wasn't finished. "You must know, my lord," Sela said to Lord Auberon's back, "that I almost daily visit Ross Bryant and his son, little Thomas. Ross has asked me to bond with him once his mourning for Bess is finished."

"And will you, Miss Meriweather?" asked Lord Auberon without turning.

"Aye, I likely will."

Her candid admission burned deeper than his impending branding. He sought her gaze, but she would no longer look at him.

"Guard!" When a soldier appeared, Lord Auberon nodded at her. "You may go, Miss Meriweather, though I will perhaps request your signed testimony later."

She nodded, and the soldier escorted her out.

"You disappoint me, Caleb." Lord Auberon turned to survey him, arms folded across his pristine chest. "I thought I saw something in you—something worthy of the Righteous. Something Pure, something…set apart."

"I could not let the woman die, my lord. I had no choice."

"So you say, Caleb, and yet you still won't tell me her identity."

"I never knew her name. She was likely from Hellebore."

"You know, the soldiers who confess to impure relations with the nightwalkers say much the same. I believed you were a better man than they."

"The Carver is a God of mercy, my lord—"

"And a God of justice." Lord Auberon circled the desk and came to stand before him. "You brought me news of a plot to attack the fort, and for that act alone, Caleb, you will keep your life. Consider my decision a *merciful* one, since members of the Righteous are judged more harshly than other men. But this day, Caleb Alexander, I strip you of any title or inheritance you might have received from your father, your membership of the Righteous, your place as my apprentice and protégé, and your rank of lieutenant. From this point on, you will no longer be considered Pure or soul-bearing, and you will be forbidden to leave Azazel from this day until your dying breath."

Lord Auberon continued as Caleb's stomach plummeted. "You will be branded twice, as befitting one whose sentence of death has been temporarily deferred—a second mercy. From that point on, you will be soulless, never to have any contact with an untainted man, woman, or child, and never again to touch the sacred words of the Carver, who gives life only to the Pure. Should you commit a further offense, you will face the death penalty."

His former mentor's face hardened. "Since you have fallen further than most men—being my second-in-command and a member of the esteemed Righteous—your sentence will include an additional component. You will be branded in front of the soldiers and flogged by mine own hand, as an example to every unbranded soul on Azazel that no man, not even the great Caleb Alexander, will be spared from the Carver's wrath."

Sela had just fallen asleep next to Roux when the pounding on the door downstairs began. She dragged a dressing gown over her chemise and hurried to the landing, where a wide-eyed Briella was watching Thaddeus unlatch and unbolt the main door.

"Is it the soldiers again?" Briella and Noemia had wept along with Tempe when Sela returned from the fort, looking no worse for wear. Not wanting to upset the little girl, Sela had simply told them that the soldiers had meant to arrest someone else. Still, Tempe had not left her side until half an hour ago. Had the pounding woken her up?

Thaddeus opened the door and three shadowy figures appeared on the threshold.

"I found him outside the fort gate, Thaddeus," a man was saying. "I'm sorry to bother you at this hour, but there were few places we could take him, and he's done both of us more than a few good turns."

Sela crept down the stairs and discerned two men carrying a third between them, who looked unconscious.

"Miss Sela," said the first man as he straightened, tipping a non-existent hat in her direction. "I'm sorry to wake you."

"Ross?" Her gaze swung to the second man, who she recognized as the former Captain Foley, though rather more disheveled and dirtier than the last time she'd seen him. "What are you doing here?"

"I don't think she should witness this," Thaddeus began uneasily, but Sela pushed past them to the unconscious man they had deposited on the longest couch.

"Caleb!" she exclaimed. He'd been stripped of his coat and waistcoat, and the shirt and breeches he wore were caked with mud and blood. Dropping to her knees beside him, she reached for his hands, only to discover what she already feared—he'd been branded on both palms. Dirt smeared the fresh weals.

Tears slipped down her cheeks, but Sela was heedless of the men who watched her. "I didn't think Lord Auberon would go so far with his own protégé."

Ross spoke more to Thaddeus than to her. "He was tossed outside the fort like yesterday's rubbish. Besides now being one of the soulless, he's been flogged to within an inch of his life."

"Whatever could he have done to deserve such treatment?" Thaddeus scratched the back of his neck. "No man of his rank has ever been treated thus."

"He showed mercy," Sela said, and then the sobs choked out her voice. She looked up at the three men, seeing Jax standing next to Briella. "I know he was one of the white fists, but Caleb is a good man. Please, we cannot turn him away in his hour of need."

"I don't intend to," Thaddeus replied, then turned back to Ross, whose gaze rested on her. "Thank you for bringing him to us, Bryant, Foley. Rest assured we'll look after him."

"Nay," Ross said, still looking at Sela and her hand resting on Caleb's shoulder. "With your arm as 'tis, Thaddeus, you'll be hard-pressed to tend him. I'll stay and help you wash his wounds, and Foley can keep a lookout for any soldiers. Do you have a bed for him?"

"Aye, upstairs."

Ross faced her. "Miss Sela, what comes next is not for any young woman to witness. He is badly injured. But perhaps you could heat some water, boil some cloths."

Briella slipped a steadying arm around Sela's waist and helped her to her feet. She was kind enough to answer Ross on her behalf. "Aye, Mister Ross, we'll do what we can."

Chapter Seventeen

The red fox curled on the edge of Caleb's bed, almost atop his blanketed feet, was a puzzlement. If Roux was here, where was Sela?

As he surveyed the small, shadowed room, he answered his question almost immediately. The woman sat in a chair next to his bed but was slumped forward over the edge of the mattress, her hand clutching his bandaged one. He almost pulled it away, but then he realized.

He was branded now. Just like her.

The sense of loss that accompanied that revelation was crushing. He felt a stinging betrayal, an overwhelming wave of anger, and yet…was that absence of a weight on his shoulders relief? How could he be *relieved*?

Sela lifted her head, and immediately a line appeared between her brows. "Caleb?" Her tone and touch were featherlight as she stroked the back of his hand. "Do you remember what happened?"

"Aye." He wouldn't likely ever forget. The double branding in front of every soldier Lord Auberon could summon, and the humiliation of being stripped half-naked and flogged till the soil at his feet was muddy with rivulets of his own blood. Lord Auberon had even taken his signet ring, the one that matched Tucker's. But someone had brought him to Sela, and washed and bound his palms with fresh linen, and bandaged his back. He could feel the tight bands of fabric across his chest beneath a soft, open-necked shirt that smelled like lavender. "Where am I?"

"The house of Thaddeus. Ross and Captain Foley found you and brought you here."

He stiffened. He was being sheltered by a former murderer, a past accomplice to the father of the very man who had threatened Sela. How far had he fallen?

"I can't stay here." He began to struggle into a sitting position, but she easily pushed him down again.

"Don't be a fool. 'Twas Thaddeus who took you in and agreed you should be cared for."

A former murderer now willingly permitted his house to be turned into a hospital? Caleb frowned.

"You're safe, Caleb. Truly. Thaddeus tended your wounds himself. And Ross, too. If they meant to do you harm, why would they aid in your healing?"

He allowed his suspicion of Thaddeus to be eroded by his greater jealousy of Sela's intended. "Bryant is here?"

"Nay, he and Capt—*Mister*—Foley returned to their homes a few hours ago. 'Tis early morning now."

He reached out and touched her hair. "Did the soldiers hurt you?"

"Nay." Still, her eyes were puffy. "I'm so sorry for what happened. I thought Lord Auberon would be merciful to you."

"As did I." He fingered the shorter locks, recently trimmed to a uniform length. "You cut your hair?"

She swallowed. "Aye, I felt like a change."

She was lying. Still, he felt some satisfaction that the woman who concealed the truth so defiantly from Lord Auberon could not easily hide it from him. "Was it the soldiers? Or Auberon?"

Finally, she shook her head. "Nay, 'twas Uriah. He came to see me…to offer his protection in the battle to come. He didn't hurt me, only threatened to do so in the future. He cut off part of my braid to take back to Liri."

Rage simmered in his gut, though he was comforted by the lack of fear in her eyes. Sela would not be easily cowed.

Yet a moment after his observation, a hint of vulnerability entered her face. "Why did you kiss me when your future is spoken for?"

"'Tis spoken for no longer, Sela."

It was a mercy that he had thought to write to his father before meeting with Lord Auberon, in the event that he lost everything. In that lengthy missive, sealed with his own ring and given to a soldier who Caleb knew would see it delivered, he'd rejected his arranged Binding and conveyed his sorrow for disappointing his parents, but he had another young woman in mind. He had said nothing of Sela, or the choice he'd made to save her life, but Lord Auberon would likely pen his own letter following Caleb's branding.

He only hoped the news of his demise would not kill his ailing mother.

"Do you love her? The woman you're pledged to?"

"Nay. To the best of my knowledge, I've never met her. But I'm not pledged to her…not anymore. I wrote to my father before I confessed and broke off the arrangement. And besides, Lord Auberon was very clear that I will never be allowed to return to the Old Town."

"But you were going to. Why didn't you?"

He sighed. Aye, he had wanted to return, to convince the elders of what Lord Auberon, in all his admirable fervor, could not yet comprehend. That the Carver was not a God of lots, or unjust punishments, or partiality…but of mercy.

"'Twas not sin to save your life, Sela. I know now that there is no difference between branded and unbranded—not in the eyes of the Carver. 'Twould take much more than a branding to deprive us of our Carver-given soul. But still, I could not live a lie, pretending I was the same man who came to Azazel months ago. If I returned to Eremia, I knew I would overlook the wrongness of the lot. I would surrender myself to the wrong destiny. I would…forget myself.

"And so, I confessed all to Lord Auberon—though he does not know 'twas you I saved—hoping that he would see that I was no less in possession of my soul than I was two sevendays ago. Hoping he would see the error of his ways and condemn the lot. Instead, he condemned me."

"But the terrible punishment—"

"I'm no coward, though you would be easily forgiven for thinking it of me, given my actions of late. Especially since I concealed the truth of my impending Binding from you—an omission for which I would seek your forgiveness. I wasn't sure how to tell you."

"I will admit, I did think you a coward. But I never wished this fate on you." She traced the bandage covering his palm. "When I think of everything you've lost—"

He couldn't allow himself to follow her into that rabbit warren. Instead, he met her eyes—her frightening, fierce, yet beautiful eyes. "You told Lord Auberon that you would bond with Ross Bryant. Did you mean it?"

"I'm not sure that I can bond with any man, Caleb. I…I have to check on Tempe now." With a regretful look, she slipped from the room.

He let her go. Why? What did she fear?

In the void left by her absence, he recalled his brother's face. He would never see Tucker again. Aye, his soul was intact, but what of his heart, which felt like it had been rent in two? The ache of loneliness swept over him.

What he would give to hold the words of the Carver, which he'd treasured from boyhood. Though he'd committed many of the passages to memory, the confiscated extracts were the greatest of losses. On Azazel, his soft hands—trained for a lifetime of scholarship—would need to turn themselves to farming and industry. He was not afraid of hard work, but already he felt his bond with the Carver slipping away from him.

As Roux slept on at his feet, he gazed at the bandages, and the strange sense of relief returned to him. There was one advantage to the soul marks on his palms, and only one. As a condemned man, he was free to bond with a branded woman—even the one woman who'd always been denied him.

If Ross Bryant didn't claim her first.

Caleb lasted less than two days in bed before he was up again, helping Thaddeus and Jax with various chores. Sela tried to keep Tempe from wandering to the windows to watch him move about the yard, but in vain. Never had the Remenant sheltered someone of such high standing. Though Caleb moved stiffly, and Thaddeus admonished him to take it easy more than once, he worked hard, weeding Noemia's entire vegetable garden and turning the earth in the bare patches ready for planting before the sun had set on his fourth full day.

At the end of another distracted lesson—for Sela and Tempe both—she dismissed the young girl to play and watched from her bedroom window as Tempe headed straight for Caleb. Even Roux had abandoned his usual place on her bed to scamper around Caleb's heels as he pulled weeds and turned shovelfuls of rich, dark earth. Sela watched as he knelt to scratch the fox around the ears with obvious affection. When Tempe emerged, he smiled and said something to the girl that made her laugh.

"How was my daughter today?" At Briella's voice behind her, Sela turned, but the woman came to stand at the window. Together, they watched as Caleb pointed to something in the dirt and Tempe knelt beside him eagerly, heedless of her clean dress.

"She attends to some lessons better than others."

Briella smiled. "He is certainly an intriguing guest. And remarkably strong, despite his injuries…and his former occupation."

Sela studied Caleb. Aye, he was healing quickly from the flogging and branding, but some wounds were yet to scab over. He was desperately uneasy at being in Thaddeus's house, despite the welcome he'd been given, and the devoted following he'd gained in Tempe and even Jax. He might have fled, had he been able to move from his bed those first two days. The first time he had met Noemia, the woman had asked to touch his face so that she might imagine what he looked like. While he'd submitted to her examination, Sela had seen his discomfort, the same expression he wore when he studied his newly branded palms.

While he was respectful and courteous to Thaddeus and Briella, he continued to hold them at arm's length, as if he only saw them through the lens of their former occupations.

Briella's lips pursed thoughtfully. "He's asked to work in the fields alongside Thaddeus tomorrow."

"Tomorrow? Nay, 'tis too much, too soon."

"So my brother told him." Briella sighed. "It might be good for him to get away from the house for a while. I know he is troubled by our pasts."

"Briella, I am sorry—"

"Nay, Sela. There's no need to apologize." She gazed out the window, smiling faintly as Caleb tugged on a carrot and handed it to Tempe, not even flinching as her hand brushed against his. "The true face of a man is always revealed when he plays with a child. Caleb Alexander is Carver-fearing and will recognize his prejudice soon enough. The Carver is kind enough to point out such shortcomings to the one who truly seeks His face."

Thaddeus and Briella spoke of the Carver as often as Caleb did, though Sela hardly knew what she thought of their statements. Did she believe in a deity who had condemned Liri to exile and lifelong suffering? But if it was the Righteous and the priests who had done the wrong, and not the Carver Himself—

Even so, why had the Carver not intervened? What of Noemia's three lost children? Or Briella's fatherless daughter? And Bess Bryant, who would never see her son's first birthday, thanks to Uriah Smith's cruelty?

And now Caleb…

"'Tis time for Tempe's bath and supper," Briella said with a sideways glance at her. "Why don't you go down and tell her?"

Sela smiled. "I know your intentions."

"My intentions?" Briella echoed innocently, gliding out of the room. "I don't know what you mean."

By the time Sela had reached the back door, Briella had already called Tempe to her bath. Sela knelt to hug the girl, who planted a muddy kiss on her cheek and sped past to the kitchen. Picking her way across the garden, Sela looked up to find Caleb paused in his work and leaning on his shovel, watching her.

The candle-burning scholar had rather easily morphed into the hardworking farmer, she thought, glimpsing his shirtsleeves rolled up to his elbows, his tanned forearms, and the healthy sheen of sweat on the bared vee of chest below his throat. His hair was still tied back in a queue, but it was windswept and curling on his brow. Only the slight crease of his forehead testified to the pain he must feel from his wounds.

"'Tis late," she said, stopping in front of him. "Why don't you come in?"

Nodding, he plucked the shovel from the dirt, gathered up the rest of his tools, and carried them to the small shed that leaned against the back of the house. Returning to her side, he brushed the dirt from his breeches, wincing slightly.

"Briella said you plan to work with Thaddeus tomorrow."

"The garden is finished," he said with a shrug.

Spotting raw, unbandaged flesh, she reached out and seized his hands. "Caleb, your *palms.*" Besides the brands, there were so many blisters that she suddenly understood the wince she'd glimpsed before.

"They will heal."

"Or become infected. Come inside and I'll tend them for you."

"*Caleb?*"

They both looked up to see a red-coated man standing only yards away, mashing his hat between his gloved hands. A large sack sat at his feet.

"Beck," said Caleb, but without moving forward to greet him. "What can I do for you?" His tone was distinctly wary.

Beck stepped closer, and Sela saw the anguish twisting his features. "Though I would understand if you didn't believe me, Caleb, I swear I didn't betray you." He stuffed his mangled hat beneath his arm, hefted the bag, and handed it to Caleb, who took it reluctantly.

"What is it?"

"Your things. When I heard of your confession down at the fort, I guessed Lord Auberon wouldn't be as generous as you hoped. I managed to hide most of your belongings before the soldiers arrived to confiscate them. Those extracts you used to pore over night and day are in there too. I saved them all." He gave a low laugh. "Lieutenant Killian used to hide smuggled cargo beneath the loose floorboard under his bed. You can thank his dearly departed soul for the temporary hiding place."

Something stole over Caleb's face, like a condemned man learning of his reprieve, and a smile curved his lips. "Thank you, Beck. You have no idea what this means to me."

Beck returned the smile. "You're a fool, Caleb."

"A fool for the Carver, aye."

The lieutenant's gaze strayed to her. "Miss Sela. How are *your* wounds healing?"

"Well, thank you."

"I must say, I am pleased to find Caleb here with you." Smirking, he gave her a suggestive wink. "Fool as he is, he'll make you an excellent bondmate."

Caleb scowled. "Quiet, Beck."

Beck's smile didn't dim. "Well, I must be off, before Lord Auberon's spies witness me associating with the tainted and brand me too." Despite his lighthearted manner, his eyes were solemncholy. "I wish you both the very best, and I'll see you…when I see you."

"Thank you," Caleb replied, nodding at the sack in his hands, and Beck gave a quick bow and set off up the hill. For a long moment, Caleb stood gazing up at the outpost, blazing in the last light of the day, the sorrow evident in every line and angle of his body.

Sela took his arm. "Now let me see those hands of yours."

And he turned away and consented to be led inside.

After he'd stowed his belongings beneath his bed and washed up as best he could, Caleb found Sela in her bedroom. She was waiting for him with a bowl of warm water, a jar of salve, and a roll of bandages. She motioned for him to sit on her bed and then pulled up a chair next to him.

At the first contact of her fingers on his palm, he flinched, not only because of the blisters and the brand, but because he was still unused to touching her. She said nothing, but swallowed her lips, the pulse at her throat throbbing.

"I cannot work with bandaged hands," he said as she began to clean the wounds. Though, he admitted silently, he'd worked for months with gloved ones.

"Didn't the healers who trained you warn of the dangers of infection?" she countered, and he fell silent. After a long moment, she looked up. "I'm sorry. I shouldn't remind you of what you've lost."

Hadn't he said the same to her, months ago? "You meant no ill by it."

To distract himself from the pain, he watched her. He had to admit that Thaddeus and the others had looked after her well. She was no longer painfully thin, as she'd been on the *Deliverance*, or pale with the lingering effects of fever. Her eyes were bright and her hair lustrous, no evidence of the gunshot wound beneath her dark blue gown. When he'd asked after her stitches, she said that Thaddeus's sister had taken them out for her. Even the cut on her wrist was healing well.

Though she noticed his attention, and colored under it, she said nothing as she gently smeared salve across his palms and bandaged both hands, leaving his fingers free. Finally, she leaned back. "Now you can have your supper," she declared, like he was a small child ready to receive his reward for good behavior.

He didn't move. "Sela. You know that Smith plans to attack

the settlement. Though Lord Auberon has been warned, Smith will likely still proceed with the attack before spring comes, just as you overheard. He won't have the manpower or the guns before then, but he'll need to strike before Lord Auberon's reinforcements arrive from the Old Town."

She nodded.

"Thaddeus has contacts on the far side of the island. There's a small settlement there, Anjelica, known for being a place of relative moderation and restraint. He wants you and the others to travel there, with the boy, Jax."

"And what of you and Thaddeus?"

He sighed. "Some of the settlement men, including Bryant and Foley, want to join with Smith against the soldiers. That can't be allowed to happen, and Thaddeus, for one, agrees with me. Both of us must stay here and try to sway the settlement men before too much blood is shed."

"And Beck?"

"I'll warn him personally. For now, 'twould be best if he stays in the fort."

"I can fire a gun as well as any man. I can stay here with you and fight."

"Nay. Smith will be counting on your stubborn insistence to stay, and you'll only put the other men in danger trying to protect you from him. Besides, Anjelica is not completely safe, as no place on Azazel is safe. Thaddeus needs you to protect the women and little Tempe, alongside young Jax."

"And you agree with his plan?" She chewed her lower lip.

"Wholeheartedly."

She grimaced. "When does he want us to go?"

"By winter's end, four months from now, I'll have escorted you there. You need only stay a few months, until the fighting is over and order is restored. When 'tis safe again, I'll come for you."

"And if Uriah gains the upper hand?"

"Then I'll still come for you." Though every muscle rebelled against him, he reached out and threaded his fingers through hers.

She didn't resist him. "And I'll find a way to take you and your sister from Azazel."

As she blinked away tears, he pulled her to her feet and into his arms. She pressed her cheek against his chest, and her breath warmed the column of his throat, fanning a fire he hadn't known was smoldering fully to life. Sliding his hand beneath her head, he tilted her face until his lips hovered over hers. His arm around her waist felt her tremble, and he caught his breath at the trust in her eyes. She'd never looked at Ross Bryant so, nor Ezekiel North.

Aye, she cared for him, more than the firebrand would likely ever admit.

A second before he kissed her, he hesitated. There were still secrets between them, and she'd confessed to murder, though ever he chose to forget it. And forgetfulness was the mark of a fool. Sela's well-honed skills in war and weaponry—clearly evident in the altercation with Smith's men—caused him to wonder about the details of the attack she'd not yet relayed to him. Torn between admiration and doubt, he closed his eyes and rested his forehead against hers. Even that small liberty felt wrong.

Feeling her stiffen, he opened his eyes to a gaze glittering with violet fire. She was angry, and with good reason. "Sela, I—"

"I think you've said enough." She extracted herself from his embrace and fled the room.

Tucker had always praised his steadiness, his lack of double-mindedness compared to other men. The Caleb of the Old Town never doubted his judgment. What was it about Azazel—about Sela—that threw everything into chaos and uncertainty? That cast doubt on everything he'd once believed? Why did the brands on her palms lead him to distrust her and second-guess himself, when he knew how unfairly the soul marks were bestowed…his own plight being a case in point?

Knowing that he'd just shattered Sela's fragile trust in him, Caleb propped his elbows on his thighs and laid his aching head in his bandaged hands. And, for the first time since he'd learned of Tucker's absolution six years ago, he surrendered himself to the fierce emotions surging through him, and he wept.

Over the next two sevendays, Sela carefully avoided him, though she continued to visit her friend Esther, and Bryant's young son…or Bryant himself. Briella and Jax both went with her, sometimes bringing the little girl, Tempe. Tempe, who was as eager for Caleb's presence as Sela was for his absence.

The days with Thaddeus in the fields beyond Belladonna were long, with plenty of time for thought, which was both a blessing and a curse. It was because of Thaddeus that Caleb had been given work in the first place, and his influence prevented the other hands from beating him to death the first day he appeared at the farm. How strange that a doubly branded man—a murderer—now vouched for Caleb's worth, rather than the other way around.

"Thank you," Caleb had said to Thaddeus when they were finally alone. The man was well-built and strong, but with only one usable arm, Caleb doubted he could protect either of them in a serious altercation.

Thaddeus nodded. "Work hard and give them time to come to their senses. They will soon realize that you are the same as they."

Caleb's mouth curved wryly as he understood that Thaddeus intended the words for him as much as for the other hands. Everything he'd read in the Book of Souls supported the equality of man before the Carver, but he found it difficult to believe such an assertion when years of learning still drummed their steady rhythm across his mind, ordering and patterning his every thought.

Even with Thaddeus vouching for him, the settlement men and women tended to shun him, perhaps fearful that he was an ambidexter who spied for Lord Auberon. Those who he'd tried to help before his branding, like Bryant and Foley, were more welcoming, but he sensed they were still uneasy. Many a trip to Belladonna for Thaddeus resulted in the hurling of verbal insults and stones. He'd flinched but not retaliated, having often witnessed the cruelty of the soldiers and done little to prevent it.

Aye, he deserved their wrath. And Sela's, too.

Two sevendays after he'd arrived, on their rest day, Briella took him aside and asked him to escort Sela to Bryant's house.

"'Tis about to rain," he objected. Though it was late in the season for 'sooners, the clouds gathering overhead resembled the same ones that would abruptly empty their wrath on unsuspecting travelers. He'd been doused by many a similar one during his first months on Azazel.

"I know, but Sela is determined to visit little Thomas. He was dauncy last sevenday, poor thing."

"You honestly believe she'll want me along?"

Briella frowned. "'Tis time you two made amends."

Caleb nodded, but when he met Sela outside on the porch, her displeasure rivaled Briella's. "I don't need your help." Turning, she hurried down the stairs.

He caught up to her easily, keeping pace as they descended the hill. She moved faster than any 'sooner. "Where's Roux?"

She barely glanced at him. "Playing with Tempe."

He kept silent until they had passed the settlement, then he took her arm and pulled her off the path. It was growing darker, and the wind had picked up as they walked, pelting them with fat drops of rain.

She tried to jerk her wrist from his hold, but proved no more successful than she had the first time she tried the maneuver. "Let go of me."

"We have to find shelter."

"There's shelter at Ross's house."

"It'll storm long before we get there." A rumble of thunder, much closer than the last, seemed to prove the truth of his words, and she finally shrugged.

He led her to a small cave he'd found on one of his early morning runs, large enough for a man of his height to stand without slouching, but no more than ten feet deep. By the time he reached it, they were both half-soaked, and Sela was shivering. When he tried to give her his cloak, she pushed him away. "Like I said. I don't need your help."

"You'll freeze to death before you accept it?"

"I'll freeze before I accept anything from you that you would rather not bestow."

Guilt softened the anger spiraling through him. "I'm sorry, Sela. I don't know what came over me. I regret my hesitation…more than you know."

She crossed her arms, but the fight seemed to go out of her. "To you, I'll always be unworthy."

"That's not true."

"Aye, 'tis. So long as you see yourself as irreparably tainted, you'll see everyone else that way, too. And the more you try to set yourself apart, the more you'll push all others away."

He frowned. "'Tis not wrong to pursue a life of purity."

"Purity, Caleb, or *quarantine*?" When he didn't answer, she stepped closer. "For you, like all of the Righteous, 'tis a case of once impure, always impure. You'll never see Briella as anything other than a nightwalker. And Thaddeus a murderer. And me…" Her eyes filled with tears. "To you, I'll always be a sinner too."

"Thaddeus took me in. He likely saved my life. I'll forever be grateful to him."

"So says your fine, reformed mind, but what of your heart? What of your eyes that disapprove and your hands that hesitate to touch anything you might once have called unclean?" She seemed to choke on the next words. "Including me?"

As the rain faltered, she moved to pass him. "I'll see you at Ross's."

"Nay." He seized her shoulders and held her firmly before him. When she winced, he remembered her gunshot wound, and slid his hands down her arms to rest above her elbows. "Don't go to him."

"Why?"

It was well past time to bare his soul to her. "Because Ross Bryant doesn't love you the way I love you."

She stared at him, more hurt in her eyes than he believed was possible for anyone to bear. "Don't play with me, Caleb."

"I would never play with you, Sela." He stepped closer, his hands encircling her waist. "I've loved you since before the *Deliverance* sailed into this bay. You even caught my attention six years ago, not because of your eyes, but because you had a passion for the Carver that matched—nay, exceeded—my own."

She wilted a little. "I don't believe in the Carver the way you do."

"If you don't believe in Him, why are you so mad at Him?"

Her shoulders sagged, the passion he'd admired a moment ago now doused by some weighty care. How did the fire in her come and go so easily? Yet he knew she cared for the Carver, just as she cared for him.

He knew she loved, because of how deeply she hurt.

He leaned down and kissed her forehead, then her cheek, then her mouth. When she finally met his eyes, he summoned his courage.

"Bond with me, Sela." This time, he kissed her with every ounce of his passion. "Bond with me for real, not for pretend."

Chapter Eighteen

Lightning flashed in the distance, and at the accompanying growl of thunder, the rain began to fall in earnest. Sela broke away from the kiss and stared at Caleb, wondering if she'd heard him correctly amidst the din.

"What did you say?"

He pulled her close and leaned in to speak in her ear. "Bond with me."

She shivered, despite his warmth. "Because you want to keep me from Ross? Or Uriah?"

"Because I want you for myself."

He gazed steadily at her, and her eyes dropped to his boots. She knew he was neither impulsive nor flippant. If he wanted to pursue her for the Binding, he meant every word. But did he really know his own mind?

"I don't want to be with a man who sees me as sullied."

"I don't see you as sullied, Sela." He fitted his palm over hers. "And if you are, then I am as sullied as you." He scraped his fingers back through his hair roughly. "Surely you see that there is already a bond between us."

One objection overturned, her mind swiftly moved to another, but this one, she could not confide. To bond with Caleb, or any man, might lead to a child. How could she tell him how much she feared Noemia's fate? To lose even a single child to the lot, as Liri had…she could not bear it. She would rather remain childless.

"Tell me what you're thinking." He stroked her cheek. "I want to share your burdens."

"You can't." When he opened his mouth to object, she spoke first. "Can I think about your request?"

"Of course." But the concerned look remained.

When the storm passed, she asked Caleb to wait outside Ross's hut while she visited, and he reluctantly agreed. She told Ross that she could not bond with him, but he was far less easily persuaded, and it was half an hour before she rejoined Caleb. They headed back toward Belladonna, Caleb's arms swinging at his sides, his hands occasionally clenching as he ran his fingers over his roughened palms. Lightning flashed in the distance like the wink of a lighthouse.

"Aren't you going to ask me what I said to Ross?" Sela asked him, sensing his restlessness.

"I'm guessing you'll share when you're ready."

Tears swelled unbidden in her eyes, and she turned her head to hide them from him.

"Sela?" He sounded concerned. "Are you all right? What did I say?"

"Nothing."

Teodoir had said the same thing when she and Cadence had sought sanctuary with him, just after she'd accidentally killed Joss Brigham. Was it a nudge from the Carver, as her father used to say? A sign that she needed to be honest with Caleb?

Stopping in the middle of the path, she turned to him. "'Tis not nothing. I owe you the truth about what happened back in the Old Town."

"What truth?"

She turned her hands palms-up. "Why I was branded. You say you love me, but you don't know the full story yet."

She wanted him to insist that he would love her regardless of what she'd done—perhaps his love was as conditional as she feared it was—but he simply nodded, then waited patiently for her to speak.

"My sister Cadence and I attended the mandatory religious classes at the seminary, with Father Monroe as our instructor. Usually, especially on the days when night fell early, my brother would come for us in the afternoon to escort us home. The streets of the Old Town are dangerous, as you likely know. But one afternoon, my brother didn't come."

She told Caleb of waiting for Liron as a thick fog descended, then her realization that her brother wasn't coming. Her fateful decision to hurry home unescorted instead of calling the priests.

"Before we'd gone far, a man accosted us. He was wealthy, but he'd clearly been drinking, and he tried to…he tried to…" She shook her head, banishing the fear that swirled around her even now. "I told Cadence to run, but she just stood there. I defended myself with the knife I kept in my boot, but then he came for me again and pinned me to the ground. We struggled, and in the process, he fell on top of my knife. At first, I didn't realize that he was dead. I thought I'd only wounded him. But when I saw his eyes…" She shuddered.

"What did you do?" he asked softly, the question emotionless. Was he quietly furious on her behalf? Or did he doubt her account?

"At first, I ran with Cadence to the house of my mentor, Teodoir. When he'd calmed us both, he said exactly what you said before—that I could tell the truth when I was ready. I told him what happened, and said I wanted to run away…or hide. He said that I couldn't ask Cadence to lie for me, but he was fearful of the soldiers, too. He took me home, and we told my parents what happened—and Liron, when he finally returned. Liron wanted to take me to the mainland, but after what Teodoir said—"

"You had a change of heart."

She nodded. "I left home before any of the others were awake, save Roux. I presented myself to Father Monroe at the seminary, and though he was sorrowful for what happened to me, he had no choice but to give me over to the soldiers."

The blood seemed to have drained from Caleb's usually tanned face. "And what of your trial?"

"'Twas skewed against me from the start, for the man I killed was training to replace the high priest."

"*Josiah Brigham* was the man you killed?"

She nodded, fear throbbing through every vein at the memory

of the man—and his father, who, disgruntled with the justice delivered her, had ordered her death. "Did you know him?"

"Aye, I knew him." His voice was grim. "Joss was my cousin."

"I thought you died," Caleb managed amidst the chaos erupting in his brain.

Sela stared back at him, white with shock. "*Died?*"

"Though I didn't know 'twas you who killed him, I knew of Joss's death. Since I was preparing for Azazel, Tucker went to your trial on behalf of our family. When he returned, he said you'd been sentenced to death and would hang in the morning."

Shock morphed into confusion. "I don't understand. The high priest did sentence me to death, but 'twas commuted to exile straightaway. Tucker must have been there to hear it, because he spoke to me directly afterward."

"My brother *spoke* to you?"

She nodded.

"What did he say?"

"He gave me a letter to give to Liri but said little else. Just that he would not deliver it himself. I wondered, when I first saw you on board the *Deliverance*, that he didn't give it to you."

"Do you still have this letter?"

"Nay. 'Twas destroyed in the storm that tossed Molly overboard."

He shook his head. Mysteries abounded, not the least of which was why his brother would lie to him about Sela's fate. Why had Caleb not thought to ask the name of the condemned woman? He returned his attention to Sela, who had gone as pale as he had when he realized she was his cousin's murderer. Nay—accidental killer.

Did he believe her?

She sounded genuinely grieved. "I'm sorry, Caleb. I had no idea Joss Brigham was your cousin—or Tucker's—or I would have told you the truth when you discovered my second brand."

"I met Joss only twice. Though our fathers were brothers, I barely knew him."

Her fingers gripped his arm. "But you knew his character and reputation?"

"Enough that I asked Tucker to plead for mercy for you on my behalf. Though I didn't know you were Liri's sister at the time."

Her face fell. "Tucker said naught at my trial."

Caleb's heart clenched. Tucker had said the exact opposite to him. If he believed Sela, he would be calling his own brother false.

"Why would my brother lie to me, Sela?"

"I don't know," she replied, clearly anguished. "There were many at the trial who were afraid for their own necks. Liron said that Lord Brigham was close to several others, including Lord Auberon, who'd apparently advocated for my death."

If that was true, Caleb had unknowingly devoted himself from the very beginning to a corrupted man.

"Her presence here must be difficult for you, Caleb." Lord Auberon's words to him as he watched Sela aboard the *Deliverance* suddenly made sense. At the time, he'd supposed that his mentor thought him vulnerable to lust, but Lord Auberon had been speaking of his cousin's death. Why had the man not corrected him when he failed to recognize Sela as Joss's killer?

Instead, he'd encouraged Caleb to watch Sela. Had Lord Auberon wanted him to fall in love with her? But for what purpose?

"You don't believe me, do you? Tucker's word and Lord Auberon's both stand against mine...not to mention that Joss himself also stands between us."

He studied her. She'd left her knife at the scene of the crime. Only the most foolish murderer would ever do so. And she'd turned herself in, knowing that she might be condemned to hang, when she could have run away with her brother. She'd shown more courage than he had when he confessed to his mentor. And all in defense of her eight-year-old sister—firstly, when the young girl's life was threatened, and secondly, when Sela's freedom would mean forcing her sister to live a lie.

It was eerily similar to his own rationale for approaching Lord Auberon.

"Why did they not question your younger sister, Cadence?"

Her eyes narrowed. "None at my trial had any thought of justice."

After a long moment, he sighed heavily. "I believe you, Sela." She'd shared the truth without any prompting. And everything he knew of her to date suggested she was fiercely honest, except when she lied to protect him.

"But you're still angry."

"At Joss and his wickedness, not at you." It was true. Though, but for Joss's actions, he might never have met Sela.

Nevertheless, what more could possibly come between them?

"I won't ask you to choose me over your brother."

He reached out to touch her, but his body once again betrayed him, and he hesitated. She looked at his hand, pain twisting her features.

"I care for you, Caleb," she said at last. "Aye, far more than I care for Ross, which I told him just now. But until we can touch each other without flinching or faltering, I cannot bond with you."

Emboldened by her admission, he faced her directly. "Then bond with me in name only. At least until we are both healed of the past enough to desire more."

Though desire would be no issue for him at least, he understood the magnitude of the wall that lay between them—the importance of rebuilding her trust. If it took months—years, even—he would sacrifice all for her. And he would show her he loved her, regardless of Joss Brigham or Tucker Alexander or anything else that threatened to keep them apart.

Indecision flickered across her face, warring with a fear he didn't understand. What did she yet keep from him?

Yet the realization that she was afraid crumbled a little of his own anxiety, and he reached out to hold her. She trembled against him, and after a long, terrifying moment where he feared she would reject him again, her arms slipped around his waist. When she finally spoke, there was no longer any trepidation in her voice.

"Aye, Caleb. Then I'll bond with you."

What had she done? Sela had thought her gunshot wound painful, but the Binding was infinitely more so. She had innocently admired Noemia's tattooed finger without any comprehension of the agony that had accompanied the elaborate design.

In Eremia, it was customary for the Binding to be symbolically tattooed on the fourth finger of the right hand, though the wealthy often wore gold or silver bands instead of undergoing the painful procedure. On Azazel, jewelry was scarce and what little could be found was expensive. Since she'd known of his privileged status, Sela was surprised that Caleb agreed to the tattooing procedure so readily. Back in Eremia, his family could well have afforded a gold ring.

A few days before their Binding, Briella had summoned Sela into the kitchen, which had been scrubbed clean a sevenday ago when Caleb and Sela had walked home together and announced their intention to pursue the Binding.

Briella had smiled at Sela. "Are you ready?"

"Nay, but I'm hoping you've done this before."

After tracing a design on her skin with a pencil, Briella had mixed black ink with water in a small dish. When she'd produced a sharp, pointed object—three needles tied together—Sela had cringed, but Noemia had gripped her arm and squeezed her reassuringly.

Pursing her lips, Briella had stretched the skin on Sela's finger, making it as tight as possible, then held the bundle of needles at a right angle to the skin and pricked her deeply. A bead of blood swelled from the incision and Briella wiped it away. Sela winced and chewed the inside of her mouth, wondering if Caleb had showed any discomfort at the perforation of his skin.

"Are you all right?" Briella said, her voice compassionate.

"Aye." Sela gritted her teeth. "Go on."

After half an hour, she was ready to weep. She watched as Briella wiped away the blood and rubbed the ink mixture into the deep needle marks. When Sela could stand no more, Briella washed her hand with water mixed with rum and announced she was finished. Smiling to herself, Briella carefully bandaged her finger, telling Sela that she could take it off at the Binding ceremony.

Sela rotated her right hand, wondering what design lay underneath, since she had not dared to watch. "Where did you learn to do this?"

Briella's smile faded. "All nightwalkers are marked thus," she replied, though she didn't indicate the location of her own tattoo. "We learn the trade from a young age."

Ever curious at Briella's mysterious past, Sela had wisely closed her mouth and helped the women clean away the bloodied fabric before scrubbing the table again.

Even with the settlement inhabitants in a state of unrest over Uriah's warmongering, the members of Thaddeus's household had been overjoyed at the news of her decision to bond with Caleb.

Noemia had smiled broadly and immediately began preparations for the small feast that would follow their ceremony, while Briella hugged her tightly and eyed her gown, as if sizing up her measurements. Jax had looked crestfallen, though Caleb's offer to help him muck out the horse stalls that afternoon—a much-hated chore—had gone a long way to softening the blow. Tempe danced around her and begged to pick the flowers, while Roux barked and ran even larger circles around the room. Caleb, who had taken Thaddeus aside, later told her that the man had agreed to conduct their ceremony.

Sela had scarcely seen Caleb, who rode out with Thaddeus almost every day, and she was fearful that harm would come to him. Rumor had it that Lord Auberon had recalled many of the soldiers from the other settlements to guard Belladonna and the fort, fearing Uriah would strike before spring.

Sela only thought of Liri. She had not attended her sister's Binding, and now Liri would miss hers. Though she knew her family would have greatly approved of Caleb, a loneliness dogged her as the day approached. None of them would know of her Binding, and if there were children…

She had been surprised that Caleb suggested bonding in name only, and nearly rejected the idea, since she knew it would never be a permanent solution to her fear. But the sincerity in Caleb's expression had swayed her, and she wondered if she might one day confide in him. She knew there were methods to avoid having children—beyond the obvious—though they weren't always reliable, as Tempe's existence attested. Perhaps Briella would know more.

Sela blushed. There were other ways around the lot. Many women had successfully hidden their pregnancies and their children from the soldiers, since there was no census on Azazel. Perhaps she could do so as well. Having watched Caleb with Tempe, how could she deny him the chance to be a father some day?

She woke the morning of the Binding without the impending dread of the past sevenday weighting her chest. Oddly well-rested, she wished that she could see Caleb, but he had stayed the night with a friend of Thaddeus.

When Noemia checked on her, she imagined her mother bustling into the room, talking about some delicious ingredient with which she'd recently experimented. Tempe's boundless excitement mingled with Cadence's sweet voice as she chattered about the embroidery on Sela's purple gown and stroked Roux's soft fur. Briella, tightening Sela's stays until she could hardly breathe, was a slightly more unexpected replacement for Liri, murmuring both gentle words of encouragement and sly words of instruction for when she was finally alone with Caleb.

Before she could slip the purple gown over her head, the door opened and Noemia came in, something draped over her outstretched arms that resembled both the twinkling silver of stars and the gleaming brilliance of spun cloud.

"I can't see it," the older woman said with a smile. "But by the reaction of the few gathered downstairs, I'm guessing 'tis lovely."

Briella and Sela exclaimed together, and even Tempe paused in her chatter to inspect the gown, which looked as if it had been stitched for a queen. With reverence, Briella lifted the dress over Sela's head, and she stared at herself in the looking glass.

Low-necked in the current fashion, with full skirts and close-fitting sleeves that finished in lace cuffs and tiny embroidered flowers at the elbows, the white gown seemed to shimmer as she turned, and she realized that sequins had been sown into the V-shaped bodice and the front pleats of the skirt. Falling in graceful swells of fabric to the floor, it fit her unusual height perfectly, unlike Briella's gowns, which were always a little short.

"She's beautiful, isn't she?" Noemia said, breaking the silence.

"Aye." Briella sounded distinctly tearful. "Aye, she is."

"I don't understand." Sela submitted to their ministrations as Briella guided her to a chair and began on her hair. "I was going to wear the purple gown."

"Mister Alexander had something special in mind," Noemia replied, still smiling. "He had it made for you using the dimensions of one of your gowns."

"He had it *made* for me? But 'twould have cost a fortune."

"Aye," was the only reply.

Sela thought of Beck and his rescuing of Caleb's belongings, and remembered the gold coins Caleb had offered her his first day on Azazel. Had he brought much money with him from the Old Town? Why had he spent so much of it on her?

And *white*. White was purity, the color of the Righteous. What did he mean by ordering her a gown in such a color? Certainly, she could never wear it again, unlike her violet gown, a pretty but practical hand-me-down from Briella.

"Did he mean for it to be this color?"

Noemia nodded. "'Twas his only specification to the dressmaker."

As tears threatened, Sela focused on Briella's earnest face as she artfully arranged her hair and stuffed pins into the gleaming mass to secure the elegant style. Since Noemia had taken Tempe to the kitchen to feed Roux, the two women were alone.

"Thank you, Briella." Warmth swelled in Sela's chest as the woman moved around the room, picking up undergarments and stowing them away. "Thank you for everything."

Her grin was distinctly impish. "Thank your future bondmate. Is there anything you want to know?"

Sela colored. "Nay, thank you." She couldn't tell the woman the truth of her agreed arrangement with Caleb—and she doubted Briella would understand her fear.

Outside her door, Tempe waited with a bouquet of wildflowers, and Sela smiled and kissed the girl's forehead. A shy Jax, dressed in his sevenday best, offered her his arm. He would soon be as tall as she was.

Thinking of a young Liron, she let him escort her down the stairs and to the garden, where a party of thirty or so had gathered.

The Remenant had been kind to many in Belladonna and the surrounding settlements, and despite their tainted pasts, Thaddeus and Briella were highly esteemed. Noemia had worked for days to prepare the feast that would follow the ceremony, which would continue well into the night. Those Carver-fearing inhabitants of Belladonna who did not frequent the taverns had little occasion to celebrate, and every Binding was ample reason for merrymaking.

In the middle of the knot of people on the stretch of grass stood Thaddeus, so tall and straight-backed he reminded her of Teodoir, or perhaps her father. He smiled and looked to Caleb, who stood at his left.

Their gazes connected at the same moment, and Sela was pleased to see Caleb's eyes widen. His broad shoulders filled the red coat of an ordinary lieutenant, embroidered with silver thread and studded with silver buttons above a neat ensemble of pressed waistcoat, ruffled shirt, ceremonial sword, and white breeches. His chestnut hair was neatly restrained in its usual queue, but tied with a black ribbon that matched the hue of his freshly polished boots.

Was the coat Beck's doing? She hoped that none of Lord Auberon's spies would glimpse him wearing it, since in doing so, Caleb demonstrated outright defiance of his former mentor's authority.

Jax escorted her through the throng of people, which parted and then closed behind them. The young man bowed and placed her hand in Caleb's while Sela passed her bouquet back to Tempe, who stood with Noemia and Briella. Roux sat beside the little girl, his bushy tail swishing back and forth like the pendulum of a grandfather clock.

Caleb took possession of her elbow as he turned her to face Thaddeus, his voice low in her ear. "You look more beautiful than I could have even imagined."

"Thanks to you." Her lip wobbled a little, but she smiled her gratitude at his generosity, then made a show of inspecting him. "Roux is going to love your coat."

He grinned, but his eyes shone intensely as Thaddeus began to speak.

The words of the lower-class Bindings were always few, most preferring to focus on highly symbolic rituals the people could understand. After several solemncholy words and a blessing, Thaddeus reached out and laid Caleb's right palm atop Sela's smaller one, positioned so that the fingers of one hand touched the underside of the other's wrist. Producing a length of cord from a hidden coat pocket, he slowly wove the strand around their flattened palms, beginning at Caleb's wrist and finishing at hers. The crowd gathered around them abruptly quieted. This was the most sacred of moments.

"Long ago, the Carver instituted the Binding so that two might become one." Thaddeus laid his hands atop theirs and closed his eyes. "The knots the Carver ties, let no man or woman seek to undo."

Caleb looked into her eyes, baring his soul to her. Hope and trust and love and desire mingled in the blue depths. The warmth of his hand bled into hers, and for a single moment, as the pulse at his wrist beat through the tips of her fingers, her palm felt indistinguishable from his.

Then Thaddeus was unwinding the ceremonial cord and winking at them both. His eyes lifted to survey the crowd. "My dear friends, I am delighted to present to you Caleb and Sela Alexander. May the Carver bless them and grant them long life together, and may He grace their union with many children."

Sela blushed, wondering if Thaddeus would utter such an enthusiastic blessing if he knew about their agreement, but Caleb only smiled. The small crowd burst into cheers, and Roux broke away from Tempe to prance at Caleb's side, as if he suddenly felt the need to compare coats.

Caleb reached for her hand and carefully unwound the bandage around her finger. Sela leaned close to inspect the tattoo and found it almost a duplicate of Noemia's, though a slightly more inflamed version. According to Briella, it would take some sevendays to heal properly. Taking Caleb's hand, she unwound his bandage and discovered a larger version of her own band, though without the double knot.

"How did you stand the pain?" she whispered. "I nearly strangled Briella more than once."

He grinned. "That's easy. Pain is but temporary, Sela. I simply imagined you waiting for me at the end of it."

Chapter Nineteen

At some point, after Noemia had stuffed him with more food than he ever wished to consume in one sitting, Caleb drifted back into the main room, only to find it utterly transformed. The chairs had all been pushed back to make space for the dancing, and the women had even hung lanterns and chains of flowers around the room.

A fiddle struck up a lively tune, accompanied by a woodwind pipe and several instruments he hadn't seen before, and Caleb felt his blood start to thrum. Thaddeus twirled Noemia around the dance floor, the woman wearing an outrageously yellow gown that clearly no one had thought to dissuade her from donning that morning. Several other couples had already joined them, including Jax and Tempe. The little girl was coaching her older friend in the steps of the dance, while he seemed to be doing more than his fair share of stepping on her feet.

Across the room, Caleb's bondmate appeared, the white of her elegant gown snagging his attention almost immediately. Beside her, Thaddeus's sister whispered something in her ear, and she shook her head emphatically. Was it something to do with him? He crossed the room to her side and Briella nodded at him and stepped away, leaving them alone.

"Anything the matter?"

"Nay."

A more honest answer was not long in coming as a woman's voice broke out in accompaniment of the other instruments. Briella had a fine contralto voice, and she was joined by the mezzo-soprano tones of another woman Caleb didn't recognize.

Sela tapped her foot in time to the music, a rousing tune where the dancers stomped their feet and men swung their partners high in the air as onlookers cheered and raised their glasses in approval, occasionally joining in with a particularly stirring chorus.

Early on in the evening, Caleb had noticed a solemncholy Ross Bryant, to whom he had yet to apologize for stealing Sela, and the former Captain Foley. Both men kept to themselves in the corner, though Bryant frequently stole glances at Sela. No doubt he fiercely regretted bringing Caleb's unconscious person to Thaddeus's door and helping Caleb to remain among those of the living.

Sela had formally introduced Caleb to her friend Esther, who was as shy and skittish as Jax, but soon relaxed around him. Caleb noticed that Briella greeted the younger woman as warmly as any other guest, as did Thaddeus.

He glanced at his bondmate in time to see her lips move wordlessly. Was she mouthing the words of the song? "Do you know this one?"

"Aye."

"Briella is a fine singer, but I think she would enjoy having another person up there."

"Nay, Caleb. I can't sing. Not when Liri is still…"

He understood. She'd been solemncholy at times throughout the day, likely remembering her family, as he was remembering his.

He slipped his arm around her waist. "Would you like to dance, then?"

She looked up at him and some of her sadness melted away. "Aye, I would."

Taking her hand, he led her into the middle of the room. He'd spoken the truth to her before—it was worth any pain to have her in his arms, tucked close against his chest as if he were her anchor in a storm. The white gown fanned and pressed against his thighs as she spun, then returned to him. She danced as gracefully as she walked.

He pulled her closer as a slower song began. "Who taught you how to dance?"

"My father and my brother. And you?"

A playful grin danced on his lips. "My mother. She insisted Tucker and I learn so we wouldn't disgrace ourselves with the first woman we invited to dance."

"You dance even better than you fight."

"Is that a compliment?"

She laughed. "That would depend on how well you fight, wouldn't it?"

He felt a heavy hand on his shoulder, and Thaddeus spoke into his ear. "She's here."

"She came after all?"

"Aye. She's in the kitchen. She says she couldn't get away before now."

"Thank you, Thaddeus." He turned back to a surprised Sela. "Come with me. I have something to show you." He tugged on her hand and she followed him to the kitchen, weaving between guests who variously smiled and winked suggestively.

He opened the door and motioned for her to enter ahead of him. "Think of this as a bonding present."

"But Caleb, you already bought me the dre—" She halted abruptly as she saw the woman standing on the other side of the room. "*Liri?*"

He smiled to himself as the two sisters ran to each other and embraced. It had taken some effort to track down Liri in Smith's camp, especially as she was rarely left alone. But several days ago, he had found her, and Liri had promised to try and attend at least part of their Binding celebration. Caleb had wanted Liri to be there when Sela woke in the morning, but he knew everything depended on Smith's whereabouts, and whether or not she would be able to get away.

Liri held her sister at arm's length and admired her gown. "Sela, you look so beautiful. I only wish I could have come earlier."

"Can you stay?"

She shook her head. "Uriah will return to the camp soon, and the children are sleeping and don't know I'm here. If Uriah was to get back and find me gone…" She shuddered, and Caleb felt a wave of pity for her.

Sela hugged her again. "Thank you for coming. To have you here…it feels as if I'm a little more whole."

"You can thank your bondmate for that." Liri's eyes sought out Caleb in the shadowed kitchen. "Uriah plans to attack by the end of winter. He nearly has the manpower, and the weapons, too."

Sela spoke before he could. "Lord Auberon has recalled more soldiers to defend the fort. And the settlement men—"

"None will be able to stop him." Liri sounded exhausted, as if she'd been running for years and had only just stopped to catch her breath.

Perhaps she had.

"We'll be careful," Caleb assured his new sister-in-law. "I'll keep Sela safe."

The kitchen door opened a crack and Liri shrank into the shadows.

"Sela?" Briella's voice. "Why don't I help you out of that gown so you can leave with Caleb when you're ready?"

"Nay, I—"

Liri stepped forward. "Go, Sela. I'll be here when you get back. I promise."

As Sela darted away, her sister faced Caleb with a wry expression. "I see you failed to take my advice."

"Didn't you ask me to look after her?"

"From a distance." She sobered. "I was sorry to hear of your branding, Caleb. Was Sela the woman you saved?"

"Aye." He wouldn't tell Liri that Sela had nearly died trying to rescue her from Uriah. The poor woman bore enough guilt already.

"Thank you," she said after a long pause, her voice quivering a little. "From the way my sister looked at you all those months ago, I didn't think Ross Bryant had much of a chance anyway."

He smiled sadly. "I meant what I said before, Liri. I mean to stand up to Smith. Promise me…promise me you'll seek us out if you're ever in trouble. If not for your own sake, then for the sake of your little ones."

She met his gaze, but seemed to look through him instead of at him. "I don't want to put Sela in more danger, Caleb. Or you."

"You're my family now, too. I would give my life to protect you both."

Sela reappeared, wearing a purple gown that matched her eyes and carrying a small bag. His heart leaped, and he fought to keep his breath even.

"I must go now," Liri said, allowing Sela to embrace her one last time. She whispered something in the younger woman's ear, and Caleb watched Sela sag a little.

Then the door clicked closed and Liri was gone.

Sela crossed the room to him and fell into his arms, burying her head against the soft fabric of his shirt. He expected her to cry, but she only curled her arms around his ribs, careful to avoid the healing wounds on his back. "Thank you," she whispered huskily. "I know you must be remembering Tucker."

With those words, he fell a little more deeply in love with her.

Even in her grief, she was still thinking of him.

Both of them were quiet after bidding farewell to the others and setting out on horseback to whatever mysterious midnight destination Caleb had in mind. Sela had been sorry to leave Roux behind, but she would return for him in the morning.

Caleb had lifted her into the saddle and mounted behind her, pulling her close to share his warmth. She sensed he was troubled, but she could also feel the rapid beat of his heart against her back and was pleased it matched hers.

"Thank you," she said a second time. "Was finding Liri why you were gone so often this sevenday past?"

"Aye. Smith frequently moves his campsite. Sometimes he

takes Liri and the children with him. Other times, he leaves her behind with a guard."

She shuddered, the gentleness of the man whose arms encircled her only highlighting the cruelty of Liri's bondmate.

"What did she say to you at the end?"

Sela was glad that he couldn't see the color threading down her neck. "Like Thaddeus, she wished us many years of bonded bliss—and numerous children."

He chuckled softly. "One day at a time."

She almost told him of her fear, then, certain he would not ridicule her for it, but something held her back. She forced herself not to contemplate that something further. "Where did you say we were going?"

"I didn't say. But we're here."

He dismounted and reached up for her, swinging her down easily. Distracted by her thoughts, she was dimly aware that they'd passed through the settlement to the other side of Belladonna, and had paused near the cave where he'd asked her to bond with him. The moonlight fell softly upon a small cabin, larger than Ross's hut but far smaller than the white house.

"It has a nice view in the daylight," Caleb murmured into her ear before catching her up in his arms. She gave a small squeal and batted at his shoulder, but he didn't put her down.

"I don't understand. How did you—"

"Thanks to Beck, I had a little money left over after the gown." He smiled down at her. "This house is the other reason you didn't see much of me this past sevenday. Though the swill-bellied officer who lived here formerly was reluctant to deal with a branded man, money is thankfully not considered so tainted, and he happily accepted my gold from Beck's hand."

"Beck helped you?"

"Aye. He's a good friend. A better man than most."

He took the two steps in one long leap and carried her across the small porch to the door, which he shouldered open. He gently put her down and squeezed her arm. "I'll be back in a few minutes. I need to attend to the horse."

When he was gone, she stared around. Caleb Alexander was certainly full of surprises. The lantern-lit cabin was spacious, with two rooms jutting off either side of the living space, and though modest, it was clean and well-appointed. The cupboards were stocked with food—likely, she had Briella and Noemia to thank for that—and someone had stacked a tidy pile of split logs next to the hearth ready for burning. Presumably the same person who had lit the lanterns for them.

Crossing to the larger bedroom, she peeked inside. It was a plainer version of the room she'd awoken in at the outpost, but with a beautifully embroidered patchwork quilt atop the large, netted bed. She dropped her bag beside the door, swallowing a large lump in her throat.

At the sound of boots behind her, she turned to find herself face to face with Caleb. He glanced behind her to the bed. "We must've been bonded longer than a day, Sela, since I already know exactly what you're thinking." He smiled, though a little ruefully. "There's a bed in the other room. I'll sleep—"

"Nay." She reached out and touched his arm. "There's no need to sleep elsewhere."

His eyes widened. "You mean—"

Her face went hot. "Nay, I'm not dissolving our agreement, I simply meant—"

"I understand." This time, his grin was almost mischievous, though she thought she also glimpsed disappointment. "Shall I help you undress again?"

Rolling her eyes, she pushed him away, hearing his deep laughter as he strolled into the other room. He had lived too long with Beckett Arkwright. Shutting the door behind him, she took advantage of his absence to hastily undress, shivering in her chemise as she braided her hair. How had she managed to forget her dressing gown on the one night she sorely needed it? She was safety tucked beneath the covers and had even blown out the lantern when the knock came at the door.

"May I come in?"

"Aye."

Caleb slipped into the room carrying a second lantern, which he stowed on a small table next to the bed. She tried not to watch him as he shucked his coat, waistcoat, sword, boots, and stockings. But when he slipped his shirt over his head, it was all she could do not to stare, gaining a far more comprehensive view than the day she'd seen him bathing at the beach. Beneath the terrible wounds of his flogging, which she'd briefly glimpsed before as Ross and Thaddeus tended to him, his muscles were taut and well-defined.

What did scholars do back in the Old Town—practice tossing heavy tomes to each other?

He turned, caught her staring shamelessly at him, and grinned. "Reconsidering our agreement, Sela?"

Her mouth fell open, and she forcefully averted her eyes from his bare chest. "You sleep without a shirt?"

"You make me sound like a savage." He dragged the ribbon from his hair and slid into bed beside her, thankfully not stripping past his breeches. "I'm simply a practical man at heart. I have to save my shirts for when you get injured in foolish altercations with land pirates."

Her blush began again in earnest as he blew out the lantern. Why had she agreed to this? Perhaps she *should* ask him to sleep in the other room. She shivered, dragging the covers higher up her chest.

"Winters are not so bad on Azazel," he murmured. "But I can start a fire, if you wish."

"Nay," she managed at last. "There's no need for a fire." Embarrassment kept her warm enough.

But after ten minutes of shivering, she felt him turn to face her and remembered that he was a light sleeper. "I'm sorry. Am I keeping you awake?"

In answer, he reached out and pulled her back against his chest. She startled and he flinched, but not, she thought, because he still considered her tainted. Was it true that he'd never been with a woman? Feeling his heart outpace hers, she guessed it was so.

How rare a man he was anywhere he lived, but especially on Azazel.

One of his arms curled around her waist and the warmth from his skin bled into hers until the trembling eased. His other arm braced against the top of her pillow, and she felt his fingers slip into her hair, loosening the braid. His gentle caresses threatened to steal her wakefulness, and she fought the wave of exhaustion sweeping over her.

Aye, she knew now why the women of Azazel risked having children, especially if their bondmates slept without shirts.

But for Caleb's sake and her own, she had to remain strong. Because after everyone they'd lost—parents, siblings, friends, mentors—neither of them could afford to lose even one more.

She woke with the light, which filtered into the room through pretty yellow curtains that brought to mind Noemia's gown the day before. More of the good woman's handiwork? Despite the chillness of the air, she was blissfully warm, her heartbeat steady beneath her palm.

Nay, not *her* heartbeat. She froze.

Though she didn't remember moving in the night, somehow she'd come over to Caleb's side of the bed, and she was now snuggled closely against him, her cheek resting in the hollow of his shoulder, the fingers of her right hand fanning out across his bare chest, which rose and fell steadily. His right arm encircled her back and came to rest on her hip, while his left hand was draped loosely across his stomach.

She would have shifted away, but a quick glance at his face showed he was still asleep. She took advantage of the fact to study him, from tousled hair, to thick, dark eyelashes, to a strong jaw now shadowed by a day of stubble. Though his features mirrored his brother's, Sela had long since ceased to notice the resemblance between them. Caleb was fire to Tucker's ice. But what would he do when he woke and found her touching him?

The pattern of his breathing changed and she soon had her answer. His eyes slid open, and when he saw her proximity to him, he smiled lazily. "Good morning, beautiful Sela."

"Sorry," she said, and went to pull away, but the arm around her back tightened and he tugged her closer.

"Stay. Please."

"I thought you said you were a light sleeper. Why didn't you push me away when I came onto your side?"

His fingers slid into her hair again and he smiled flirtatiously. "Did you want me to?" He chuckled. "I foolishly hoped you sought me out for affection and not for warmth."

"And if 'twas the latter?"

"Then I'll gratefully receive whatever gift is freely given."

Sela laughed, and as if they moved of their own accord, her fingers strayed to his stubbled cheek, tracing the line of his jaw. She raised herself on her left elbow and a spark lit in his eyes. Stroking a lock of his hair, she found it thick but softer than she'd imagined. In answer, his hands slid around her waist.

Oh, she was a fool.

"You know," he said seriously, "though circumstances on Azazel have driven us together, Sela…if I'd known you back in the Old Town, I still would have pursued you for the Binding. I decided as much while we were aboard the *Deliverance*."

Then he'd given his heart to her long before she was even aware of his regard. Even if he doubted everything else, he had known the truth of his feelings.

"Though I'm guessing I would have needed to ask your father's permission, and your brother's, too."

Something stirred at their feet and Caleb jerked upright, pulling her back against him protectively.

He laughed a moment later, the tension easing from him. "I wondered if Roux would truly stay with little Tempe."

Her fox, who'd been curled up on the end of their bed, stood, stretched, then offered them both a congenial smile. When her bondmate grinned back, the fox bounded over and all but jumped into Sela's lap, licking her face with a vulpine purr that would have roused the dead.

"Did you think to ask Roux's permission?" she asked Caleb before being batted with the fox's bushy tail. "He's very picky when it comes to strangers."

In answer, Roux launched himself against Caleb's chest, giving him a cheek full of fox slobber before shrieking and leaping from the bed to run circles around the room.

Caleb raised an eyebrow at her. "Was that it?"

"Aye." She laughed, inwardly thanking the fox for having prevented her from doing something stupid, like baring her soul to Caleb. "That was it."

Chapter Twenty

His life with Sela had settled into a strange rhythm. Since it was not safe for her to be alone, he escorted her to the white house each day so that she could work alongside the other women while he went with Thaddeus and Jax to the fields or completed all manner of mundane chores. Caleb and Sela would frequently eat with the others before making their way to the home that he hoped would be safer after Uriah Smith was soundly defeated.

Before winter ended, he would need to escort her and the others to Anjelica, and he loathed to leave her, feeling the approach of spring like an immovable deadline. Each night she slept at his side she became more a part of him, and though she had said nothing to dissolve their agreement, he sensed she wanted to. Though he knew something held her back, he also saw that pushing her for the truth would only heighten her defenses. So instead, as the nights grew colder, he simply held her, grateful that the Carver had given him the strength to allow her the space she needed.

The settlement men remained undecided in their support of Smith or the soldiers, and Caleb and Thaddeus spent every evening they could spare visiting houses, trying to sway them for peace. But the cruelty of the soldiers had increased of late, even for minor infractions, and it was difficult to persuade a man that Smith's tyranny outpaced Lord Auberon's when he was nursing wounds from a recent flogging. The inhabitants of Belladonna—who had borne the brunt of the fort's wrath for years—wanted revenge.

And Caleb could hardly blame them.

Would it be wiser to move the women and children well before winter was at an end? Selfishly, he'd kept Sela with him, even rejecting Thaddeus's generous offer to stay at the house with the others. Perhaps he should speak to Sela about going sooner.

Near the middle of winter, he awoke one night to a frantic knocking at the door. As Roux leaped to the floor, Caleb pulled on his boots and shirt and reached for the flintlock he kept loaded and primed beside the bed.

"Stay here," he said to Sela, who'd awoken, and slipped into the main room where he lit a lantern.

The sight he glimpsed through the window was not what he'd expected, and he quickly opened the door wide, lowering his flintlock. Liri stood on the rain-soaked threshold, clutching a small child in her arms and holding the hand of another girl, surely no older than five years.

"I'm sorry, Caleb," she said simply, and burst into tears.

"Come in, please," he replied, noting a darkening bruise on Liri's cheek and a bloody scrape on the back of her hand.

Gliding into the room wearing a dressing gown over her chemise, Sela bolted forward to hug her sister. "You're soaking wet! Quickly, come warm yourself by the fire. I'll get some blankets."

While Caleb stoked up the fire and heated water for tea, Sela tucked blankets around Liri and her girls, the occasional exclamation of delight bursting from her lips as she studied the children.

"This is Anwen." Liri indicated the sober-faced older girl, who looked much like her mother, with damp blonde hair and serious green eyes. A large bruise on her cheek was twin to the one on her mother's face. Liri handed her younger daughter to Sela and the girl immediately latched both hands around his bondmate's neck. "And this is little Sela, named for her aunt. She's just turned three."

Both Selas turned to face him, and he sucked in a breath. Already tall for a three-year-old, the girl had Sela's straight black hair and sweet features—even her unusual violet eyes. Seeing the light of vulnerability in his bondmate's expression, something that had previously been a puzzlement to him clicked into place, and he stood and came over to them, kneeling in front of his older niece.

"Would you like to see something amazing?"

Reluctantly, the girl nodded, her eyes watching every movement of his hands. Careful not to startle her, he whistled softly for Roux, who came running from the bedroom. Both girls squealed as they sighted him. As if sensing their fear, the fox put on his gentlest demeanor, and soon he was curled in little Anwen's lap while the girls nibbled on some bread Sela had brought them.

When his nieces were finally asleep in the second bedroom, snuggled up with Roux, Liri closed the door and came out to face them. By the light of the lantern, he glimpsed dozens of bruises smattering Liri's face, collarbone, and arms. Caleb's fists clenched behind his back. For a man to do such a thing to any woman, let alone his own bondmate…

Sela hugged her sister close, but Liri was the first to pull away. "I know I shouldn't have come," she said with a quick glance at him, "but the girls—"

"You did the right thing," Caleb assured her. "You're safe here."

Liri sniffed, and some of her timidity hardened into outright defiance. "Though he has always been cruel to me, Uriah has never once raised a hand against our girls. But tonight, he was drinking, and Anwen said something—I don't even remember what 'twas. But he was so angry, and he struck her on the cheek—you have likely already seen the bruise."

Sela's eyes flashed. "He's a monster."

Liri nodded. "I knew I had to escape before he harmed the girls further."

"How did you get away?" Caleb asked softly.

"Uriah's sister, Elsie, is kind to me—as kind as Uriah is brutal. She and some others helped me to leave while Uriah was unconscious. Though when he wakes in the morning…" Her gaze moved between them and she looked faint. "I fear I have put you both in danger."

"Nay, Liri." Caleb glanced at Sela. "I thought to take Sela to Anjelica soon, perhaps even tomorrow. It will be no trouble to take you and your children with us."

"Tomorrow?" Sela stared at him. "I didn't think—"

"Let us sleep on it," he said quickly, seeing Liri's shoulders sag.

"Aye," Liri agreed, her eyelids already shuttering. "We will sleep on it."

While Sela helped her sister into dry clothes, Caleb latched and bolted the door and dragged a heavy chair beneath the handle for good measure. Finding his sword, he stashed it beside his bed with his flintlock and knife, glad he would sleep between Sela and any intruder. Though he doubted there would be any sleep for either of them tonight.

When Sela finally entered their room, she looked weary and ashen, as if the fire had once again left her. She slipped into bed beside him and quickly sought his arms. He leaned back against the headboard, relishing the feel of her.

"Thank you," she said at last, her eyes dry but oddly vacant.

"Things will look better in the morning. I'll not let any harm come to your sister or her children."

She swallowed. "Uriah beat her. She lost her unborn babe because of it."

Heat swirled through him, though he tried to mask it. She needed his steadiness, not his righteous ire. "Smith is another kind of evil."

He pulled her fully into his lap, caressing her cheek with one of his newly callused hands as she leaned her head against his shoulder. She was slightly damp from the child she'd held so closely.

"You fear the second lot, don't you, Sela?"

She stiffened and raised her head, searching out his face in the semi-darkness. "How did you know?" If a voice could be soulless, Sela's was a likely candidate.

"I saw you holding your little namesake with the same fear in your eyes as when you touch me…or I touch you." He gentled his tone. "Do you fear bonding with me in truth because we might lose our child to the lot?"

She hesitated, then released a long, slow breath. "Aye." Her hands curled around his neck. "Liri lost her eldest, a boy and twin to Anwen. Noemia lost all three of her children. I could hardly bear to lose our son or daughter. And so I thought…"

Understanding swept through him. But how could he reassure her when he feared the same? *Carver, what is Your will in all of this? You give and take away. Would you even take our child?*

"I'm sorry, Caleb. I should have told you before I agreed to bond with you."

"'Twould have changed nothing."

"Nothing?"

"I would have pursued you just the same." He stroked her hair. "I can't take away your fear, Sela—or my own—but the Carver promises to do so. For He does not give us a spirit of fear, but power and love. Whatever the future holds, I believe 'tis for our good."

"How can the taking of a child from his mother's breast be for her good?" She buried her face in his neck. "I don't understand."

"Nor do I," he confessed. "Not truly. But 'tis said that there will come a time soon when all will be made right. Perhaps that is the good the Book of Souls spoke of, long ago."

After Uriah makes war on Belladonna, Carver? Are You in support of revolution when the government is evil and corrupt?

Sela's tears trickled down the collar of his shirt and he hugged her closer. There was a way to comfort her, but not when she was still so lost and bound up in so many fears. Perhaps once Liri and her children were safe from Smith's grasp, he could take Sela to Anjelica permanently. And if there was a child—or children—they could face Lord Auberon and the lot together.

"Please don't leave me," she murmured once she was relaxed in his arms and nearly asleep. He doubted she would remember her request in the morning. "I don't want to go to Anjelica, Caleb."

"I'll never leave you." He kissed the top of her head, choosing to let the second statement go unanswered. "I promise."

"Don't make promises with your lips that you can't set your mind to keeping," she mumbled, as if quoting a household prophet.

And then she was asleep.

Before the sun had fully hauled its bulk over the lip of the horizon, another visitor arrived unexpectedly on their doorstep.

"Come in, Thaddeus," Caleb said, glad that Liri and her children were still asleep, probably exhausted from their nighttime journey.

Sela bustled about, steeping tea. She handed a mug to each of them, then sat next to Caleb. "Is everyone all right, Thaddeus?"

"Aye, they're fine, though Briella is feeling poorly again." Thaddeus looked to him. "I came about Smith."

"His bondmate and daughters are here," he told the older man. "Smith beat Liri and struck his own daughter. They sought refuge with us last night."

"Aye, I suspected they might be in Belladonna after what I heard."

"What did you hear?"

"Smith knows his bondmate has gone, and given Sela and Liri are sisters, he's likely guessed she's here."

"I thought to take them to Anjelica today."

Thaddeus scratched the beginnings of a beard. "Nay, Caleb, there'll be no taking anyone to Anjelica, not now. Smith's men are watching every road and mountain trail into Belladonna." He sighed heavily. "From now on, no one leaves this part of Azazel without Smith knowing."

On Thaddeus's advice, they agreed to move to the white house for the time being, which was a far more defensible location, especially now that Liri and her children were with them. Besides, there would be several guns at the house, and they would have a better chance of defending the women and children.

Caleb had chided himself multiple times for leaving the removal of their loved ones to Anjelica so late in the season, though likely Liri's leaving had sparked Smith's retaliation— another burden of guilt for the woman to shoulder. *"He thinks of naught but possession,"* Thaddeus had told him sevendays ago, as Caleb guessed he'd told Sela, and he resolved not to let either woman out of his sight.

Thaddeus stayed to escort them back through Belladonna, though seeing how Liri's girls feared the large man, Caleb was almost sorry he had. Liri, looking dauncy and still weary, hugged her eldest daughter close in the wagon Thaddeus had brought with him and now drove with his good arm, while Sela walked beside Caleb holding her namesake, who clung to her like a barnacle to a ship's hull.

Over his bondmate's shoulder, the girl's violet eyes followed Roux who capered about, trying to snatch a butterfly from the air. She giggled, happily unaware of the troubles that dogged her mother and older sister.

Caleb sighed as they passed the taverns, then neared the outskirts of the settlement. So far Liri, with a shawl covering her hair and her face buried in her daughter's tresses, had gone unnoticed. But if Smith's spies heard where she was…

He glanced behind them. So early in the morning, hardly anyone moved about. Only a lone soldier stood in the middle of the muddy street, wearing polished black boots at odds with the muck and a white coat that blended in with the pale dawn.

A *white* coat?

Caleb swung around and took in a head of tamed copper hair followed by a pair of icy blue eyes and a mouth that had dropped open in shock.

A soft gasp broke from the woman beside him.

"Tucker," Sela whispered.

His brother had come to Azazel.

Sela watched Tucker walk toward his brother as the color seeped from Caleb's usually tanned face. Behind them, Thaddeus had paused with the wagon. Did her sister now witness the reunion of the brothers?

I would spare you this pain if I could, Liri.

"Caleb!" Tucker neared them, his deep voice possessing an almost boyish hesitancy. "I just arrived on Azazel this morning. I'm so glad to see you well."

"How are you here?" Caleb had hardly moved from Sela's side. She looked around. Where was Roux? The fox had suddenly disappeared, probably to chase a rabbit.

Tucker paused. "I received a letter saying that you were dauncy and like to die. I came on the first ship that was set to sail."

"As you can see, Tuck, I'm hardly dauncy."

Tucker frowned, then moved to embrace his brother, but Caleb only held up his palms, as Sela had the day she found Liri.

A rapid montage of emotions crossed Tucker's face as he looked from Caleb's branded palms, to his plain, roughly spun coat and clothes, and finally to Sela. When he glimpsed her, his features hardened.

"So, you found Sela Meriweather." He all but spat the words. "I hoped you wouldn't, though I've since discovered you sailed to Azazel on the same ship."

Caleb's arm curled possessively around her waist and pulled her close. "Sela *Alexander*. She's my bondmate, Tuck."

"Your *bondmate*?" Tucker's gaze flitted to the tattooed band on Caleb's finger. "You bonded with the very woman who murdered your cousin?"

"Aye, the same woman whose name and true fate you deliberately concealed." Caleb's gaze turned steely. "Why didn't you tell me that Joss's killer was Liri's sister?"

Some strong emotion—spite, perhaps—clawed at the sides of

Tucker's finely wrought mouth. "Because I feared the very circumstance I see before me now."

"You told me Joss's killer was to hang."

"Aye, and she should have." Tucker scowled at Sela. "If she had hanged in truth, none of this would've happened."

"Take that back," Caleb growled, and Sela glanced sidelong at him. She'd never seen him angry—not like this. "You said you pleaded for mercy for her."

"She deserved none." The hatred in Tucker's eyes was so potent, she found herself physically recoiling from her brother-in-law. "She's a *murderer*."

As Caleb clenched his fists, Liri's younger daughter began to cry, gazing at Tucker with wide eyes and a trembling mouth. Tucker glanced at her and grimaced. Then, as if realizing that the girl was too old to be Sela and Caleb's daughter, he looked past her to the wagon.

"*Liri?*"

Sela did not need to turn to know that her sister stood beside the wagon. It was a lot to take in at once for any man, but especially so for Tucker, whose wrath had suddenly dissolved into shock again.

"Mister Alexander." Liri, though pale and ailing, was more composed, holding Anwen on her hip as casually as if she compared different types of potatoes at a market. "I hope you are well."

He studied her bruised face and the marked face of her daughter. "Who hurt you, Liri?" For once, he seemed oddly anguished. His gaze on Anwen's face was particularly intense.

"My bondmate," she replied, without ceremony. "Caleb and Sela have taken in my daughters and me."

Despite Sela's fear of Tucker, her pity for him in that instant was genuine. To find out that the woman he had loved—and likely still loved, if the expression on his face was any indication—was bonded and mother to the children of another man… It rivaled his shock at learning his beloved brother was branded.

Though Caleb was just as lost to him as Liri.

"If you would excuse me, Mister Alexander," Liri said, politely cold, "I must be getting away." Taking her younger daughter from Sela, she returned to Thaddeus, who helped her and the girls back into the wagon.

"Go," Sela heard Caleb say to the older man. "We'll follow."

Tucker tracked the wagon until it was out of sight. Seeing the misery in his eyes, even Caleb had softened. "Who wrote the letter that told you I was dauncy, Tuck?"

"'Twas an anonymous note. I thought it might have come from a doctor." The fire in Tucker's voice rekindled as he looked Sela over. "Perhaps another of your bondmate's many deceptions."

"Your anger at Sela is misplaced. 'Twas not for her that I was branded." Caleb slid his arm around her shoulders. "I chose to give up my place."

"And was it worth giving up everything you had for her to warm your bed, Caleb?"

Caleb's hands bunched, but Sela stepped between the brothers. "You insult your brother's honor and good judgment, Tucker."

"Nay, Sela." His eyes were colder than she'd ever seen them. "I only insult you."

She tried to understand the reason for his anger. "I kept the letter you gave me for Liri. But 'twas damaged in a storm on the way here."

"Damaged, or deliberately destroyed?" Tucker asked, his voice mocking.

"Damaged, I swear. Liri knows nothing of it."

"So says the harlot who stole my brother's future."

Her blood heated. "I'm neither harlot nor thief, Tucker, but you are no better than my sister's bondmate, since you did *nothing* to save Liri from Azazel or any other fate. Your brother is a worthier man than you'll ever be."

Tucker's slap across her face surprised her, not only because he condescended to touch her, even with gloves, but because his hand had seemed to come from nowhere. Were her reflexes dulling? She lunged at him, but Caleb grabbed her, thrusting her aside as he sought vengeance in her place. Instead of punching his brother, he gripped the front of Tucker's white coat, drawing so close their noses were only inches apart, though Caleb stood an inch or two taller.

"Touch Sela again, and you'll answer to my fists, unbranded soul or not." Caleb let his brother go and shoved him backward in disgust. Tucker stumbled, trailed a glove along the ground to steady himself, then gained his balance.

"You would choose a woman over your own brother?"

"I trusted you, Tuck, and you lied to me. Turn your wrath on yourself." Coming to her side, his arm tightened around her again. "Go find Lord Auberon at the fort. Perhaps he can lend you a mirror and show you at least one of the things that makes a man sick to his stomach on Azazel."

Roux trotted back to them and Sela bundled him up in her arms, fearful that Tucker would shoot him. But Tucker was too busy staring at his brother to even notice the fox.

As much as she despised Tucker, she could see the grief in his eyes beneath the anger. And whatever Caleb maintained to spare her his brother's wrath, Sela knew that at least a part of it was her fault.

Aye, and her fault alone.

Chapter Twenty-One

Sela yanked on a large weed, nearly tumbling backward as the roots came free more easily than she'd anticipated. Righting herself, she tossed it aside and reached for another, relishing the warm caress of the wintry sun on her back. From the house came a bubble of laughter—Tempe, maybe, or even Anwen.

To spend so much time with her sister, after six long years of separation, was a gift Sela could scarcely comprehend. While Briella remained dauncy—the two women had barely spoken to each other when Liri and her daughters first arrived at the house— Liri had recovered quickly. Tempe and Anwen were the same age and played well together, while little Sela usually trailed her aunt about the house, or her aunt's unusual pet. Roux frequently went into hiding to escape the children whose new favorite game was to pull the fox's tail, and twice Sela watched him leave with her bondmate for the fields.

She sighed. Caleb had discovered her fear, but had done nothing to persuade her to change their arrangement. Was it because of Tucker? Since his brother's coming, he had changed from a cheerful companion to a moody recluse, and Sela missed the easy camaraderie and intimacy that had begun to grow between them.

"You're getting very tanned, Sela." Liri bent to grasp a weed beside her.

"Am I?"

"Back in the Old Town, you were always so pale."

"Weren't we all?"

As the two sisters laughed, Liri shaded her face with her dirt-streaked hand. "Caleb is a good man."

Sela reached for another weed, shaking free the earth that still clung to the roots. "Aye, he is." She risked a glance at her sister. "I'm sorry about Tucker."

Liri sighed. "Despite how he appears, there is some good in Tucker still. The boy I fell in love with is still there, but weighted by much sorrow and anger. If he lets it, it will destroy him."

"You were in love with him, then?" Sela whispered.

"Aye," Liri said at last. "I would have bonded with him, had it been poss—had he asked it of me."

Sela reached for another weed, but her fingernails grazed only earth. "I still don't understand why the Carver allowed you to be branded."

"Perhaps 'twas because I…" She trailed off and looked away. "Perhaps we will never truly know the reason, at least not in this life." That very same life seemed to drain from her eyes. "I am only sorry to put you all in danger. If not for my coming here, you might be safely in Anjelica by now."

"You already know my answer to that, Liri. Don't blame yourself for Uriah's wickedness. Besides, if you hadn't come, I never would have met my namesake."

Liri's smile was small, but wistful. "When I named her, I never expected that she would know you. 'Tis a gift."

"Sela?"

They turned to see Ross Bryant, and Sela watched her sister tense. She was always on edge, startling easily, and more frequently falling into her sightless episodes, as Sela called them. In those states, she seemed to see even less than Noemia.

"Sela, if you don't mind…I would speak with you alone."

Liri stiffened, but Sela nodded at her. "'Tis okay. I won't be long."

Hardly reassured, Liri crossed the garden to the back porch and disappeared inside. Sela turned to face Ross.

"What can I do for you, Ross?"

She kept her tone light, but the man's expression remained serious. "I'm sorry to trouble you like this, but there's something you should know." He glanced at the pile of weeds, then followed the stains on her apron to her face. "You remember Hiram Foley, aye?"

She nodded.

"Well, a ship has sailed into Belladonna's bay, captained by a good friend of Foley's. When the captain found out what was done to his friend…" His eyes flashed and he tossed his head. "Needless to say, the captain has offered passage to Foley and a choice selection of friends who wish to escape the coming war. Little Thomas and I are going to join him."

"But none of us can escape the island. If he's caught—if you're caught, Ross—you'll almost certainly be killed. And Thomas—"

She had seen more bodies dangling from the hanging tree in recent sevendays, like limp washing barely stirring in a dull breeze. Not to mention the human skulls atop the stakes that had greeted her when she first came ashore. When she'd asked Caleb about them, he admitted that the soldiers hung or impaled anyone who tried to escape Azazel, as well as those who aided them. The penalty was clear to every ship's captain who made berth on Azazel, and it dissuaded most. But now Ross wanted to risk his life—and his young son's.

"We won't be caught, Sela. Foley's friend will be careful."

"And where will you go?"

A hint of a smile appeared on his sun-roughened face. "There are places in the world beyond Azazel, Eremia, or the mainland. Places where a man—or a woman—can be free."

"But the Old Town—"

"Says that most of the world is ocean—aye, I know. Wouldn't you like to be part of the adventure that proves them wrong?"

She frowned. "Part of what adventure?"

"There's a place for you, should you wish it."

"For me?"

"And for Caleb," he said, but it sounded as if he was grinding out the invitation. "And your sister and her children, too."

"Have you mentioned this to Caleb?"

Ross hesitated. "Nay."

"Because there's something about this plan you've failed to share with me?"

"Because he was one of the Righteous," he replied flatly.

"You don't trust him?"

"Nay, Sela. He's a fine man, and I'd be lying if I said I didn't admire him, but…I'd appreciate if you kept the details to yourself. At least for now. We don't want to frighten Foley's friend."

"I'll ask him." She watched Ross gaze at her tattooed band with something like regret.

"No doubt he spun some mighty fine cheek music to win your hand," Ross said, but he was gone before she could say anything else.

After reassuring Liri of Ross's friendly intentions—though she said nothing of his offer—Sela decided to ride out to the field where Caleb was working with Thaddeus. It was not far, and she needed a break from the monotony of tending the garden and teaching the children.

"Caleb told you not to go anywhere alone, Sela," Liri protested as she mounted Jax's horse, hitching up the skirts of her gown so she could ride astride. "At least take young Jax with you."

"I'll be fine, Liri. I'm well within the boundaries of the settlement, and I'll be back before dark, I promise."

Liri's next words were drowned out in a flurry of hooves and dust.

Sela rode as quickly as she dared, marveling at the speed of Jax's horse. The settlement of Belladonna crouched at the base of the mountains she'd glimpsed her last day aboard the *Deliverance*, but to the south of it, beyond Ross's hut and the cabin she shared with Caleb, were vast stretches of farmland, which Caleb said also extended beyond the mountain range. She'd never been farther than her ill-fated excursion to Hellebore, which was still on their side of the mountains.

She wondered about the wilderness that was reputed to lie

beyond. Was it truly as impenetrable as everyone suggested? To access the other settlements, most chose the treacherous and longer coastal routes, which were fraught with danger and prone to rock falls that could easily crush a person. Some opted to brave the jagged reefs that surrounded much of Azazel, sailing or rowing through precariously shallow channels to enter the various coves and bays. Aye, there was a reason that visitors to Azazel usually came and departed via Belladonna—even smugglers.

Nearing the fields, she slowed the horse, then dismounted. Whatever she said to Liri, she'd never been this far, not even with Caleb when she accompanied him on his morning runs.

The tangled mass of green and brown before her was an impressive sight. Taller than any man and grown so close that no one could force a path between the stalks, the dense crop would be sure to harbor many of the snakes and vipers that called Azazel home, as well as the dozens of species of brightly colored birds that roamed the island. Sugarcane, Caleb called it, and it was not nearly as pretty as the tidy rows of corn her father grew back home. Instead, it was as wild and unruly as everything else that flourished on Azazel.

Hearing voices coming from the thick of the crop, she found a narrow path between two vast squares of sugarcane and tethered the horse to a slender palm tree. If any snakes appeared, the beast would undoubtedly startle, possibly trampling both her and his slithering assailant.

"Caleb!" she called, starting down the path, and the voices stilled.

"Sela?" Her bondmate sounded far away. She picked up the hem of her dress and headed in the direction of his voice.

"I'm coming!" she yelled, just as she burst into a small clearing.

"Are you, Sela?"

Hearing the orotund voice behind her, Sela spun to see Tucker, looking hot and uncomfortable in his white coat. He strode forward until he stood only a yard away. A bead of sweat meandered lazily down his temple, and he brushed it away with one swipe of his gloved hand. No doubt he wished he could dispose of her as easily.

Unfurling her fists, Sela mentally rehearsed the sequence to access the knife in her boot. "You followed me?"

Tucker nodded. "I wondered what important business had you riding like a lunatic through Belladonna."

"And are you satisfied now? I only came to find Caleb."

"To find Caleb, or to aid pirates?" He glared at her. "I know your sister is bonded to Uriah Smith."

"Uriah is a devil, or didn't you see Liri's bruised face?"

"Into what chaos have you thrust my brother, Sela Meriweather?"

She backed away a step. "Caleb and I have naught to do with Uriah save our intervention in saving Liri and her daughters."

"Or so you say." His cold eyes swept her disdainfully. "Uriah is reputed to be a very handsome man, Sela. Perhaps you have as much a weakness for a beautiful face as your sister does."

"How dare you!"

White hot anger crowded out the last of her reason and she lunged for him, but he quickly sidestepped her, and she tripped over a clod of earth. She recovered her balance, turned, and faced him. A winsome breeze fanned across her skin, cooling a little of her ire, and she hauled in a deep breath.

"Whatever you may believe about me, you have no right to question the decisions of a woman you abandoned."

"What was I supposed to do, Sela? Get myself branded and go into exile along with her?"

"Your brother never hesitated to do the same for me."

A darkness stole over Tucker's face, so cold it even dried the sweat beaded on his forehead. "So, Caleb *was* stripped of his soul because of you."

"Aye, he found me after an altercation with Uriah's men. I wasn't breathing… I was dying. Caleb lost his status among the Righteous because he chose to save my life. And because he later confessed his transgression—if a transgression it even was—to

Lord Auberon. A man just as evil as Uriah Smith."

"You could hang for those words."

"Then hang me. Perhaps, then, your brother will be rid of his affliction."

He moved so fast, Sela was barely aware that he no longer stood before her. Grabbing her wrist, he wrenched her arm until it twisted at an unnatural angle behind her back. "Don't tempt me." He wrapped his other hand around her upper arm, but his distaste in touching her was clear. He threatened murder, not ravishment.

"You would avenge Joss?"

He twisted, and she gasped in pain. "Joss, aye…and Caleb, too. You've bewitched my brother." Despite his unspoiled appearance, he smelled unpleasantly of sweat and mud. How could her sister have once loved this man—and claimed to still see the boy that had been?

More importantly, how had a man like Caleb been so close with Tucker, who hurt her with callous indifference?

"You're wrong, Tucker. Not just about Caleb, but about me."

"About what am I wrong?"

"Caleb saved my life, not because of duty, but because he loved me." Her voice was tremulous and reedy. "As I love him."

He twisted harder, and she whimpered in pain. She felt his hot breath against her ear. "Love, Sela? You *seduced* him."

"Are you angry because Caleb chose me, or because Liri chose Uriah?"

He gripped her so tightly she feared he'd break her arm. "I would have provided for her, even on Azazel. The mother of my—"

He bit off the words, but he had said enough, and his admission proved him more despicable than she'd first imagined. The pieces fell into place.

Just as something hard plowed into Tucker's back.

Tucker's momentum pushed Sela to the ground, and Caleb summoned every ounce of willpower to prevent him from killing his brother. Had Tucker broken Sela's arm? The blow to his back had broken his hold on Caleb's bondmate, but Caleb knew from numerous past scuffles that Tucker recovered quickly. Caleb grabbed his brother's coat, ducked to avoid a left hook to the head, and planted his right fist in his brother's chest.

Tucker skittered back, winded.

Caleb lunged for him again, but Sela once again placed herself between them. "Nay, Caleb. He didn't hurt me." Though the way she cradled her right arm attested otherwise, he stilled, remembering the brief exchange he had overheard before intervening.

Sela faced Tucker. "Anwen is your daughter?"

As Caleb hissed in surprise, Tucker scowled. "Aye."

"She doesn't look like you."

"Nay." Tucker's expression turned wistful. "She looks like Liri."

Caleb stepped to Sela's side. "You mean to say that Liri was pregnant when she left the Old Town? With *your* child?"

"Aye," his brother replied mutinously. "Though not far along."

Disgust at what his brother had done warred with Caleb's instinctive pity. Tucker had not only dishonored Liri by taking from her what no woman should yield, save to her bondmate, but he'd all but shunned her when she was chosen in the lot. How desolate she would have felt, how utterly forsaken—

Sela's voice was rigid with anger. "You are despicable."

Aye, Caleb agreed with his bondmate. "How could you, Tucker?"

Flinching at Caleb's use of his full name, Tucker glowered. "I would have provided for Liri and our child, though she refused my help. I *loved* her, though I was too young to realize how deeply."

"Is that why you refused to come to Azazel?"

"I thought to be like you, Caleb, knowing my weakness in the face of temptation. I knew that if I came here, I would too easily succumb… I would no longer be Pure."

"I am *nothing* like you." Caleb grimaced. "You know as well as I that to enter the ranks of the Righteous, a man must not have known a woman outside of the Binding. You lied to them about your past?" He surveyed Tucker's white coat. "You're lying still?"

"Since I am still in possession of my soul and you are not, 'twould seem that both of us have weaknesses we have never admitted to." Tucker's gaze strayed to Sela. "And none any worse than an illegitimate child."

"Children," Sela corrected. "Anwen is a twin."

"A twin?" Disbelief colored Tucker's face.

"Aye, Anwen is sister to a boy, Liron, named for my brother. He was taken in the second lot and returned to Eremia."

"A son…" His lips parted. "I have a son?"

"No more precious than a daughter." Caleb drew close to Sela, who had gone quiet. "Your selfishness would have put Liri in an impossible position when she arrived on Azazel. Have you ever considered that 'twas *you* who drove Liri into the arms of Uriah Smith?"

His brother's face turned ashen. Liri might have been able to hide her pregnancy on the sea journey to Azazel, particularly as malnourishment stole extra pounds, but once she arrived…she would have had no way to provide for herself or the babies.

Did Smith know that Liri's twins were not his? He must…

When the silence stretched to a full minute, Caleb pulled his gaze away from his brother. "Of all the things you could have proved yourself to be, Tucker, I never thought you a coward. Touch Sela again, and I'll tell Lord Auberon what you should have told the Righteous."

He turned, steering Sela ahead of him. Though he knew he was not soulless by virtue of the branding, the ache in his chest had never protested the fact more strongly than it did in that moment.

They found Sela's horse, but she indicated that she wanted to walk. Caleb led the animal along the path back to the settlement, grateful that after hearing Sela call his name, Thaddeus had excused him from his labors to accompany her home. Only when he heard her cries of pain had he realized she was not alone.

He had not expected her assailant to be his own brother.

Watching her test her arm, he frowned. "Did Tucker hurt you?"

"Nay."

Not believing her, he paused, handed her the reins, and took her arm. Trying not to hurt her further, he felt along the length of the limb, probing for broken bones.

She winced as he tested her shoulder. "The muscle is only strained, Caleb. 'Twill heal, along with all else."

Except that Tucker's actions had damaged Sela's sister so irreparably, he doubted she would ever heal. No wonder Liri could hardly bear to be around other men…

And Caleb was the brother of the man who'd abandoned her.

After this, how could Caleb reclaim the easy friendship he and his brother had once enjoyed? Tucker's callous actions contradicted everything the Righteous stood for…that Caleb stood for.

"I'm sorry he hurt you," he whispered. "I don't know who Tucker is anymore. Or if I ever knew him at all."

"Tucker has his own hurts to contend with."

Aye, he did.

"Ride with me," he said, after a long moment of studying her shoulder. "There's something I want to show you."

"You're not angry with me for coming after you?"

"You should have taken an escort. But you know that already." He allowed a small grin. "Besides, part of me is flattered that you desired my company."

Her eyes were warm. "I always desire your company, Caleb."

His breath hitched and he helped her into the saddle, then

mounted behind her. Turning the horse away from the settlement, he tried not to dwell on the way she leaned back against him, or on the passionate declaration he'd overheard.

"Where are we going?" she asked as they passed the cane fields and began to climb a twisting path to the southern headland. She was forced back against his chest.

Aye, this was one of his better plans.

"There's a clifftop beyond, half-hidden by that hill you see to our right. Though 'tis not easily found, 'tis the site of an old outpost, once used by the soldiers but now fallen into disrepair. It will have a nice view of the sunset…and everything else."

She murmured something which was quickly snatched away by the wind, and he turned his attention to guiding the horse along the rocky path.

He was rewarded by her soft gasp when they reached the top of the hill, an even higher perch than the one where he and Beck had resided. He helped her down and watched as she turned in a circle, surveying Belladonna and the bay—the northern outpost and fort crouched on the opposite arm—as well as the mountains towering behind them.

"If you look through there"—he pointed through a gap in two of the tallest mountains— "you can catch a glimpse of the heart of Azazel beyond."

She followed his index finger to the haze of emerald green, more tangled jungle than desolate wilderness, and pockmarked with low-lying fog. White-tailed eagles circled the crowns of the mountains but did not descend to the jungle beyond. Despite the fearsome rumors, he longed to explore the place that every other man dreaded and avoided.

"How do you reach it?" Sela's voice indicated she possessed the same sense of wonder, mingled with healthy trepidation.

"There are several passes through the mountains, though many of them are steep and rocky, and I don't recommend them to you for a pleasure stroll."

Taking her arm, he steered her to the edge of the cliff. Far below them, sharp rocks pierced water that was so deep, it was closer to black than blue. Sela glanced at the crumbling stone outpost, a mere shadow of the one that had housed him on the opposite side of the bay. "'Tis beautiful."

He supposed it was, crusted with moss and overgrown with weeds, in a whimsical kind of way. He was drawn to Azazel's rugged beauty, the same way one admired the intricate pattern on the back of a python. But he much preferred to look at Sela, who sank to the ground in a puddle of dark green skirts, gazing out at the orange- and purple-streaked sky as if she recognized it for was it was—a canvas of the Carver of Souls Himself.

Dropping to the ground beside her, he slid his fingers through hers and was surprised when she squeezed his hand and leaned against him. "Thank you for showing me this, Caleb."

"I've wanted to share it with you for a long time—almost since the beginning."

She glanced up at him, then, as if just remembering something. "Ross came to the house. He and Foley and some others are going to try and leave Azazel."

He frowned as she explained the details. "He offered us a place? And Liri and her daughters, too?"

"Aye. 'Tis why I came to find you."

"What would you choose, Sela?"

"I'll follow where you lead." Her casual brush against his arm stirred his blood.

"And I'll only lead where you would follow."

"'Twould be dangerous."

"I'm not afraid of danger." At least, he wasn't for himself. He reached out and stroked her cheek. "Like you, I don't believe in running from my problems." He sighed deeply. "There will soon be war on Azazel, and many innocents will be swept up in it. I have spoken with the Carver before on this matter, and I don't believe the answer is to leave…at least not yet. Not while Smith still threatens the settlement. And now Tucker—"

"I don't want to leave the Remenant either," she said, and he smiled at her odd name for their friends. She leaned into his caress.

"Then 'tis agreed—we'll stay on Azazel…for now, at least."

"Aye, 'tis agreed."

He was the first to break the silence. "So," he remarked casually, "you love me."

Her cheeks borrowed several hues from the sunset. "You heard that part of my conversation with Tucker?"

"Aye. I already told you I'm easily weakened by flattery."

"I didn't see you skulking around in the sugarcane."

He grinned flirtatiously. "Perhaps my training in the art of war was more thorough than yours. Maybe I could teach you what your brother evidently lacked."

She poked him in the ribs, and he gave a howl of protest and dragged her onto his lap, tickling her mercilessly. Squealing, she shoved him away, but she lost her balance and fell against him. They rolled together, and he easily pinned her, though he was careful not to crush her with his weight.

He plucked a twig from her hair, followed by a piece of moss. She had gone very still, watching his every movement. "Are you avoiding acknowledging the truth of my statement, Sela?"

"I thought 'twas a question." Her lips quirked.

He lightly swatted her nose. "'Twas clearly a statement." He sighed theatrically. "There's so much to teach you, I don't know where to begin."

"Aye, I love you, Caleb." She reached up and brushed his cheek. "I've long loved you."

He had dabbled in words all his life—the words of the Carver, the Righteous, the priests…even his own. He had reveled in them, finding a beauty in written language that surpassed all other created things. But his love for Sela, like his love for the Carver, was something that defied—nay, transcended—any words that might attempt to capture the sentiment, and so words, at least for the time being, were rendered utterly useless.

She gasped as he found her lips, but her resistance lasted barely a second before she slid her hands into his hair, tugging him closer, willing him to taste her. She slipped the tie from his queue and dark-brown mingled with ebony-black in willful, glorious abandon.

He pulled back slightly, and a frown stole over her features as he reached for her hands. Pressing a kiss to each of the brands on her palms, he hoped she understood the significance of the gesture.

The soul mark meant nothing to him.

Relief mingled in the purple depths of her gaze and she smiled hesitantly. "Caleb, what you have lost—"

"I consider nothing against what I have gained." He stroked the silken lengths of her hair, then slid his fingers down the graceful curve of her neck. "The Carver is still with me, and with you. And He has mercifully given us each other. We need only to be thankful."

He extracted his gloves from his pocket. "I've kept these for the day when I could truthfully tell you that I no longer desired the things I once did, Sela—a position of great standing, the respect of my colleagues—widespread renown, even."

She took the hand he offered her and followed him to the clifftop. Drawing back his arm, he hurled the gloves over the cliff with every ounce of strength in his body. Satisfied, he watched as the hateful things tumbled to the rocks below. Seeing tears in Sela's eyes, he led her to a safe distance from the edge again. Before he could pull her close, she was in his arms.

They needed to be getting back. All manner of animals and wild men came out after nightfall, and he had only a flintlock and sword to protect them. Besides, Smith's men could be anywhere…even this close to the settlement.

"Thank you, Caleb."

He tugged Sela a little closer, liking the way her arms banded around his waist, her cold nose tucked against the warm column of his throat. He moved his hands from her back to her hips, admiring her curves. Did she want to bond with him in truth?

Give her time, was the immediate reply, and he bid his hands halt in their exploration. Holding her would have to be enough…for now.

He studied the lengthening shadows.

Aye, he could afford to hold her a little longer.

Chapter Twenty-Two

Caleb sat on the back porch of the white house and watched Anwen and Tempe play together in the twilight, feeling a strange twinge in his chest at the sight.

Thaddeus had spoken truthfully—Smith's men now guarded every path and trail into Belladonna. In response, Lord Auberon had recalled most soldiers to the fort, and despite Caleb's anger at his brother, he hoped that Tucker—and Beck—had gone with them. It would not be not long until the reinforcements arrived.

What stayed Smith's hand? Surely it did not serve his plans to put the settlement on high alert, readied for his coming. Or perhaps he thrived on the fear of others.

But innocent women and children were in his path, and Caleb hated that they were now in danger.

The wooden slats creaked as Liri sat beside him. She gathered her knees to her chest, looking impossibly small and frail.

"Your daughter recovers well," Caleb said, glancing at his sister-in-law. "And yourself, too."

Most of the bruises on Liri's face had faded, though he sensed the lingering effects of Smith's ill-treatment remained.

"'Twas good of you to take us in."

"I only did what Tucker should have done." Caleb hesitated. "I'm sorry he abandoned you and the babes to Azazel."

"He told you?"

"Aye. And he's sorry for his actions, though his apology isn't worth much in the face of his neglect." He watched Anwen—his brother's daughter, he realized, and his niece by blood as well as through the Binding—jab at the dirt with a stick, Tempe leaning over her shoulder to read what she'd scratched there. "He didn't know of your son."

Liri's lower lip trembled. "I received no further word once Liron was taken. I hoped my family might recognize the unusual name and claim him, but they may have changed his name. I'm not sure even I would recognize him now."

There was a chance that Liri's infant son had not survived the return trip to the Old Town, but he would not mention the possibility—she had enough grief with which to contend.

"When this is over, I'll send back to the Old Town for word of him. And Tucker might agree to try to find him once he returns."

She studied him, as if something had suddenly occurred to her. "You said before that Sela was the woman you saved from death, Caleb?"

"Aye."

"What was she doing when you saved her?"

He sighed. It would serve no purpose to conceal the truth. "She came for you and the children at Hellebore."

"Sela was injured trying to rescue *me*?"

He nodded.

"I told her to stay away."

"'Twould seem that she rarely listens."

Liri gave a timid laugh. "Aye, she was like that as a child, too." Her tone sobered. "She could have died—she would have if not for your intervention, Caleb."

"Sela loves you," he replied, simply. "She would always sacrifice herself for you. Even at the cost of her very life." He shrugged. "Besides, 'twas not my intervention that saved her. 'Twas the Carver's."

His sister-in-law inverted her hands and studied the brands on her palms. "I don't deserve such devotion—or such mercy. Not after everything I've done."

"None of us do," Caleb replied automatically, but he squeezed his hands closed. It was still easier to forget that he was branded. To pretend that he was back in the Old Town, surrounded by family and friends.

That those same people didn't now consider him forsaken by the Carver.

Liri stood. "I hope we are worth your sacrifice."

The soft words brought his head up, and he opened his mouth to insist that they *were* worth it—that Sela and her family were everything to him.

But Liri was gone.

When everyone had retired to bed, Caleb made his way upstairs, feeling weariness in every line of his body. The men had taken to keeping watches through the night, Bryant and Foley and others— who'd planned to leave Azazel on the night of the morrow—even bedding down in the main room to take their turn protecting the women and children. It would not be his shift until the early hours of the morning, and he was determined to get as much rest as he could before then.

All thoughts of sleep fled as he neared the room where he and Sela had taken up temporary residence and heard the music emanating from within.

He paused near the door. Someone was singing, so beautifully it tugged—nay, wrenched—every tendon and fiber of his heart. The woman had a fine soprano voice, the finest he'd ever heard, even compared to the choirs of the priesthood and the Righteous. High like the warbling of a bird, yet not shrill. Though the words were muffled, he could tell it was some kind of lullaby.

Caleb pushed open the door and slipped inside, thankful for bare feet that masked his approach. Sela sat on the edge of their bed beside a child who was her twin in every way, stroking the girl's hair.

It was her—his bondmate—who was doing the singing.

He stood for a long moment, listening to the sweet lilt of her voice, so rich and pure he wondered that it didn't shatter his heart into a million pieces. Though she sang quietly, she sang with abandon, and he felt as if he was glimpsing the true Sela at last.

She turned, then, and blushed to find him watching her, but

she only held a finger to her lips. He stepped forward, gathered Liri's sleeping daughter in his arms, and carried her to Liri's room, where his sister-in-law gratefully accepted her.

Returning to his room, he closed the door behind him.

"So," he said, with a grin to mask his astonishment, "you sing much better than I do."

"You can sing?"

Caleb laughed. "Not at all."

"I'm pleased to finally find you mediocre at something." Sela smiled ruefully. "I didn't know you were watching me."

"If you did, would you still have sung—for me?"

She ventured close. "Aye. If you'd asked, I would have." She lifted her head, and the trust in her eyes stirred something in him. Aye, trust, along with something else of which he'd seen only flickers, but not yet witnessed in full flame.

Then she abruptly turned away, crimson flooding her cheeks.

Retreating to the shadowed corner of the room, she reached behind her for the hooks of her gown and he understood her embarrassment. He crossed the room to her.

"Let me," he said lightly, surprised when her hands dropped obediently to her sides. "Did you know that green is my favorite color?"

"Green?"

"Though these days, violet is a close second."

She slipped out of the gown, then turned to face him, seemingly unaware that she was only in stays and petticoats. "Oh?"

"The exact color of your eyes."

Caleb watched her gather her breath, suspecting she was gathering courage as well. "Dark blue is my favorite," she whispered. "Before you and after you." She lifted a hand and traced the section of his cheekbone beneath his eye. "If I was Liri, your eyes would remind me of the rush of an underground river, deep and steady, always knowing its way and course."

"If you were Liri?"

"From her birth, Liri sees colors as sounds, and vice versa. I don't know the name for her condition, but it troubles her little."

He tucked the information away to think on later. "What else is on your mind, Sela?"

Though he knew what she wanted to say, he needed to hear her say it. Brave in all else, she seemed oddly shy on this one matter, though he understood her reticence. In sharing her voice, she'd bared her soul to him. On the other aspects of bonding…

Hesitantly, she lifted her eyes to his. "Though like any woman, I fear the lot, I would not live my whole life in fear of it. Seeing my namesake in your arms… I will trust the Carver to make a way for us." She reached for his hand and stroked the tattooed band circling his finger, now fully healed. "Should you wish it as well…I would bond with you in truth."

"Aye." Cradling her face, he pressed his forehead to hers. "I wish it."

Her last piece of resolve melted away, and she kissed him. All timidity banished, he was surprised at her passion. Responding to it, he would have carried her to bed, but for the sudden frown on her face. She stepped back, her eyes searching the room.

"What is it?"

"Have you seen Roux?"

Caleb shook his head. "Nay. The last I saw him, he was in the garden with the girls."

"Now that I think of it, I didn't see him at supper. And he always comes in at night."

"You search the house, and I'll call for him outside. Perhaps someone locked the door and forgot to let him in."

As she pulled on a dressing gown, he left the room a little reluctantly. Perhaps this was part of the fox's plan to keep them separated, though he'd not appeared to resent Caleb before. He grinned. Perhaps the clever Roux feared an onslaught of offspring that would be forever pulling his tail and chasing him around the garden.

Aye, that was it.

On the back porch, he called for the fox, eyes roving the

backyard silvered with moonlight. With such excellent hearing, Roux would surely hear Caleb's voice. When no bushy-tailed animal came running, he searched the garden, but found nothing save a pair of rabbits that scampered away from the reach of his lantern. By the time he returned to the porch, Sela was standing there, her arms wrapped around her shoulders.

"Any luck?"

"Nay." Her voice sounded as if it belonged to a ghost. "You?"

"I haven't heard anything." He followed her to the front porch, and again they called into the darkness. Caleb had alerted Thaddeus, who was taking the first watch. The man had not seen the fox since the afternoon.

His heart clenched. Could Sela bear to lose another thing precious to her?

Sela started walking in the direction of Belladonna, hardly aware that she was still in her slippers.

Something rustled in the bushes to their right, and she turned toward it with an expectant expression. Hearing what Sela had likely not—the click of a gun—Caleb moved to her side, reaching for his own flintlock and cocking the trigger. Pushing her behind him, he aimed the gun at the bushes.

"Who's there?" he said loudly.

No answer came, and the rustling eased.

Keeping his weapon trained on invisible assailants, he guided her back to the porch. He must warn Thaddeus of a possible intruder. Though it could easily be one of the bedraggled youths from the settlement who had attacked Sela her first full day on Azazel.

He felt her sigh.

"I can't imagine where he's gone," she said despairingly, gazing toward the settlement and fort crouching below them, shrouded in shadow. "He's never been prone to wandering off. Besides, he knows of the danger beyond."

Caleb took her hand. "We'll find him, I promise."

And then the sound of cannon fire split the air, and the darkness surrounding the fort flared to life.

Chapter Twenty-Three

As Sela listened to the report of cannons and guns echoing across the bay, Caleb straightened, the former weariness she'd glimpsed in him ebbing away. He pulled her back to the safety of the house, taking her by the shoulders when they reached it.

"Listen to me, Sela," he said urgently. "You must promise me that no matter what happens, you will stay here with the others."

"I can help you. I can fight."

"Aye, and you likely will before night's end, in defense of your sister and Briella and the others. When that time comes, I'll call upon your skills. But please…promise me you won't do anything foolish."

Seeing his concern, she nodded.

He pressed a fierce kiss to her lips. "I love you." Then he bundled her into the house.

Inside, all was chaos. Half a dozen men, including Jax, stood with their noses to the windows, loading and priming weapons. Noemia appeared to be arguing heatedly with Thaddeus as he steered her from the sitting room. At the top of the stairs, Briella stood in a dressing gown, holding Ross's son, Thomas. Tempe stood beside her wearing a nightdress and a fearful expression.

As Caleb joined the men, Sela headed upstairs. Inside her room, she dressed quickly, abandoning the dark green gown Caleb had admired in favor of the men's clothes she'd acquired sevendays ago, when she'd realized how much women's clothing hindered the defense of oneself and one's friends. She stowed her knife in her boot and pocketed the small flintlock Caleb had bought for her. By the time she emerged, Liri was standing beside Briella, holding her two wailing daughters and looking more uncomfortable than fearful.

Realizing that she'd rarely seen the two women interact in all the time that Liri had stayed at the house, Sela briefly pondered the reasons for their estrangement before taking Anwen in her arms.

"Shh," she reassured the girl as the usually stoic Tempe took up Anwen's tears. "'Tis okay, Anwen. We're safe."

Though for how much longer, she did not know.

Briella smiled, but without her characteristic warmth. "Perhaps we should find Noemia's kitchen and have a little something to eat and drink."

"Aye, that's a good idea," agreed Liri, though she was deathly pale.

As the party headed downstairs, Sela gripped her sister's shoulder. "I won't let anything happen to you or the girls. I promise."

"Don't make promises with your lips that you can't set your mind to keeping," Liri returned, though no smile graced her beautiful face at the quoting of their mother. "Nay, Sela, you might promise, but Uriah is…" She swallowed. "I've known he would come for me. If he does, there's nothing you can do to stop him."

Sela stroked the gun in her pocket, lighter than a pistol but as easy to fire. She refused to fear her sister's bondmate. "I can kill him."

"Oh, Sela. Always so brave." Liri studied her with a fond expression, and Sela had the distinct impression that her sister was memorizing her features again. "I love you."

"You say that like 'tis a farewell."

Liri move to glide past her. "Aye, I fear 'tis."

As the night came alive around him, bringing hundreds of soldiers from every direction, Tucker fought his way through the onslaught to the commanding officer's house. The sharp, acrid tang of gunpowder that accompanied the thick white smoke stung his nostrils, and he discerned charcoal, along with the sulphur and the saltpeter that smelled faintly of urine. The fort had numerous cannons, and the added protection from the cannons of the two warships anchored in the bay would likely keep the land pirates more than occupied.

Nodding at the two soldiers stationed outside Lord Auberon's door, he pushed it open, only to find a flurry of activity within.

In the center stood Lord Auberon, still fully dressed despite the late hour, and as impeccably groomed as he had been that morning. Around his desk gathered several officers of varying ranks, all talking over each other.

"My lord, despite what Captain Foster says, the pirates *do* pose a threat. There is word of at least a hundred men, though more may yet be in hiding. And they have cannons—"

"Not so large as ours, Lieutenant Griffin." A short man smirked. His red coat sat uneasily on his shoulders, his collar askew, as if he'd dressed hurriedly. "And we have decidedly more of them."

"My lord," a thickset man offered, planting meaty palms on Lord Auberon's desk. "I request permission to lead some of our cavalry against the pirates. To finish the scum permanently."

"Permission is denied, Commander Judd. We will stay inside this fort, surrounded by the guns Captain Foster so generously described for us." He looked past the men to Tucker. "You are all dismissed. Attend to your orders."

"Lieutenant-Commander Alexander," Lord Auberon said when the officers had departed. "I had hoped to speak with you."

Tucker eyed the large map spread atop the desk, pinned down by several tiny weights shaped like anchors. "Is it Smith's men who attack the fort, my lord?"

"Aye, but 'tis in vain. They can burn the settlement if they like, but they will never get within a hundred yards of our guns."

Tucker thought of Liri—and their daughter, Anwen—and grimaced inwardly. "What of the innocents?"

"Innocents?" Lord Auberon frowned. "The only innocents are here in the fort, my son, behind gates that will never yield to

Smith's puny cannons." He fingered his freshly shaved chin. "You are concerned for your brother?"

Tucker nodded.

"Ah. I had hoped to speak to you of Caleb."

"*Now*, my lord?" Tucker asked, glancing behind him. Did Lord Auberon not realize they were in the middle of a firefight?

"Aye, now is as good a time as any." He came around the desk and crossed his arms. Though he was shorter than Tucker, Lord Auberon was nonetheless an impressive figure. "Your brother accompanied me on the crossing from the Old Town, months ago now."

"Aye, I know."

"Though I have no idea who sent you the letter saying that your brother was dauncy, Tucker, there is an unexpected blessing in it. Long before we reached Azazel, your brother was warring with himself over something he knew he should not want."

"Sela Meriweather." He spat out the name like it tasted of gunpowder.

"Aye, Sela. Your cousin's own murderer—or so I recently discovered. At the time, I assumed she was one of the lot. Condemned, aye, but harmless. Caleb was drawn to her almost from the first time he sighted her. I admit that I encouraged your brother to watch her for flaws, to discover the limits of her morality, in the hope that his disappointment would lead him to see her as you and I see her. Instead, he only wanted her more. He was willing to forfeit his own soul for the sating of earthly passions. And so she was the undoing of him."

"Caleb is deceived, my lord."

"Aye, and greatly so." He stroked his whisker-less chin. "Though your brother can never return to his place among the Righteous, there *is* hope for him, Tucker. If you could persuade him to set Sela aside, there might be a measure of…forgiveness. I can promise nothing, but the Carver is merciful. Especially since your brother once showed such great promise."

Lord Auberon held aloft a signet ring that Tucker immediately recognized as Caleb's. Had his brother abandoned it so easily?

Tucker considered the man's offer. Was he willing to betray his brother's bondmate in exchange for even a fraction of Caleb's soul?

"Aye, my lord. I will do as you ask." He paused, remembering Liri. "What will happen to Sela?"

"Unfortunately, Caleb denies that Sela was the woman he gave up his purity to save. Therefore, I have no case against her."

"Sela herself admitted it to me," Tucker said readily. "I would willingly attest to her guilt." He took the ring Lord Auberon offered him, sliding it onto the finger next to his own.

"Good." Lord Auberon webbed his gloved fingers together and smiled. "Well done, my son. I can see you have as much aptitude as your brother—perhaps even more so. When you have completed your task, we will speak more of your potential…and your promising future."

Tucker nodded, bowed, and left the room.

He frowned as he stepped out onto the compacted dirt. Something was wrong. The fort's cannons had not fired for many minutes now, and the sounds of fighting that had before been localized to the exterior of the fort, where Smith's men had first attacked, now seemed to emanate from within.

From within?

Retrieving his flintlock, Tucker hurried toward the parade ground that had been clogged with soldiers in red and black coats not so long ago.

Instead, he found it swarming with pirates.

The soldiers appeared to be fighting each other as much as they were fighting the intruders, and Tucker's throat clenched at the sight of so many men already sprawled in the dirt, bearing wounds from sword, bayonet, flintlock, cannon, and knife. How had the pirates gotten inside the fort?

His answer came a moment later as more shots rang out. Some of the soldiers had gone over to Smith and now fought on *his* side.

Backing away, Tucker noticed a pirate coming toward him,

his face contorted in a war cry. Raising the flintlock, Tucker cocked the trigger and fired at point blank range. The man slumped to the ground, bleeding from the forehead, and Tucker drew his sword. There was no time to reload.

He had to warn Lord Auberon that the battle had turned against them.

But when he returned to the commanding officer's quarters, the two soldiers who had been guarding the door were crumpled on the ground, unconscious or dead. Shoving open the door, he was startled to find a man standing behind the desk. Not Lord Auberon, but another man with a dimpled smile who beamed as cordially as if he'd just invited Tucker to take tea with him.

"Good evening, Lieutenant-Commander Alexander," Uriah Smith said, flicking his wrist. "'Tis good of you to finally join us."

He heard the rustle of feet behind him, but, surprised, he turned too late.

Something heavy slammed into the back of his skull, and he lost consciousness to the sound of Uriah laughing as cheerfully as if he'd just bested the devil.

"They've taken the fort."

Caleb turned from the window, stunned by Ross Bryant's report. The man had gone to spy on the battle between Smith's men and Lord Auberon's soldiers and returned gasping for breath, as if he'd run full pelt up the hill.

"The fort? *Nay.* The warships anchored in the bay—"

"Are equally disabled." Bryant dragged his fingers through his barely tethered hair. "Smith must have had saboteurs stow aboard them, ready to overpower their crews at the first sign of the attack."

Thaddeus sank into an armchair, his flintlock musket laid across his lap. "You saw the fort then, Bryant?"

"With my own eyes." He collapsed in the chair opposite. "Smith's men are torturing the officers and branding or killing the soldiers at random. Much of the fort burns with unholy vengeance."

Caleb jerked to his feet. *Tucker...*

"And what of Belladonna?" This came from Foley, hunkered down by the window.

"So far, Smith's left the settlement alone. Rumor has it that many of the settlement men have joined him."

"Though few will likely stomach what follows," murmured Thaddeus.

Caleb knelt beside him. "My brother's down there. I have to save him." Had Smith guessed that Tucker was the father of Liri's twins—and her former sweetheart? If Smith captured him, the truth could cost Tucker his life.

Foley stood, massaging his sun-reddened neck. "Captain Ward's still anchored in the bay. Though our plans were for tomorrow, and for a safer harbor, there's time to leave yet. There'd be room for all of you who wished to go."

"I thought there was space for only a few."

"Aye, but I've had word that the captain has managed to acquire another ship, a smaller vessel that might do for a shorter voyage."

Caleb's gaze strayed to the staircase Sela had ascended half an hour ago as she tried desperately to keep the children occupied. "Thaddeus?"

The man's grim eyes raised to his. "More than most, I know what will follow tonight, Caleb. If the fort has fallen, and the settlement men have joined the side of evil, there is naught to stand against Smith. If we want our women and children to be safe, we must leave Belladonna—at least for now."

"We can sail to Anjelica," Caleb put in. "Take the seaward route."

"If Smith has taken Belladonna this easily, then the rest of Azazel won't be far behind." Thaddeus rubbed his incapacitated arm. "Best we leave while we have the chance."

"But if we're caught leaving Azazel, all of us will be hanged." Caleb looked around the room. "Without question."

"We won't be caught, Alexander," Bryant insisted, a fierce look on his face. "And if we are, better to fight to the death in the pursuit of liberty than in this stinking hellhole, torn like a scrap of meat between two dogs."

Thaddeus gave a slight smile. "You're quite the revolutionary, Mister Bryant."

"Aye," was all Bryant said in return, though Caleb saw him briefly glance toward the staircase. Perhaps he hoped that his revolution would cost Caleb his life, thus gaining him Sela.

Nay, he chided himself. That was unfair.

"Then 'tis decided." Foley brushed dirt from his knees. "I'll send word to Lucius Ward. Though it'll be risky going through the settlement, perhaps we'll go unnoticed amidst the confusion."

Caleb turned and found Sela standing at the base of the stairs. He crossed the room to her, taking her in his arms. "Gather your things, quickly. We're leaving here soon, all of us."

"If you're coming with me, I have all I need." Then a crease appeared in her forehead. "*All* of us?"

"The fort has fallen. We're leaving Belladonna." He quickly explained their plan. "Before we set sail, I'm going to rescue Tucker."

She gripped his arm. "I'm coming with you. I have to find Esther. She wouldn't come with us before, but now that Belladonna is threatened—"

"Nay, Sela. 'Tis too dangerous. I'll look for your friend and bring her to you."

"She won't come with you unless I'm there."

"Your friend was present at our Binding. She knows me."

"Aye, but you were once a white fist, Caleb. She won't trust you."

He sighed but had to admit that she was right. And how could he ask her to leave her friend when he refused to leave without Tucker?

He eyed her men's clothes—far better-fitting than the ones she'd worn before, though she would never pass as a man with the obviously female shape forced by her stays. Her ingenuity made him smile despite the dire circumstances.

"Very well then, but stay close to me."

She clutched his sleeve. "What of Roux? I still haven't seen him."

"He has a good nose. Wherever he's wandered off to—whatever rabbit he's gone in search of—he'll be able to track us."

The rest of them quickly made their preparations, made easier by the fact that each of them had had a bag packed for sevendays now, and Noemia had already stashed ample supplies of food into several more.

"I'm coming with you, too," said a voice beside him, and Caleb looked down at the lanky youth, Jax, wearing a determined expression and gripping the hilt of a sheathed sword far too big for him.

"Nay, Jax. You must see the women and children safely to Captain Ward's ship."

The boy frowned as Thaddeus came alongside them.

"Jax is right, Caleb. You could use our help."

"Only after the others are safely aboard." Caleb looked to Bryant holding his young son, Liri with her daughters, Briella and Tempe, and finally the blind Noemia. "I won't risk anyone else's lives."

Thaddeus nodded. "We won't sail until you arrive."

Seeing the futility of arguing otherwise, Caleb bobbed his head and reached for Sela's arm. "Come on. There's no time to lose."

Wordlessly, she accompanied him down the hill, moving with admirable stealth in knee-high boots which matched his. Her long hair was bound at the nape of her neck, and somehow, she'd acquired a sword, which was belted at her hip. She glanced back at him and her eyes sparkled, unafraid.

He moved in front of her, and as if by silent agreement, they headed for the taverns first, keeping to the shadows that cobwebbed the lampless streets. Hopefully, after they saved

Esther, she would leave him to pursue Tucker alone.

He quickly saw that Foley had been right—the streets of Belladonna were a flurry of confusion, and several isolated buildings were already burning. Had the pirates torched them, or the soldiers? But it was the pirates who paraded freely through the settlement, taking prisoners and firing upon any who resisted. Caleb recognized several settlement men with them, as well as a few soldiers.

Though he tried to shield Sela from the worst of it, Caleb knew she witnessed women being dragged from their homes and protestors shot where they stood, whether man, woman, or child. Dozens of men had swarmed the taverns, looting their supplies of rum, whisky, and tobacco, and a chill stole through him. He suddenly wished he had never given in to Sela. If they detained them and discovered that she was a woman—

Seeing a crowd of men gathered ahead, he pulled her into an alley, his heart hammering so fast he feared it would give them away. They crouched in the shadows as indiscernible voices lashed out in the night.

"We have to get closer," Sela whispered, slipping out before he could tug her back.

Silently, he followed her to the alley closest to the throng and melted against the wall next to her.

At least two dozen men were gathered in a circle around a large fire that had been built in the middle of the street, no doubt fueled by the whisky and rum that flowed unhindered from the taverns. Near the center of the circle, closest to the flames, stood four men, all with their gloved hands tied behind their back, three of whom wore the red coat of a lieutenant. The fourth wore a white coat smudged with dirt and blood.

"Tucker," he hissed as Sela's fingers wove reassuringly through his. How could he save his brother from two dozen pirates?

A tall man stepped forward. Caleb recognized Uriah Smith, wearing an elaborate hat he'd evidently pilfered from one of the officers. The triangular gap formed by his mostly unbuttoned coat revealed a multiple-barreled flintlock at his hip opposite a sword as wickedly curved as his mouth.

Sweat trickled down Caleb's neck. Where was Lord Auberon?

One of the pirates retrieved something from the fire—a rod with an end that glowed fiercely. Taking the brand, Smith shoved the first lieutenant to his knees. The firelight glanced off a wine-red birthmark and Caleb caught his breath. Sela's hand in his tightened.

"Curse the day you were born, Smith," Beck snarled. "As I imagine your mother has often done."

Smith laughed and grabbed Beck by a fistful of sandy hair, baring his cheek. "Aye, she did." The surrounding men guffawed.

Sela pressed her face into Caleb's chest as Beck screamed, the smell of burning flesh nauseating them even from yards away. Caleb clenched his fists as Beck struggled to remain upright. Finally, he raised his head, half of his face an angry red burn. What kind of brand had they used on him? Not the soul mark, but the brand used to mark animals.

Beck spat at Smith's feet. "Burn in the hottest fires of Hel, Smith."

"Perhaps you can stoke up the flames before I get there, Lieutenant."

With his most charming smile, Smith withdrew his flintlock, cocked the trigger, and fired. Caleb suppressed a howl as his friend slumped forward lifelessly, his hands still bound behind him. The remaining two lieutenants whimpered in fear, while Tucker stared ahead, his jaw tight.

Sela's body had grown rigid with fury, and despite his grief, Caleb recognized the change—from ice to fire. Grabbing her around the waist, he held her tightly against him.

"Nay, Caleb," she muttered, trying to wriggle out of his grasp. "I must do something."

He dragged her deeper into the shadows. "Aye, but this isn't like the lynching from months ago—the pirates are out for blood tonight. Listen to me, Sela. You promised me you wouldn't do anything foolish."

She stilled, but her body remained taut. "He *murdered* Beck."

"I know." He kept his voice to a whisper, though he didn't trust it not to shatter amongst the stench of human smoke and gunpowder. "But you won't bring him back by throwing your own life away." Turning her to face him, he held her close, brushing away her tears. "We need a plan."

"Aye, a plan."

And another shot rang out.

Chapter Twenty-Four

The shot was quickly followed by another, and then a third. Screams tore apart the night like carrion birds fighting over a hunk of meat. Caleb edged toward the opening of the narrow alley, and Sela tried to peer over his shoulder.

Glass shattered, and then something exploded in a whoosh of flame. Caleb pressed her back.

"What was that?"

"A grenade," he replied softly.

Liron had told her about the deadly weapons—hollow iron balls filled with gunpowder and ignited by a slow burning fuse. Had the pirates raided the armory? More explosions followed and men scattered like bats stirred from a cave. What was happening?

"Stay here," Caleb whispered, but she ignored the command and followed him out of the shadows.

Though smoke choked the air, she could see that the ring of pirates had disbanded to fight a group of men who had approached from the other side of Belladonna. Mere farmers and tradesmen, they wielded garden tools and kitchen knives instead of swords, pistols, and muskets, but they'd managed to capture the pirates' attention, at least for now. Caleb stole forward to where the two remaining officers knelt, hands bound but unguarded.

"Caleb?" Tucker's head came up as Caleb darted behind him and quickly sawed on his bonds with his knife, avoiding looking at the section of dirt where Beck lay sprawled.

Sela worked on freeing the other lieutenant. The ropes were so tight she wondered if the men would be able to use their hands.

Instead of thanking her, the officer she'd freed grabbed her shoulders, putting her fears about his wellbeing to rest. "You little—"

Stepping between them, Caleb shoved the man away. "Get gone," he barked. "Find a rock to crawl under until this is all over. Or better yet, stay there."

As the officer disappeared, Sela faced Tucker, who rubbed his wrists and watched her with a hateful expression.

"This is no place for a woman, Miss Meriweather—"

"*Alexander*," Caleb corrected. "There's no time for cheek music, Tucker. Let's go." As if to prove his point, Caleb raised his flintlock and fired at something behind Sela. A man dropped to the ground clutching his side.

Tucker grabbed a sword and a pistol from a man lying prone not far away, and Sela drew her own weapons.

The two brothers surged ahead of her, engaging any who came at them, pirates and soldiers and settlement men alike. Did they know the men they were fighting?

She squinted through the smoke. Sparks from the pirates' fire had spread to a nearby roof, igniting more explosions as the flames licked through the tavern. Men and women burst from the building, their skin streaked with soot. The powdered faces of nightwalkers gleamed eerily, their painted lips a slash of blood, shadowed eyes glittering like gunpowder. Screams issued from the second and third floors, no doubt from those still trapped inside. A wave of heat rushed over her, thicker than any front of humid air, and she realized that this was the tavern she'd stayed in her first night on Azazel.

Esther...

Stowing her weapons and stumbling forward, she grabbed the first nightwalker she came across and spun her around. Caramel-brown hair hung in disarray around the woman's ashen face.

"Esther Gray. Please, have you seen her?"

The woman stared, but shook her head.

Sela forced her way through the crowd, questioning. The fifth woman, a nightwalker with flaming red hair, finally nodded.

"Aye, miss. I saw her upstairs. I don't know if she got out."

The roof of the tavern was now fully alight, and the surge of people streaming from the building had slowed. Sela glimpsed the handless giant called Reed and the greasy man who had offered to show her around.

But no Esther.

She lurched forward, raising her arms to protect her face as she ran up the steps and plunged into the burning building.

"Sela!" A man's voice sounded from behind her—Caleb's?

She ignored it. Tucker would probably prevent him from coming after her. Choking on smoke, she darted across the first floor, skirting the dozens of tables and chairs in disarray and the thoroughly ransacked bar. A well-dressed man was sprawled across the stained wood, blood blossoming from a wound in his back—Murphy? One of his hands was fisted around a coin attached to a metal chain.

Dodging several more bodies sprawled across her path, she peered through the gloom to the staircase that led to the upper floors. And her heart sank.

It was already on fire.

Hearing screams from those still trapped above, she searched for a way past the burning timbers, to no avail. Sooty tears streamed down her cheeks as the screams of fear turned to howls of agony. Was Esther up there, dying?

"Carver, have mercy!"

She coughed, braced herself against a table, and nearly tripped over another body. A low moan emanated from the slumped figure and Sela dropped to her knees. Carefully, she rolled the person into a supine position.

Her heart leaped as she studied the powdered face. "Esther!"

Unconscious, Esther barely stirred, and Sela quickly looked her over, growing more aware of the flames crackling overhead. Any moment, the roof could cave in, crushing them both. Esther seemed uninjured, but she lay almost in the middle of the path from the stairs to the exit. Had she been trampled?

Sela tried to heft the woman's dead weight, but her shoulder— not yet fully healed—howled in protest. Rolling Esther into a sitting position, she bent and draped her friend over her good shoulder. Her lungs burned from the smoke, and she coughed again. Now, if she could only get to her knees....

"Sela!" Caleb appeared through the smoke, holding the collar of his shirt against his mouth and nose. "What are you doing?" But he glanced at Esther and thankfully asked no further questions. He easily lifted the woman, Esther's limp head falling against his shoulder. "Come on!"

She followed him from the burning tavern, surprised that he could carry an unconscious woman nearly at a run, wincing as drifting sparks found her hair and exposed skin. They burst into the cool night air just as the tavern exploded behind them. Still at the top of the steps, the force of it jerked them from their feet, propelling them through the air to sprawl in the dirt.

The building crackled with fresh vengeance.

Esther moaned again, and Caleb winced as the woman tumbled from his grasp. By the looks of it, he'd taken the brunt of their fall. But by the time Sela scrambled to her feet, he was on his own, lifting her friend with only the slightest of grimaces.

"You'll have to defend us." He nodded at her sword and hefted Esther over his shoulder. He would have one spare hand, but it would be difficult to fight while bearing the woman's weight.

"Lead the way," she replied, never prouder to be Caleb Alexander's bondmate than in that moment.

Turning, he forced a path through the fleeing settlement inhabitants, and Sela pressed close beside him, Tucker somewhere to Caleb's left.

To most, her sharp sword and small flintlock were enough to dissuade others from challenging them, but twice she crossed blades with men she suspected were pirates, and a third time with a soldier who looked more terrified than the inhabitants of Belladonna. Since it was difficult to prime and load her flintlock in the fray, she tried to save the weapon for dire need.

With every sweep and thrust of her sword, she thought of Joss Brigham and hoped none would die tonight because of her.

Passing the settlement, Caleb melted into the shadows again, and she suddenly knew where he was headed. Thankfully, their cabin had not yet been looted or torched, and the road was eerily quiet after what they'd witnessed.

Tucker strode into the cabin like he owned it, shadows bearding his face despite the light the lantern threw his way. His mouth twisted in revulsion as he watched Caleb lay Esther in one of the armchairs.

"She's a *nightwalker*."

Sela glared at him. "Aye, and you're a liar and a hypocrite, but we still saved your muddy hide."

Caleb suppressed a smile. Tucker's lip curled, but he made no move to approach her.

Esther stirred to life, and her eyes widened as she saw them leaning over her. "Sela?" She forced herself upright and winced. "What happened? Where am I?"

"Shh, you're safe. You're at our cabin."

Once they'd established that she had nothing more than bruises and a small cut on her temple from being knocked to the ground as the others fled the tavern, they quickly told her of Foley's plan. Her eyes widened, her even teeth nibbling at her lip.

"I can't go, Sela."

"You want to escape Azazel?" Tucker turned to Caleb, his voice dripping with disbelief as he ignored Esther's soft statement. "If they catch you, you'll be killed."

"If we stay, we'll die anyway." Caleb crossed his arms, his only injury from the altercation with the pirates a shallow scrape on his elbow. "I glimpsed Smith before, though luckily he didn't see Sela. But he'll come this way, and when he finds us—"

"*Luckily* he didn't see Sela?" Tucker frowned. "Why would *she* matter to him?"

"Because of Liri," Caleb replied. "Smith's wanted Sela from the beginning."

"And because I shot him the first time I met him," Sela added, pleased to see Tucker's face purpling. It was then that she noticed him cradling his right hand. Was he injured?

"And where is Liri and our daughter?"

"Liri and her *daughters* are on their way to Captain Ward's ship. There's space for you, should you decide to accompany us." Caleb's gaze softened as he looked to Esther. "And you, too."

"A ship full of nightwalkers and murderers?" Tucker's nose wrinkled. "My reputation would be permanently tainted."

Esther flinched.

"I'm sure once they know how pleasant you can be, Tucker, they'll keep their distance." Caleb's sarcastic tone surprised Sela.

As the brothers continued their argument, Sela crouched beside her friend. "Come with us, Esther. 'Tis no longer safe here."

"I…I can't. What would the others think of me, Sela?"

"You heard Lieutenant-Commander Alexander," she replied, scowling at her brother-in-law. "There will be plenty of nightwalkers aboard."

As Esther hesitated, Sela tuned into Caleb and Tucker's conversation, which had taken a calmer turn.

"If I come with you," Tucker was saying, "then I won't be leaving Azazel forever. I have to return and find Lord Auberon."

"Then you haven't seen him?"

"Not since the start of the attack."

Caleb looked thoughtful. "If Smith had captured him, we would know. Perhaps he's gone into hiding."

"Aye, perhaps. His reinforcements are due any day."

"Then 'tis decided. You'll come with us, at least until 'tis safe to return."

As the others readied to leave, Caleb reached for Sela.

"You were very brave," he said into her ear so neither his brother or Esther could hear. "And exceedingly foolish."

She smiled at the admiration in his blue eyes. "You came back for me."

"Aye, Sela. I'll always come back for you."

He kissed her lightly on the lips, and would have taken her in his arms, but Sela glanced over his shoulder to see Tucker glaring at her. She pulled away, and Caleb turned to look at his brother.

He frowned, his hands around her waist tightening.

"Tucker has a long way to go. Though no greater distance than that which I myself have already traversed."

"Nay, you are nothing like him, Caleb. And you have never been."

Though Caleb was surely aware of his brother's ire, he pressed his lips to hers again. The softness of his mouth reminded her of the pledge she'd made to him back at the house, and she shivered with anticipation. Tucker was nothing to her, except as a relic of Caleb's past and a man whose worth shriveled when compared with that of her bondmate.

Her bondmate, who remained unconvinced of the ugliness of Tucker's soul. "Perhaps Azazel will be the making of him, Sela."

Sela glanced over Caleb's shoulder again. The hate remained steady in Tucker's eyes, like a spirit level that found its equilibrium no matter the circumstances.

"Or his unmaking."

As the first rays of dawn smudged the horizon, they crouched in the twisted undergrowth nearest the docks and their assortment of dilapidated sheds and warehouses, not far from the hanging tree. Surprisingly, most of the shore, including the docks, had been deserted, though the sounds of drinking and carousing drifted to them from the warships anchored across the water.

Sela shivered.

How many of Belladonna's inhabitants were involved in the looting, raping, and pillaging that went on in the town? Gunshots still fragmented the night, startling flocks of gulls that had settled on the thin strip of beach into flight. Several fires still burned sullenly, but they had not spread to any more buildings.

"'Tis quiet," Tucker observed.

"Too quiet," agreed Caleb, frowning.

"I can see the docked ship over there." Esther pointed into the gathering gloom at a jetty that jutted out into the bay like a spindly, malformed arm. "And the second, smaller vessel is next to it."

Sela glanced at the lightening sky. "We have to go while 'tis still dark. If we wait any longer, we'll be seen."

"Though I hate to say it, she's right."

"Why thank you, Tucker." She smiled sweetly at him, and he scowled.

Without further ado, Tucker stood, breaking cover. As a figure moved on the shore, he raised his arm and fired. Sela flinched as the shadow dropped to the sand.

Tucker's aim was as good as his brother's.

Caleb steered Sela and Esther past Tucker, but said nothing about the dead man. Would he, too, have killed a man in cold blood? A chill wind rose up, shrieking through the palms, and Esther pulled her shawl tightly around her.

Near the end of the long jetty, a man waited, holding a flintlock. Sela squinted through the lingering fog, a legacy of one of the several still active volcanoes that ringed the island.

"Don't shoot," Caleb murmured to Tucker and lowered his own weapon. "Thaddeus," he said, with warmth. "You kept your word."

"Aye, though we got here only moments ago." Thaddeus lowered his voice. "Have you seen Liri and her daughters?"

"She's not here?" Caleb's voice brimmed with concern.

"Nay, we split up, so as not to attract too much attention. Liri and the girls were to be escorted by Bryant."

"And what of little Thomas?"

Thaddeus jerked his thumb behind him, where a fully rigged schooner bobbed alongside a much smaller sloop. Sela glimpsed several people huddled together next to the vessels. "My sister took him so that Bryant would have his hands free to fight if necessary." His gaze strayed to Tucker, but he said nothing at the sight of one of the Righteous.

The blood drained from Sela's face.

"There's no time," Caleb said. "Get the others on board the schooner and leave. No point in all of us staying."

"But if there's trouble—"

Caleb glanced at Tucker. "We can handle it."

Thaddeus frowned, but finally nodded. While the fog swelled around them, Sela hugged Noemia, Jax, Briella, and Tempe, and kissed Thomas's velvety cheek. She was surprised when Thaddeus's good arm enveloped her shoulders.

"Stay safe, Sela," he murmured into her ear. "We'll see you soon."

Once she'd sighted Briella, Esther had been persuaded to leave with the others. Sela watched her friend hesitantly board the shadowed vessel, hearing Captain Ward's orders relayed by his officers across the main deck. She tried to forget Esther's ominous parting words.

"Hurry, Sela. Smith is looking for you."

"Don't you want to leave with them?" Sela eyed Tucker beside her, who only squared his shoulders and crossed his arms.

"I stay with my brother."

On that count at least, they were united. She watched the ship glide out of sight and into the mass of fog that had descended over the bay, feeling an odd sense of loss. Aye, she would see her friends again. But what of Roux? And Liri?

Hiram Foley had stayed behind to captain the smaller vessel with several other men acting as crew, and he called to Caleb to help him ready the single-masted sloop. Caleb frowned, clearly reluctant to leave her with his brother, but she waved him away.

"Go. I'll be fine."

Caleb leveled a look at his brother. "*You* could help Foley while *I* stay with Sela."

Tucker shrugged. "I know little about sailing." He raised his hand and she glimpsed a bloodied bandage. "Besides, I'll be of no use handling the ropes."

Begrudgingly, Caleb's gaze moved from Sela to his brother. "Look after her, Tuck. Please."

A muscle jerked in Tucker's jaw, but he nodded, perhaps softened by Caleb's use of the familiar nickname.

Sela primed and reloaded her pistol, then retraced their steps down the jetty a way, searching the fog for Liri and the others. At least they no longer had to fear the revealing light of dawn.

Tucker followed, glancing doubtfully at her pistol as he primed and loaded his own. "Are you sure you know how to use that?"

"Aye."

"Shouldn't you—" He broke off, no doubt hearing the footsteps and yells that had her straining her ears and eyes to pierce the gloom.

"Sela!"

Hearing Liri's voice, she stuffed her weapon into her coat pocket and started forward. "Liri!"

Her sister emerged through the fog, holding her youngest daughter and tugging a white-faced Anwen behind her. She looked exhausted. Behind them, Ross stumbled along like a man running from demons, his palms bloody, clutching a wound on the side of his thigh. Where was his sword?

When he looked up, Ross's eyes were frantic.

"Run, Sela! He is just behind—"

The resonant voice that followed his warning was sickeningly familiar, coagulating her blood and rendering her inert. Memories of another time—and another man emerging through the fog— returned to her with the force of a blow. Was it Liri she sought to save, or Cadence?

"Miss Sela. How good of you to wait for us."

Chapter Twenty-Five

Sela watched as Uriah Smith detached his large frame from the cobweb-like fog that tethered him to the mainland. He had discarded the ridiculous hat and affable smile from before and now wore a fur coat like the ones Sela had occasionally glimpsed on fine ladies in the Old Town. Two burly men flanked him, though she guessed that more came behind. His flintlock pistol, with a beautifully carved silver muzzle depicting the head and maw of a dragon, rested almost lazily in his hand.

As Ross groaned and dropped to the planks, Sela returned to herself and stepped in front of him, forcing Liri and the girls behind. Surprisingly, Tucker came to stand beside her, his flintlock trained on Uriah.

Uriah curled his lip, but the full extent of his disgust was reserved for Liri, who cowered with her daughters next to Ross. "Where do you think you're going, witch? Don't you know there's no place you can go that I will not find?" His gaze strayed to Sela. "Though I'm pleased you led me straight to a far sweeter prize. One that will put up a lot more of a fight than you have of late, my dear."

Sela raised her flintlock. "Come any closer and I'll shoot."

His dimpled smile was patronizing. "You should know better than to challenge me, sweetheart. After all, I have the best aim of anyone on this Carver-forsaken island." He fingered the collar of his fur coat.

Nay, not a coat.

A fur scarf.

A *red* fur scarf.

For a long moment, the world stood still, and then six years' worth of pain rose like a 'sooner, swamping her with wave after wave of emotion until she felt like a brace of seaweed tumbling helplessly in the surf. She opened her mouth, but her tongue refused to work.

"Roux?" she finally choked out, unable to comprehend what her eyes told her. Bile swelled in her throat.

Her beloved pet, her confidante, her friend…but wait. Where was the white tip on the end of the tail?

"Was that your name for him?" Uriah lifted the fox tail and rubbed it against his branded cheek, closing his eyes as he inhaled the scent. He sighed with pleasure. "He'll keep me warm for the remainder of the winter. As will you, Sela."

A guttural cry tore from her chest, and she fired the flintlock. But the wash of tears across her eyes made her blind and the shot went wide of Uriah, instead hitting the man to his left. Tucker's shot finished the pirate, who keeled over and landed in the water with an agonized yell and a distant splash.

Why had he not fired at Uriah?

As Uriah advanced slowly, she grabbed Tucker's sleeve. "Get them to safety." She shoved him backward. "Take Liri and go! I'll distract him."

She drew her sword. It would be useless against Uriah, who could fire several shots before reloading, but she had nothing else.

She had to save Liri and her daughters.

Tucker hesitated only a moment before he turned and made for Liri. While Ross hauled himself to his feet, Tucker glided past him, gathering up Anwen with one sweep of his arm and dragging Liri, who held little Sela, along the jetty toward the sloop.

"Sela!" Liri cried, but the desperation of her call was quickly smothered by the fog. Like Sela with Caleb, Liri had no hope of freeing herself from Tucker. Besides, she had to see that Sela's actions would save her daughters.

Ross staggered forward, as if to lunge toward Uriah. The pirate calmly raised the pistol and fired. Ross fell, clutching his shoulder.

His *shoulder*.

From all she knew of him, Uriah didn't miss.

Sela met the pirate's eyes and was chilled by the utter emptiness she saw there. In the center of the darkness, she glimpsed a flicker of something that whipped the dread in her stomach into a maelstrom.

What had Liri said of Uriah's color?

"Black, Sela. Complete, utter, soulless black."

"He thinks of naught but possession..." Thaddeus's words, truer than she'd realized, though she sensed it was both a desire to possess and a hunger for retribution that drove Uriah Smith. How much would he make her suffer before she died?

Her palm holding the sword hilt grew sweaty, but she gripped it like a lifeline. If she died, she would die bravely, and she would do her best to take Uriah with her.

For Bess. For Roux. And for Liri.

The silver mouth of the dragon was wide enough to swallow her whole. She faced it, thinking of the richness of the dark blue ocean on a summer's day—the way that light pierced a body of velveteen water one had previously thought without color, irradiating hundreds of particles suspended in its brilliance. Was that why the Carver had given her Caleb, if only briefly? To show her that she had a soul?

Uriah's eyes flashed dangerously. "Yield to me, Sela. You cannot defeat me."

Aye, she was nearly powerless. But there was one greater than even Uriah Smith, and He had the power to save her if He chose.

Carver, have mercy on me.

Her last thought before she charged was of Caleb.

At the sound of twin shots, Caleb stiffened and peered through the gloom. Had Sela and Tucker wandered from their position beside the sloop? The fog was now so thick that he could barely see more than a few yards in front of his face. But they'd been there the last time he looked, waiting for Liri and the others.

"Hold," he said to Foley. "I'll see what's wrong."

Drawing his pistol, he leaped from the boat to the jetty, only to see Tucker emerge from the fog, half-dragging, half-carrying Liri and her daughters. Liri looked wild with anguish.

"Where's Sela?" Caleb demanded. "And Bryant?"

"Bryant is almost certainly dead," replied Tucker, grimly. "As for Sela—" A third shot rang out and he winced. "We were attacked by Smith. Sela is holding him at bay so that we can get away."

"You left a woman behind to do a man's job?" Caleb shoved past his brother, but he'd only sprinted a few yards when Tucker tackled him from behind.

They crashed to the planks, the breath whooshing from his lungs. Tucker took advantage of his windedness to dig his knee into Caleb's back. "Don't waste her sacrifice, Caleb. Sela wanted us to save her sister."

"Coward," he ground out, and wrenched his body so that Tucker fell sideways. This time, Caleb dove for his brother, landing a right uppercut in his chest, followed by a punch to the stomach. Tucker bellowed in pain, but fought back, sinking a left backfist in Caleb's jaw. The two rolled, each fighting for dominance as the fog swirled around them. Far below, water lapped against the wooden supports. Liri screamed for them to stop, while her daughters wailed.

Caleb thought only of Sela, alone with Uriah Smith.

His next punch found the underside of Tucker's chin, and his brother fell back, clutching his jaw. A shudder ricocheted through the planks beneath Caleb's feet, and he fought for breath, using his body weight and Tucker's injured hand to pin his brother. A fraction taller, Caleb had ever proved the stronger man, though it pained him to use force against his brother.

The brother who had betrayed him.

"Get into the boat," Caleb said to Liri over his shoulder. "I'm going after Sela." Liri handed her daughters to Foley and the other men, but remained close by. Did she think she was going to accompany him?

"That woman doesn't deserve you," Tucker said, testing his bruised jaw, the extent of his conviction—and his hate—unnerving Caleb. How could he have entrusted Sela to his brother, injury or nay? "Don't go after her, Caleb."

Caleb's fingers curled around Tucker's bare throat. "I asked you to look out for her. I should kill you for what you've done."

He squeezed once and stood just as the sound of cannons shattered the silence of the bay for a second time. Had the soldiers risen up against the pirates? But nay, the cannon fire came from further out—near the entrance to the bay.

Janus Auberon's reinforcements had arrived.

Momentarily distracted, he didn't notice that Tucker had also clambered to his feet, nor that his brother had reached for the butt of his flintlock.

"Caleb!" Sela's voice split the fog, filled with so much agony and desperation, he was briefly lost.

"Sela!" he yelled back. "I'm coming!"

"Watch out, Caleb!" Liri cried.

Just as he turned his back on Tucker, searing pain knifed the rear of his skull. He crumpled, his cheek smashing against the wooden planks. The air was smacked from his lungs a second time.

As he fought for breath, the fog shifted and parted, and further down the jetty, he discerned a tall man holding a woman whose unbound hair hung like a curtain of silk over the man's thick arm. As pain rippled through his head, he watched her struggle to free herself.

"Caleb!" Her anguished scream briefly cleared the fog in his brain, and he propped himself up on one elbow. The vision shimmered and swayed, and he groaned, fighting to stay conscious. He had to save Sela…he was her only chance.

He *loved* her.

"Sela," he whispered, weakly.

And then the world faded to black.

As distant cannon fire lit up the bay once more, Tucker watched Smith carry a now unconscious Sela toward Belladonna. Was she dead? Nay—if she were, Smith would have left her on the jetty. Two of his men shouldered a groaning Bryant between them and dragged him away.

Why did Smith not pursue Liri and the children he believed were his? But Tucker knew—the reinforcements from the Old Town had arrived. Smith would need to act quickly to consolidate his power.

Besides, the pirate had his prize. Lord Auberon would be pleased to learn of Sela's fate. And Tucker would have his brother back, once Caleb came to his senses.

As Tucker gazed down at his unconscious brother, he felt a prick of remorse. Whatever her other sins, Sela had been brave to take on Smith by herself. Unspeakably foolish, but undeniably brave.

But she'd also willfully, knowingly caused the downfall of his brother, a man who had the potential to lead the Righteous itself. Without her gone, Caleb could never reclaim his former position.

He turned to see Liri watching him, tears streaming down her cheeks, her body rigid with fear. He stepped toward her and she startled.

Tucker held up a gloved hand, gentling his voice. "There's nothing to fear, Liri. You and your daughters are safe. Caleb is only unconscious." He holstered his flintlock, regretful only that he'd had to resort to such violence.

She stared back at him, and he flinched as he recognized her expression for what it was—revulsion.

"How could you?" she whispered. "They went back for *you*, Tucker." She choked down a sob. "You're just like Uriah. Nay—worse."

Her words cut into him, rousing his anger and reopening old

wounds. He forced his mind to the present. With the reinforcements newly arrived from the Old Town, Tucker would be safe once more, but not Liri and her daughters...*his* daughter. He needed to find a safe place for them—on the mainland, perhaps, since the closest port was two sevendays of sailing from Azazel— and then he would return to Azazel with Caleb.

"When I can, Liri, I'll come back for your sister. But for now, you must see that Sela's sacrifice buys our freedom."

She extended a shaking palm, revealing her brand. "As my sacrifice bought yours, six years ago?"

A chill thicker than any fog descended on his heart and he ignored her challenge. Instead, he set his aching muscles to hauling Caleb to the waiting sloop. Foley frowned, but he and another man reached out for his brother's body and lifted it on board.

Aye, Tucker would make them understand that what Sela had done, she had done for *all* of them.

Tucker returned for Liri, who still stood rooted to the planks. She hugged herself, looking toward Belladonna as if she yearned to follow Sela, but then quickly glancing back at the sloop where her children waited. Her face creased with sudden determination.

"I'm staying here," she said, "and I'm going after my sister."

He caught her up in his arms, and though she struggled, she was no match for his strength. Feeling the brush of her bare cheek against his, he hissed and shouldered her more firmly, trying not to touch her lest he become as tainted as Caleb.

"Sela!" Liri screamed, her tears drenching his collar. "*Sela!*"

He climbed aboard the sloop, still clutching the wriggling woman.

In time, Liri would forget her sister.

And Caleb—his beloved brother, who deserved the world— would be free.

Chapter Twenty-Six

Once again in the lair of the lion, Liron dragged his hood over his hair and pushed into the crowd milling around the docks of Consuela. Weaving through hundreds of sailors, dockworkers, merchantmen, and craftsmen, he ducked beneath two men carrying a long wooden plank and skirted a tangled pile of nets left in a treacherous mass for someone's ankle to collect. He wrinkled his nose at the stench of rotting fish that pervaded the harbor. He much preferred the clean draughts of the open sea, laced with salt and flavored with possibilities.

Though it was nearing twilight, he set about questioning sailors and workers, knowing he did not have a moment to lose. Once the prince had revealed himself to his men, it would be difficult to gain an audience with him. And Liron could not risk being sighted by the very navy he'd deserted.

After half an hour of dead ends, the Carver tossed him another breadcrumb.

"Magnus, ye say?" A lank-sleeved man with a mouth filled with yellow and silver crenellations untwisted a fraying rope with surprising deftness, despite his missing arm. "Aye, I spoke wit' a Magnus yesterday who fit yer description." He pointed a gnarled finger toward a tall-masted schooner several hundred yards away. "I couldna offer him passage, so he headed thattaway."

Liron nodded his thanks and went on his way, surprised at the man's words. Prince Magnus wanted passage from Consuela? Where was he headed? And why would he not utilize his own ships?

Was he so afraid of betrayal? Or fearful of the crowds? He was royal, after all, and people were always drawn to royals, not only because of their prestige and wealth, but for their gifts of prophecy and healing.

The port was crowded despite the late hour, and it took him a long time to reach the schooner the lank-sleeved man had indicated. Seeing the ship's sails fill with wind, he picked up his pace. Was it departing?

Finding the somewhat isolated jetty that led to the schooner, he ran down the uneven planks, only to find that the ship had already pulled away.

Shoving back his hood, he waved his arms and jumped up and down, heedless of the half-dozen dockhands who had paused in hefting cargo and untying ropes to watch him.

"Hi!" he shouted. "Stop, please!"

The ship maintained its course, and he briefly considered jumping into the deep water and swimming after it. But though he could keep himself afloat, he was no swimmer, and he'd seen numerous sharks on the crossing from the Old Town.

But as he peered after the ship, he saw a tall man on the main deck turn to look at him.

Liron started. *Prince Magnus.*

Even at that distance, and after eighteen years, Liron recognized the man. He stood with his hands curled over the rail, a closely trimmed beard masking his expression. Did he remember the boy he'd saved?

Liron's heart sank. He had failed his sisters a third time.

Someone tugged on the edge of his coat and Liron turned around.

"Are you all right, Mister?"

It was so like what the prince had said to him, all those years ago, that he was briefly lost in his recollections. He became dimly aware that he spoke to a boy, younger even than the powder boys that the navy employed on their warships, and so thin he seemed all knobby elbows and dusty kneecaps.

"Do you know where that ship is bound, young man?" Liron nearly smiled as he remembered Prince Magnus's address of him at a similar age.

"Aye, sir," replied the boy, looking almost wistful. "It goes to the prison-island, Azazel."

"Azazel?" He glanced back at the ship, only to find it had nearly disappeared into the sunset. Why was the prince headed for Azazel? Could it be that he went for the same reasons as Liron? That he would at last fulfill his promise?

"One day soon, you and your sisters will be free. I give you my word."

Aye, and Prince Magnus was a man of his word.

Liron's vision cleared and he realized the boy was staring up at him expectantly. "Thank you, young master—"

He stopped mid-sentence and stared.

The boy was a perfect replica of himself at the same age. Dirty and disheveled, with pants that hung shy of his ankles and a nearly threadbare shirt, but with the same onyx-black hair Liron shared with Sela and the green eyes that mirrored his twin's.

It can't be...

"Are you all right, Mister?" the boy repeated, this time clearly concerned for his sanity.

"Your eyes," Prince Magnus had said once. *"They tell me everything I need to know."*

Liron shook himself. "I'm fine, thank you. Where is your mama, young man?"

The boy shrugged. "I don't have one."

"She's dead?" His chest tightened.

"Nay," the boy replied. "On Azazel." His features turned solemncholy, and he seemed far older than five or six years should have made him. "I was brought here when I was only a baby. Mother Phoebe looks after me now."

Clearly not very well, Liron muttered inwardly, but said nothing. At least the boy's speech bore a hint of refinement. He knelt beside the lad, shoving his hood all the way back to expose his own features. "Do you see our resemblance, young man?"

The boy's eyes roved over his face. "I've never peered into a looking glass, sir."

"You are the exact image of me when I was your age. We have the same hair, the same eyes, even the same chin."

The boy's eyes widened until his eyebrows were nearly swallowed by a coal-black fringe. "Are you my papa, then?"

Liron's heart gave an unexpected jolt. What would Etta say at the sight of this child, so like him? She would think he'd strayed from her. "Nay, young man. But I believe I'm your uncle. I think your mama is my twin sister." He gentled his voice as Prince Magnus had. "Do you remember your mama's name?"

The boy shook his head. "'Twas long ago, sir," he said, once again pensive. "But I think I remember her face. She was very beautiful."

"Aye, she was."

Was he wrong to hope? Could this be Liri's son? How had her child come to be taken from her—and from Azazel? And to Consuela, of all places? He was clearly fatherless, and everything seemed to suggest that the boy was Liron's nephew. But there was one important question he hadn't asked.

"What's your name, young man?"

Would Liri have named her son after someone she knew? Their father, perhaps, or grandfather? Perhaps it would provide a clue to the boy's true identity.

The boy smiled, and despite a missing tooth, his broad grin was all Sela. In that moment, Liron saw the coin that hung from a leather cord around the boy's neck, not so smudged that he could not discern the name scratched there.

Liri Meriweather.

"*That* question I can answer, Mister. My name is Liron."

Acknowledgments

Of the eight books I've written to date, *The Soul Mark* is the closest to my heart. After spending twelve and a half years on my first book and nine months on the second, this, my third book, took only six weeks to write…mainly because it felt like it simply poured out of me, a story that was being discovered rather than dreamed up, unravelled rather than imagined.

But after this book was written, it was difficult to find it a home. It was a very unique kind of story—a historical fantasy, a blend of romance and adventure and deep spiritual themes that seemed to resist easy categorization. Eventually, I decided to enter it into Mountain Brook Ink's Fire Award, and when it advanced at each stage, I was stunned. Finally, when I won the competition and Mountain Brook Fire offered me a book contract, I couldn't believe it.

As soon as I began to work with MBF's team, I realized *The Soul Mark* (then titled *The Rendering*) had found the perfect home. The MBF team have worked so hard to make this book what it is today. To Miralee—thanks for taking a chance on an Aussie author halfway across the world! To Alyssa—without your edits, this book would not be the polished product it has become. Your editing commentary made me smile and giggle and your encouragement kept me marching through what is normally a difficult and stressful part of the publishing process. I plan on framing your comments one day.

Thank you to Julia, for the stunning character art. You really brought the characters and the world of Azazel to life!

A special thank you to Misi, who I first met through the Fire Award and who has become such a dear friend, even though we live in different countries and time zones. Thank you for your excitement about my books, your support of me as an author, and your wonderful friendship. I can't wait to see your brilliant books out in the wild someday! Readers, if you haven't yet heard of Misi's amazing ministry to Christian sufferers of chronic illness, go check out The Valley and sign up for their newsletter: graceinthevalley.org. You will not regret it.

To my readers, some of whom have read multiple stories from me now—thank you so much for your support of my author journey. I hope you can bear with me through yet another cliffhanger (please don't blow up my letterbox), and Sela and Caleb's story is going to end well, I promise.

I want to thank the usual gang who champion this writing gig of mine, including an amazing cast of family and friends (you know who you are!). A special shout out to my mum, who read a decent chunk of the initial manuscript and loved the story—an absolute miracle since she always falls asleep partway into *The Lord of the Rings*. (And if the combined heroism and physical beauty of Aragorn and Legolas can't keep you awake, then there's really no hope. ☺)

To my amazing husband, to whom this book is dedicated and who formed much of the inspiration for the character of Caleb Alexander (my favorite hero so far). You are truly my Samwise Gamgee in the wilderness, and the way that you've been there for me over the past nine years of our marriage is incredible. Thanks for reading every single one of my stories and always reminding me to "include more of those lush descriptions." Oh, and thanks for not squirming too much at the Romance and Kissing in this book. The many sword fights in this book and the sequel are for you (the extended car chase scene will happen one day, I promise).

Finally, to God, the Carver of Souls by whose grace each of my books has been written and contracted, and who first led me into the wilderness several years ago in order to guide me to the Living Water that would truly satisfy. Thanks for taking away what I thought was good so that I would reach for what was better. And thanks, as always, for providing a way back to Eden and to You. Soli Deo Gloria.

- Jasmine

About the Author

Jasmine's writing dream began with the anthology of zoo animals she painstakingly wrote and illustrated at age five, to rather limited acclaim. Thankfully, her writing (but not her drawing) has improved since then. Jasmine began writing her first proper novel at age fourteen, which eventually became her debut fantasy series, The Darcentaria Duology, which was published in 2021.

Jasmine completed her Bachelor degree in English Literature and Creative Writing in 2012. Also a qualified psychologist with undergraduate and postgraduate degrees in clinical psychology, Jasmine's dream is to write stories that weave together her love for Jesus, her passion for mental health, and her struggles with chronic illness.

When she isn't killing defenseless house plants, Jasmine enjoys devouring books, dabbling in floristry, playing the piano, eating peanut butter out of the jar, and wishing it rained more often. Jasmine is married to David, and together they make their home a couple of hours north of Sydney, Australia. You can stalk her on social media or visit her official website at www.jjfischer.com, where she's always open to swapping good memes, talking about chickens, or whingeing about Luke Skywalker.

Find Jasmine Online:
Official author website: www.jjfischer.com
Facebook: www.facebook.com/jjfischerauthor
Instagram: www.instagram.com/jjfischerauthor
Twitter: twitter.com/jjfischerauthor
Pinterest: www.pinterest.com.au/jjfischerauthor
Goodreads: www.goodreads.com/author/show/20763565.J_J_Fischer
Amazon: www.amazon.com/J-J-Fischer/e/B08P12SJ8W
Bookbub: www.bookbub.com/authors/j-j-fischer

9 781953 957320